C000252580

ELDER

Judgment, Revenge, Rewriting Destiny

Jordon Genetski

Map of Verbenia

*Just something to note: the Fair Folk, the Sidhe, the Aos Sí, are NOT human, nor do they appear human. They are sacred beings, and many appear animalistic. This is a work of fiction with various themes and Faeries taken from Celtic Mythology research. Please do not go out of your way searching for these creatures because of what you read in a book. They are dangerous. Do not say the name of the Nuckelavee out loud (you'll see).

The Elder Tree, *Ruis*: Judgment, Revenge,
Rewriting Destiny

For my parents and my dear friend Allison. When my wings were clipped, you taught me to trust the winds again.

To the years we've lost, and the future we'll conqure.

CHAPTER ONE

Eadha

"Alright, ye two, back to the barracks. Next pair, into the pit," the warlord's voice boomed in my ears as I held my friend Séamus in place to my chest, my dual swords in a cross to his neck. Sweat dripped off of my face, and I tried to stabilize my breathing as I laughed.

"Checkmate," I whispered as I kicked him away with a grunt and wiped the blood dripping from my lip.

Séamus tousled the snow out of his fiery red curly locks and laughed, "I think I won that time."

Despite his towering size and cut build, he had grown too soft to deliver the final blow in sparring. In war, that was a different story; but as the warlords have said: "Treat the pit like battle, those who are weak will die in it."

"Oh, did ye now? Is that why I could have snipped yer neck clean off yer shoulders just now? Almost fifty thousand years, my friend, and ye still cannot best me." I laughed and walked in stride next to him, coming up to merely his breastbone.

I looked up and studied his face. He had delicate features besides his angular jaw. His cheeks were round and boyish, and his mouth was full and mischievous. He was undoubtedly handsome, almost angelic looking, and rather cute, thanks to his curly red hair and pink cheeks. He could have any woman he wanted. However, I did not remember the last one he so much as spoken to.

"What a painstaking fifty thousand years they have been. I may never know how yer still alive, but good on ye for not looking a day past twenty. And don't berate me for not wanting to stomp yer skull in, I truly dream of it, but some of us still have a heart even in war, *Eadha*." I hated how he enunciated the syllables of my name to make a point; *Eh-yuh.* It made me feel like a child who was being scolded by her parents.

Heart had no place in battle, it would get him killed, and he knew it. But it was not like we had to worry about any great wars. Our leaders had done all they could to turn the vicious, bloodthirsty warriors of our kind into mere bodyguards.

Séamus stopped in his tracks and looked down at me. "The Tiarna wish to speak with ye, by the way. Want me to come with? It sounded serious."

Ah, *the leaders.* The Tiarna were the most powerful of the High Druids and chosen by the gods themselves. They came from bloodlines as old as the earth and were born with more natural abilities than I could count. The bulk of their magic was gifted to them by the old gods and goddesses. Faolan worked with Arawn, the god of death and wrath, who also ruled the Otherworld. With the god's gifts, he could snap his fingers and send anyone into their next lifetime.

Aerona worked with Macha, goddess of sovereignty. The two deities only worked with the Tiarna, for the conduits that held their magic would burn if they were not strong enough. I tried to spend my days away from them, but they did call on me occasionally. How could they not? I led their Laoch, their armies. The same armies they had stagnated in the mud, rotting away.

I shook my head. "No, I can handle them myself. Work on yer dagger attacks. Yer a brute, yes, but ye lack in quick footwork. I took ye out with speed. I'm sure our lovely twins would take to the pit with ye to help with that."

He scoffed and pushed me. "I'd rather cut out my own throat than work with those buggers."

Whatever Séamus was, the twins Donnan and Dolan were a mirror opposite. Small, quick, ruthless, and a pain in my backside, like two cockroaches that have survived the tests of time. I had a love-hate relationship with them, but they were in my tight circle, along with Séamus and my dear friend Lana. Unlike Séamus, Lana, and I, who joined the Laoch legions as outsiders, the twins were born and raised into it.

I waved a hand and pulled out my Druid Stone. Through my eyes, it was a glowing orb of blue and gold, able to focus my magic, so I did not have to resort to spell work and incantations. To anyone not of Druid birth, it looked nothing more than a mere rock.

"Practice all the fun and creative ways ye speak of killing them then, see ye at the palace tonight, yes?" I asked, as I opened the veil that separates our world from what lies beyond.

Séamus looked me in the eyes with concern but gave a slight smile. "Are ye sure? I know how ye get with them."

I shook my head. "I don't hate them, Séamus, if that's what yer asking. We go through this every time. I can face my own parents without yer help."

With that, I tore through the darkness of the veil, away from our humble war camp to the palace of the monarchs. I reflected on my words and wondered if they were indeed a lie. I certainly did not hate my parents, but I hated their actions for many years. When our nation was ripped from our hands and our people slaughtered, we demanded justice and retaliation. All of their promises of such things fell empty.

They plunged us into hiding, to live a life of false normalcy on lands that were not our own for centuries. We wanted war, but they made us stifle away our longing and work to rebuild. And so, rebuild we did. Our people were resilient and our numbers vast, but at the cost of erasing ourselves from history and living in shadows to protect us all.

I knew I truly did hate it here at the palace grounds. It was a representation of everything I was not: proper, eloquent, and beautiful, everything my parents probably wished I was, instead of the savage Laoch I grew to be. But I would not change that for a second.

I opened the door to the throne chambers and bowed at the waist before my parents. "Yer *highnesses*," I mocked with a wave of my arm, avoiding my eyes from lingering on the mural behind them, the mural that held the eyes of my twin and the happiness that had since been lost in mine.

"Eadha, must you be so insufferable? And it is pronounced *your*. A Laoch you may be, but a High Druid born. I pray you speak with the likeness of your parents in our presence," my mother, Aerona, said with a smile. Although she never came out and said it, I knew my mocking the throne pained her. I only did it to protect myself from ever gaining the title "Tiarna" like them. The title that was rightfully my brother's.

I smiled back and crossed my arms. "About a few centuries too late for that lecture," a lecture I received with every visit.

The Laoch spoke "improperly," so said the Druids, but being around them more than my parents for my whole life had caused their tongue to rub off on me. My rolled r's and closed, elongated vowels reminded my parents that I became everything they wished I would not, as if the blue war tattoos were not enough to do so. Though they always supported me in my decisions to fight for our people, there now was no heir to the throne after my brother fell.

My heart ached as I wished to see my parents more, but the pain of seeing them and paintings of the life we once lived was too much to bear even after all these years. I visited them often but decided to spend my days in the war camps with my circle of friends.

My father, Faolan, smiled at me and said plainly, "Things have been stirring up across the Fae realms, and the Circles have been seeing unusual traffic into the human lands. We do not feel comfortable with Lana going to trade anymore over there. You will be going this afternoon."

I raised an eyebrow and narrowed my gaze. "What do ye mean *things* have been stirring up? What things? How are Fae able to go through the wards of the Circle?"

My father looked at me with the same intensity I have only seen one other time in my life. "I had a vision this morning, the first in many years. Sabriel is going to attempt to open the sacred Well of Bríg."

My stomach dropped, and I forced my knees to lock so they would not give out. That Well sat on the land of our ancestors and connected our world to the Otherworld. If Sabriel had found a way to open it, any amount of ancient filth could step over and wreak havoc on the world.

"Why-how do ye know?" I asked breathlessly.

He looked down his nose at me and pursed his lips. "Aside from my vision, there have been reports of Sluagh entering the human realms. The wards over the Faery Circles are fading, and only a great deal of magic can accomplish that. Temples are being raided across Verbenia, for what, we do not know."

My radiant mother, trying to keep her face as still as a pond, narrowed her gaze to me as well. "As you know, we have not attempted to reclaim our land because our magic is expended every day to keep us hidden and protected. We also lost many Druids the day Sabriel invaded our home. But we have spent enough centuries rebuilding. If he attempts to open the Well, we will need to move in. We will not allow anyone to experience the same brutalities he unleashed onto our people."

My heart flipped, and a grin began to brim my face. "I've been waiting a lifetime for this," I whispered.

Finally. Revenge for killing those I held dear to me, revenge for my capture, revenge for desecrating our sacred land. After all of these years, we may move from the shadows that bind us into the light of the world once again.

"Get to the merchants and get us the gold so we survive this winter, then we can speak of these pressing matters. With the Sluagh off their leashes, you will need to tread lightly. Do not, under any circumstances, use your magic against them. *Behave yourself* this time," my father instructed coldly.

I wanted to snap back that it was only *one* shop I

lit on fire the last time I went to trade, and I should have never been reprimanded in the first place, but I could only muster a nod before leaving.

Almost fifty thousand years ago, Sabriel, a Fae from the north, invaded our lands, wielding magic never before seen by my people, and killed all in his sight. He sought out my parents and the heir to their throne to end the Druid reign. While my parents escaped, my brother and I were not so lucky. Sabriel captured me, tortured me, and left me to die. My parents have since hidden our people away as a means of "protection," but Sabriel was responsible for my brother's death, and I never forgave them for not fighting back. Part of me knew that they could not bear to lose another child to the hands of that monster, but the day for retribution could very well be upon us.

I hastily packed a few fruits and changed my clothes. Winter was brewing in our lands, so I could only imagine what it must be like in the human realm. I chose fur-lined black leathers for my coat and pants over the long sleeve shirt I wore in the pit. As I looked in the mirror, I could not help but frown. I had the slightest of beauty from both my parents, a heart-shaped face, soft cheekbones, yet a strong jaw.

My lips were petal pink and rather full against my icy pale skin, but a savage still sat on top of the beauty that could have been. I had a blue tattoo on my face, over my left eye of various dots and swirls but, despite that, Séamus was right. I did look young. I felt young sometimes, despite how old I truly was. I could thank the lack of a childhood for that. The inner bairn within me yearned to escape its cage, but the monster guarding would not relent.

My body was lean and strong, with a slight curve to my hips. It was no wonder I have not taken a husband. I was no stunning Druid beauty, just a plain Laoch warrior, and I was proud of it. I tied up my snow-white hair into a braid at the crown of my head, two braids on the sides, and let the rest flow down. I had always wondered what I would have looked like with my mother's frosty curls instead of my father's pin-straight white hair. Nevertheless, time to quit sulking on vanity and do the task I was assigned.

I quickly glamoured the various blue markings over my body and held the scent of my magic close to me. "Alright then," I said to myself in the mirror before holding my Stone and passing through the veil to the human realm.

I blew a searing hot breath into my frozen hands and cursed the winter that plagued these lands. I looked around at the many faces around me, making sure no one saw the steam from my magic breath. The fur-lined leather coat and pants I wore laughed at my attempts to stay warm. It was barely even November, and the land was covered in snow and ice.

Trade was the same every other week or so. Someone, usually my friend Lana, brought goods and spices crafted by our people and sold them for gold and materials across human continents. It was the only way we were able to flourish since hiding. We made our goods as human as possible to not raise suspicions and have moved to different lands whenever we have traded in one place for too long. We had no one else but the humans to turn to for bartering, and without them, we surely would have perished.

"Oi, Jameson," I called. The young merchant boy looked up from his book and greeted me with a smile as I set my sack down on his stand. He was handsome for a human with short, cropped brown hair and a sweet young face that was not hardened by poverty like many boys around him. His father was a master merchant and had always been well off.

"Oh, Ev, it's been a while. You know, everyone still remembers what you did six months ago, probably not the best idea that you're here. No Elaine today?" Jameson asked.

Ah, Elaine, my dear friend Lana's alias. Lana became a little bit of a bridge between humans and Druids through the years. She was incredibly diplomatic and never raised any suspicions of our existence, unlike a few rowdy Druids. Of course, I meant myself. No one could hate or be suspicious of Lana. She was too kind.

I shook my head. "Only me from now on till Elaine can come back for me. And that old gasbag had it coming. Shorting *me* on coin, hah! Anyways cloth, crafting metals, pelts, um let's see, some of the jewels ye were looking for, chainmail, ye name it. Same selling price as always. Gold for the jewels, no trade."

He inspected the sacks of goods and handed over a large burlap of gold coins, far more than I was expecting to receive, but Lana had been sweet on this boy since we started trading in this area, and he had always given us more coin than he should. "Will you ever tell me where you find such exquisite items?"

I gave him a polite smile and packed away the gold into my bag. "Thank ye. I'll be seeing ye next month."

Before I could turn on my heels and leave, Jameson grabbed my arm. "You're a mercenary, yes? Have you heard the rumors?"

I bit my bottom lip and shook my head. "No, can't say I have." My heart stayed steady, but I felt his begin to race through the ground.

"Creatures have been spotted around here. Winged beasts. They have been crossing our borders from the Circle, or so they say. Not many, and those that claim they have spotted them, seem a little less than sane. But, it is still causing a stir around here," he lamented with wide eyes.

My blood ran cold. Even though my father warned me, they still terrorize my memories. The Sluagh. "What kind of winged beasts? What do ye know, child?"

"White grotesque beasts with tattered wings, and the snout of a serpent. You'll be safe in your sailing, will you?" His face was so innocent and full of hope. I prayed that innocents not be withered by war. I hoped to cap whatever it was brewing in the western Fae seas very soon.

"Have ye heard anything of the Sidhe? Um, or as you call them, Elite Fae? Have they crossed the borders as well?"

Jameson shook his head. "No, ma'am. I did not know they still lived. I thought Faery Circles were just a bedtime story. It makes me think this all a joke from some of the kids in town."

Damn. Of course the Fae would do nothing more than sit on their arses while the lackeys from their lands terrorized the humans. "Stay out of the forests and away from any Faery Circles, ye hear me? And tell everyone ye know. I'll be seeing ye next week."

Many wards still protected the Circle of rocks in the forest just south of the market; however, something seemed off about it. As if there were the essence of a hole in the magic guarding it, a door waiting to be opened. The magic that created this pocket was not that of the Elite Fae that put the wards in place. It was chilling magic. A magic I felt the day life as I knew it ended.

"Sabriel," I whispered. Dread rose within the pits of my soul as the scent of it made my stomach turn. What should have been my eighteenth birthday celebration was desecrated by this vile sorcery.

But why was he poking around the human realm? I thought he was content hiding in his hole all these years. The Circle was created to separate the realm of the Fae from humans. No Elites or lesser beings were able to step through it. What could Sabriel possibly want here? The Fae were obviously doing nothing to protect their borders. They were putrid beings with no sense of morality, so of course they would let this happen.

A twig snapped behind me, and my dual swords spun into my hands as I assumed a defensive stance. No one stood at the origin of the sound, but I could feel eyes roving my body, assessing me. Their magic, their glamour, poured off of them like a cheap perfume.

"Out from behind the veil then, and face me head-on, ya coward." My stealth and ability to disappear would not help me when my enemies lurked behind the veil I used for cover.

With a snap of white light, the beasts the merchant boy spoke of appeared. A troop of ten towered above my head, axes raised, snouts foaming. White as the snow around them, and their wings flapped about in the rushing wind. Some say the Sluagh were dead risen, fallen being of grace, but they were just monstrous lesser Fae working for Sabriel.

"A peculiar scent you have," the leader of the troop sneered, with a voice that could have chilled a roaring forest fire. Four archers, six brutes, and a rule from my father forbidding me to use my magic on this side of the Circle or against those that sought to slaughter us if they knew our kind still existed. If even one got away from this fight after I used my magic, they would run back to Sabriel, and he would know my kind still lived.

"I forgot to bathe last night. My apologies," I spat out and gave a sarcastic smile. Every step back I took, they matched. I made a quick note to avoid the Circle looming behind me in the snowy mud.

The pack leader cackled. "A lesser Faery, perhaps? Either way, a good snack before our journey home."

I knew the day would come when I had to face these beasts again, but no amount of sparring could have prepared me to fight those that murdered the ones I loved, that took away my home. Panic began to rise in my body. An archer fired an arrow, but my swords were quicker, and I batted it away with the flick of a wrist. Two brutes charged me. With one hand, my blade stopped an ax, and the other sliced through a face. A quick stab through a leg, then after a spin, a skull. The screams of the Sluagh jolted the memories of that haunting battlefield to the forefront of my mind, and I could not help but run.

They were quicker than me; curse my father. I

would not die here by not using my abilities. I focused my breath and willed the winds to drive me ahead of them. Images of blood and ruin clouded my vision, and my chest tightened as I panicked. The screams of family and friends rang through my ears in an attempt to send my mind back to the day of the invasion. I fought for my vision not to go dark from terror. The winds drove me faster and faster until I collided with a mass in front of me and heard the crunch of my nose breaking.

"Ah!" I grunted as my hands sprawled out in front of me to break my fall. Droplets of blood leaked from my nose and hit the snow like rubies in a sea of diamonds. A woman moaned in pain and held her head as she flipped in the snow. "Oi, ye okay lass?" I asked.

She turned to me and gave me a half-smile. Her face was radiant, sharp, and wonderfully golden. Her hair was a lovely honey color match, and her clothes were ornate, though I could tell they were battle leathers. As she moved her hair, I glimpsed through her glamour and saw her pointed ears, and my eyes found themselves rolling. *A cursed Sidhe; an Elite Fae.*

"I'm okay. I'm sorry, I didn't see you. You were running so fast, I-" she stammered.

I got up and glanced behind me, and the specks of white in the distance grew closer and closer. I wanted so badly to leave her, abandon her, as her kind did to us. But I did not have it in me. I would not see another suffer at the hands of those beasts. "Well, ye better get yer legs warmed and ready for a run. Now."

I gripped her arm and pulled her along with me, gathering back the speed of the howling wind. A buzz zipped past my ears and another. The archers were firing as they struggled to keep up.

"Iron bolts!" the Elite panted out. "How are you running so fast?"

"Shut yer gob and run!" I shouted with a groan.

I thought the Elite Fae were the fastest and strongest of their kind, but this woman weighed me down. I could not keep dragging her like this; the Sluagh were gaining on us. A sharp pain tore through my side, just past my kidney, and slammed me into the ground with a cry. An iron bolt now pointed through my abdomen.

"Shite!" I cried. The Elite Fae woman looked at me in horror and drew her sword as I hobbled to my feet.

"End them," the leader of the troop instructed, and then we were surrounded.

I unsheathed my swords. The thirst for the blood of these creatures replaced all panic held in my body. Every attack was blocked and countered, arrows were dodged. The Sidhe woman kept pace with me, a strong fighter indeed, but I was wounded and could tell she was no warrior.

At last, only the leader and one other stood. He lunged at me, and I crossed my swords over his axe and kicked his knees back. As he crashed down again, one of my blades blocked, and the other drove deep into his side. His ear-piercing squeal could have melted my brain right out of the side of my head. As he faltered, I plunged my sword into his neck and collapsed, clutching my side.

The woman rushed over to me after she took out the last one standing. "I can heal you. It may sting."

I shoved her hands away and noticed the blue tattoos on my arm. My glamour was fleeting with my strength. I curled my lip. "Piss off if ye know what's good for ye. Slimy Sidhe."

With a deep breath and a cry, I broke the tip of the iron bolt clean off, not caring if she noticed my strength, and pulled it out of my body. The snow around me melted as a sea of red stained its purity. I could heal myself. I did not need the help of a sniffling Elite. Why was she here? How did she pass through the wards?

"I'm not like them. I'm an Elite. I won't hurt you." Before I could protest, her hands gripped my wound, and it disappeared with slight pain. She then twisted my nose back into place. "There. Thank you for saving me. I couldn't have taken them all on by myself."

I looked her up and down and pushed her away again. A screech from in the distance had me on my feet and marching away so I could travel home. "I know what ye are. That's why I'll say it one more time. Piss. Off. I have no business with yer kind."

She ran ahead of me with her arms out, halting me in my path. "Please, I can't get back through the Circle. I came here after the Sluagh and thought there were only two or three. Don't you have to go back as well? How did *you* get through the wards? You look human, but you-you were impaled by iron. You broke the bolt clean in half."

I stopped in my tracks and drew my sword to her throat. "Ye'll forget ye saw me today. Do ye understand? I don't come from Verbenia or any other lands in which your filth dwells. How ye get back is no concern of mine," my words attacked her like the venom spat from a viper.

She looked behind me as another squeal sounded. "Well, I know you don't come from here. Help me get back, and I'll forget I ever saw you."

I searched her eyes for deceit and could not find any—only fear of what would happen if I left her to the Sluagh. I sheathed my swords on my back and sighed. "We'll have to wait for them to pass, lest ye want another fight on yer hands."

Her beautiful face lit, and she held out her hand. "It's a bargain then?"

I pushed her hand away and let out a low snarl. "I don't need a bargain to keep my word." Now, off to find a hole to hide in while these beasts storm through the forest.

CHAPTER TWO

Eadha

We sprinted to a nearby cave, moved rocks over the entrance, and waited. I did not let my eyes off the woman or move my hand from the dagger attached to my thigh. She studied me while fastening a veil around her hair. It must have come off when I collided with her. I've heard of some Fae veiling their hair for modesty, so I looked away until she finished.

"My name is Áine," she said warmly.

How dare a Fae take the name of one of our goddesses. I shrugged and shook my head, the corners of my mouth pulled down. "Don't care." I did not want to know who she was.

Áine scoffed and rolled her eyes, picking at her nails. She did not look pompous or too terribly awful. Her cheeks were rather round with a natural rosy blush, and her red lips were striking against her darker skin that was the color of strongly steeped black tea with just a splash of cream. Her features were angular but not as aggressive as most Fae. The ornate battle outfit she wore proved she was here for a fight, yes, but there was still the question of how she or the Sluagh got through the Circle, and why they were here.

"If we are going to be in here a while, can I at least know your name?" Her eyes were, in fact, kind. They looked like bright pools of golden honey, and her mouth twitched into a half-hearted smile as she inched away from the door, closer to me.

I raised my dagger to my lap and cleared my throat. "No. How did ye get through the Circle?"

Áine smiled warmly. "Question for a question, how about that?"

I let out a long sigh, keeping my blade stiff in my hand. "Eadha. My name is Eadha. How did ye get through the Circle?"

She pursed her lips to the side, and she began picking at her nails again. "The wards are slipping, and we don't know why. I was able to slip through, but I couldn't get back in. See, there is an Elite Fae across the oceans on our lands who-"

"Aye. Sabriel," I interjected. "I figured the wards weren't slipping, and he was probably chipping away at them. I smelled the stench of his magic the second I got close. What all do ye know of him? How is he doing this, and why? What does he want here?"

She clicked her tongue. "From what my husband, Rigel, has been saying, the Sluagh have only crossed the Circle one other time. We still don't know why. Alright, my turn for a question. What, um, what are you? Do you come from Aerras? I felt the wind pushing your sprint."

I choked on the saliva in my throat and got sent into a pathetic half laughing, half coughing fit. Aerras, the Kingdom of Wind. Home of the most haughty of all the Elite Fae. I could see where her assumptions came from. Those that dwelled there bore the power of the wind.

"No, gods no. I do not come from Aerras. But *you* healed me, so ye must be a Ruling Fae's daughter with that power. Ye have eyes of honey, golden hair, sun-kissed glittery skin. I assume you come from...Fossera, yes?"

The Elite Fae that dwelled in Fossera had the healing powers of light. Although, the leathers she wore were black, crested with red gems, and did not reflect the land of sand and sun. Images of winged beasts lined her vambraces, and her armor was imprinted with feathers.

She stiffened with my words and turned her face to look through the cracks of the makeshift door. As the light from outside hit her face, I could see the glittery freckles on her skin and how young she truly looked. Fae were immortal, but they became rough and callous with age, much like myself. She seemed sweet and beaming with youth.

"Yes to both of your theories. If I could hide where I come from like you, I would. My love is the ruler of Tenebris. As you can see, that posed some conflict. Needless to say, I had to fight to get out," she said solemnly.

Whatever warmth she began to make me feel chilled with her words: Tenebris, the Land of Darkness, the kingdom my parents were the closest to, worked with even, that betrayed us. I wondered what scum was leading that nation now.

Áine must have seen the look of disgust on my face, and her smile vanished. "My husband is a great man and an impeccable leader. He saved me when I had nothing and no one. My father fought against closing off the Fae lands, I'll have you know, unlike Rigel," she paused and looked me in the eyes. "What do you have against our kind? You called me a *Sidhe*. If you speak my people's old language, you must-"

I put a finger over my lips as sniffing ensued outside. With a wave of a hand, I willed the winds to carry our scent away from our cave. Once the heavy steps retreated, my finger fell. Áine's question almost made me smile. I would need at least five hands to list every reason why I hated her kind.

"I speak *my* language. And Rigel? Is that the name of the walloper in charge over there now?"

She cocked an eyebrow at me. "Rigel was crowned about five centuries ago. You said you don't come from Verbenia or anywhere on our lands. Where *do* you come from? You have magic from what I can see and feel."

I did not know if it was the sweetness of her voice or the truth in her eyes, but I found my anger slipping. Maybe, just maybe, the gods crossed our paths today. She seemed genuine enough. Perhaps we could form an alliance. After all, war was won with numbers and expendable bodies. I would need both.

I sheathed my dagger and narrowed my gaze. "How old are ye lass?"

She stirred, and her cheeks blushed a rosy pink under her light bronze skin. "Fifty-two. But I'm not naive. I've seen my share of atrocities and pull my weight in my kingdom."

Goddess above, I was right in my assumptions of her being young, but she was still a bairn compared to how many years I had on this earth. It almost made *me* blush. Maybe Áine could be useful to me. I would not abuse her kindness, but I needed to take what I could get. This "Rigel" seemed to be monitoring the situation at the borders. If he had information, I would like to know about it. I could use whatever armies her land held and lose less of my men in the conflict.

I took a deep breath. "I'll make ye a bargain since yer kind loves doing such things. I'll tell ye what I am, but no one can know. It needs to stay between *you* and *me*. A whole nation depends on it. In exchange, if need be, I can call on ye without question. And ye can call on me." She held out her arm, and I shook her hand; a white light of magic bound her word to mine.

I took another deep breath and glued my eyes to the rocks covering our entranced. "I'm a High Druid. Well, born a High Druid. I joined the elite army of our kind, the Laoch, when I was just shy of twenty years."

Her brows furrowed, and her head cocked to the side. "A Druid? The Druids went extinct centuries ago. From the very little I learned in lessons as a child, there is no history or record of them existing, save for first-hand accounts passed down."

I nodded and chuckled. "Aye. We made sure to wipe our existence after the invasion. What ye call Kamber Island, we called home. Covalla. The closest thing to the Otherworld ye can get on this earth."

A snort sounded from Áine. "Nothing delightful about that gods' forsaken land. What happened?"

I flicked my gaze to hers. "Sabriel happened. He came out of nowhere from the north and invaded. He just started slaughtering any person in sight, wielding a dark magic my parents have never seen before. If it weren't for that magic, we would have ground their bones to dust. Many lesser and High Druids worked with yer kind, but no one came to our aid that day. So, to answer yer question, that is why I hate yer kind. Ye killed us, " I did not hide the anger in my voice.

She scooted closer and placed a hand on my knee, but I recoiled. "So, are you the same as witches then?

Humans wielding magic?"

I could not help but glare at her and roll my eyes. "No. We are comparable to yer priests and priestesses. Only we don't work on *behalf* of gods and goddesses. We work *with* them. Well, the High Druids do. Lesser Druids will work with Fae, daemons, and other beings of the like. Our powers are gifts from those we work with, although High Druids are born with some abilities. My father is a seer, for example, and I have stealth abilities."

Áine shifted onto her knees with a baffled look on her face. "How come nothing of your existence survives? There are no writings, no documents. I never even learned about the invasion." I could see a look of concern flash in her eyes, and maybe even a splash of guilt.

"My parents are the most powerful of our kind; the Tiarna. They were able to move our entire capital city through the veil and ward it from being seen or tangible to anything other than Druids. They also wiped away our manuscripts and history so Sabriel would believe us dead, and no other beings would set out to find us. Every day they work to keep the wards in place and keep the knowledge of us gone. Their strength never fully recovered from that day."

She stared at the ground, taking in my words and choosing her next questions carefully. Why I was so forthcoming about myself, I did not know. I would much rather be out there, killing those beasts, breaking their legs, and taking them hostage. But a group is too much for me to manage without magic. If one survived and made it back to their master with the knowledge of the magic I used, my peoples' safety would be jeopardized.

"Do you know why he invaded your lands? Why haven't you gone back?" She gazed up at me like a child listening to a riveting bedtime story.

My face fell further, and I looked her right in the eye. "We were sacred, coveted people. Yer kind came to us in search of seers and spellmakers. My parents are ancient and some of the most powerful rulers my people have seen. We were not immortal until they forged a spell to make it so. *That* is the kind of power they have and what many lusted after. They work with deities that ruled over yer kind when they walked the world. Many have tried to infiltrate our lands and steal our secrets, but only he succeeded. We were too weak to go back on our own," and soon, we would have no choice.

A dainty hand grabbed my arm, and Áine sighed. "Thank you for confiding in me. I could not imagine if my home was taken from me, well, I had to escape mine."

I was relieved to change the subject from my past to hers. "Well, tell me about it."

She took off and unleashed the story.

"It's simple, really, at least to me. My father took me to Tenebris for a meeting about two decades ago. I saw Rigel and fell in love with him at first sight. I have an older brother, Norr, who would be taking the throne from my father, so I thought I could leave and not be missed," her smile fell, and she hugged her knees tight. "My father resented it. He kept me from seeing Rigel. Locked me away is more like it. Luckily his Ravens helped me escape and-"

I shook my head and held up my hands. "Hold on, hold on, Ravens?"

She chuckled. "Well, they're Vespairans, not Fae. I

don't know what they are or where they come from, but they call themselves Ravens. They look human, with rounded ears and soft faces, but have beautiful black feathered wings. Well, almost all of them. Mindless brutes, some of them are. But they saved me, and tensions have been high between our lands ever since."

I raised an eyebrow. "Mindless brutes? Sounds like the Laoch, ye said only some of them had feathered wings?"

Áine twisted her mouth and sighed. "Rigel has two of them working in his court: Sorlin and Corvis. Sorlin is...insufferable, to say the least. Amazing fighter, head of the Raven army, but could use a good ass-kicking now and again. Corv is a different breed. He has wings that are, well, they look like the Sluagh, but they didn't always look like that. He is a talented veilwalker, and his mother was a wraith. I love them both dearly."

Bat like wings on a Raven? *Wonder what happened to him.* If I made an ally out of Áine, I wondered if the Ravens would be included in her fleet. That would be the kind of manpower I would need. I felt content sitting here and chatting with her. I was tempted to feel a bit treacherous to my people, but talking to her made me feel like I had an ally I could trust.

"The daughter of the sun fell in love with the son of the moon. How precious," I said with a sarcastic smile. If love were ever in my cards, I would want such a heart pulling tale.

"We have a bond I just can't explain. We feel each other's pain, happiness, even dreams. I couldn't stay away. My brother has been relentless in trying to get me to come home. I love Rigel so much I couldn't imagine leaving."

I nodded. "We have a word for that kind of bond. *Anam Cara.* Means soulmate, other half, or even eternal friend. It's a rare, magical bond, almost unnatural. We believe ye have yer other half since before yer born, just have to find them. Of course, ye could always detest and reject them but, to each their own."

She went on about how she loved her old kingdom of Fessera but had an affection for Tenebris that had no bounds. She told me about her close friends and family, and I actually enjoyed listening. I believed when the time came, if I ever were to call on her, she would answer. I did not realize how late we had been talking until the shadows outside shifted with the dying sun.

"Well, we should get ye back," I said, standing up with a grunt. My feet tingled from having sat on them for the past few hours.

"Yes, Rigel will be worried. I-I came here without him knowing. I just saw those beasts flying over our lands and couldn't let them go through the Circle."

I knew I made the right choice in trusting her. "Well, I can try and open the wards, or ye can walk through the veil with me. Yer choice."

She looked at me, wide-eyed. "You're a veil-walker? I'll take my chances with the Circle. Tearing through the veil always frightened me."

I nodded, and we made our way to the Circle. I was never afraid of that thin veil that separated our reality from the darkness on the other side. It was hard learning to keep my footing as the winds and darkness ripped past me, but once I mastered it, I became our most vital spy. The Laoch generals could not wait to send me to do all of their dirty work for them. Instead of walking through it, I soared, almost as if I could snap my fingers and appear at my destination. I even mastered the technique of slipping just past it, to disappear. I scared the daylights out of my mother with that trick more often than I was willing to admit.

The Sluagh have since passed. Where they went, I did not know. While hiding in the cave, I heard no screams or cries of pain, so I could only assume they crossed the borders looking for something. The wards on the Circle were meant to keep Fae and others of the like confined into their lands. I still did not know how Áine passed through, but her people were spell breakers, so that may have been the answer.

I pulled out my Druid Stone once we arrived at the Circle. When the Fae crafted it, no one thought to ward against the Druids. We have long hidden away and out of memory. I focused and opened the Circle with a flash of white light. "Ye never told me how ye got through, lass. Yer kind isn't supposed to be here on this side."

She huffed and brushed a few strands of hair out of her face and tucked them into her veil. "I followed them through. I felt a hole and pushed past it, but it closed off as soon as I broke through to this side. *They* closed it off."

I turned to leave, but Áine let out a gasp. "Wait, our bargain. How will you call on me?"

"The wards are only going to get weaker. Every other week we make trades at the market just north of here. There is a young man named Jameson, leave a letter with him if ye need me. Pass through and glamour yerself before going. If *I* need ye, I'll send a letter through the veil."

She nodded and grabbed my hand. "Thank you, Eadha," and with that, she left.

I was unsure if my parents would approve of the decision to take on an ally without their knowledge, but if we are going to war, we would need all the bodies we could get.

When I returned to the palace, the sun had set, and I retreated to my room. I willed the candles to spark and illuminate the way to the bath. As the water filled, the weight of the day crashed down into me, and a warm tear fell down my face, and my body began to shake with my sobs.

I choked today. I let the past chew me up and swallow me whole. I ran when I should have stood my ground against those oversized white bats. All these years, I lived and breathed training and fighting. I was my people's greatest warrior, and all I could do was run and hide. I hid in a cave with one of the beings I was supposed to hate. All I could do now is hope Áine's honeyed personality lived true, and that I did not betray my people today.

I jolted as a knock sounded at the door, and Séamus poked his head in. "Yer home late. Trade didn't go smoothly?"

I quickly wiped my eyes and faced him. "Was fine, if ye can see I'm a tad busy right now," I said flatly and motioned to the bath that was now close to overflowing.

His green eyes pierced me down to my core and found my dishonesty. "What happened Eadha?" A demand, not a question.

What should I tell him? That I was a coward? That I ran from the same beasts I should want to roast on a spit? A tear threatened to plague my eyes again, but

I quickly subdued it.

"The wards on the Faery Circles are slipping. Well, on the one I found at least. I-I had to fight off a group of Sluagh, then hide from some more."

His already pale skin drained of color at my words. That fateful day probably flashed in his eyes as he staggered back. "Sluagh?" he whispered, "How? Why are there Sluagh in human territories? Did ye tell the Tiarna?"

I shook my head. "I just got back. I don't know how sensitive this information is, Séamus, so keep it between us. My father had a vision; he said Sabriel was going to attempt to open the sacred Well on our homeland."

I could have sworn I saw Séamus flinch. "For what reason?"

"That day he invaded, he captured me and questioned me on the whereabouts of my parents. He needed the power of the Tiarna for something. What if he wanted to open it all along? He wanted so desperately for me to tell him where my parents were. He has been ransacking temples across the Fae lands. I bet there are troves out there just as powerful that could break the wards on that Well."

The wards on the Circles were powerful. It would only make sense that Sabriel was using them for practice. The question was, who or what exactly was he trying to release from the Otherworld?

Séamus narrowed his gaze. "What will ye have us do then?"

"It's not up to me," I said exasperatedly.

"After what happened on that island, ye know our people look to *you* for leadership. Yer parents know it too. We move on yer word. This is bigger than keeping our people secret and safe. No one will be safe if he opens that Well."

I was no leader. A leader would not have given up the secret of their race's existence on the whim that some Fae would help them go to war. A leader would not have run away today.

"Well, we may have help if we must attack. I met an Elite out in the woods today. Married to the High Lord of Tenebris, daughter of the High Lord of Fossera. She seemed sound enough, and we made a bargain." If a look could slice me dead, I would be cut in half by Séamus's eyes.

"What bargain?"

I chewed the inside of my cheek and contemplated my next words. "I told her who I was, and she speaks of it to no one. In return, I can call on her for aid. She was genuine in her words, and I saw no ill intent in her eyes."

Séamus chuckled and wiped his mouth. "I take back what I said about you being a leader. Yer daft is what ye are. Fosserans are the sirens of the earth. Trickin' ye with their beauty and sweetness only to trap ya like a bug in a web. They are despicable creatures. And she's married to the Lord of Tenebris? Do ye forget what that court did to us? To *you*?"

He was right. The High Lord of Tenebris sold our people to Sabriel in exchange for power. It was not only reckless but incredibly stupid of me to trust the words of a Fae, given our history, but I did not have a choice.

I sent Séamus my own death inspiring glare. "Ye will not speak of what happened to me. Especially when what *I* did saved *yer* hide. Get out. Speak nothing of what I told ye tonight."

After giving me a look of disdain, he left my bathroom and slammed my bedroom door shut. I knew the reputation of the Fosserans, but somehow Áine was different. I blocked out all thoughts of betrayal and reveled in the idea of having an ally in the Fae lands and the armies that came with it. When my group of four, Lana, Séamus, and the twins, were not all trying to kill each other out of boredom or spite, we did get along quite nicely. But we would not be enough to stop a being from the Otherworld alone.

One of the perks of staying in the palace was the bed. In the camps, we slept in our tents on the ground, no bath for days and hardly any change of clothes. If my fellow Laoch did not accept me as one of them with open arms, I would not be surprised if they tried to kill me for retreating to a palace now and then. They understood my circumstances. I was the daughter of our rulers.

The sheets were warm and inviting, but my racing mind prevented me from sleeping. Talking to Áine today made me lust for the life I could have had. My twin brother Tadhg would have taken the throne when the god and goddess chose to work with him. He would be alive and would be beaming with joy as he received his title. I would cry with pride for my brother and whichever woman he chose to marry. Of course, I would have to hate her because no one would have been good enough for him. I would have become a Laoch by training and going through initiation, working my way to the top instead of having to knock on death's door at the hands of Sabriel. I would not be physically scarred for the rest of my life.

I would have fought many battles for my people and protected others instead of standing in the mud, hiding. I would never have had to cover the shame permanently marked on my back. Maybe I would have even taken a husband. My parents would have decided it was their time to cross over into the Otherworld after seeing my brother crowned and married. Life would have been so easy and free of pain, and I could have enjoyed my young years.

Love was a trivial and childish thing for me to have thought about in these times. There was something about how Áine spoke of her husband, Rigel, and her people that gave me a sense of longing. I wanted someone to speak of me the way she did of him, her love. When this was all over, I hope one day someone lights up for me the way she did for him. If I were beautiful like my parents, it would come easy to me, but a savage Laoch covered in blue ink marks I would remain.

I was not ashamed of my marks. They each symbol an act of valor committed and reminded me why I had chosen to stay alive all these years when I could have quit; my people needed me. Every day my power grew as the ones I worked with bestowed more gifts upon me, and I would give every drop of it to protect my people. My eyes grew heavy, and the sound of distant waves on the coast lulled me to sleep.

The night spared me a nightmare and instead plagued my slumber with a peculiar dream. I was standing in the grand courtyard, walking down an aisle. In the end, my parents were ready to join me in unity with a man. Deep within my belly, I felt a tug. As if a thread the size of a hair was wrapped around my insides, pulling me further ahead. Hot tears stream down my face, but they were tears of joy. The man offered me a hand, and I accepted it, beaming with happiness. When I turned to see who my love was, he was a figure made of soft blooming shadows.

I could not help but chuckle when I woke up. There have only been a few dreams that haunted me at night. Some happy, but mostly nightmares. My more joyous dreams were me sitting in a cavern, in which I have never been, that was illuminated by glowing crystals, with a waterfall cascading down in front of me. Sometimes I read, and sometimes a voice read out loud to me. They were my best dreams. Then, of course, there were the nightmares of the invasion and what happened to me. This dream was new, yet it felt oddly familiar. There would be a time to ponder its meaning, but now, I needed to meet with my parents to find out what all they knew of the looming threat in the southwest.

My closet was riddled with impractical Druid fashion of tight hugging dresses and silks, but I shoved a few of my go-to outfits in there. I wore a plain blue cropped shirt with sleeves that cut to my elbows, exposing my mid-drift, black suede legging, and a sleeveless wolf pelt as an overcoat. Though sometimes a different cut or color, this was my usual attire and what the women of the Laoch wore.

Winter just hit our lands, but I had no problem warming myself with my magic. I cursed my hair as I pulled it all in one unruly braid going down my head. On my left wrist, I put on my family's torc that signified my status as a High Druid. It was a simple white gold band with sapphires on each end. After strapping a dagger to my thigh and my swords to my back, I went off to find my parents.

Séamus, Lana, and the twins stood with my parents around the large table in the war room. I gave Séamus an: "If ye flapped yer gums to them about what happened, I'd gut ye like a fish," look. He returned my gaze, with expressions telling me to calm down.

"Eadha, welcome. Everyone be seated," my father motioned for me to take my place. "Since I know my daughter all too well, I assume you, Séamus, learned about the threats brewing on the dark island. And since I know *you* as well," he nodded to Séamus, then looked to the others, "I assume you three are also aware?"

Lana, Donnan, and Dolan nodded slowly, avoiding the daggers Séamus and I were shooting out of our eyes at them.

My father huffed. "That's what I thought. What is conversed about in this room does not leave. Lest Aerona and I subject you to the punishment Eadha sees fit. Donnan, Dolan, that means you." Donnan gawked as if he had not gone and blabbered our plans to other Laoch, but Dolan smacked him in the back of the head. I motioned for them to stop being children as my father continued.

"As of now, the vision I had is the only one concerning Sabriel. Whatever trove he has in his possession that gives him this dark magic, prevents me from seeing him and his paths. The future can change, and what we need to focus on now is finding what gives him his magic and bringing a piece of it back to me so we can track his movements."

Lana shot her deep sapphire eyes to me, wide as saucers, and cleared her throat. "Ye want us to go to the island? And search around right under the bastard's nose?" She draped a lock of her straight, auburn hair behind her ear.

My mother took a deep breath. "It's what needs to be done. Even if we cannot prevent him from opening the Well, which I pray we do, knowing when he will strike and knowing what he is trying to bring out will help us fight and survive. Eadha, you have spies, and you have stealth. You have two veilwalkers that can bring in Donnan and Dolan. It's all your call. Gather all the information you can, and when you have a plan, come to us for approval."

My friends looked at me the same way they did all those years ago, ready to fight by my side. "Alright then. I'll send out spies across Verbenia, see if his plight spread to the Fae lands. We can ask around for what temples were raided and what was stolen. If I sense any danger, anything we are not prepared for, I go myself."

Séamus scoffed. "Well, what all do we have to lose? If we die, we have thousands to take our place. This is what we have been preparing for. We all go, or nothing. Whatever Sabriel lets out of bed, we'll have a kettle ready for some tea and hope it's quite jolly."

Lana held back a smile and nodded in agreement, but I found no humor in his words. I saw what Sabriel was capable of. I saw what he wished to do to our kind. I would put my head on a blade before allowing any of my friends to experience that horror. I simply nodded, knowing that I would lock them away when the time came and go myself if I must.

"Then it's decided. Faolan, if you could please get out the map, let's go over what we already know," my mother said, turning to my father. He pulled out the

map of the Fae land, Verbenia, and we began to make
our plans.

CHAPTER THREE
Eadha

Weeks turned into months, and months turned into years since the day I met Áine. Five, to be exact. I never told anyone other than Séamus about her. I knew many of my people would instead march to their graves than side by side with a Fae. I used to think of her often, but only on days when we spoke of the looming possibilities of war. Today was one of those days.

We had no progress in finding the motive behind Sabriel's wanting to open the Well. The spies of lesser Druids and myself had not seen the Faery Circle crossed by any entities since I met Áine in the woods. The good news was, the Sluagh had not been crossing into the human lands, and the wards remained intact. As for the bad news, there had been a silence across Verbenia. Sabriel had most likely found whatever he needed to open the Well, and now we were just waiting. The Laoch grew restless waiting for the order to strike and worked tirelessly to train for the battle that may lie ahead.

The sun beat down on the war camp, and the winds blew the scent of honeysuckle on the breeze. June had proven to be a mild summer month, though I lusted for autumn's delicate chill to creep into our lands soon. The sun had always been unkind to my fair skin.

Lana had pestered me every day she saw me of my plans for the five of us going to the island. If I told her, then that meant the plan was spoken into existence, and it would not be enjoyable. It took five years for me to come up with this. Five years of studying and sneaking, but I feel I had finally cracked it.

‡

"So, what yer saying is, ye have no plan," Lana said as she bit into her apple and stared blankly at me.

As June began and the days crept closer to Mabon, the autumnal equinox, Lana stopped eating and sleeping regularly. She did not think anyone noticed, but I did. Her dark blue eyes were garnished with purple rings beneath them. Although, the three blue ink slashes she had over each eye did an excellent job of hiding them. Her round face turned sharp as her features jutted out little more than usual, and her thick auburn hair grew thin. She looked absolutely exhausted and would spend hours finding work to do to keep herself occupied. It was a ritual we all shared and spoke nothing of.

I rolled my eyes and crossed my arms. "I cannot just waltz into the most guarded and protected lands in all the world, search for whatever it is Sabriel used to take us out, and somehow break off a piece of it and bring it back for my father. I'm good, but I'm not *that* good. I do have a plan."

She just shrugged, her blue eyes not meeting my gaze. "Well, ye had five years of sniffing about, and ye found nothing. So now what?"

I scoffed. "I didn't find 'nothing,' I found the raided temples in the Fae lands had nothing stolen. So maybe Sabriel has not found what he was looking for."

Lana stood and shook her head. "But there has been no word since. He clearly has what he needs. Every day we wait is a day closer to him opening that Well and-"

"*I have a plan*," I said aggressively. "But it involves stealing from the Fae *and* the Tiarna. So if ye wouldn't mind letting me finish and keep yer voice down, I'll tell ye."

Her mouth dropped, and she nodded, eyes beaming. I took a look around and pulled her into my tent. "What if we destroy the Well."

Lana cackled with her hands on her stomach and wiped away fake tears. "Oh yeah, while we're at it, let's fight the Morrígan, or ask yer father to call on Arawn for a cup of tea. I'm sure the god of death and revenge prefers chamomile."

While the thought of my father's patron sipping tea in a garden made me chuckle, I grabbed Lana by the shoulders and shook her a little. "Lana, yer forgetting who my parents are. My father *works* with Arawn. He is one of the most powerful deities. As myth tells, Arawn possessed a cauldron of great power when it had all its pieces. If what they say is true of him, I think the power of that cauldron could break the Well."

Lana pushed me away and brushed wrinkles out of her blue tunic. "That's just a myth."

I gawked at her. "Oh, so we have Bríg's Sacred Well, the portal to the Otherworld, but magic cauldrons are just taking it too far for ye? We lived on the same land of the gods from before once stood. Their treasures are there. It's why we were invaded in the first place."

"Okay, okay, but Arawn is a wrathful god who will only work with the Tiarna. The only reason there *are* all-powerful Tiarna is because of his and Macha's magic. Unless you plan to take the throne and go through the rite, how will you wield his cauldron? Doesn't legend also say it was broken and given to the Fae since he ruled over them?"

I already had those I worked with, though I had not spoken to them in more time than I was proud to admit. If I took the title, it would break our working bond, and I would lose the power I worked tirelessly to acquire, or worse, they would kill me. Plus, my brother was being groomed by the god and goddess for the title, not me.

I huffed. "The seven jewels that lined the cauldron were each given to one of the Ruling Fae and one to the Druids when the gods left this world many millennia ago. If I can steal each jewel and reunite them with the cauldron, we may be able to destroy the portal. The gods have us, so they don't need to come back. *We* do *their* bidding. It will work, I know it will."

I realized the weight I was putting on all of my friends' shoulders. Being off of our lands caused many Druids' magic to grow weak. Séamus, who worked with Badbh, goddess of war, rage, and fury, lost a portion of his magic. One of the only reasons we made it out alive the day of the invasion was because of his ferocity and weapon forging abilities. But even he could no longer call upon his matron. The only thing that had saved them from losing everything was the Druid Stones we all held, keeping what little connection we had to our deities and magical beings. Lesser Druids, who worked with Fae like Lana, lost almost all of their magic.

Lana worked with Fosserans and had healing abilities. After the war, her Stone allowed her to heal herself slowly but could no longer heal others. She yearned to work with Airmed, the goddess of healing and resurrection, but she was born of lesser blood and could not hold such power. However, Donnan and Dolan were not Druids, and their strength and speed all came from the breeding of Laoch. At least our armies would hold firm if we went to war.

I was lucky. I was the only High Druid that did not work with gods, so my abilities held true. I was the first Druid to ever work with the four Dragons of the elements: Cré, Aer, Uisce, and Tine. They called on me as they wished and granted me a piece of themselves that lived within me. They did not control the elements; they *were* the elements. The power that they gave me was not magic, but something else. Something I could not explain, like a piece of the universe itself, lived in my soul.

Lana brushed her hair out of her face and nodded. "I'll follow ye to the grave, and ye know that. If this is what ye think is best, then tell me what I need to do."

A smile spread across my face, and I squeezed her shoulders. "I'll figure out how to get the stones. Hopefully, my stealth will be enough. Then, I'll need ye three to come with me to the island. We will have Covalla by the end of autumn. I promise ye that."

"Aye. Well, do ye have the weapons for Jameson? I'm going to trade in three days, and ye still haven't given them to me. And I won't tell Donnan and Dolan about this. Ye have my word. If ye tell Séamus though, he won't let ye go through with it."

Séamus would indeed be a problem. He knew me so well. It would be hard to hide anything from him. Part of my words to Lana were lies. I did not intend to bring any of them with me. I just needed to get the Laoch under control long enough to plan my leaving.

I looked back at her and smiled. "That's why I say let me handle the stones. Weapons are in the east barracks. Are ye going to be warming that human boy's bed after, or no?"

A shove on my back made me stumble, and Lana pushed her middle finger into my face before leaving. The only happiness she had found in the last six months had been from Jameson. I was glad for it. She loses herself so quickly this time of the year. The five of us did not speak about that day and how it had affected us. We made a silent vow that we would not be the same as we once were and never would speak of the horrors that they saw me endure so they could escape.

Lana, Séamus, and I were aspiring rowdy Laoch before the invasion, but Lana was always the more gentle and tender of us. As a healer, I could not imagine what it felt like being surrounded by so much carnage or what leaving me behind did to her. If Séamus or the twins suffered, they did a brilliant job hiding it, but I do not doubt their nights were filled with the same nightmares as mine.

As I walked through the war camp to meet with my spies, people stopped and bowed their heads to me. The Laoch were growing restless and bloodthirsty since word got around that we were planning on moving in on Sabriel. My people had always been divided into groups: the Laoch, the Druids, and the plainsfolk. Warlords governed the Laoch, Druids had the council, and then the plainsfolk, Druids born without magical abilities, had their representation. But, all answered to the Tiarna.

When I returned to my people, all of them looked to me for leadership and guidance. Some even called *me* Tiarna. As much as I despised it, it warmed my heart that my people were finally united despite the circumstances.

I walked into the area of the camp that housed my spies. Some were Druids turned Laoch, and others were Druids who pledged their services to me, but all were veilwalkers. Séamus looked up and silenced the commotion in the room.

I cleared my throat. "Alright, I called ye all here in secrecy. What is spoken about in this room will not leave. And if it does, ye'll be thrown in the pit with Séamus and me and will fight to the death. Are we all in agreement?" My tone, flat and cold, made the color in their faces drain as they nodded.

Séamus raised an eyebrow and took a seat. The only person I could trust fully with my plan was Lana. Even to Séamus, I needed to lie. He would never let me go through with such a risky strategy. None of my friends could know I intended to go to that island by myself.

"Good. I need each one of ye to go to one of the Fae courts and give me the locations of a stone. It will be heavily guarded and filled with vicious magic. Ye'll tell me where they are all being held, but do not attempt to steal them."

Séamus looked at me as if he could read my thought to see what I was planning and clenched his jaw. As High Druids, we were in the same classes as younglings, learning our history and the gods we worked with. He knew what those stones were. He wisely did not speak about his speculations.

One of my spies raised her hand. "Are these stones dangerous? What will they look like?"

I nodded. "Aye, they are dangerous. That is why ye tell me where they are and do not touch them. I do not know how they look. I can only assume the stones will reflect the Ruling Fae that hold them. Use yer gods given stealth and get out swiftly. If ye come across anything ye cannot handle, ye leave. Figure out amongst yerselves who goes where and leave soon."

And with that, I left. Séamus followed close behind and yanked my elbow, bringing me to a halt. My eyes rolled, and I sized him up. My friend he may have been, but I was still general, and my word was law. If he had a problem with it, no amount of violence would sway me.

"And what are ye planning on doing with these stones? Don't ye dare think me an eejit. I know what they are," his voice was forceful and forbidding.

My lip curled. "Don't worry about me. If I get these stones, ye'll know full well what I am planning. Until then, shut yer trap and do yer job. The brutes are looking shabby and soft thanks to ye."

A sword met his hands as fast as lightning and held it to my throat. Red crept into my vision as my fingers twitched over my dagger.

"For how many years, Eadha, have I been at yer side, watching ye carry these people on yer back? How many years have I sat, watching ye destroy yerself, saying nothing? How many years have I lived with the memory of my best mate chained to a post and bleed to the bone, only to leave her behind? I can only imagine what yer thinking on doing, and I assume ye think yer doing it alone."

The steel of my dagger let out a scream as it slid down his sword, and I kicked him back. Many Laoch drew their weapons and glued their eyes to us. The blue tattooed bear made from various knots and swirls down Séamus's torso flexed with his deep, heaving breaths.

My breath was uneven as I shook with anger. "Ye will not speak to me about what I do for my people! Whatever I do is no concern of yers," I yelled and swung at him with my blade.

He laughed. "Oh, that's rich, isn't it? Yer *my* Tiarna. To the Otherworld with whatever blame and hate ye harbor in yerself that blinds ye from seeing that. *You* are the one we look to for direction, for leadership. To me and everyone else, our job is to protect *you,* like it or not. Everything ye do is my concern. Gods, even yer parents believed ye to be the heir ever since ye were born!"

His voice grew, and my knuckles turned white as I clutched my blade. The torches around us swelled with my breaths as the ferocity of the fire coursed through my veins. "Ye have no idea what yer talking about. I will not have anyone touch those lands until it is safe. Our people have suffered enough."

He stepped forward, and the cold tip of his sword kissed my neck. "No, *you* have suffered enough. I won't tell the Tiarna what ye plan on doing. But when the time comes, I am coming with ye. I'll follow ye if I have to. Try and stop me, and ye will see just how 'soft' I have grown."

I waved away the few Laoch that held their swords aimed at Séamus. "We will see about that," was all I could whisper.

"Aye, we will. Ye know I am right. Ye just don't want to admit it. We have a chance to go home, Eadha. We have a chance to be the great nation we once were. I want this as much as anyone else, but ye cannot do this by yerself."

My dagger once again greeted his sword, and with a grunt, I kicked him away in the stomach, making him stumble back. "Ye will not be telling me what I can and cannot do by myself. If Sabriel is opening that Well, who knows what will come crawling to his side. We cannot chance this, Séamus," my voice turned gruff as I yelled, and sadness raked my throat.

He got into a defensive stance, ready to strike. "Aye, we cannot chance it. And we will be going through with yer little plan, *together.* I stood by yer side in battle, and I will do it again. Ye gave everything that day so I, and many others, could live. I'll take a sword through my own heart before I see ye suffer again. Ye hold a guilt within yerself, and it is a guilt that will get ye killed. Ye do all these reckless acts, and ye say it's for us, yer people...but I have half a mind to guess ye just want to end yer life, but have no heart to do it yerself."

Those were the words I needed to hear for my chains to break. I lunged at him with a primal scream, and sparks flew as my dagger shrieked against his blade. Séamus was strong, but the great Dragon of Earth granted me the strength of mountains. With every blow, Séamus grunted and momentarily wavered, but there was a reason he had the mighty bear tattooed on his torso. He would protect his family with a force that could level mountains even if he was saving them from themselves.

Before he returned my attacks, my dagger was sheathed, and my swords whirled into my hands, blocking his assault. He wound up his blow and swung at my head. I had to jump back and roll to avoid his sword hammering through my skull.

A voice thundered against my eardrums and made me jump. "Hey, hey! Git yer childish scrap out me camp before I unleash the shadow hounds on ye!" A hand pulled my left wrist and forced me to face the warlord of our camp. "I dinna care who yer parents are, lassie. Yer my general, I command ye. I willnae tolerate this insubordination in me camp. Séamus, go scrub the blasted stalls till I can eat me dinner off the floor. One speck of mud or horse shite and ye'll be thrown in the pit with Eadha, killings go, since ye think so highly of yer skills to antagonize her."

The warlord threw my hand away. I knew Séamus would not back down. If we continued fighting, we would kill each other. I backed away, pulled out my Stone, and tore through the veil to my room at the palace.

As soon as my feet connected with the cool tile floor, my knees gave out, and tears of anger stung my eyes. Séamus was wrong. He could never have been so wrong. I harbored justified guilt. Because of me, I had to hold my twin brother in my arms as he took his final breaths. I could not do enough for my people, and many lost their lives. My friends were captured because I was too weak to save them.

My sobs burned my chest and I could not control my shaking. None of this was supposed to happen. I was supposed to turn eighteen, live my life, not be captured or forced to rot in the shadows. I never learned how to enjoy life all these years because all I wanted to do was have it end. I was permanently frozen at the age of twenty and never learned how to even be that age. I only knew desolation, pain, and failure. How could Séamus not see that?

The shame of that day of ruin was carved into my back from the torture I endured, and I deserved every scar. Not only did I fail my people that day, but I also failed them again in the woods five years ago as I panicked and ran. How dare he soil the title of Tiarna with my name.

I was no Tiarna. I was no leader. I was a coward in warrior's clothing.

CHAPTER FOUR
Corvis

Rigel paced back and forth across the floor. His mouth was pulled into a tight line, and his silver eyes flamed with intensity. Our lands were hit again, no doubt by the rats from Kamber Island. The treasure hold was infiltrated, but nothing was stolen. The same as what happened to our raided temples, only this time was different.

Whoever broke in went right under our noses and did not trip any alarms. They had to have been a trained emissary and possibly a veilwalker. Word had been getting around that Sabriel was planning something on his island, and we didn't know what. It was big, and we had a feeling some of our neighboring courts may have been a little bit more than aware of the situation.

Rigel stopped and pinched the bridge of his nose. If his hair were not already silver, the stress he was under would have surely turned it gray. "I just don't understand. This is the third time this month alone our borders have been crossed. We saw a small clash between our men and the Sluagh, and grimy magic is just pouring off of that island. Not to mention, some humans were killed two weeks ago, and now their rulers are blaming us Elites. It's like the wards we repaired five years ago did absolutely nothing. Whatever this is, we need to act quickly, and we need to act now. So, ideas.

Go," the High Lord of The Moon pointed to us, but we all kept silent.

Áine looked between Vela, Sorlin, and I holding her stomach as if she were about to vomit. My brother Sorlin shrugged and flexed his feathered wings. "I say we go in there and ask the bastard just what in the gods' names he thinks he is doing and promptly end his life."

Vela snorted, her ruby eyes flared. "Oh, yes, Sorlin, please do. Send us a postcard while you're over there before he guts you like a fish," she always spoke plainly, with little to no inflection, and managed to terrify all of us with her stillness.

Rigel clapped and brushed his hair back. "Alright. Love intensity, let's keep that spirit, but we know what Sabriel is capable of. Our charming daemon, Vela, is right. He would obliterate any of us if we so much as step on his island. He would see us coming from a mile away. There has been speculation circulating some of the courts, but I did not want to cause unnecessary fear by informing you all. But by the looks of it, the rumors may hold true."

I placed a hand on my knee and cocked my head to the side in surprise. Whatever rumors Rigel had heard have not yet reached my ears. As the spy of Tenebris, that was strange.

"Enlighten us. My ears across the lands have not heard any rumors," I said.

Rigel crossed his arms as he leaned a shoulder against the wall. "There is a Well on that island. It connects our world to the Otherworld. Some have been saying he has been trying to open it for many years and will never succeed. Others say he has all he needs to do so and is only waiting for the right moment to strike."

Sorlin crashed down onto the couch next to me, and his feathered wings rustled as they brushed against the leather. "Yes, yes, and I'm a Lady of the Lake."

"One ugly Lady," I said under my breath.

His fist connected with my shoulder, but before I could raise my hand, Rigel pinned it to my lap with his magic. "Sorlin, you're a beautiful Lady. Cov, knock it off. Vela, you're the one older than dirt here, no offense, maybe you could shed some light on this gossip?"

Vela reclined in her chair. "The Well exists, though he cannot open it. You need the magic of a Druid Tiarna, and they have been dead for centuries. He probably has been invading our lands to find something comparable to their power," her red eyes scan Rigel intently, and I could see the slightest shudder. Why we ever decided to welcome a daemon to our group that we were all equally terrified of, I would never know. She had been alive as long as life itself, or so it seemed with how much knowledge she held.

When Rigel was crowned, tensions were brewing across Verbenia, and Tenebris did not have a stable army. He had to leave his court to fight in a few battles with Sorlin and me but could not leave the court unprotected. He struck a deal with Vela, and since then, she has been a sort of guardian for Tenebris even after the wars. I never knew why she stuck around after the deal was done, but we were all secretly glad for it.

Áine's eyes grew weary, and she sat down, hugging her shoulders. Her honeyed bronze skin paled by Vela's words. "What would happen if Sabriel opened it, Vela?"

The daemon shrugged. "Nothing much, unless he has something waiting on the other side. The gods would never come back. However, the Otherworld isn't all sunshine and rainbows. There are dark pits that hold kind like mine, and worse. But, you know, home sweet home."

It was my turn to shudder. What would Sabriel possibly want behind the gates of this Well? Since I have been alive, he had been nothing more than a nuisance. The worst he had done was aid the Fosserans and Eotians when they fought to keep the humans living in our world as laborers and breeders. He had aired his grievances about the Circle more publicly than those opposed to it, but a nuisance he remained.

Vela's crimson gaze shifted to mine. "I see that look in your eye, boy. Do not underestimate that Fae. He has committed atrocities none of you know anything about."

"Well then, what do you suggest we do?" I shot back at her.

She sighed. "The only thing we can do is wait and tighten our borders. None of us are strong enough to take on Sabriel, not even me. I bet he is even rallying an army. If he intends to open that Well, We can only assume he is planning some act of war. Even if we send in the Ravens, we will lose half alone to his numbers. I doubt any of them would agree to fight on his territory either way."

Áine took in a sharp breath and paused. "What about a small team? What if Corv sends in some of his veilwalkers to get more information?"

I shook my head. "All veilwalkers are not like me. I have yet to find one that can stand in the folds of the veil as stealth."

She twisted her mouth to the side and reclined

back into her chair. "We are the most powerful beings I know. I'm sure there is a way to stop this from happening. A small team could be able to sneak in and kill him."

Áine looked to her husband Rigel, and he huffed. "If we all go, no one would be here protecting the people. Vela would have to stay, then that leaves us four. Two Vespairans, a dream-threader, and a light-healer. To stand any chance, we would need Vela with us. I can only tap into so many beings' minds at once, and even then, who's to say he hasn't warded against our kind?"

Áine shuffled in her seat. "We cannot just sit here and fight off more Sluagh while something bigger is brewing. We will end up expending more men than we can afford if we are about to enter an all-out war. I have half a mind to think that is exactly what Sabriel is doing, picking us off to lighten our armies. The Fosseran and Eotian lands remain untouched. Corv, can we get some of your spies in their lands?"

I nodded. "Of course."

Sorlin grunted. "I agree with honey cake over here. We can't just sit here, Rigel. This needs to be dealt with immediately. Let me go over there and-"

Rigel cut him off. "Absolutely not. I do not doubt your abilities, Sor, but I will not put you into the belly of the beast when we have no idea what exactly Sabriel is cooking up. I like the idea of a small group of us going in and taking him down from the inside, but we would need help. Maybe another Ruling Fae, from Aerras, perhaps? Cazara and I have grown close over the years, and I am sure she will join us."

"No, I don't think we can ask that of her. She is a queen with no husband, no one to watch and guard her lands while absent. Aerras would be a target if things do not go well over there," I said plainly. Cazara was the High Lady of Aerras and close friends to Rigel and our court, but it was unlikely she could do anything more than spare a few fighters to take with us.

Sorlin shrugged. "Arbres? Addax could be useful. Islands are made of rock. Rocks are his thing, it could work."

I let out a laugh. "Are we just going to forget how the last time we saw Addax, you destroyed his estate after losing a game of cards and have since been banned from his lands?"

He gawked at me and scoffed. "*I* did not lose. I was played. First of all, it was cheating, and I wanted my five hundred pieces back. Second of all-"

"No, I would rather not see Addax unless it was essential. I wasn't there, and yet somehow, I got blamed for that whole mess. That leaves Eotia and Fossera, but we don't know where their allegiance lies. It certainly is not with us," Rigel said.

We all looked around the room, hoping some ideas would start to flow, but all came up short. When my eyes fell on Áine, she was biting her fingernails and looked as though she was about to burst.

"Áine, do you have something on your mind?" I asked.

Her face turned a deep shade of red, and her hands fell to her lap. "I-I may have someone who can help."

Rigel crouched next to her and placed a hand on her knee. "Well, enlighten us, love."

She leaned forward and looked between us all. "You treat this information with the utmost secrecy, and it does not leave the five of us, do you understand me? I have treated you all as friends throughout my years here, but this is the first order I give any of you as Ruling Fae. You are not to speak of this to anyone. I made a bargain and to tell you, would break it."

We all looked around and nodded. I rested my chin on my hand and pulled my leathery wings in tight as I leaned forward. It took a lot for a Fae to break a bargain. Whatever this was, it was serious. Áine giving us an order made this all the more serious as well.

She took a deep breath. "Do you all remember that day about five years ago in November? I believe it was? When I crossed the Circle after the Sluagh?"

Rigel laughed. "You mean without my knowledge or any protection? How could I forget, darling."

Vela let out an annoyed groan. "Get to the point."

Áine shot them a warning look and continued, "I met a woman. Well, she ran into me, and fought off the Sluagh. She took them out in seconds. A horde of ten, just obliterated them…some she didn't even touch. Others she gave a quick few jabs and had them paralyzed. I never saw anything like it. She wasn't a Fae, at least, I thought she was until she told me *what* she was."

Sorlin raised an eyebrow and leaned in closer. "Well, the suspense is killing me."

"Sor," Rigel quieted him. Áine was visibly uncomfortable telling us this story as she was fidgeting in her seat and not making eye contact with either of us. What could be so troubling that she could not speak to us about it?

She took one last deep breath and looked around the room. "She told me that I had to forget what I saw and forget her, but I had to know. We were stuck in that cave together, and she held a dagger to me the whole time. She hated me, but I didn't know her. I had to know why she felt such contempt for me and how she took out those thugs. I don't know what she saw in me or how she trusted me, but she told me that she...she told me that she was a Laoch, of the Druid army."

Vela roared with laughter and clapped her hands together. "Oh, that's rich. A savage warrior of a race that has been dead for what, almost fifty thousand years? Shows up in the human realm, and you just happened to run into her?"

I went to open my mouth, but Rigel spoke first. "Vela, explain, please. Laoch? Druids?"

Vela rolled her eyes and flipped her short pale blonde hair behind her ear. "Oh, you should know the history, Rige. Sabriel killed the Druids when he invaded their island. Loach is just what they call their warriors. When they were alive, Druids were our connection to the gods and goddesses. They worked with some Fae, practiced magic, yadda, yadda, yadda. They were mighty and deadly, depending on who they worked with. Your great-grandfather worked with the High Druids, I believe. I personally worked with them on occasion. Did this *Laoch* give you a name?"

Áine's cheeks grew red in color, and she resumed her fidgeting. "Eadha."

Vela stiffened with Áine's words and narrowed her gaze. "What did this woman tell you?"

She shrugged. "I didn't pry. She told me she was there the day of the invasion of Kamber Island and that her parents moved their entire capital city away and warded it so heavily no one but their kind can visit it. I forgot the word she called them. Teh, um, ter, tar-"

"Tiarna," Vela cut her off.

"Ah, that's it," she answered with a snap of her fingers.

Sorlin's eye glassed over, and he began to stare off into the distance. I didn't blame him. I had trouble wrapping my head around this conversation. My kind did not have proper lessons like the Elites we worked for. All of the words Áine and Vela exchanged were foreign to me. I heard stories growing up of the Laoch, but they were just stories. The ancient warrior race was extinct and had been for a long time. They were lethal and would put my kind to shame on a battlefield. I had no idea they were connected to Druids, and I was not sure even I fully understood what a Druid was.

I cleared my throat. "Growing up, we spoke of the Laoch as if they were a myth. They were the beings that our trainers said would come to kill us if we brought shame to the warlords in battle. I didn't know they were even immortal."

Vela sighed. "They aren't really, but they aren't human either. They are their own race. Anything can kill them, save old age. It wasn't like that until Faolan and Aerona, the Tiarna at the time, cast a spell of longevity for their people. Those two were truly unstoppable beings, so I doubt they let their pure bloodline turn savage with a Laoch if this is all true."

Áine scoffed and gripped the arms of her chair. "I could *feel* the power radiating off of her. Her words were true. Let me send for her, and you'll see for yourselves."

Rigel shook his head. "This seems too risky. We do not know who this woman is working for or what she truly is."

I nodded in agreement. We had a real threat looming over our heads. I trusted my leaders with my life. However, banking on the idea that some mystical woman, who should be dead, would come to save us made me nervous.

Vela got up and began to walk out of the room. "That island is warded against our kind, but probably not the Druids. If what Áine says holds true, that woman may be able to slip in and out. After all, they know how to wield the troves of the gods. She could be of use to us," she closed the door behind her as she left.

Rigel rubbed his temples and took Vela's seat. "We don't even know if she would be willing to help us."

"We made a bargain that we could call on each other for help. Corv can take me through the Circle to where she instructed me to drop correspondences. I've been practicing my spell breaking. I can manage the Circle," Áine explained.

I looked at Rigel and nodded. "I can take her through the veil. If this woman agrees to a meeting, Sor and I can stand guard."

Áine winced. "Yeah, about a meeting. Eadha holds a sort of loathing for our kind. She held a sword to my neck and threatened me until she felt safe enough. I think it would be best if she met with just Rigel and me. Under no circumstances should you," she pointed intently at Sorlin, "be anywhere in sight until she agrees to work with us."

Sorlin's arms shot up, and he glared at her. "Rude. I am offended. I am a wonderful host, thank you very much."

I kicked his leg and let out a small laugh. "Last time we had an outsider in this house, you threatened to rip out their eyes and eat them if they touched your oatmeal, Sor."

"I think it is fair for me to want to enjoy a copious amount of sweet cream oatmeal in the morning without worrying if there will be enough," he said as he crossed his arms.

Áine pinched the bridge of her nose. "Oh, gods above save us."

Rigel sighed and pulled out a pen and paper. "Alright, honeycomb, get to writing, and say a prayer for us all."

After our meeting, I made my way up the stairs to the left-wing of the house where Sorlin and I stayed. As I was closing my door, a foot stopped in the doorway, and Sorlin barged in. It was always taxing to have him in my room. Not that I didn't care for my brother, I did. He was just a raging ball of unkempt foolishness and exhausted me.

Sorlin smiled and widened his eyes. "So, a Laoch. Are you terrified or excited?"
He walked over to my desk and pulled the sheet off of my mirror. He inspected himself vainly, then tied the top half of his black coily hair that sat just above his breast bone into a lazy bun before crashing onto my couch.

I clenched my jaw. "I'm indifferent."

His mouth fell open. "We heard their stories growing up, thought they were fireside tales, and now we get to meet one? Come on, man, I'm excited. Wonder if she'll spar with us. Oh! Do you think I could kick her ass? Probably could," he added with a chuckle.

"Let's just see how this goes. The Laoch are savages, and you heard Áine, that woman seems to hate the Fae. We are nothing more than barbarians to her, and you, you're insufferable," I pulled him up by his elbow and escorted him out of my room.

He winked and pointed a finger at me. "Very true, but how can you not be the least bit enthralled about this? I'd like to see just an ounce, maybe a dash, a tinge even, of emotion from you."

I gave him a fake smile, showing all of my teeth, before shoving him through my door and locking it. Although we call ourselves brothers, we were simply orphans who found solace in each other at our war camp growing up. We couldn't be more different. He was loud, overbearing, and animated about everything. I never found the need to keep to anyone other than myself. He had the deeper complexion of the Vespairans while I probably looked sickly next to him. He also had coiled, raven black hair while mine was loosely curled, maybe even just wavey. The biggest of our differences were the wings.

I walked over to my desk and groaned before pulling the black sheet up. My eyes caught a glimpse of my reflection, and I paused before fastening the sheet. I spread my wings and inspected them in the mirror. They were leathery and bare of the luscious black feathers of my kind. Every day I teetered back and forth between accepting my form or being repulsed by it.

I didn't envy Sorlin's wings. In fact, I was a stronger flyer. I just wish I didn't bear a permanent reminder of Fae brutality on my back. When my wings were ripped off and replaced by these monstrosities, my kind rejected me even more than they already did for being a half-breed. I never knew my mother, but I knew she was a wraith. It was not hard for me to find out considering my skills in veilwalking, and when the shadows started unfurling from my body, that was all I needed to know to figure it out. I was a target ever since. Only purebloods were allowed to live in our camp, but Sorlin protected me every day until we were enlisted into the aerial army.

I fastened the sheet back over the mirror and began planning to take Áine across the Circle. Sorlin was the general of the Vespairan army, a brute, standing a few hairs taller than me and built a bit more muscular than I was. *I,* however, was the spy of the court. I worked in the shadows and did the dirty work for Rigel, who took every advantage of my half-blood. I knew that when he sent me to protect our Lady, it was because whatever entity we ran into, he wanted subdued and brought back for interrogation. An interrogation led by me.

Sorlin could maim many opponents in battle but would always morn those he killed. I saw and experienced more evils than him in my years in this world and have become numb to the acts of violence we have seen together. He wasn't able to break people as I could.

The human world was dangerous for our kind for many reasons: besides the fact that most humans would hunt and kill Fae if they had a chance to do so, the Sluagh were now off their tethers. If we came across one of them, I would have to break from the shadows and fight them. That would surely attract unwanted attention.

I spent the rest of the day plotting every possible outcome of this trip, marking hiding points and Circle locations, so if we needed to run or fight, we would be prepared.

In the morning, Áine was dressed and ready,

waiting in the parlor with Sorlin, Rigel, and Vela.

Rigel rubbed his temples and shook his head. "I don't want to lean heavily on this theory, no offense darling, and suggest we go forward with my plan on finding a solution ourselves."

Vela rolled her eyes. "And what plan do you have in mind, *my liege*?"

Sorlin chuckled and groaned. "I say we all had a good run. Five hundred something years isn't too bad. If Sabriel is planning on destroying the world, I say let him."

How these four personalities all fit in one room, I may never know. Although there have been many physical altercations throughout the years, we all got along pretty well despite being obligated to work with each other.

Áine huffed and grabbed my elbow. "Ha-ha Sorlin. Rige, you have to trust me on this. We are bound by a bargain. She can and *will* help us."

Vela clicked her tongue. "But Druids aren't bound by Fae magic. Many High Druids are more powerful than your kind. If she does indeed come, it would be of her own will. What I'm saying is, she tricked you. You're the only one bound by the magic of the bargain."

I felt Áine's grip tighten and saw her mouth go ridged from irritation. "Bargain or no bargain, I consider her a friend after that day. She didn't have to save me, but she did."

I cleared my throat and looked down at her. "It has been five years. Do you even know if she still trades at this market? Have you kept any kind of contact with her?"

Foserrans were not like Áine. They used their

warm and inviting exterior to their advantage. They were cunning swindlers and cold, ruthless people. Áine was sweet, like steaming honey milk. She saw the good in everyone, so if this woman tricked her, she would be heartbroken for some time.

She looked up at me and smiled. "Let's go. Please do not go so fast. I hate the other side of the veil."

I nodded. "As you wish."

CHAPTER FIVE
Corvis

I navigated to the Circle Áine directed me to in Eotia. The fire-wielders' kingdom was completely underground, but we were still cautious walking through their lands. Once we stepped out in front of the Circle on our side, Áine looked as though she was about to vomit. She was clutching her stomach and scrunching her face. I couldn't help but chuckle.

"The veil isn't that bad, my Lady," I said as I held out a hand so she could lead me through.

"Of course it is. You feel like you're falling the whole time, plus, I don't have wings. I'm not used to that feeling. And stop calling me that Corv. We're all friends. You're too proper," she grabbed my hand and paused. "Now, last time, I couldn't get back through, but the wards feel a little bit more stable now."

Nervousness tinged my stomach as she grasped my hand. I would not be able to help us get through if she got stuck. I was an excellent veilwalker but could not cross the Circle through it. I was sure someone a bit more talented in the skill could, but for now, I just hoped Áine had this covered.

As we stepped through, it felt as though hands grabbed all around my body, pulling me back, like I was not welcome. I was yanked and groped in unsettling ways and couldn't help but shut my eyes.

Áine noticed me stumble and called back to me.

"It's the wards. Just hold on I'm almost through."

I could only nod and focus on keeping my breakfast down. After a good struggle, Áine grunted and pushed us through, falling onto a muddy forest floor.

She laughed. "Now I'm the one telling *you* it's not that bad."

I brushed off the dirt from my pants and shivered, "It felt like someone was grabbing and pulling me back."

"Well, you get used to it. Get to the shadows and follow close behind. The market is only a mile or two north."

As I used the abilities inherited from my mother and turned to shadows, Áine glamoured herself. Her ears now round and her clothes simple and light. When she was anywhere but our home in Tenebris, she wore a headcover over her hair, secured around her chin. Although she has tried to distance herself from her homeland, she kept her people's customs close to her heart. She turned behind her, looking for me, and nodded before heading off north.

Áine was the newest to our group of misfits. Rigel took on Sorlin and me in his court when he first came to power, but we were great friends beforehand. The two of us were a tad too cautious when Rigel married Áine, thinking she was a spy from Fossera. After some time, we have grown as close as we could be since. I knew Áine thought of me as a friend, but I worked for her. She was the High Lady of my lands, and I treated her as she should be treated.

Her sugary exterior was a camouflage to the strength and power she harbored within. She could handle this trip on her own, and Rigel knew that. We just needed to make sure if any filth from Kamber Island showed up, we could capture it. That would send a message back to that bastard, Sabriel, that we were not ones to go to war with.

In the market, no one batted an eye at Áine, but we kept our distance. Her glamour hid her Fae features well, but some humans were sensitive to energies that were not of their kind. Some turned their heads but did nothing more than stare.

"Where is this merchant?" I asked, looking around. If humans figured out what Áine was and attacked, fighting them would break many rules set in place for our kind, and a new threat would arise.

She looked around and squinted. "Um, I'm not sure. Excuse me?" She flagged an older man down as he was walking by. "I'm looking for a young man named Jameson."

The man looked her up and down suspiciously, and I tightened the grip on my sword as I moved closer to her. After what seemed like an eternity, he grunted and pointed to a brown-haired boy in the back of the market. She gave him thanks and hurried along to the stand. I wanted to follow the man and find out if he would tell anyone of any suspicions he had, but Áine would not be able to find me in the shadows.

The young man looked up from his ledger and smiled at her as she approached. "Can I help you?" He asked.

She cleared her throat and pulled out the letter. "Yes. Is there a woman who comes here to trade? Um, she has white hair, fair skin, and is rather hostile?"

He laughed. "White hair and hostile? It sounds like you're talking about Ev. Is everything okay? Is Elaine still coming to trade today?"

Áine nodded and smiled. "Oh, yes, everything is fine. I just have a letter I need to get to her. She told me I could leave it with you."

When he reached for the letter, their hands brushed. His face fell, and he yanked his hand away, taking the letter with him. I pulled on Áine's elbow as a way of telling her we should leave, but she resisted. My heart began to beat rather fast as the boy's eyes traveled Áine's body.

She rubbed her hand and forced a surprised expression on her face. "Oh gods, did I shock you? I'm sorry. Wool and iron rings are not a good combination," as she pulled her hand down, a metal band was now glamoured in place on her middle finger. "Can't be too careful. I've heard terrible stories of Faeries in these parts."

Good girl, I thought. Jameson chuckled nervously and rubbed the back of his neck. "Ha, yeah. Uh, I'll give this to her. H-have a good day."

Áine smiled and turned on her heels. "I know you can hear me, Corv. He suspects something. We got to hurry," she said in a hushed tone.

"Don't walk too fast; don't hold your head down," I whispered into her ear.

She nodded and confidently walked through the market. People stopped and stared, whispering into each other's ears. I was sure her Fae ears could hear precisely what they said as she stiffened and quickened her pace.

"Just keep going. You're almost there," I grabbed Áine's elbow to keep her close and held my breath as we crossed out of the market and into the forest. "Hold on."

Walking to the Circle would be too risky. If someone saw her disappear, so be it. At least we would make it back home without a fight. I snaked my arm around her waist and pulled her into the shadows across the veil. She flinched and shut her eyes hard as we quickly passed to the Circle.

"Okay, your turn. Hurry." I pushed Áine to the Circle and glued my eyes to the north. It was probably a mile away from the market, so we had about ten minutes before someone was bound to be here investigating.

"Gods, I can't-the wards, they're stuck. Give me a minute," a light flickered on the Circle but quickly died as soon as it started.

"Well, my Lady, we have about nine before we have company," in the distance, the heavy footsteps of horses shook the calm forest and the sound of men shouting grew closer and closer. "Make that one minute. Áine, I can't glamour myself, and the wings are not easy to hide."

She grunted and struggled to break the wards. Sweat started to glisten on her forehead; horses crested the hills, and I drew my sword.

"Áine!" I pressed.

"I-I got it!" She grabbed my hand, and we rushed through the white light of the Circle. Going back through to our side was easier than coming from it. It accepted us vigorously, welcoming us with open arms. We were forcefully pulled through and thrown onto the ground. Once Áine and I had a moment to gather our surroundings, we let out a half-hearted laugh.

"I won't tell him if you won't," I said as I extended my hand.

Áine caught her breath and placed her hand in

mine. "Agreed. Everything went as smooth as silk," she said with a wink.

"Do you think this woman can help us? What was her name again?" I asked as the winds of the veil rushed around us.

"Eadha. If she can't, I don't know who can."

###

Rigel was waiting for us once we walked onto the balcony of the parlor. His face instantly relaxed as Áine burst through the door and into his arms. "How did it go?" He asked with a kiss to her forehead.

She shrugged. "Fine. Boring."

He shot me a look. I only nodded and sat down on the couch, knowing he didn't believe that for a second. "Darling, Vela wishes to speak with you about this Druid. She's in the study and rather cranky. Tread lightly."

We all knew what that meant. Áine was to go into another room while Rigel got the truth out of me. Áine looked at me wide-eyed and blushed, giving a sympathetic smile before retreating.

Rigel clapped his hands together and sat across from me. "So, what *really* happened?"

I sighed. "They knew. We ran. We made it out."

"And the letter?"

"Delivered, but who knows if that boy is going to give it to her. I couldn't get a good look at the mob to see if he was a part of it."

Rigel rubbed his temples and let out an exasperated groan. "Okay, well, now we wait. Thank you for going with her."

I nodded. "Of course, it's my job."

"Corv, you have every right to refuse or speak

out against any task I give you, and you know that. Sure I pay you, I am using your skills. But I could have asked any half-wraith to be my spy, and I chose you. My friend."

I chuckled. "Because you know so many Vespairan-wraith hybrids?"

"Well, I guess the wings are a plus, huh?" He looked me up and down and rested his chin on a fist. "Hey, you've been a little...distant lately."

Here we go, I thought to myself. "I'm fine. Busy, but fine. I appreciate the concern, though it's not needed."

"Just, promise me once all of this is over, you'll take a break? You deserve one, and you've done more for Áine and me than anyone has these past few years. Don't tell Sorlin I said that," Rigel smiled, but I knew he wasn't making a suggestion. He was *telling* me to take a break.

He had been dogging me to take one ever since we retrieved Áine from Fossera two decades ago, but I had no reason to. If I was not working myself raw, I would stew over things I could not change and let my guard down. It was not safe for anyone in our group if Sorlin and I were not in our best shape.

"Rige, I don't need a break. I'm fine."

He looked at me with concern in his eyes. "You're tired. And you never had a chance to rest since even when we were kids. I mean, you didn't even take the proper recovery time from-"

"Don't. I'm fine. Are we done?" I squinted my eyes at him, and my face faded of all expression.

He huffed. "I can always order you to go on leave or not call on your services. I've known you almost five hundred and fifty years, and you never once have taken a day off. It's not healthy."

I stood and paced. Why was he bringing this up now at the start of a possible war? "You can order me off of tasks, but that doesn't mean I won't find more to do. What will I do on my break Rige, see all of the family I don't have? Dote over my loving non-existent wife?" My voice rose, and I could hear Vela and Áine stop their chatting from the study next to us.

Rigel stood slowly and put his arms out to the side. "*We're* your family, so don't even go there. And if you took a break, maybe you would be able to find a wife."

I laughed sarcastically. "Oh, of course, I could. I would love to find someone to enjoy for more than one night. However, have you thought maybe *this*," I gesture to my ragged wings and swirling shadows around my body, "maybe a tad bit of a deal-breaker?"

He shrugged. "You've had many lovers. Don't deny that. Look, after we are done with this threat, you are taking a break. I'll lock you in your room and have Sorlin guard the door if I have to. You're tired. And not just physically...look, Corv, I'm a dream-threader, you know this. Part of that includes the unfortunate abilities to enter some people's dreams. I know your nights are getting bad again."

I tightened my fists and clenched my jaw. I was not about to have this conversation with Rigel. This was an issue between me and a glass of ale. "And if you think stopping my work is what I need, then you don't know me at all. I'm leaving, unless you would like to *order* me to stay."

We stared at each other for a few minutes, but neither made a move to talk. I bowed my head and retreated to my room. Unfortunately for me, Sorlin was waiting at the top of the stairs.

He crossed his arms and leaned against the railing with a teasing smile on his face. "Yelling at Rigel before five? While sober? You want him to kill you in the ring tomorrow morning, or what?"

"Leave it be," I said as I pushed past him.

He followed closely behind and closed the door after him. "Was it about the human lands?"

I shook my head. "He wants me to take a break. I respectfully declined."

"Well, you could use one. My room is right on the other side of this wall. I know how little sleep you get. You *have* been acting a little detached. Are the nightmares coming back?"

I knew he meant well. The only reason he knew about my nightmares was because of one liquor induced, crying filled night between the two of us. I'm surprised he could even remember I told him about them since I held his hair back most of the night while he blacked out and proposed to the toilet.

"The fact that you can remember *that* and not my birthday, really says something about you, doesn't it?"

He roared with laughter. "At least I get the month right."

"Sometimes. And no, they aren't back. Well, I have had strange dreams, but that is a conversation I will have with a bottle of gin and not with you."

Sorlin sighed. "Just wished you would let one of us in sometimes. I've known you my whole life, yet I feel like I barely know you."

"Why are you getting so sappy right now? It's almost insulting that you two think I can't handle myself." I went to open my door and push him out, but he blocked me.

"Fine, let's just drop it. What strange dreams have you been having?"

"Out," I turned him by his shoulders and gave a swift push between his wings to shove him out the door.

"Hey, Rigel? Can I help you kick Corv's ass tomorrow in training?" He yelled rather loudly as he was walking away.

"Of course!" Rigel faintly yelled back from wherever he was downstairs.

My eyes almost rolled into my brain as I shut the door with a grunt. This "house," as Rigel likes to call it, was more of a palace carved in the middle of the coastal city of Oneiros. It only housed Sorlin, Vela, and I, and maybe a few servants. Even with all this space, Sorlin managed to pick his residency right next to mine. At least Vela had the smart idea of taking up a whole floor to herself.

I walked over to my liquor and broke out a bottle of gin. I could lie to Sorlin all I want and tell him my nightmares weren't back, but Rigel said it himself. He had been seeing into my dreams and knew the truth. Thankfully they have not been too regular. What I told Sorlin was partly true; I had a strange dream popping in and out of my mind.

I brought the bottle to my lips and took a swig of the floral liquor, savoring the burn as it traveled down my throat. I closed my eyes and lay flat on my back as I pictured the images from my dream. I had only experienced it maybe twice in the past month, but it was always the same: I stood standing at the edge of a grassy cliff watching waves crash against the rock below. The sun was burning an intense sunset blush, and clouds wisped past in the breeze. I could never move, but I was not afraid. There was someone with me, but I never knew who. The scent of cedar and fresh rain tingled my nostrils, and for some reason, I felt at home. As if I have come to the end of a long and exhausting journey.

Maybe it was how I fantasized death, or perhaps it was what lies beyond this lifetime into the next. Whatever it was, I woke up feeling happy and refreshed. I wished I knew how to trigger it more often to drown out the nightmares.

I heard the shifting of paper on my desk and opened one eye to see that a letter appeared that was not there before. "Must be some good gin," I said with a laugh.

I closed my eyes, but my daydreams once again were interrupted by the clanking of metal against wood. A pen and inkwell had appeared on top of the parchment. I set my bottle on my nightstand and clutched my sword as I slowly approached my desk. Rigel's residences were protected against veilwalkers and warded against those who do not have permission to enter. Not even Rigel himself could send me a letter through the veil in this house.

The stationary was plain white, with a blue wax seal. There was a vertical line with four horizontal lines going through it embedded in the wax. The stationary simply read "Áine" across the top of it. On the back, read a peculiar name I wouldn't be able to pronounce if I hadn't been able to put two and two together. But why did it end up on my desk?

"From, Eadha," I read out loud. I turned on my

heels and set out to find Áine.

In the dining room, Sorlin had a sandwich half stuffed down his throat while Áine and Rigel were drinking tea. I held up the letter and cleared my throat.

"Look what I just got," I said, waving it around.

Áine almost spat out her tea as she raced over to me. "Already? Well, that boy did say someone was going to trade today. Okay, okay, let me get my tea ready in case this goes bad," she waved her hand over the table as she sat down and her tea was piping hot. "Alright, read out loud."

I cracked the seal and opened the letter. After my eyes grazed the gist of the words, I had to bite my lip to suppress a laugh bubbling in my chest. Vela sauntered into the room as if she was listening to our conversation from the other side of the wall.

"Um, it says, 'Áine, you can go jump in a shallow grave if you think I am stepping a single foot on that gods-forsaken continent or that manky no good city you live in, ever again. I would rather thrust knives into my eye sockets and plummet off a cliff face first than meet the slimy bastard that rules your lands. Our bargain is done; you weren't to speak of my people or me to anyone. You're on your own.' Uh, she spelled a lot of things wrongs, if that makes anyone feel any better about that."

Sorlin clapped his hands together, breaking the silence in the room. "Can we hire her? I like her."

The color drained from Áine's golden bronze face. "I can fix this. I just need to send another letter."

I shook my head and placed the letter on the table. "Áine, no, we can't. The humans could see through your glamour. If you go back, they'll have your head on a spike."

Rigel rubbed his hand down her back. "We tried, now we figure out our plan. Corv? Vela? Any suggestions?"

Sorlin scoffed. "What about me?"

We all looked at him with raised eyebrows until he shrugged in agreement.

Vela sighed. "All we can do is fight to keeps our lands secure or find a way to stop Sabriel. He will see us coming regardless. Even if we manage to get there, we don't know the extent of his magic. I think the best bet is to forget about Sabriel entirely and focus on what we can control. The Well."

Rigel waved a hand. "What, like destroy it?"

Vela shrugged. "Seal it, destroy it, doesn't matter. We can't afford a war. Verbenia is too divided. We don't even know if Fossera and Eotia are on his side or not. I don't think we can fight him *and* them."

Sorlin stirred in his seat. The once easy-going man turned to the ruthless general of our armies. "She's right. We have the manpower, yes. But Eotians are fire-wielders. They can take out fleets with a snap of their fingers. If we had any chance of winning, we would need the Fosseran healers. Cazara will help us if we ask her, and I'm sure Akamu in Cascata will help if she will. Addax is a hard maybe, but if we have their tree fighters, game over for Sabriel."

Áine slammed her hand on the table with anger spread across her face. "And what if it is not enough? What if Cazara refuses? What if my father joins arms with Kamber Island? It won't be just one battle. They will pick us off like pests. Miniscule attacks are already thinning our armies, and we still know not where they come from. I am the Lady of this court, and I am *telling* you all that I will be sending another letter tomorrow, and that is the end of it. Not just for me, my court, my family even, but also for her. Her people deserve to go home," she stood and walked to the door. "Rige, I'll be at home. Don't even think about staying here tonight." The hurt in her voice rang through every corridor.

As Áine walked out, Rigel grimaced in his seat and looked between us three. "You know it's serious when she pulls the High Lady card. She never does that."

"I'll follow her, Rige, don't worry," I said.

He shook his head. "She isn't the dainty flower she fronts herself to be. She is more than capable of going by herself. I'll wait on the other side of the Circle in case she gets stuck, but only if I can't convince her not to go," Rigel let out a loud groan and yanked his hair, "gods, I'm too lazy for this. Why can't the world end when I'm dead?"

Sorlin rose from his seat and snorted. "I'll get in contact with the armies in Aerras and Cascata. If we're going to war, might as well have the cool people on our side."

"Keep it quiet. We can't have Eotia or Fossera knowing we are rallying. They may try to convince Addax and the Arbres army to join them," I instructed him. He nodded and walked to the balcony, unfurled his wings, and jumped into the air.

"Corv, get your spies to keep a close look on the coast and the southern border. Any sightings of Fosserans, you come to me. How did you get that letter, by the way?" Rigel asked.

I shrugged and looked at the parchment. "It just

appeared on my desk. But as far as I know, the attacks have been coming from Kamber Island. I just do not know how they keep getting in. But I assure you, Sorlin and I will make sure word does not get to our enemies."

He patted me on the shoulder. "Well, I'm going to go see if there are blankets set out on my couch for me. Head to the coast and the borders. Training at seven tomorrow?"

I nodded and headed to the balcony, becoming incredibly conscious of the large wings hanging from my back. I had neglected my flying lately, and if I didn't keep up with it, Sorlin would definitely be able to pummel me in the ring. My heavy wings stretched to either side as the wind passed around me.

I jumped into the air and headed off to my spies.

CHAPTER SIX

Eadha

The sun danced across my eyelids as I shifted in bed, but I realized I was not surrounded by the smell of dirt and sweat or lying in a sleeping bag. There was a rough carpet scratching against my skin and multiple eyes on me. I opened one eye and scanned the room to find my father staring down at me and Lana with her hand over her mouth, shaking her head. *Oh no, what now?*

I slowly got to my knees and smiled. "Well, yer looking rather cross, eh?"

My father held my gaze and jutted his hand out to Lana. "Leave the letter and see yourself out. Tell Séamus he will be in charge of the Laoch until further notice."

My heart dropped, and I jumped to my feet as Lana handed my father a familiar silver envelope and left mouthing: "Sorry." A letter? Did he find the one Áine sent last week, or was this a new one? Why would she send another? I made my point as clear as day that I was done with her.

"Now, before you speak, I know this is not the first letter you have received from Verbenia. You'll tell me why you have these in your possession and the nature of the first correspondence."

My eyes shifted from the letter to his pale blue eyes, and I thought of all the ways I could kill Lana for giving him this knowledge. "It was a letter asking for help. To aid Tenebris in this possible war." I prayed she spoke nothing of my plan to stop Sabriel.

A chair appeared underneath me, and an invisible hand pushed me down as my father stepped closer to me. "And why would Tenebris know of you and ask for aid? And why would you decline?"

I tugged on my invisible restraints and narrowed my gaze to my father. Tiarna or not, if he wanted to play this game, it would end badly for him. "Because I helped their Ruling Fae. When you sent me to trade five years ago, I ran into the Sluagh. The woman somehow managed to cross the Circle and got stuck. We hid, we talked, and ended up making a bargain. I would tell her who I was, and she would tell no one. In exchange, we could call on each other for aid."

He clenched the letter in his fist. "So you are breaking a magical bond? Do you understand the repercussions of such things?"

My mouth dropped. "Excuse me? I'm not bound by Fae magic, and you know this. Besides, *she* broke the bargain. She told others of me, of our people. The bargain is off."

He curled his lip and towered above me. "If you think for one second that our armies are enough to fight whatever Sabriel plans to unleash from its tethers behind that Well, then you have no business being the general of my armies. Let's read this letter together, shall we?"

I stared in disbelief. After all that I had done for our people, he dared to speak to me in such ways? I closed my eyes and started to untangle the magic binding me to my seat while he read the letter aloud.

"'Eadha, please, you don't understand. Rigel is

planning on just rallying troops and fighting. The people of Verbenia have seen too much war and hardship throughout the years. I know there has to be another way. I don't know how, but I have to have hope. Our people don't need to fight anymore, but if they have to, we will not make it without extra support. Please reconsider. You helped me once, help me again. From Áine.'"

I looked him in the eye and began to shake with anger. "How many years have ye kept us in the shadows? How many years have I seen people around us slain by war, starve from hunger, and burn from anarchy due to our absence? How many years did I *beg* ye to please let us fight for our homeland so we can support those around us? And that is coming from *me*, someone who *despises* the Fae. I wouldn't have gone through what I did had they came to our side and fought, but it still pained me to see their people suffer while the Ruling Fae sat on their thrones. So forgive me for taking a page out of your book, father, for deciding to sit on my arse doing nothing. I know how the Fae are. They are tricksters and cheats. She broke the bargain, so I'm covering my hide."

He tightened my invisible bindings and gazed at me with disgust. "All of the outcomes of this problem end in war. There is no stopping Sabriel. We must band together and hope we can fight him off. How could you not realize this? Some people see you as Tiarna, but you know nothing of it! You do not know what it takes to lead a nation, to keep your people protected. You have to make sacrifices, but you know nothing of the word."

My magic surged through me like a crack of lightning. I broke the ties my father had put on me and sent a wall of air towards him, pushing him back. Using my abilities to circle a force around his throat, I stood above him and as he clawed at his neck.

"You will not speak to me of sacrifice! What happened to me on that island is forever marked on my body. I gave *everything* for my people that day, for *you* even. I fought to keep them safe on the battlefield while ye sat in this palace. While Sabriel beat me and tortured me, ye sent no one after me!" Blinding rage scoured through my body as I tightened my magical hold around his throat.

"I held Tadhg, yer son, in my arms while life fled his body. How dare ye tell me I don't know sacrifice!" My voice broke, and a tear streamed down my cheek.

My father gasped for breath as I released. His bewildered eyes met mine, and he struggled to rise. "Get- get out of my sight. Séamus is in charge until you return from Verbenia."

I scoffed. "I won't be going to Verbenia."

I pulled out my Druid Stone, but my father grabbed my elbow and pulled me back to him. "You're not the Tiarna. I still give you orders. Until the day you take this throne, you do as I say. I am ordering you to go to Tenebris."

I laughed. "Fine then. I invoke the council to discuss this. We'll see what they have to say. Let me know, eh?" I shot him one last look of venom and disappeared to the camp to find Lana.

I had no idea why he would want me going to Tenebris. Although, it would bring me closer to the stones of Arawn that I would need to complete my mission. Staying with Áine could guarantee my safety while looking for them. But she betrayed me and my trust.

When I got to Lana, she was waiting for me at my

tent with a look of horror on her face. "Eadha, the letter was mixed in with the coins. I wasn't expecting another one after what Jameson said happened the last time, and I didn't think that Sidhe would send another one. He didn't even tell me there was a letter in there."

I waved her off. "It's okay. I didn't expect another letter, either. Didn't Jameson say the town's men chased after her? Intending to capture her and burn her at a stake?"

She nodded. "Aye."

When I pulled my tent cover away, I groaned and rolled my eyes. One of the twins sat on the ground waving at me, and a headache had begun to throb behind my eye. It was Dolan. The only way to tell the two apart was by their Laoch tattoos. The most notable one would be Dolan's blue line going from his hairline to his wait, whereas Donnan's face was bare but had a blue knotted hawk around his neck.

"Surprised yer not dead," Dolan said, brushing his shaggy black locks out of his eyes.

"I'm sure I will be after the council meeting," I said flatly.

Lana gasped. "Eadha, ye invoked the council? That's a sure way to get ye thrown out to Verbenia. They've been hounding yer parents for years to get us out of hiding."

I shrugged. She was not wrong. The council never understood my parents' reasons for hiding us all these years. The Druid council was our democracy, and all voted for us to storm the island many centuries ago, but the Tiarna selfishly declined.

"I just need to buy myself some time. One Sidhe is fine. I can handle that, but if I'm forced to stay in their lands, I'm bound to kill one of them. I can't stand them."

Lana nodded and crossed her arms. "What happens when Séamus finds out about ye leaving?"

I scoffed. "What do ye mean? He doesn't control me, Lana."

"No, I know that. It's just that what happened to ye at the island shook all of us to our core, but it affected Séamus differently. He always saw ye as our glue. When he thought ye dead, he wasn't himself. He will worry about ye deeply while yer away. We all will, but especially him."

Séamus. He was our brute with a heart of gold. I was not ignorant. I knew he cared for me differently than our friends. I also knew he never wanted to lead our armies but, if I was gone, he was the acting general, and if I died, even worse. He would have the title permanently and was too gentle for that.

Dolan cleared his throat. "If it's any consolation, I say go. I won't miss ye. It'll be like a grand holiday away from the thing that fuels my nightmares. I'm still not over the time ye tied me up, drizzled me with honey, and threw me on an anthill."

I was about to make my rebuttal, but something on his arm caught my eye. A fresh blue marking sat against his pale skin in the shape of a wolf.

"Dolan, what is that? You received a mark?" I asked evenly, but my heart began to race.

We receive our blue tattoos as Laoch after performing acts of bravery. There was a big celebration for it, but I heard no such thing happen. The wolf was the guardian of family and tribe. My stomach fluttered in a slight panic as I scanned the room and did not see Donnan.

He looked down at his lap, and Lana put a hand on his shoulder. "We had orders to scout the ruins of a temple in the human lands," Dolan said with a twitching mouth. "We went in with a few other Laoch. Yer father wanted to know why it was raided a few months ago, but it wasn't empty. It was a stronghold for at least fifty abominable beings, and there were only five of us. Donnan was instantly hit with an arrow. He's fine now, healing. I had to fight us all out."

How was I not informed of this? Five of my men not only left the island on others' orders but were attacked as well? Donnan and Dolan may be a nuisance, but I loved them dearly. If anything were to have happened to them...

This was the last straw. I gave my life, and I gave away the person I used to be for my friends' safety, and now even that is fleeting. The power the great Dragons bestowed upon me many years ago began to stir beneath my skin. Sparks spit from my fingertips, and I felt the waves surrounding our island swell, and the air whirled around my tent as fury scoured through my veins.

Lana looked up as the sounds of nature bellowed around us and locked eyes with me. "To the Otherworld with the Tiarna. I believe ye can stop this. The Sidhe woman can better help ye get those stones than we can. Stop this, Eadha. I want to go home."

I nodded and grabbed her hand. "We're going home. I promise. Tell Séamus that if anything happens to me, if I can't stop whatever filth comes crawling out of that Well, he continues the assault as planned. Scour the island, reclaim it, and send troops to Verbenia to fight. Whatever ye do, do not come for me."

Dolan furrowed his brow, and his eyes turned sad. "Y-yer leaving? Actually? I thought it was a joke. What are ye planning, Eadha?"

I gave a stern yet playful look. "Dolan, I give Lana full permission to beat ye into yer next lifetime if ye and yer brother don't behave. I hope I see ye both again, but if I don't, I spent the best years of my life with ye," I placed a hand on both of their shoulders. "I wouldn't change a thing. If the next time I see ye is in battle, fight hard, fight strong, and die a swift death."

They nodded to me, but before they could say anything, I tore through the veil to send a letter to Áine and Séamus. The letters were simple: to Séamus, I thanked him for all he had ever done for me and apologized for the fight we had weeks ago. I instructed him to send my things through the veil once I sent word through our Stones. To Áine, I simply told her I would be there.

War was coming, and I would give my life to stop it. Áine was right in saying our people have fought too hard for too long. Her people deserved a time of true peace, and my people have been hiding in the shadows, powerless for long enough. Soon, we would rise again.

I looked over my map of Verbenia. It was old, but it would do. I needed to plan how and when to retrieve the stones. Tenebris, the Land of Darkness, would be my first stop. It sat on the northwestern coast of the continent, the closest court to Kamber Island. Its people were dream-threaders, able to shift others' minds to see different realities. Their pale skin, silver hair, and eyes made them look as otherworldly as their abilities. At the time, the High Lord of their lands worked with my father and abandoned us when we needed them the most. What was the name of the new Lord Áine married? Nigel? Rigel? Hopefully, he was less useless than his forefathers. I'd be able to retrieve his stone first.

Next would be Aerras, the Court of Wind. They have always been close with Tenebris, though they dwelled in the continent's southernmost mountain ridge. The people of Aerras were snobbish, prudish, and somewhat strange looking. Their skin was painted with the blushy hues of a birthing sunrise, and their hair was a striking strawberry blonde. I always called them "the pink people." They considered themselves above the other lands because of their ability to wield the wind as a shield and believe it to be the noblest element. How the Fae acquired the abilities of the Dragon Aer, I would have liked to know. I would need to visit them next.

Cascata would be after. The Islands of Mist. Cascata sat next to Tenebris to the northeast coast and was a collection of islands in a pocket of land. Much like wraiths, they could turn to rain mists in the blink of an eye to avoid damage in battle, or to sneak into places where they did not belong. They were beautiful people with luscious tan skin and the most intriguing eyes. As far as I knew, they had a blood bond with Aerras. If I secured Aerras as an ally, I would have Cascata.

Hmm, Arbres. Home of the tree warriors and largest court in Verbenia. The land spread from the coast to the neighboring Fae country. I did not know much of this land. I only knew it sat in the middle of Verbenia and was neutral in its endeavors, aiding the highest bidder. I did not know their likeness or abilities. I would have to ask Áine how to proceed.

Eotia and Fossera would be the most challenging two to infiltrate. My spies were not able to locate their stones. Eotia was the Land of Flame. They resided under Arbres to the left. Their hair and skin was as dark and mysterious as the sea, and they wielded the power of the flame. Truly terrifying, but not outright evil. Eotia was the home of wraiths, and their rulers are elusive as shadows themselves. They worked with many of our kind and have searched for us since we disappeared. I believed Fossera corrupted their High Lord many years ago and only worked with Sabriel because of it.

I did not know how to go about entering Fossera. Tensions seemed to be high between Tenebris and them, from what Áine told me. Their people were healers and curse breakers and fought side by side with Sabriel on occasion. I would retrieve their stone last, for Áine's sake. Who knew what would happen to her if we showed up unprepared.

I marked all I needed on my map and sent my letters through the veil. Like clockwork, Séamus appeared in my room. "Yer leaving?" he asked, holding my letter in his hand.

I nodded. "Prepare yerselves. I'll do my best to hide my identity, but people are going to know we exist. Even those we wish wouldn't."

He twisted his mouth from side to side. "Please, Eadha, please come back. Be the hero that comes home. Be the one we carry through the streets, singing yer name...not in a box to yer grave."

I bit my lip and nodded. Séamus had always tried so hard to love me. Either like a brother or friend, but he always restrained himself, and I did a great job of pushing him away. I did not know if it was because he never wanted to replace Tadhg in my life, or maybe it was because he was just as broken as I was. I would miss him the most.

"Séamus, I promise I'll do whatever it takes for us. If that means giving my life, so be it. But I will see you again, either in this life or the next." I walked up to him, wrapped my arms around his neck, and pulled him in close.

My face buried in his chest as he held me, swinging back and forth. This was not only going to be difficult for me, but also for my friends. We have never been apart for more than a few days, and we always knew we were coming back. Now, I was not so sure if I would. I just hoped wherever I ended up, I could watch them reclaim our home.

I pulled away and stared into Séamus's deep emerald eyes. Reaching up and pushing his red curls out of his eyes, I brushed a tear off of his stubbly cheek. I loved Séamus. He always fought for me, protected me, and helped me through the worst nights. When I would wake in a cold sweat screaming, he would rush through my door and hold me until morning.

There have been a few drunken nights where we explored each others' mouths, thinking we were more than friends. But we would always laugh at the awkwardness and utter absurdity of just how much intimacy we lacked. I would miss him dearly and would worry about him every day.

"I don't accept that as an answer. Yer the most powerful creature I've had the pleasure of knowing. Ye'll live until ye stop fighting. Tell me everything I need to do for ye. I'm yers to command. *Tiarna*," he said and bowed his head.

My cheeks heated, and I dropped my hand. Hearing someone call me that word always sent a chill up my spine. "I'll be leaving either today or tomorrow. If anything happens to me, just know I'll be fighting till my last breath. I want ye to be my successor. General, heir to the throne, the person that keeps our group together, all of it. I know it's a lot to ask, but I trust no one else to lead our people to greatness."

Séamus nodded and grabbed my hand. "I'll do it with pride. Be safe. Fight strongly and die quickly." The little motto the five of us adapted held a special place in my heart and made me smile.

"I'll try. Go. Whatever bags I have here, send them to me when I give the word. Don't forget."

I turned away from him, but he gently tugged my arm to face him and braced my shoulders. "Eadha, I'd go to the darkest pits of the Otherworld for ye, and I know ye'd do the same for me. I'm not going to let ye leave this world before ye know happiness and warmth. I don't care where ye find it, and I don't care how. But either before or after this war, be happy. Do it for me."

He gave me one last hug and left, a piece of my heart going with him. A tear tugged behind my eyelid. I did not deserve him as a friend. He was too good, too pure for the likes of me, and was everything I was not. I envied his ability to see the light through this darkness. He spent all his time with our group and me, giving up so much for us. I don't even think I have ever seen him take a lover. Guilt raked through my body as I wondered if it was my fault. Was he too preoccupied making sure I was living my life for him to enjoy his?

As much as I wanted to mourn my going, as much as I wanted to keep his sweet face in my mind, I needed to focus. There would be a time for sorrow, just not now. I opened my weapons cabinet and surveyed my options.

I settled on my bow and arrows, a few throwing axes and knives, my dual swords, and a hidden blade I could connect to my wrist or the bottom of my shoe. I knew there might be a few formal events I would have to attend, so I thanked the gods for my High Druid blood and packed the finest dresses I owned. Other than that, a few measly pants, shirts, and tunics. Lastly, my armor.

I changed into a worn blue cropped tank with a collar that circled my neck, brown leggings cut to my knees, and my sleeveless fur jacket that stops just past my waist. Gone is that hopeless girl chained to a post in prison. Gone is the girl cowering in the shadows.

The age of the Druid was dawning. I would bring my people home. Or so I hoped.

CHAPTER SEVEN

Corvis

I wiped the sweat dripping off of my forehead with my shirt and tossed it aside. Sorlin chuckled as he leaned his head back to stop the bleeding from his nose. "Good session, although I didn't appreciate you taking it to the skies. I wasn't prepared for a fly. I think you broke my nose."

A laugh escaped my chest. "Maybe you should stop underestimating me and realize I can kick your ass." My wings tingled as the summer breeze curled around them. I was less out of shape than I thought I was, which was good. Now that we have a looming war in our midst, Sorlin and I would be training rigorously and would soon be spending more time at our childhood Vespairan war camp.

"Race you down?" Sorlin asked with a grin. I nodded, spreading my heavy wings, and leaped into the air. I could hear him scream something about cheating, but I didn't care. I forgot the joy flying brought to me, how free I felt in the sky. My wings have regained almost all of their strength, and I could outfly Sorlin. I landed on the parlor balcony with him following seconds after.

"You cheated," was all he said, pushing me aside.

I stumbled and flared my wings to keep my balance. "You said race. I raced."

"Yeah, but I didn't say 'go'. You broke the cardinal rule of the race: someone has to say 'go'." Sorlin's hands were out to the side, and his eyes were wide as if he were genuinely upset.

I held my hands to my chest. "My heart said, 'go'. That's all that matters."

He raised his eyebrows and followed me as I walked past him. "What? No, that's not all that matters if no one says 'go' how are we supposed to-"

Sorlin was interrupted by a small envelope dropping in front of us. On it held the same blue wax seal and the strange symbol embedded in it. I looked at my brother and picked up the letter.

"What the goddess is that?" He asked.

I bent over and inspected the letter. How does this woman keep slipping these past the wards? Why are they coming to me? "It's from the woman. Áine went yesterday to drop off another letter, remember?"

"Well, open it. What does it say?" He asked, reaching for the envelope.

I pulled it slightly away from him. "Not for you. I'm taking this to Áine. Are they at Rigel's place?"

"I assume so. Race you there?"

I rolled my eyes. "Are you going to whine about me not saying 'go'?"

He ran to the balcony smiling. "Okay, ready?"

I ran and leaped over the balcony into a free fall, spread my wings, and glided over Oneiros. The city was beautiful in the daylight. The buildings were all a greyish purple tone, and the streets were lined with blue goldstone and labradorite. Even during the day, the city sparkled, and the skies sang with the hue of otherworldly greens and purples. I was proud to call this city my home. Not many of my kind had the privilege of dwelling outside the camps.

I felt a force collide with my shoulder, and I wavered in the air as Sorlin took his place next to me. "Cheater! Have you no shame?!" He yelled over the thundering winds that rushed past us.

"Absolutely not!" I called out with a chuckle and dove down to Rigel's house on the far side of the city. This was the quieter, more homely side to the east, nestled close to the mountains that encased Oneiros. An Elite and a ruler he may have been, but he never wanted the title. He wanted nothing more than to live out his days pestering Sorlin and me, traveling, and going on adventures.

He was a kind and casual ruler but knew when to force his hand. The other Ruling Fae were wary of him because he never put on a show. Lax, he may have been, but Rigel had always known when to spare lives, when to take them, and when to walk out of them. Many left his court when he was crowned. They thought he didn't live up to his father's legacy. He was the youngest and weakest son, but all his siblings died either by each other's hands or by war. I pitied him sometimes, but I held him in the highest regard.

His house was simple, no bigger than a large cottage nestled between a few shops. While us delinquents lived in his forefathers' palace, he lived in a quaint two-story home. His house was protected by the same as the palace; no one could enter through the veil or mist their way in. I couldn't even take my shadow form inside.

Sorlin crashed into the ground glowering at me like a child who had just lost a game as I knocked on the door. "Grow up," I snapped at him.

He scoffed. "Big words for a cheater."

My eyes rolled, and I pushed past Rigel as he

opened the door. "Just accept the fact that I am still the stronger flyer."

Sorlin contemplated his words, but we silently agreed not to pursue the conversation further. There was only so far we could joke about wings and flying before the words started to sting.

"Ah, I missed training this morning, I see," Rigel said as he closed the door and walked with us to the parlor. He even looked simple in this house. His silver undercut hair was slicked and neat as always, but he wore a casual black tunic embroidered with red and silver flowers on the collar. Nothing compared to what other Ruling Fae wore.

Áine greeted us with a warm smile, and Vela crossed her arms, looking us up and down. I held the letter up in my hands.

"A response, I assume," I stated.

The color drained from Áine's face as she rested her head on her knuckles. "Oh, gods. Alright, lay it on me. What does it say?"

I cracked the seal and took in the room before reading the two simple words written on the paper. "It says: 'Piss off.' Not quite sure how to take that."

Sorlin sprang out of his chair with a grin. "Again, can we hire her?"

The corner of Áine's mouth slowly lifted, and her eyes widened. "That-that's a yes. I feel it in my bones. That's a yes!" She clapped her hands together and laughed, but all I could do was raise an eyebrow to Rigel, who reciprocated my confusion.

Vela was the one who spoke up, "I'm sorry, what? In what language does 'piss off' mean yes to you?"

Áine waved a hand. "Eh, it's good enough. A disgruntled yes, but still a yes. I feel it. Okay, she told me the last we spoke that if I called on her, she would be able to find me through the magic of the bargain. You, and you," she pointed to Sorlin and me, "better be far away from this house when she comes, as I have said before. We need her to like us."

Sorlin dramatically gasped. "If you don't want this ray of sunshine here to sweeten the deal, don't come crying to me when she declines to offer us her services."

I chuckled and stuck my arms out. "What's wrong with me?"

She shook her head. "I haven't decided yet. I just know you'll cause trouble somehow."

Vela stood up and intertwined her fingers in her short blonde hair. "So we are just letting this woman into our lives, claiming to be part of an extinct race of people? I know I pushed it in the beginning, but now that it is actually happening, I don't have a good feeling about this." I could have sworn I heard a tinge of concern in the monotone of her voice.

Rigel smiled and propped his legs up. "I just love our little adventures, don't you?"

Vela shot him a look of hate and rolled her ruby red eyes to face Áine. "I know the name in which this woman bears. I know who her parents were, who they worked with, and have seen their power. If she is as spiteful of your kind as you have stated, she could snap you in half with magic alone. And if she is a Laoch, she could do it with her bare hands. Who's to say this isn't a trap?" Vela's tone was flat and direct. Only when she was angry could you hear the echoes of the ancient spirit she truly was.

Áine folded her arms and stood. "Well, good thing we have a half-wraith that can hide in the shadows and be sure nothing happens."

"I can't shadow turn in this house or the palace."

Rigel nodded. "I can lift the wards for you during this meeting. I think it is for the best. Do you know when she will show up?"

Áine shook her head and took the letter from my hands, inspecting it. "No, maybe today, maybe tomorrow, but I don't know. I think it's best if we just hang around here and wait. I doubt she will send word when she is coming."

Rigel looked at Sorlin and pointed to the door. "You heard the lady. Scram. Go do whatever it is you do in your free time."

"Just a whole lot of this," Sorlin moved his fist up and down in an obscene gesture as he stood. We all groaned and averted our eyes before he kindly stuck his middle finger in the air and walked out the door.

"Gods, he needs a woman," Rigel said. "He needs someone else to bother. Burn off some of that smart-assery." He opened his palm, and a flick of purple light reached my eyes and disappeared. I felt a sort of restraint flee with it. "Wards are thinned. Don't make your presence known during this meeting and stay in the shadows unless things get ugly."

I nodded and watched as I turned my arm to shadows to test my abilities. "Of course."

We waited for the rest of the day, sitting, chatting, and planning, but the woman never showed. The day turned to night, and we all fell asleep. Thankfully, my dreams were kind. I had my lovely dream of that cliff, only it was different this time. The landscape seemed closer, almost more lifelike. That sense of peacefulness wrapped around me like a blanket as I watched the waves crash against the rock. Closer and closer, I moved to the edge of the cliff as if I was being guided by an unseen hand.

I didn't know what came over me or what made me shoot up off the couch and go run up to Rigel's bedroom in the morning. I didn't know what intuition I had just unearthed, but I swung open the door, and the couple jumped.

My eyes were wide, and I was slightly out of breath as my consciousness crept back into my brain and drowsiness faded. "She'll be here soon," was all I could say.

Rigel rubbed his eyes and looked out at the morning sun. "How do you know?"

I shrugged. I didn't know how to answer that question. "I-I Just know."

Rigel nodded with a look of suspicion. "It's showtime, I guess."

We barely had enough time to get dressed and sit down in the kitchen before that feeling returned. It wasn't painful; it was just as if something in the back of my mind was telling me she was coming. As if I had sensed her presence before, and I recognized it. It was a peculiar feeling. Rigel nodded to me, and I turned to black misty shadows hiding in the corner of the room. Áine sat next to Rigel at the end of the table with one chair across from them.

"Are you sure, Corv?" Rigel asked, looking in my direction.

"Yes. I don't know how I am, but yes. I just, I feel strange," I called out to him.

Áine gave me a smile and stirred in her seat. "I just hope this all goes smoothly and no one gets hurt. I don't particularly feel like healing anyone today. I have a question for you, though, Corv."

"Yes?"

She picked at her nails and turned to where I stood. "Why did the letters go to you? Both of them, they both appeared to you. Do you know why?"

I was about to open my mouth, but I stiffened as a familiar scent filled my nose. I knew I had never smelled it in person, but it stuck to me like a distant memory—the scent of a stormy cedar forest. The veil shifted; we all felt it.

"Did you lift the wards for her?" Áine asked.

Rigel shook his head. "No."

With a flash of light, the most alluring woman I have ever seen appeared at the head of the table in the empty seat. I was momentarily taken back, but my fingers danced around my sheathed sword as I remembered my purpose for being here. The woman's pale face was stern and angry. The top of her snow-white hair was gathered into various braids and exposed the tension in her clenched jaw.

She had an intricate blue tattoo on her face. A swirl of fine lines and dots extended from her left eyebrow to the top of her softly carved, pale cheekbone, like blue ink dripped into a bowl of milk.

I wondered what all the markings meant. She was covered in them. Her biceps were colored in blue, reflecting line work. Five large dots went from the back of her right hand to her elbow. It was hard for my eyes not to linger as the dark blue was striking against her pale skin.

Áine cleared her throat and smiled. "Eadha, thank you so much for coming. It's great to see you after the time that has passed. This is Rigel, High Lord of Tenebris, and my husband. Rigel, this is Eadha."

Eadha didn't move a muscle, only looked between the two Elites that sat in front of her. Her body language gave away nothing, and I made a note of how strong she looked. If things went south, I would struggle to keep her at bay. The childhood stories of the mighty Laoch filled my head, and for the first time in many years, I was intimidated.

Rigel smiled and leaned back in his chair as he brushed his already slicked hair back. His silver eyes looked Eadha up and down, most likely assessing the danger presented in front of him. "A pleasure. May I ask how you were able to veilwalk into my home?"

Eadha shot a deadly gaze to his eyes and shrugged, her face unchanged. "Did ye ward against Druid magic? If not, there ye go." She looked over to Áine. "Ye look tired."

She spoke with a voice that wasn't too high or too low and had an accent I had never heard before. It was hard for my ears to adjust and make out what she was saying. As she brushed a hair out of her face, I noticed more blue lines on her palms going up to her inner forearm, matching on each side, but the top of her left arm was bare, like untouched snow.

Áine nodded and sighed. "Well, we are dealing with a lot here. I can imagine you are upset that I told them about you-"

"Oh, there's a them? Not just this bastard?" Her lip curled, and she looked in my direction, raising her eyebrows. "Is one of them hiding in the shadows over there?" She asked with a lazy point. I gripped my sword but maintained my stealth. I had to admit, I was afraid. If the stories of her kind were true, I was not so sure my sword would be of much service.

Rigel propped his ankle over his knee and rested his hands behind his head, looking utterly bored. "Truly, it is a pleasure," he said quickly while clearing his throat, "as you can imagine having someone as mysterious as yourself in my home would be foolish without a bit of protection."

She snorted. "Aye, it would be." She continued to look right into my eyes as if she could see me. I couldn't help but shiver as no one has been able to sense me in the shadows before. It was unsettling to know that stealth would be of no use around her.

Áine shot her husband a look warning him to shut his mouth, and he wisely obliged. "They can be trusted. They are family and had to know. Look, yell at me all you want for doing it, but we need your help. There are rumors that Sabriel is planning on opening this-this Well. No one knows why, no one knows what he is planning on drawing out, but it could be bad. Large scale war, bad."

Eadha chuckled, and her face turned dark. "Do ye think I'm some bumbling eejit? Ye think I don't know of Sabriel's doings and taking steps to prepare?" Her voice was disdainful and rough. I did not take kindly to anyone speaking to my High Lady with such disrespect.

Áine clenched her jaw, and Rigel stiffened. "I would like to know the steps of preparation you are taking," he said calmly. "I have many questions, but can we start with that?"

Eadha sighed. "My father is a Seer by nature. But

It's impossible for him to see past whatever magic Sabriel is holding. He wanted us, well, me, to go to the island and grab a piece of his trove so we can map his movements during the fight. We have numbers. Druids, plainsfolk, and Laoch alike are prepared for battle. I, for one, am planning to prevent it."

Rigel nodded. "Well, we are in agreement then. We both do not wish to fight. How can you prevent it? If you don't mind me asking. There is no living history of your kind. I don't even know how your magic works. I was informed that you work with the gods and goddesses. I can only imagine the power-"

Eadha put up a hand to cut him off. "My parents work with the god Arawn and the goddess Macha. I work with Dragons."

I silently choked and stifled a cough as I took in her words. Dragons? Surely she must have been joking. Dragons were a myth. Well, I guess she was too, and yet, there she stood. The shock I felt was written on Rigel and Áine's face as well.

Áine's brows pulled together, and she stammered. "Dragons? As in *the* Dragons? The four that legends say control the elements? Those Dragons? I did not know they were real."

Eadha grinned. "Aye, they grant me knowledge of the elements, and I use that in my fighting. More specifically, strength from earth, balance from air, speed from fire, and grace from water. They will fight with me in the war."

I had so many questions I wish I could ask. I wanted nothing more than to break from the shadows and ask of all the adventures she had seen. It almost pained me to think that if she decided to leave, I wouldn't have known all of what she had done in her life.

Rigel nodded slowly. "They will fight with...with *you*," he pointed, "meaning they are real tangible beings and not just...spirits? Interesting. So you have elemental magic?"

She shrugged. "Depends on yer definition of magic. I don't think so. I am capable of taking out almost any opponent if that is what yer asking me. I'm a High Druid by birth, so I was born with innate magic. I have stealth abilities and an impenetrable mind. Not that anyone would want to venture in there."

A long pause birthed the room as Rigel looked intently at Eadha, and his silver eyes glowed. He was testing her words, but she merely smirked. "That was a valiant effort, High Lord. Well, let's all just shut our gobs. Ye want to prevent war. If we cannot do that, then I need to be in Verbenia to fight, and well, yer already here. Someone has to make sure ye all don't get slaughtered before the fun begins."

Áine smiled. "Is someone forcing you to do this??"

Her face dropped. "Of course, I'd leave ye all to die if it were up to me. But, I made a promise to someone dear to my heart that I would come back alive. I'll need help to do that. So, since I am forced to be at yer service, I'm yer ally unless ye turn me away. Yer court and yer people have my protection. Under one condition."

Rigel waved a hand for her to continue.

"Ye listen to me, and ye work with me. Feel free to weigh in options and command yer own people, but big picture, I am in charge. This involves my people now, who I will protect with my life. I am much older than ye laddie, I've seen horrors ye cannot even imagine.

Ye need to trust me, or I leave." Her words chilled my bones.

Rigel...come on, I willed. He had to accept. I knew we could not stop this on our own, and I didn't want to see what would happen if we tried.

He smiled, his teeth gleaming. "Well, I'd love a good Dragon show, so how could I resist? Agreed."

Eadha nodded, and Áine rushed to her with open arms. Rigel looked in my direction and gave me a dismissing nod. I lingered for a moment; Eadha's eyes seemed to meet mine one last time before I disappeared into the veil and headed back to the palace.

Sorlin and Vela were bickering in the dining room when I flew through the balcony.

Vela was on her feet and grasping my shoulders within seconds. "Well? Was she what she claimed to be? Is she going to help us?"

I nodded. "She didn't look like any being I have seen before. She walked through the veil to get into Rige's home, and not even you can do that, so I assume she is a Druid. And yes, she is helping us from what I can tell."

A wave of relief washed over her face, and she smiled. "Good," she let go of my shoulders and sauntered out the door.

Sorlin shivered. "I don't like her, Corv. She creeps me out. She threatened to eat me before you showed up. Anyways, tell me everything," he bit his lip with eagerness and lifted his heels up and down.

"She is intense. Powerful as well, I assume. She could sense me in the shadows and is seemingly impervious to Rigel's magic."

He opened his eyes wide and clapped his hands. "I'm excited."

Before I could answer, one of the housemaids cleared her throat behind us. "Lord Rigel asks that you retreat to your rooms. His guest is coming and staying in the wing opposite of yours, and he wishes you not to meet her until dinner tonight."

Sorlin groaned and grabbed me by the collar, pulling me with him out the door.

"Hey, let go," I pushed him away, but he held tight.

"You aren't telling me everything. There is something else. What is it?"

I scoffed and shoved him hard, breaking his grip. "There is nothing more. Leave me be."

I went into my room and shut the door. I always strived to maintain a mask of neutrality on my face, but Sorlin knew better. There *was* something else, but I didn't know how to describe it. Seeing her there in person was like seeing an old friend from a faded memory. She looked so incredibly familiar, but I knew I have never seen anything like her before.

No...I have *felt* her before. I just didn't know how, and I could not remember when. Being in a room with her was like standing next to a force of gravity. She had a sort of pull that I couldn't explain. Not to mention the feel of the magic pouring off her body was foreign, yet I felt as though I had experienced it before.

My heart stopped as I recalled her face. *Her eyes.* They were an ombre of color. No, not color, a *picture.* A grassy green cliff overlooking the sea's crashing waves and clouds blowing past a fiery setting sun. The landscape moved as if it were alive within the confines of her irises. I felt as though I was standing on that cliff, watching the sunset, watching the grass blow in the wind, and watching the waves crash against the rock. I had never seen anything like it.

Only I have. I *have* been to that cliff; it was the same cliff I have dreamt of in the past. Or at least it looked like it. How could her eyes hold so many images? As I looked at the covered mirror, I became conscious of the mangled wings I carried on my back and snapped my whirling thoughts to a halt. I was not here to explore the meanings of dreams or play with the new toy in town. I had a job to do, and we were on the brink of war.

Though I was unsettled, and I had questions, she needed to be watched like a hawk. I didn't fully trust her or her motives. I didn't know why she is so vaguely familiar, but it didn't matter. One of the most deadly breeds of warrior was now living in my house. Though she seemed blunt and genuine, I couldn't help question why she agreed to help us so easily. The aggression and rigidity she expressed during the meeting begged me to think she may not be able to settle her differences with the likes of the Fae. She looked like an incredible fighter. I would hate to see her skills used against me, let alone her magic.

Eadha claimed to have stealth abilities, which gave me a reason to keep her closer to me and away from the others. She could work alongside me for the time being until I could trust her.

CHAPTER EIGHT
Eadha

Rigel informed me that I would be staying in his palace. Much like he did not ward his private house against Druid magic, the palace was unprotected. True to his word, two female servants were waiting for me. They were both lesser Fae and looked to be of this court with dark gray hair but slightly darker skin than Rigel, but still had the otherworldy fair skin of this court.

The taller of the two smiled and extended a hand to the stairs behind her. "Welcome. I will show you to your room." The shorter servant kept a lingering eye on me, darting between all my weapons. I lifted my eyebrow to her and followed the taller one.

The palace was beautiful and highly reflected the land in which it sat. The walls were a deep midnight blue, and the floors were tiled with a bluish-green iridescent stone. It was quite lavishly decorated with art, vases, and sculptures and a complete turnaround from the modest cottage the Ruling Fae, Rigel, lived in. Everything about him was rather plain compared to this. He was undoubtedly handsome, but the clothes he wore were simple, and his house was not decorated with anything other than memories. Why would he not live here?

I cleared my throat as we ascended up the grand staircase. "Will I be living here alone?"

The servant shook her head. "No, members of

Lord Rigel's court live here. They dwell in a separate wing than you will," her voice was like velvet against my ears, but I knew Fae; beautiful to trick you from what they really were. Even though I pledged my services to Rigel, I considered myself in the heart of enemy territory and would not be letting my guard down for anyone or travel without a blade. I wondered how vast his lands were and just how many Fae's movements I would be mapping over the next few days to ensure my safety.

As we arrived at the top of the stairs, the servant turned right, but before I took a step to follow her, I stopped. The air escaped my lungs as a peculiar sensation took over me. It felt as though a thin thread was pulling me to the left-wing. When Áine called upon me, I was able to follow that same feeling from our magical bond to her; but she was not here.

I moved to follow the thread, but the tie collapsed as a soft hand touched my shoulder. "Miss, the High Lord wishes you not to meet the others until dinner tonight. Please, follow me," the servant's voice was frank and impassive as she pulled me along.

Others? Must be the members of his court on that side. They probably possessed something of importance that I needed, something my senses were leading me to. I made a quick note of approximately where I thought the pull originated and followed the woman down the hall.

The servant opened a door and led me into an ornate bedroom. My mouth fell open as I took it all in. The walls were a soft dove gray, with heavy golden curtains on the doors leading to a balcony. The floor was a gold and blue marble, and the large bed, a silky midnight blue. I peeked into the exquisite bathroom and found a sizeable gilded soaking tub resting beside floor to ceiling windows. If it were not for my noble birth, I would say I did not belong in such extravagant living quarters.

The servant began laying out a gaudy and rather tight dress onto the bed. "Ach, no, no, no. I have my own clothes, thank ye, that will not be necessary. And no, ye will not be doing my hair either," I said as I noticed a brush in her hand.

Her pale eyes closed as she nodded. "Of course. If there is anything you need, you can ask us. My name is Thela, and the other you met is Cari. Feel free to call whenever you need. Down the stairs is a library, and the floor above you is off limits for your safety, unless you are invited." She picked up the dress and walked out of the room, the door closing behind her.

I snorted. "My safety. What ye got up there, an imp?" Out of the corner of my eye, I saw the bags that I packed at home appear on the bed along with a note from Séamus. No seal, no stamp, no envelope: *"Don't die before I can kill ye for leaving. Get back soon. I already want to throttle Donnan and Dolan."*

I smiled and clutched the first of the five blue filled circles I had marked on my arm that represented him. I really hoped Lana could manage to keep them all from massacring each other, but then again, who would be watching her?

My chest began to tighten slightly once the reality of my situation hit me: there was no turning back. I was to live in Verbenia, in the same court that hung us out to dry. I was going to go to Kamber Island and stop Sabriel, or die trying. When I fought the Sluagh five years ago, I choked. If that were to happen when I face him, I would jeopardize my whole nation. He would know we exist and would not rest until he found our island. He most likely grew in power, but so did I. He would not hold me captive again.

I shook my head to snap out of those thoughts. I needed to focus on the task at hand: unpacking and surviving this dinner. Maybe I'd even get Rigel's blasted stone tonight. I shrugged off my coat and started tearing apart my bags. The bulk of my packing was my weapons and dresses. I figured I would find myself in a situation where they would be necessary, but my gods, why were they made with so much fabric? Thank goodness there were two wardrobes in this room.

The balcony caught my eye, and I walked out onto it and shuddered in the breeze. I've been to this city once before, as a prisoner. Back then, it was dreary, stale, and rather dark. The High Lord of this land I met all those centuries ago was spiteful and cruel from what little I saw before killing him. I should probably keep the killing part to myself around here, though. Now, the moon shined even as the sun was high. The sky danced with color, and laughter rang from the streets below. The pathways looked like they were carved from the same stones as the tiles down in the foyer. It almost reminded me of my home, Covalla. Though I was not here on vacation, I would love a chance to explore the city a bit, but there would be a time to do so. Now, to spend the rest of the day unpacking, sharpening my blades, and reading whatever books were on the nightstand.

A knock sounded on my door, and I jumped out of my light slumber, clutching my dagger. Thela opened the door and smiled politely. "Dinner will be in fifteen minutes. The dining room is on the ground floor on the opposite side of the parlor, feel free to wait there for the others," the tension slowly left my body as I gave her a dismissing nod.

My room had turned into a golden wonderland as the setting sun shined through the door while I was asleep. My body did not want to leave the comfort and warmth of the bed, but with a groan, I slid out and headed to the wardrobe. Was this a nice dinner? What would I wear? The thought of a dress made me nauseous.

I decided on a light blue tunic that cut to the top of my thighs with sleeves that ended at my elbows, and grey pants hugged my legs. In case anything turned hostile and I needed to run, I chose thin practical boots that climbed to my knees.

I took a moment to look in the mirror. I was not displeased with my body. In fact, I loved how strong it looked, but I wished it was more feminine at times. The tunic outlined a nice curve to my waist, but I could still see the muscles carved under the fabric. I was not huge by any means, not like Séamus. I had a small frame and was a tad short compared to most Laoch, just rather cut and lean.

Donnan and Dolan used to joke and say I was the tiniest thing that would ever kill them. I smiled and brushed over the other dots on my arm, one for each of my friends and my brother. May the gods grant us more time together on this earth. I combed out my hair and braided the top half, letting the rest flow. After strapping on a belt to hold my dagger and fastening my swords to my back, I headed out of the room.

Cautiously, I looked over the railing and heard

someone shuffling about in the front room. Neither Rigel nor Áine's magic was anywhere to be felt in the palace. *Hmm, must be someone from his court,* I thought.

I opened the now-closed door of the front room to investigate, and there stood a rather tall man wearing a tight black tunic that exposed his muscular frame. He had to have been one of the Raven's Áine mentioned when I first met her on account of the man's massive black feathered wings. Sorlin, I believed his name to be. He was quite large like Séamus, but not as tall with luxurious bronze-tinted skin and striking amber-yellow eyes.

He turned to look at me with a wide grin and brushed back his long, black, unruly hair. "Ah, so *you're* the talk of the party," his voice was animated and low.

My lip slightly curled. I expected something more menacing from the elite aerial army of Tenebris. He looked nothing more than a large human with wings, only more alluring than an ordinary human. He had trimmed facial hair, a cut jawline, and a set of lips that just looked like they got him into trouble. They probably got him that scar going diagonally across his mouth.

My fingers automatically touched the top of my dagger as I made my way across the room and sat in a chair, his amber eyes never breaking my gaze. "So, strong silent type? That's fine, I can respect that. Although, I don't like the way you're clutching your blade at me, in *my* home."

I huffed and leaned forward, my blood beginning to heat. "I can do a lot worse to ye in *yer* home, with far less than a blade, sir," I said evenly. Sorlin's grin increased, and he took a step towards me, "I reckon ye'll be staying right where ye are, eh laddie?" The hilt of my dagger now fully in my hand.

His mouth fell, and he began to analyze me. "You're going to threaten me in my own home too? I don't know what land you come from, but we don't take too kindly to that around here."

"It's no threat. It's a warning. Ye can take it or leave it. I've eaten many birds in my days, though a little wriggly, I always managed to pick their bones clean," I said, gripping the arms of my chair. Tension began to build in my body. I felt as though I could snap at any second.

Sorlin took another step, all but a few feet away from where I sat. I rose as he pointed his finger at me. "Look, this whole 'new chief in town' front you have was cute, but now I'm starting to think you don't actually know who you're-"

"Ye'll be putting that finger down before I rip it off," I cut him off and lessened the distance between us. My stance widened, and I shifted my gaze to his hands, keeping a close eye on any weapons he may reach for. Anger clouded my brain, and I felt my mouth twitch.

"Oh, you'll...rrrrrip it off, will ye? What if I don't put it doon?" He said in a way to make fun of my accent. He made two pointing motions before my blood boiled over and red overtook my vision. I simultaneously grabbed his finger with my left hand and punched his diaphragm with my right, sending him a few feet away from me. He looked at me bewildered as if he could not believe someone like me pushed someone like *him* away with just a punch.

I wiped my hands together and smirked at him. "Now, yer lucky I didn't rip-"

Sorlin lunged for me, and I bent just in time to grapple his knees and push him up over my head, but he quickly caught me by the waist and took me down with him. I was under his knees, but I locked my legs around his waist. His eyes no longer showed jest but shined like a predator about to devour prey. I let him manage one punch before I threw him to the side with my legs. The taste of blood covered my tongue and stung my lip, but through that punch, I gathered all the information I needed. I felt his weak points.

We pounced and crashed, pushing with all our strength, neither one yielding. I slid my hand down to his elbow and squeezed the pressure point I felt when he punched me. Sorlin cried out; I kicked his knees back, tackled him, and pinned an arm down. My fist collided with his nose multiple times.

He grunted and tried to buck me off, but I held my ground and sent a few strategic punches to his dominant arm, right on those pressure points. Sorlin thrashed his head in pain and hollered through clenched teeth. His wings began to push him up, so I slid my knees higher to pin them in place. I recoiled my arm and my fist collided with his face, over and over again.

A strong hand abruptly grabbed my wrists, and an arm hooked around my waist, pulling me off of the Raven.

In front of me, Sorlin thrashed against Rigel, who was now holding him back. "I can't move my arm!" Sorlin yelled with the look of absolute murder in his eyes.

I grunted and pushed against the force that was holding me in place. "I told ye to get yer manky finger out of my face, now look what happened!"

Rigel chuckled and grunted as he struggled to keep Sorlin away from me. "Áine, I'm having the best time. I-I'm glad-we, ah, decided to...to do this." His silver hair was wildly out of place from the struggle.

Something cool and soft danced across my cheek, and out of the corner of my eye, I swore I saw a shadow graze past my vision. I nearly jumped out of my skin and I broke free to look at what was holding me back.

A male Raven stood in front of me with his hands up to show he was not a threat. I have never seen a face quite as gracefully carved as his. He looked maybe a few years older than me but not as old as Sorlin. Unlike his winged ally, his eyes were a blazing deep orange. I could have sworn they widened a bit before returning to neutrality. His black hair was slightly curled but was shaggy and danced around his eyes, unlike his brute companion's wildly curly long hair. His cheeks were high, somewhat hollowed, and his jaw gently sloped to his softly pointed chin.

Around him bloomed the black inky shadows that graced my cheeks. His wings were bat-like in their structure, bare of any feathers, and rather leathery. This was the man Áine spoke of before, Corvis. He was considerably paler than the other Raven but not as fair as Rigel or myself. It must have been the wraith blood Áine stated he was mixed with that caused him to look so different than Sorlin.

"I don't know who you are, but anyone that beats the piss out of Sorlin is a friend in my book," a chilling female voice said. A blonde woman came sauntering into the room with an eerie grin on her face. She looked human but had a peculiar feeling accompanying her, probably due to the red eyes that were analyzing me from head to toe. She was about my height and rather plain looking.

I've felt her kind of presence before as a babe. I knew her. I've met the daemon before when she was possessing a different body.

"I'm Vela. Truly, thank you for your work. He had it coming," she wiped what I assumed was blood off of my lip, and the sting vanished. "This is Corvis, Corv as we all call him. The lesser of the three male evils in the house, well, depending on his mood."

Corvis extended a hand to me. "A pleasure to meet you." His voice was deeper than Sorlin's and smoothly angelic compared to the raspy voice of the other Raven. I clutched his hand and flinched as his shadows curled around our embrace. "Sorry. I can't control that," he said with an emotionless half-smile.

I pulled away with a nod and surveyed the room. These were the companions I would be plagued with for the foreseeable future. Perhaps it could have been worse.

Vela nodded to Sorlin. "The beast you brawled is Sorlin. He's all talk, just ignore him, and he won't bother you," I looked over and jeered in his direction.

"So, Sorlin, finger-pointing? Is that what we are resorting to now?" Rigel released him and fixed his sparkling silver hair.

"She started it," Sorlin murmured as he walked out the door, moving his fingers and circling his wrist.

"Eadha, can you just...not pick fights with anyone?" Áine asked with concern twisting her face. I looked fairly underdressed compared to the gold and white dress she wore. In fact, she was the only one who wore any kind of ornate clothing in the room.

I scoffed. "I didn't pick shite. The bastard taunted me, then got pissy when he bit off more than he could chew."

"I'll be ready next time!" Sorlin yelled from the other room.

Vela let out a growl and met my gaze. "Enough talking. The fact that you walked away from a fight with a Vespairan leads me to believe you are who you claim to be. It also helps that you are the spitting image of your parents."

I nodded. "Aye. And ye have a...new body now. And a name."

She shrugged. "Well, I've always had a name. You just never knew it. Bodies make it easier to get work done, and well, I like this one."

My lip lifted slightly, and I shuddered. *Daemons, what a cruel bunch.* I wondered if she was the one that lived on the floor off-limits to me. It would make sense for Thela's concern for my safety.

"Well, I'm famished. Shall we get on with it then?" Vela asked with a smile.

Rigel nodded and motioned to the door, which led out to the foyer and the dining room. I sat at the end of the table, with Vela next to Corvis and me across from her. Rigel sat next to me, followed by Áine then Sorlin.

It was quite a strategic placement, though unnecessary, with the three strongest beings in the room closest to me and ready to pounce if need be. I should be the one worried about these people, not the other way around. The eyes of Rigel's court members all focused on me, including the long-haired lout. I began to think I should just go home and leave them on their own.

Rigel waved a hand, and a simple hot meal of chicken, roasted potatoes, and a few varieties of greens appeared. Nothing that I would have expected a High Lord to be eating. The Fae food was truly intoxicating to smell, and I helped myself. I assumed Rigel and Áine would stay quiet through this interrogation, as they had already made up their minds about me.

Vela propped her elbows up on the table and glared at me through squinted eyes as she began to eat. "Forgive me if I tear open old wounds tonight, but I haven't seen your parents since you were a newborn. I need to know what happened that day. Why did you disappear, and how did Sabriel beat you?"

I gave her my own stare and shoved some food into my mouth. "Why didn't ye show up to help?"

She clicked her tongue and picked at her fingernails. I hated that noise; it made my skin crawl. "I'm a daemon. Whoever sells their soul to me or gives an offering, I'm bound to. At the time, I was bound to a land far from Verbenia. I didn't know you all were gone until I went to the island myself and saw the ruin," she spoke with a cold and apathetic tone. I tightened my jaw and took a deep breath, debating on how to answer her. The nightmares now only come on occasion. I bet they will grace my nights once again if I speak of that day.

"Sabriel invaded," I said bluntly. "My parents, my brother, and I went to each cardinal point in the capital city, once we realized what was happening, and walked the whole of it away through the veil. I went back with a small group of Laoch, I was not one at the time, or at least I wasn't inducted…we walked as many people out as we could before we collapsed. We were held captive and escaped. Not much more to say."

Vela nodded and gave me a half-smile. "Can you all veilwalk? What other magic do you possess?" She asked, shoveling mashed potatoes into her mouth.

All these blasted questions. This was one of the many reasons I did not wish to come. I swallowed my food and cleared my throat. "I have innate stealth abilities. And much like you lesser Faeries," I shot a glance at Sorlin, "have a trove to focus yer abilities. I have this," I pulled out my Druid Stone.

Sorlin gave a sarcastic nod. "Ah, yes, a *rock*. I can see how that is comparable to the rings that give us literal weapons."

Rigel snickered, and Corvis cleared his throat. I darted my gaze between them, and they quickly shut their mouths. "To you, it looks like a rock, but not me. They are forged by the power of the Tiarna and help many Druids keep their connections to the gods they work with. We can communicate through it as well. Without it, my Druid magic is sloppy."

"You mentioned you have stealth abilities?" A smooth male voice called out over the sounds of clanking forks and chewing.

"Ah, Corvis, meet your new partner. She can

disappear much like yourself, so I've heard," Rigel exclaimed with an excited grin on his face.

I knew there was someone else in the room during our meeting. "You were there this morning then, yes?"

Corvis nodded. His face was like stone, unreadable and unchanging as his shadows held close to his body. He did not speak, so I continued, "I didn't know wraiths bread outside of their own kind. Thought half-wraiths were a myth."

He simply shrugged. "I thought the same of your kind."

Vela rolled her eyes and snapped her fingers to get my attention. "Yes, yes, your existences cease to amaze us all, but there will be time for that later. Do you work with the god and goddess as well? Or will that be passed onto your brother once it's his time to be crowned Tiarna?"

I bit my lip and set my fork down. Tadhg...he was so perfect, so gentle to all. The proper High Druid boy who did his studies, learned the ways of craft magic, worked with many healing goddesses, and was a born leader. "No, he didn't make it through the invasion. It is unclear how the relationship will be passed down, considering my Laoch path and the working relationships I already have. I will not even consider the title at all."

The room quieted, and I hated them for it. I did not want their pity, my brother died a hero's death, and I did not need anyone feeling sorrow on my behalf. "Well, I am sorry to hear that. Who do you work with currently?" Vela asked plainly.

I pushed away my plate as a sour feeling grew in my stomach. "I work with the Dragons."

Vela choked on her food, and I heard a knife snap in Sorlin's direction. The two looked at me with slack jaws. "You work with their spirit? Like any other deity, yes?" She asked.

I smiled and snorted. "No, they are alive and well, walking the earth. I stumbled onto one by accident and almost pissed myself. Didn't know what he saw in me, but granted me knowledge of his element and sent me on to the next. I'm surprised someone as ancient and formidable as yerself didn't know about them."

Vela nodded and wiped her mouth. "Interesting. Well, it will be nice to see you unleash the tricks up your sleeve onto Sorlin. So, on court, you have your parents as monarchs and Laoch, who have their own higher-ups. Do you have just regular humans? Who all survived?"

I blinked as I took in all her questions. "Some people are born without any power and no ability to commune with spirits or other beings. Outside of immortal age, they are normal. We call them plainsfolk, but they are still born of Druid blood. Not many High Druids survived, many lesser did, but nonetheless, we regained our numbers."

Áine groaned and sighed. "Can we stop pestering the poor woman and agree this is the kind of help we need right now? I will be the first to say yes; I want her to work with us and help us. Corv?"

He looked at me blankly. "I think it would be useful to have another person of stealth with us."

Áine clicked her tongue. "Fantastic. Vela? Yes? No?"

"As long as you spend some time with me and answer all my questions, yes. Your parents...I almost considered friends. It would be nice to see your history written in the books," Vela did not break eye contact with me as she answered.

I shook my head. "Only after the war can ye write about me publicly."

She nodded and looked to Sorlin, who mumbled something unintelligible. "I'm sorry, Sor, I don't think we heard you correctly," Rigel said with jest.

"Work with us if you want, but I'm kicking your ass in the ring."

I threw a piece of bread his way and rolled my eyes. "So what are yer plans for stopping Sabriel?" I asked Rigel.

He paused and pursed his lips, contemplating his words. "Well, you tell me. So far, the only idea we had was battle. I can't bear to put my people through such things. He's probably prepared for so long that no army could compare to his."

I nodded. "Aye. Well, my plan is simple. When the god Arawn left this world, he, like many other gods, left his trove with us: his cauldron. He broke off the jewels that power it and gave one to each Ruling Fae in Verbenia. I get the stones, I get the power of the cauldron, I destroy the Well so he can't open it. Then, if we have time, I possibly take his dark magic somehow or kill him."

Rigel sat for a moment before smiling. "We discussed destroying the Well, just didn't have the means to do it. This is it. That's how we will stop him. We'll take my two Ravens and my wife to the island, but do you have anyone you could bring to replace Vela? I'll need her here guarding the city."

My first thought was a Laoch from my fleet, but no. It had to be someone powerful. It would be useful to have Lana's healing abilities. With a Fosseran with us, her magic surely would be repaired. The twins would be ruthless and attack all they saw, but I needed strategy. "Aye. My second in command, Séamus. He's a High Druid who has weapons magic much like ye," I motioned to the two Ravens before me.

Áine beamed with happiness and rubbed her hand together. "Well, you have our stone. Rigel will retrieve it tomorrow. I say we come up with a plan in the meantime to meet with Cazara. Should we tell her all we know?"

Rigel shook his head. "I say we keep Eadha's identity a secret. We will glamour her wherever we travel."

I let out a chuckle. "I can glamour myself, but I agree. Verbenia should not be made aware of my kind until it is absolutely necessary. Now, If you'll excuse me, I just need to get some air." They nodded and were silent until I hit the balcony of the dining room, then their hushed whispers began.

My hands were sweaty, and I fought to keep my breath steady. I would be traveling to every Fae court and stealing their most prized possessions out from under their noses, fighting whatever beasts they have guarding them. I have never felt more alone in my entire life. I did not realize how heavily I relied on my friends for my sanity until now.

None of us spoke about the invasion to each other, and I just realized how harmful that must have been for us all. Oh how it must have pained my parents watching me pull further and further from the light until I was consumed by the darkness. I stayed alive to spare them the sorrow of losing their last child without realizing they already had.

My brother and I were born on Mabon, the autumnal equinox, which marked the beginning of the dark half of the year. Growing up, my mother would always joke about our birthday and would say: "It's no wonder why I could never grow anything until the dark half of the year. The day you two were born was the day my garden bloomed." Now, her garden was dead and withering away.

I felt a presence approach behind me, and his scent perfumed the air: burning rosemary and lilac. I noticed it during the meeting this morning, though it wasn't coming from Áine or Rigel.

"Ye have no business out here," I said coldly as I turned around.

Corvis looked at the ground before meeting my gaze intensely. "I just wanted to apologize for Sorlin's behavior," he stopped to roll his eyes, "and his future behavior. But you seemed to have the situation under control."

"Well, what can you expect from a Fae, or, Raven, whatever ye are," I said in a harsh tone. As handsome as he may have been, he was still a representation of everything I hated.

He took a sharp breath in and cleared his throat, furrowing his brows. "I'm not a Fae or a Raven. I'd appreciate it if you would just call me by my name," his words cut through me like a hot knife, and my cheek began to sting. The look on his face almost made me regret my words.

Corvis's eyes traveled up and down my body, and he casually motioned to my arms. "What do they all mean?"

I looked down and gave a small laugh. "Not enough hours in the day, I'm afraid."

He nodded with an unwavering face of stone, but his shadows extended and swirled around him carelessly. "Well, we train at seven each morning. There is a sparring ring on the roof we go to. Hope to see you there. Goodnight," he nodded and left the balcony.

He mentioned earlier that he could not control his whirling shadows. Still, I was sure if I studied them enough, they would give me some insight into his mind —the thought of being in enemy territory and being around someone I could not gauge unsettled me.

I just hoped I could have Sabriel's head and my home before autumn. I did not know how long I would last in these lands before I did something I could regret. Now, to get some rest and prepare for the journey ahead.

CHAPTER NINE
Eadha

I jumped out of bed with a gasp and fell onto the floor, panting as the light of dawn flooded my eyes. I dreamt that I had wings. Giant, stunning feathered wings...and they were ripped from my back. I ran to the mirror and thrashed around to pull my shirt off.

"Oh, thank gods," I sighed with relief. I never thought I would be grateful to see the scars on my back. "What the shite was that?" I whispered. Perfect, these bastards were already giving me nightmares. I giggled and rubbed my eyes. This was going to be a long string of months if that oversized bird, Sorlin, was already getting into my head after the first few days.

A chill traveled down my spine as the sounds from my dream still echoed in my mind; the screaming. It sounded as if it were coming from halfway across the city, yet rang right in the back of my head. *Unsettling is what that is,* I thought to myself. I took out my Druid Stone, drew a groggy breath, and slipped behind the veil.

I could instantly feel the wards around me as I opened my door like eyes watching in contempt as I broke a rule of the house by veilwalking. Rigel was indeed powerful, it was a struggle to slip past the wards he set in place, but I did not care. I needed to find the blasted screaming that was sending ice through my veins. It appeared to be emanating from the left-wing of the palace.

As I approached the first door, the scream intensified, but not audibly. I could *feel* that it grew louder. I opened the door to find Sorlin snoring and sleeping like a baby, no sign of distress or of the grotesque nightmare I witnessed. The screaming was deafening. I slowly opened the next door but was met by nothing more than Corvis sleeping in his bed, illuminated by the light of the birthing sun pooling in from his balcony door. He turned over in his sleep, mumbled, and the screaming stopped. I quickly rushed back to my room and closed the door.

Of course. Of course Rigel would be playing some kind of cruel trick on me. I rubbed my eyes aggressively and groaned. If I went back to sleep now, surely I'd get sucked back into whatever that was. I decided on drinking some tea and doing some of my own training before the others joined me.

The two servants were already waiting in the kitchen. Did they ever sleep? Thela smiled, but Cari remained wary of me. "Good morning," they said in unison.

I gave a small smile back. "Aye. Mind showing me where to get food and maybe some tea?"

Thela pointed to the dining room. "Through the door on the far side is a small kitchen, but we would be more than happy to prepare something for you."

"No, that won't be necessary," I said as I made my way into the kitchen. I went frigid as I recounted what just happened upstairs. Maybe Rigel wanted to make a point that he could, in fact, get inside my head and attacked me while asleep. I would not put it past his kind to do such things; either way, the incident needed to be addressed. I guzzled down some bread and a few pieces of fruit before heading to the roof of the building.

The sun was incredibly warm as it rose in the sky, and the breeze decided not to come my way. I pulled at the high collar of my shirt, cursed the rays beating down on my fair skin, and gasped as I took in the city. It rested inside a ring of mountains and was nestled right by the sea. A powerful waterfall on the east most border created a roaring river billowing through the city and into the ocean that breached a gap in the western mountains. The sky was brushed with vivid purples and golds as the sun dueled the moon for a spot in the sky. A ray of green and pink light that seemed to be always visible danced sporadically across the city and carried on past its borders. It was breathtaking.

I looked at the sun's position in the sky and guessed I had about fifteen minutes before the others would be awake and rumbling up to me. My eyes fell, and my lungs drew a long and steady breath as I recited the great invocation of the Earth Dragon.

"Cré, guardian of the lands and keeper of the rock, I call on yer strength. Grant me the stability of the trees and the strength of the mountains. Give me the vision to hunt all the corners of the world. Crawl to my feet and sound the roar of creation." Although the power of the Dragons lived on within me, grounding myself and reciting their blessings gave me a boost closer to them, especially when I had gone a few years without seeing them.

I opened my eyes, and in my head, I could see everything in the palace below my feet, and the might of earth spread through my body. I touched the tattoo over my left eye and smiled. It was given to me by Cré after mastering his gift of sight. I could see everything through the earth, not with my eyes, but by connecting my energy to the rock beneath me. I took a low stance and commanded spikes to rise with my movements from the stone beneath me.

"Still got it," I whispered. I could feel the Ravens below head to a balcony to take flight, so I sent my spikes back where they came and began sharpening my blades.

"Ah, Eadha, I am so sorry. We will have to promptly reschedule your beating as I promised my Lady Áine I would work with her. Good on you for warming up though, you would have needed it," Sorlin bellowed out as he crashed into the ground.

I snorted. "I'll kill ye in yer sleep, birdman, if ye don't shut yer trap."

Corvis landed shortly after and walked over to me, wearing a tightly fitted shirt and pants. "I see you wrapped your hands already. I hope I can be a substitute for Sorlin," his orange eyes burned like embers as his face of stone held true.

I shrugged and waved for him to follow me to the ring. "Aye, ye'll do. Maybe muster a few smartarse remarks so I can get the illusion of beating *him* to a pulp."

For the first time, he lifted that emotionless mask and smirked. "I'll try my best." Corvis raised his hands to fight, and my eyes drifted to the leathery wings behind his back. My stomach dropped as I recalled my nightmare. Did that happen to him? Was that *his* dream?

I remembered Áine talking about the two Ravens when I first met her and how Corvis's wings were not always like this. A phantom pain graced my back as I recalled my own past.

Corvis cleared his throat. "Eadha? Is everything alright?" His voice carried a dash of concern.

I shook my head and pulled myself out of the trance. "Aye."

Whatever dam that held him at bay broke, and Corvis lunged at me in a whirl of fury. His moves were elegant and carefully calculated, much different than Sorlin's fighting style of sheer force. If I could not predict his attacks through the ground, I would have struggled to keep up. He was on me like a shadow dancing across the light of the sun. He would disappear through the veil, but I could feel where he would appear, and my fists greeted him each time. In an instant, he dove down and grappled my knees, pinning me to the ground; as if he could sense I was tracking his every move.

Panting and sweating, he gazed down at me with his piercing orange eyes. I gave into his gaze for a split second before my legs wrapped around his hips and twisted him off of me. The stinging sound of metal scraping a sheath filled my ears, and I quickly twirled my dual swords to my side.

He was relentless, fierce, and fast, but he could not take me down. In a spinning move, I hooked my blades to the base of his, flipped his sword out of his hand, kicked his legs out, and twisted his back to me, my swords at his throat. A signature attack I used on Séamus many times.

"You could see where I was moving behind the veil," he panted out and raised his arms in defeat. He was solid, and I could feel his muscle through the fabric separating us. If I were not given gifts of strength from Cré I would have struggled more fighting him.

"Aye. As a wraith, I think ye can relate to sensing things ye cannot see," I gasped in return.

A chuckle rumbled against my chest as I held his back to me. "Well, if I am supposed to be Sorlin, I think this is where I insult you like a sore loser."

"Get lost. I know where you sleep," Sorlin called over from his sparring ring.

Those inky shadows played against my cheek once again, and I yielded. Corvis stood and peeled his shirt from his body, wiping the glistening sweat and some blood from his forehead. His body was perfectly sculpted, and his chest carried a beautiful tattoo of a red raven. He looked like a proper hot-blooded warrior. I've been around men my whole life but seeing Corvis like this brought a tinge of heat to my cheeks, and I resented myself for it. He was attractive, but he was my enemy. I could not forget that.

"Show me your stealth abilities," he said flatly. The blood that trickled from various cuts and gashes slowly stopped and healed over, the works of true immortal blood, unlike my own. My people were charmed only with the gift of long life.

My Stone appeared in my hand, and I vanished. Looking at Corvis through the veil was like watching a silhouette play on the top of a running river. I walked in front of him to see if his wraith abilities could sense me, but his gaze did not follow. His shadows flowered out and around, cocooning him in a blanket of smoke as he became one with them. Once he passed through the veil, his corporeal form manifested.

"Fancy meeting you here," he said with a slight smirk. "Those two out there will be able to see a shadow on the ground where I stand. But you...you just disappear. I've never known anyone not of wraith blood to be able to do this."

I shrugged. "I was born with this ability. Can't explain it," I motioned to the plumage of black around him. "I thought you said you couldn't control them."

His stone face cracked, and he gave me an almost full grin. A tendril of black crept towards me and formed a sturdy grip around my wrist. My lip curled, and I tried to pull away, but it held my arm in place.

"They have a mind of their own when I'm not commanding them," he said as the smoke dissipated from my wrist.

I clutched my arm and shuddered. "Well, that wasn't a fair fight then. You were holding back."

His face fell back to his standard neutrality. "So were you," he said lifelessly and went back through the veil.

"What happened to ye?" I whispered to myself as I watched him take to the ring with Sorlin. If I were to be close with anyone here, it would probably be Corvis. It seemed as though he had the unfortunate understanding of what it's like to be scarred, to wake up in the middle of the night in a cold sweat fearing for your life. I felt oddly connected to him because of this, as if we had a cruel bond through shared pain. I left the veil and continued sparring for what seemed like hours.

※

After giving and receiving several beatings, I wearily headed back to the palace in search of Rigel. The quicker I got his stone, the quicker I could go home. As my feet met the palace's tile floors, a male's voice called out to me. "Think fast," it said, and a small solid mass collided with my temple.

"Ach! What in the bumbling, gods damn, ever-lovin' fu-,"

"Well, that wasn't very fast, was it?" Rigel asked with a boyish smile on his face.

I clutched my forehead and dabbed the slit of blood before letting out a growl in his direction. "What in the gods above is the matter with ye, ya bawbag?!" I yelled out at him.

He chuckled. "What? You look barely scuffed up from today's training. I assumed you bested my Ravens, so I had to do my own test."

I grunted and drew my dagger. "I'll roast yer Ravens on a spit if ye'll be throwing anything else at my face. What was that?"

He patted the air. "Okay, okay, calm down. It was my stone."

I scrambled around and picked up a solid black jewel the size of my fist. The magic pouring off of it was supernatural and ancient. It felt very much like my father's presence. "Alright, one down. Six to go."

Rigel looked at me inquisitively. "Six? There are only five more courts. Where is the sixth stone?"

My stomach knotted, and I winced. "With my parents. They don't know of this plan. It will be the hardest one to steal, believe me." I sent his stone through the veil to my room upstairs, and a thought dawned on me. "Hey, I thought ye weren't able to get inside my head?"

He nodded and raised an eyebrow. "I can't. I tried during the first meeting we had. Why?"

I opened my mouth to speak, but the presence of those manky birds stalked in behind me.

"Now, Eadha, I know Corvis is not the best fighter

in the world, but- ow!" Corvis punched Sorlin on the shoulder before he could finish his sentence, and he shrunk away to the couch.

Áine rolled her eyes. "Alright, children, listen up. Cazara granted us a meeting. We leave soon, and the three of you will be joining us."

My cheeks heated, and a tingle went through my body. Another stone. Two of seven. Rigel looked me in the eye and nodded as if he could read my thoughts. "No need for any kind of formalities with Cazara. She is like family. Corvis and Sorlin, *behave*."

I looked to the winged men, and they exchanged a mischievous glance. When Corvis's eyes fell on me, he dropped back to his cold neutrality. His shadows held close to his body and twitched in the air.

"Well, what are we waiting for?" I asked as I locked eyes with Áine.

She smiled and turned to her husband. "Nothing. Shall we? Eadha, will you be able to navigate there?"

I shook my head. "Never been to Aerras. Ye'll be able to walk me in?" I asked Rigel.

He looked around and pursed his lips. "Well, we can't all be strong veilwalkers as yourself. Unfortunately, you'll have to pick between one of those two to fly you in."

"Ah, well," Sorlin said from behind. He got up and walked over to the balcony, "I'll just see myself out, get a little bit of a head start. Have fun with that Corv."

I groaned and walked over to Corvis. "You can walk me in, right?"

He shook his head. "No, I'll have to walk Sorlin through when the winds get too dangerous to fly. I can't carry more than one person across the veil." He looked down at me and furrowed his brow. "You're bleeding."

I shot a glare to Rigel, and he looked away and started whistling. "Yer *Lord* threw a jewel at my head."

Corvis looked over my shoulder and gave Rigel an unreadable expression before holding out his hand to me. "Have you flown before?"

I shook my head. It wasn't a complete lie. I have flown on my own accord and on the back of Dragons. They crafted a contraption that I could summon at will to soar on my own, but I did not want to reveal my full powers to my new company. The minute they knew what I was capable of, the quicker they could learn how to take me down. The thought of trusting one of these people not to drop me left an unsettling feeling inside me.

Corvis gave me a soft half-smile and gently grabbed my arm. "I won't drop you. Let me know if I am going too fast." I felt a prick in my cheeks as he guided me to the balcony and cursed myself for it.

Áine wrapped her arms around Rigel and muttered, "Gods, I hate the veil," before the pair vanished.

An arm snaked under my knees and lifted me into a sturdy embrace. I brought my hands together behind Corvis's neck and shivered as his raven-black locks brushed my wrists. "Don't do anything stupid, laddie. I'm not that easy to kill."

He looked down at me with his unreadable wall plastered onto his face, but his shadows seemed to relax and gently flow in the breeze. "Of course, my lady."

I scoffed. "I'm not yer-"

Before I could finish my sentence, he unfurled his massive leathery wings and gave me a warm look. They were magnificent and reminded me of the Dragons. I could not imagine the work he had to put in just to keep himself airborne. No wonder these two men were built like Séamus. My disdain for him seemed to chip away as I recalled our conversation when I first arrived and the dream this morning. He indeed was not a Fae, that much I knew, and did not deserve the cold shoulder I had been giving him. I genuinely regretted being so spiteful towards him after I pieced together what I thought happened to his wings. Though, if he were anything like myself, he would not want pity.

"Hold on," he said in a low voice.

I tightened my grip, and he shot into the sky.

CHAPTER TEN

Corvis

Eadha was as stiff as a board in my arms and didn't look in my direction as we flew over Verbenia. Instead, she looked down and awed at the terrain below. The murderous woman I fought earlier was now like a child in the middle of a market, awe-struck by all of the wonders her eyes took in. As we flew over Arbres, she chuckled and pointed to all the colors of the land. Her laughter brought a small smile to my face. I knew she was frightened, being in our lands, so to see her unwind even the slightest was nice to see.

"Are you not afraid?" I asked.

I felt her exhale quickly. "No. There is very little I am afraid of...yer shadows move, ye know. They seem to flow with yer emotions."

I raised an eyebrow and stared down at her. "Is that so?" She wasn't wrong. I knew my shadows were uncontrollable, it was rather hard to focus on them at all times, but no one had ever mentioned that to me before.

"Well, what do they look like now?" I asked.

She turned her face and looked around till her gaze met mine. "Calm."

I nodded and looked at the top of her snow-white hair. "What *are* you afraid of?" I asked the question before I could keep it from passing through my lips.

She laughed and turned her face up to mine.

"Wouldn't ye like to know, eh?"

My gaze fixated forward as I concentrated on our path to Aerras. The silence between us was awkward, and I could tell Eadha would rather be anywhere but in my arms. I didn't blame her. She was a stranger in a strange land.

"Are you nervous at least? Being around all these Fae, I mean."

She shot her entrancing eyes to mine and gave me an aggressive glare. "Why do ye care?"

I didn't know how to act around Eadha. I was apprehensive of her. She had been here less than a week and kept her distance from us all, barely speaking a word to any of us. She was definitely less hostile with me than with Sorlin, most people were, but she was still so explosive. It didn't matter. All I needed to do was keep an eye on her and keep her in line to the best of my abilities.

The peachy lands of Aerras bloomed into full view as I caught up with Sorlin and the winds became violent. I clutched Eadha tightly and yelled, "The winds are going to be too dangerous to fly through! The palace is straight ahead! Veilwalk to Rigel, I have to grab Sor!"

She squinted up to me, nodded, and vanished from my arms, taking the captivating scent of a rainy cedar forest with her. Sorlin rushed over to me and grabbed me around the neck. "My hero!" He yelled in a mockingly high voice. I rolled my eyes, and my shadows curled around us, pulling us into the veil. With a blink of an eye, we appeared by Eadha's side with Rigel and Áine.

Rigel smiled and straightened the collar on his button-down shirt. "Well, this is exciting, isn't it? Who would have thought we all would be saving the world together, huh?"

Eadha snorted. "Yer just my key to get into these lands. Ye won't be getting yer pretty hands dirty on that island."

Áine gave her a small smile and fastened an ornate golden veil around her hair. "Let's just focus on what we can do now. Cazara is a lone Ruling Fae. She will probably give us her stone but will likely not travel to Cascata with us to strong-arm Akamu. I have yet to send him a request for a meeting, but if Cazara agrees to this, he will as well."

Rigel looked at Eadha. "Glamour yourself. We will call you a lesser Faery and hope for the best. Cazara would never speak of you to anyone, but we should just take an extra percussion."

Her tattoos disappeared as she nodded, and her mosaic eyes faded to plain blue. She hugged herself, looking around apprehensively as if she were shielding her naked body. I didn't know why, but a feeling of embarrassment washed over me for a split second, as if her emotions were so large they were pouring over onto me like a flooded stream after a storm.

Of course, that was not possible, but I could visibly see how uncomfortable she looked. I personally preferred her with tattoos. They made her look as lethal as her attitude. Áine clapped softly and motioned to the entrance of the palace. "Alright, let's go."

The three walked on ahead, but Sorlin grabbed my arm. "Hey, you looked good in sparring today, very lively. Dare I say I even saw you smile?"

I pushed him away and walked ahead of him. "It was nice to have a real challenge up on that roof. You and Rigel are wimps compared to her."

He chuckled and said in a sing-song tone, "Maybe Corv just likes the new pretty girl in town, hmm?"

I could tell him I preferred her company over my companions, even though I didn't know her or trust her yet, because not only was she less insufferable, but she didn't stare at my wings. It seemed as though she couldn't care less about them, unlike most people. After the accident, everyone who met me treated me like a poor victim, asking me if I needed anything or if I wanted to talk about it. I didn't need to admit that to Sorlin. We were here for war and could not afford any distractions.

I whispered low enough so the others wouldn't hear me, "She is interesting and powerful. Besides, it's my job to keep her close, so *you* don't get your throat cut in the middle of the night."

I felt pressure in my head and looked to Rigel. He was raising an eyebrow and looking between us. I simply nodded as if to say: "Everything's fine."

Eadha's eyes were wide, and I could see her shiver ever so slightly. In my head, I walked up to her and told her everything was going to be okay, that we would all be protecting her, but all I could give her was the most sympathetic smile I could muster. I felt my heart begin to race, but I was not nervous or anxious. In fact, I was relatively confident this meeting would go well. I looked at Eadha, and sweat began to break out on her forehead and felt mine dampen as well. I didn't know why I was overthinking this so much. I enjoyed being around Cazara and had nothing to worry about. It was quite strange.

Rigel pushed open the doors to the palace in the

capital city of Nuren, where Cazara and another woman stood hand in hand. Cazara was as beautiful as ever with her blush tinted skin and long strawberry blonde hair. The people of Aerras were some of my favorites, as their features were incredibly sharp and just looked so ethereal. The woman standing with Cazara waved and smiled. Her hair was short and cut close to her head and had more rosy than Cazara's, with slightly paler pink tones to her skin.

"Welcome Áine, Rigel. I see you brought a new guest with your usual entourage." Cazara's voice was as sultry and low.

Rigel beamed as he kissed her cheeks. "Cazara, it's been too long. And who do we have the pleasure of meeting?" He asked and extended a hand to the woman.

Cazara smiled and dropped a hand to the woman's back. "Rigel, I hope you will forgive me for not inviting you to the wedding as it was extremely small, but this is Brisa, my wife."

Brisa smiled and shook his hand. "A pleasure, Rigel."

"Well, forgiveness will be hard to give Cazara. All these years of friendship and I didn't get an invitation? You've been deemed 'The Lone Lady,' and now you pull out this magnificent bride?"

We all shook hands. I looked over to Sorlin, who was grinning from ear to ear as he shook Brisa's hand, muttering a multitude of congratulations. I wondered what kind of game he was trying to play, but at least it was working. Cazara seemed less agitated by his presence.

Eadha walked up to the High Ladies and bowed her head. "Thank ye for inviting me into yer home."

Brisa shook her hand. "What a peculiar accent you have. Where do you come from?"

Eadha tucked her hands into her pockets. "The northern isles. I won't lie and tell ye some tale. I need to ask ye a favor."

We all went stiff and looked between her and the High Ladies. I'm sure Rigel planned on a night of wine, food, and talking before asking for her stone. I was not familiar with the troves of the Fae, but if this stone was something that could be used to take down Sabriel, I was not sure if Cazara would part with it so easily.

Cazara flinched ever so slightly but smiled. "Well, I can't wait to hear all about it. Shall we move this to a more intimate setting?"

We followed her into a grand parlor. I caught Eadha glancing at me periodically as we walked. Her eyes were wide as she clutched her hands together, rubbing them back and forth. I have been in her shoes before. When I first started working for Rigel about five centuries ago, I felt out of place and intimidated in his court. Everyone was of pure blood and rather proper, and I was a half-wraith brute. I gave her a squeeze on the shoulder, but she quickly pulled away, glaring at me. I didn't mind. I just needed her to know she wasn't alone.

The parlor was extravagant, and everything was made out of pure rose gold. Everyone sat and made small talk. Sorlin sat with Brisa, berating her with questions about the wedding and how she met her wife. Rigel and Áine spoke with Cazara about the attacks they have experienced through their lands, but as I looked around the room, Eadha was gone. She must not have followed us into the parlor.

I smiled at Cazara, keeping my face utterly neutral. "I believe Eadha found herself lost looking for the restroom. I'll go look for her."

I shot Rigel a look and felt a pressure against my head. "*I think she is looking for the stone. Keep them distracted,*" I said to him. Being a dream-threader, Rigel could not only alter the reality of his opponents, but he could also read minds, always asking our permission before doing so. He nodded to me and tried to relieve the suspicions that had arisen in the High Ladies. Once out of sight from guards or servants, I slipped into the shadows and followed Eadha's unmistakable scent.

This could be bad. The only reason Cazara and Rigel grew close was by building many years of trust. Even if she declined to give us her stone, he would have never ordered us to steal it and eventually would have convinced Cazara to lend it to us either way. Cazara and Rigel's fathers hated each other and fought for centuries. Aerras had always been somewhat elitist, and for a while, considered fighting with Fossera and Eotia against the creation of the Circles many years before I was born.

Cazara was different and only focused on her people and what would be best for them. She was the middle of three sisters and killed her way to the throne. Unfortunately, in the Fae lands, it was kill or be killed wherever family power was concerned. She was kind, but if crossed, she would show you how cold she could be. If Eadha stole this stone, who knew what would happen to our alliance. We had so few of them in these lands, and we couldn't risk this.

After perusing the halls, following a trail of unconscious guards, I found Eadha on the lower floor of the palace picking a lock on a rather sturdy door.

I broke from the shadows and she spun around, knife in hand, and sighed once she saw me. "Ah, *you*. Help me with this."

I grabbed her arm. "What in the goddess' names do you think you are doing?" I could feel my shadows jerk and twitch with irritation.

She shrugged and pulled her hand from me. "Ye want this stone or no?"

It became apparent to me that I'll not only be keeping an eye on Eadha during her stay, but I'll need to give her a crash course on Verbenia politics before she got us all killed.

"Eadha, Cazara is our ally, our friend. If we stole from her, that alliance would end and we will then have every single court in Verbenia fighting against us. How did you even find this?" I asked, looking over her shoulder as she popped the lock open.

She grunted as she pulled the door open. "I sent my spies to every court. They located some of the stones and brought the information of their whereabouts back to me. Even yers."

I stood back, stunned. At the beginning of the month, we found one of our most sacred temples broken into, but nothing was stolen. That had to have been her people. "So you really intended on doing all of this yourself?"

She drew a sword and locked eyes with me. "If I had to. Now you can make yerself useful and stand guard, or we can cross swords and have a fair fight," she said in a disturbingly calm voice.

I marveled at her perseverance, but I was not going to be part of this. If I helped her steal this stone, Tenebris would be directly involved, so I simply stood guard and waited. Some of the incapacitated guards groaned and stirred. There would be absolutely no hiding this or coving it up if she managed to steal the trove. I wondered how she took out all of these Elites in the short time she was gone. No alarms were sounded, and I did not even notice her leaving.

These men and women all had the gift of air and would have put up quite a fight. In the many battles I have fought, there were times when I did not know If I would make it off of the battlefield, still drawing breath after fighting Fae. I knew I could feel her holding back in sparring. Someone with as much power radiating off them as Eadha could have snapped me in half with little strain. I did not fully grasp the extent of that restraint until looking at these Elite Fae strewn across the floor.

I let out a chuckle and shook my head as I recalled the stories of my childhood. Growing up, if we fell back in training or missed any marks were told the spirit of the Laoch would come and peel the skin from our bodies as we slept. I did not know if Eadha's strength or power came from her being a Laoch or a High Druid, but I believed even if she were not either of those, she would still be her own force of nature.

Eadha emerged from the room, clutching a glistening pink stone. "Now, we go and ask her for it," was all she said before disappearing behind the veil. Goddess above.

I followed her, but she was faster than me and made it to Cazara before I could grab her.

Eadha stood before Cazara, holding out the stone. Rigel and Áine shared a horrified look. "We can all sit and pretend we came here for small talk and congratulations, but there is a war coming. I can only imagine what has come crawling past yer borders from Kamber these past few weeks."

Cazara stiffened and darted a violent look between Eadha, Rigel, and Áine. "That stone you are holding is sacred."

Eadha nodded. "I know what it is. It's the key to ending this possible war ye know is coming. I need every Ruling Fae's stone, and I already have his," she pointed to Rigel.

I held my breath and placed my hand on my sword as Cazara stood. Eadha was now a part of our court, even if only temporarily, and I was sworn to protect those in it.

"You brought a stranger into my court to steal from me?" She spat out to Rigel.

He shook his head with an oblivious look on his face. "I came here to ask you for the stone. She stole it on her own accord and without my knowledge. It will be taken care of, but she is right. You told me before you had suspicions of Sabriel opening the Well on that island. We are hoping to destroy it before he can do that, but we need the stones."

Cazara stared at Eadha for what felt like hours before her face hardened. "Get out. All of you," she instructed harshly.

Eadha snorted. "I'll leave, but I'm taking this with me."

"You will drop that stone or-"

Eadha cut off Cazara by unsheathing a sword and rolling her eyes. "Or what? Yer guards are having a nap and High Lady or not, yer no match for me. I'm not trying to undermine ye, Cazara, but take this stone from me and ye'll be dead come winter by the hands of Sabriel."

My heart raced, and I swallowed a lump growing in my throat as the two women stared at each other with murder in their eyes. I had no idea what to do, and Rigel looked just as lost as I was, but oh, was he angry. His silver eyes flared, and his breaths were ragged as he tried to stifle the rage burning in his chest. As I gauged the room, I seemed to be the only level headed person at the moment and would need to break up whatever fight could ensue.

Cazara let out a long breath and crossed her arms. "If you managed to steal that without my knowledge, then you are obviously powerful or at least lucky. But what happens if you fail to prevent war?"

Eadha sheathed her sword and crossed her arms. "Then, we fight. Yer people are The Defenders. We will need yer shields of wind."

Brisa placed a hand on Cazara's shoulder and whispered something in her ear. I bit my lip and relaxed my hand off of my sword. Cazara was not happy, but she knew what would happen if we failed. Her people would have to go to war, and her new wife could potentially perish along with the rest of the world. We all knew what was at stake.

"If you plan on going to Cascata, I suggest you leave your new *pet* at home. Akamu and Natia are in a blood bond with *me*, not you. If you steal from them, they will turn you to mist where you stand. I assume you'll be going to each court?" Cazara asked, turning to Rigel.

He nodded. "Yes. We will need each of the old god's stones. I haven't made a plan for Forssera or Eotia, but I assume force will be involved. Have you heard of where their alliance lies?"

Brisa nodded her head with a grim look on her face, and my heart fell. If the healers and fire-wielders were against us, we would be obliterated. "They are together in whatever happens. They became blood bound a few months ago."

Áine bit her lip and turned her face away. I couldn't imagine what it must have been like for her at that moment as the daughter of a traitor. She always wanted to love her father and her own people how she loved Tenebris, but her father, Farhan, was a rotten man. He always sought to be the largest and most powerful court in Verbenia, waging war between various territories and slowly expanding his lands. I didn't want to know what Farhan put the High Lord of Eotia through to be blood bound, but I imagined it involved various forms of blackmail and manipulation. The High Lord of Eotia, Nago, had been terrorized by Farhan since they both took power. Nago had committed his share of atrocities across Verbenia, most Ruling Fae had, but Farhan forced his hand in almost all evil endeavors.

"Well, if anyone can break a blood bond, it's Rige. I'm not worried," Sorlin said as he made his way to the door.

Cazara sent a wall of air to the door, promptly closing it shut. "Not so fast. Friend or not, you cannot just steal from me and walk away so easily, Rigel. Who is this woman? Arawn's stone is my most guarded trove, and she sauntered off and retrieved it like nothing."

Eadha went to speak, but I found my mouth moving faster than my brain. "In due time, we will explain the nature of who and what exactly she is. All you need to know now is that she is the key to stopping this all.

We made a promise to keep her identity between us. It will ensure all parties' safety until we sort out the allegiance of Fossera and Eotia. If they are allied with Sabriel, we could all die if he found her identity."

Brisa and Cazara nodded gravely. "We really could be walking to our deaths in battle, couldn't we?" Brisa asked Eadha.

She clenched her jaw and nodded. "Aye."

I could have sworn I saw fear in Eadha's eyes, but it was quickly whisked away and replaced with anger. Cazara nodded, and the door opened. "I'll be seeing you, girl. You have my allegiance in whatever may come, but no bond can force Akamu to give you his. When you go to his side, you'll need to do some talking for him to lend his army."

Rigel nodded and brushed back his glittery silver hair. "Well, good thing we are leaving our wild card here with you while we butter up the man of mists himself."

"What?" Cazara, Eadha, and I all exclaimed in unison.

I cleared my throat and played off the shock in my voice that surprised even myself. "No disrespect to Eadha, but do you think it's the best idea to leave someone so unfamiliar here without us? Who's to say she will be here when we return?"

Eadha scoffed and shook her head. "To the Otherworld with all of ye. I'm no child."

Sorlin muttered under his breath, "Just as destructive and stubborn as one, though."

Rigel held up a hand and silenced them. "We need allies, Eadha, and you stole from mine. So to prevent any further altercations you will remain here with the High Ladies. Sorlin, Corvis, my Lady, shall we be off then?"

Eadha looked absolutely horrified, like a deer about to be mauled by a bear. I had to follow Rigel, no matter how much I disproved of leaving her here.

As I turned to leave, a hand pulled on my shoulder, and Eadha pleaded to me with her eyes. I got lost in them as sadness and fear overtook the oceans painted at their center. I could have sworn I faintly heard her voice breaking through the darkest chasm of my mind whispering, *"Don't leave me with them."*

I took a sharp breath in and turned to Rigel. *"I'll keep her close. You would never leave us behind. No need to put her through that."* He acknowledged the message I sent to him and nodded before leaving.

I was not sure what was connecting us during this meeting today; perhaps it was the veil. It had a way of weaving its walkers together in the past. Whatever it was, I had to admit I was grateful to be getting some kind of insight into her mind. It not only made her seem less unnerving, but it also made me feel less numb to the world around me to see someone as fierce as Eadha wear her emotions so openly.

She pushed past, giving me what looked like it could have been a smile, and my eyes lingered in her wake. A hand rifled through my hair and Cazara appeared next to me. "I know a wandering eye when I see one. How are you doing, Corvis? Did you fly here?"

I nodded to her and looked away. "If you are asking if I healed, then yes. It has been quite some time since the incident. I've had many years to heal. The wings are as strong as my old ones."

She smiled. "I won't press. I'm just glad to see some life in you again. Now, about that wandering eye?"

I shook my head. "No wandering eye here,

madam. Congratulations on your marriage. I hope once this is all over, we can catch up."

Cazara crossed her arms and waved me out the door. I stretched out my wings and shivered. I didn't like that the story of what happened to me in Fossera had reached the southernmost court. I hadn't stepped foot back there since Farhan ripped my wings from my back and healed new ones in place as punishment for breaking Áine out of his court. It happened two decades ago and was still as fresh in my mind as if it had been yesterday. Sorlin and Rigel pushed me to talk about it to them, but I never could. Our wings were sacred; they were what made us Ravens. As pleasant as Cazara was, for one moment, I would like to be around someone who looked at *me* and not my wings.

The only person who did that as of now, was Eadha.

CHAPTER ELEVEN

Eadha

The stone felt heavy in my satchel, and I could feel it looking at me, warning that I was not meant to touch it. I had a feeling that with each stone I acquired, the god of death would become more enraged that someone other than the Tiarna was handling the beloved pieces of his cauldron. I looked up to Rigel and Áine, and my lip curled with rage. They were going to leave me here, in an unfamiliar land. I thought Áine would have known better. She at least knew how I felt about the Fae; about her kind.

Just as I was warming up to these people, they gave me a reason to push away. Curse them for thinking I needed to be watched like some unruly child. I could feel Cazara's tension through the ground. She never took her eyes off me, and she would never have agreed to give us her stone; I could feel it. She would have turned us away or lied.

Áine gave me a stern look. "We are going to Cascata unannounced. I sent word for Akamu to meet with us, but he did not answer. Just...just leave the talking to us. If we have to resort to *thievery*, then by all means, go nuts."

Sorlin chose wisely to stay silent and only gave me a snort and the shaking of his head.

"Be prepared to stay the night. How's your glamour holding up?" Rigel asked.

I shrugged. "I could keep it up for days."

A shadow graced my vision, and Corvis stood tall next to me. I gave him one last thankful nod for not abandoning me in this place. His face was as unreadable as always, but his shadows seemed to flow slowly and relaxed before pulling tightly to his body, a silent acknowledgment.

"We will fly in. It will give you enough time to butter up Akamu before we all come knocking at his door. If you can manage to get the stone, do it. I'll need to stop by the war camp on the border between Tenebris and Cascata to see what news we have from the coast," Corvis said sternly.

Rigel nodded, grabbed Áine, and slipped behind the veil. Corvis pulled his lips into a tight line and extended a hand. "I won't say that was a smart thing you did, but I saw the look in her eyes back there. I don't think she would have willingly given us that stone had you not shown her you were capable of stealing it."

I grabbed his hand but had nothing to say to him. I knew what I was doing and did not need validation from any of these people. A hand pulled behind my knees and Corvis grunted as he launched us into the air. I kept my eyes forward, watching the colors change court to court as we moved through the skies, not realizing how quietly we had been traveling until Corvis made me jump as he called to Sorlin. "Why are you all smiley? You're grinning like a child on Yule."

I looked over to Sorlin and noticed he was rather cheery. "Cazara never ceases to amaze me," he said while shaking his head.

"Well, do explain, brother." Brother? I bet that was just some term of endearment for each other. There was no way those two men were related.

Sorlin shrugged and flexed his wings to put him into a steady glide next to Corvis. "She was just so unapologetically happy today. It makes me smile."

"And why shouldn't she be, Sor?" Corvis called back.

Sorlin chuckled. "Now, not me, but some people might call her unconventional."

"Well, I'm glad those people aren't in our company. I envy those that find love. I would never judge where they found it." I looked up at Corvis with surprise. It was just nice to hear something sweet coming from his lips. It made him seem much less apathetic.

Corvis met my gaze for a split second before I looked away. His shadows momentarily relaxed before they resumed their jerky, unsteady moments. No one was this stern for the sake of it, I knew from personal experience.

Had he always been like this? Or did he become this way after what happened to him, if that dream I saw really was his? Speaking for myself, I was turned into the harsh person I was and remembered a time when I could do nothing more than smile and dance under the moon. But something told me that Corvis had never seen an ounce of comfort in his life, even before whatever happened to his wings.

Sorlin tried to suppress a smile and flew far ahead of us. I stirred in Corvis's arms. "Kind of a rude statement, don't ye think? What was that all about?"

He shrugged and looked ahead, his stone mask in place. "Actually, I think it was quite the opposite. I'm sure there are a few Fae who might look at Cazara and Brisa with a raised eyebrow, and I am proud that I do not keep them near me. Besides, I have my suspicions about Sorlin, but they are private suspicions nonetheless. I'm sure he was just trying to-" Corvis grunted, and barrel rolled to the right, clutching me close to his body. "Archers from Arbres!" He called out to Sorlin. "Hold on!"

I looked down and a flock of arrows clouded the skies, flying right for us. "Why are they shooting? We passed through here without a problem-" I reached out and grabbed an arrow right before it could pierce me between the eyes. A tree-like warrior was etched into its sturdy wood.

"Are you alright? Did you get hit?" Corvis asked, his voice frigid and laced with concern. Sorlin joined us in the air dodging arrows, and before I could answer, a misty shield encased the three of us coming from his ring.

"I'm fine. Why are they attacking us?" I asked Sorlin.

"Well, you see, the Arbressens require a human sacrifice once every thirty years due to the trees-what do I know?! Why are you asking me?!" He snapped back. I did not think I would particularly mind if an arrow slipped through his shield and took out an eye.

I could feel Corvis stifling a laugh as he held me close, and I rolled my eyes. "Well, I'm not going to die in these skies with ye two bastards." I tumbled out of Corvis's arms into a free fall and sent myself through the veil to the ground below. Arbres was the court I was the most unfamiliar with and had no idea where their allegiance currently resided as their land bordered both Fossera and Eotia. One wrong move and my likeness and whereabouts could be sent right to Sabriel.

I appeared on the ground and held my arms up above my head. The forest was dense and rather dark as the trees blocked the soon to be setting sun. I could not see the warriors that were shooting at us, but I could faintly hear their breathing as the wind carried the sound of their movements to my ears. "Don't shoot! I come from Tenebris. I am traveling with two Ravens and the High Lord. We are just passing through."

A man dropped down from the tree ahead of me, pointing a drawn arrow to my heart. "How do I know you are not a spy? Or a second wave of infantry coming to my lands?" Second wave? The man in front of me wore a green tunic plated with gold armor and held an expertly crafted bow. The gold helmet he wore covered half of his face, but I could see his mouth twitch with the same anger that shaded his voice.

"The winged creatures that I travel with are Vaspairans, not Sluagh. Did ye recently get attacked?" I felt two forces collide into the ground next to me. Corvis grabbed my arm and defensively swung me behind him.

"Addax? Is that you under all of that metal? Finally getting down and dirty with the big boys I see," Sorlin boomed out with his hands raised.

The man lowered his bow and took his helmet off, revealing a perfect and softly chiseled face. His skin was lightly tanned. He had long, straight blonde hair, about as long as Sorlin's, and high hollow cheekbones. "You have ten seconds to get off my lands before I have my men obliterate you."

I looked to Sorlin, who put his hands up higher as armored men clattered down from the trees around us. "Sorlin is banned from this court," Corvis whispered in my ear. He stepped in front of Sorlin, who was reaching for his sword, and cleared his throat. "We were just passing through. We paid a visit to Cazara and Brisa to give them congratulations and are only trying to go home."

Addax's face softened as he looked at Corvis. "I have no qualms with you, Corvis. However, your *companion-*"

"If ye were attacked, I'd like to investigate. I am *Lord* Rigel's outside help with this impending war." I cut off Addax and held his gaze as he looked at me with perplexed eyes.

"War? What war?"

I stared at him for a moment, then looked up to Corvis to see if this man was serious. Corvis gave away nothing. "*What war?* I come crashing into yer lands, and ye were fixin' to call me a spy. Now ye have the baws to ask me 'what war'? Am I hearin' yer words correctly?" My voice became irate as I spoke, and my accent grew thick and crass with my growing exasperation.

"Eadha," Corvis warned.

Addax tensed his arrow slightly and took a step closer. "We have had a few attacks recently from some Sluagh, but Sabriel has always coveted these lands. We get small attacks once a year, maybe twice. It is nothing out of the ordinary."

I scoffed. "Ye truly do not know? Do ye not have allies telling ye of the things happening across the sea?"

As the last light of day glinted across his face, I could see that same glow of youth I saw in Áine when I first met her. This Ruling Fae was young, younger than her. He gave me a small nod. "Well, hopefully you wouldn't mind enlightening me. Men, women, lower your weapons. You two can follow me. You," he pointed to Sorlin, "go home."

I slightly stuck out my tongue and raised my brows to him, but Corvis interrupted my celebration. "With all due respect, if you listen to what we have to say, you'll want *all* of our help."

Sorlin mockingly lunged at me and stuck his tongue out when Addax begrudgingly agreed with a nod. I pushed him away with a growl. Fantastic.

We followed behind Addax and his warriors, but I was a bit confused. I always thought the tree warriors were walking trees, towering above their opponents. Of course, I have lived a relatively sheltered life and did not continue my studies past twenty, but I always pictured the Court of Trees differently. This place seemed so serene, peaceful, and quiet. I could hear birds chirping, the wind whispering between the trees, and the deafening sound of just...nothing.

We came to a line of thick trees, and with a wave of his hand, Addax sent them into the ground, and a magnificent estate came into view. It was an expansive three-story white manor surrounded by gardens and hedges. I wondered the extent of his abilities; I doubted that all he could do was command tree growth.

"Welcome to Elowen. Unlike the lands you have seen in Tenebris, we don't have too many expansive cities here, only towns and villages." Addax's armor vanished, and a gold embellished green cape flowed down his back to his knees. A gold crown with the horns of a stag appeared on his head. He was a sight to look at and was a mirror opposite of Rigel, who lived so modestly.

"It's beautiful," I said as we walked through the grand doors of the mansion. The sentries left, and he motioned for us to take a seat in the dining room.

"Will Rigel be joining us?" He asked Corvis, not taking his eyes off Sorlin.

"I, unfortunately, do not know the answer to that question. We were traveling separately," Corvis said plainly. His shadows were held close to his body. I was starting to believe that was his sign of neutrality.

Addax looked at me and smiled beautifully. "We could discuss this 'war' you speak of over dinner, yes? Are you planning on staying?"

I shrugged. "We will stay as long as we need to, and as long as ye'll allow."

Food appeared in front of us, and Sorlin started shoveling it into his mouth like the barbarian he was. I needed to rest. I could keep my glamour up for days as long as I had a break.

"So ye truly know nothing of what is happening?" I asked Addax once again.

He shook his head. "I received my title of High Lord seven years ago. I was only forty, and the court has always been neutral. I personally have not made any allies in Verbenia, and no one has approached me either." He had a somber tone to his voice and looked rather upset by his own words. I knew all too well how it felt to have no allies or anyone to call for aid when needed the most.

"Stay away from Fossera and Eotia. Ye don't need their companionship," I mumbled.

"I know all too well of their brutalities," Addax said as he looked to Corvis.

Corvis put his fork down, and his shadows began to twitch and spread a bit further out from him, probably signaling some sort of discomfort. He gave Addax a polite nod and resumed eating. If seeing his dream was not enough to guess what happened to his wings, that comment sure was. My heart broke as I recalled how I felt during that nightmare.

"Well, all ye need to know is that as of now, we are planning on taking care of the threat brewing in Kamber Island. If we fail, Sabriel is going to invade Verbenia, the human lands, and every corner of the earth he can manage," I said.

Addax raised his eyebrows and picked at his plate. "Shame what my father has done to this court. If it weren't for his shortcomings, I could have been preparing. I could have formed alliances...how do you know of this? Who are you?"

Corvis began to speak before I could answer, and for that, I was grateful. I still did not know what to call myself to keep suspicions at a minimum, "She is my best spy from Tenebris. The other courts, well, Aerras at least, are aware of the threat as well. If you are in need of a sister army, you have the dream-threaders and the Ravens at your disposal."

Addax looked at him inquisitively. "Is that a promise you have the right to make?"

"Well, I'm the general of the Raven army and haven't said otherwise, so how about that, Antlers?" Sorlin exclaimed.

I shot him a warning look, and he merely smiled and twiddled his fingers at me. "Forgive the ogre. Or ignore him as I do. It's getting late. I'm sure we can speak more about this in the morning."

Addax nodded and smiled, looking almost relieved. "Of course. I have servants waiting at the foot of the stairs should you wish to stay the night. They will show you to your rooms, though I ask you, Corvis, to share a room with your less than desirable brother in arms. If I have to rebuild this estate again because of *him,* I will not be happy."

Corvis nodded and rose to leave, dragging a protesting Sorlin with him. I sighed and stood. "Thank ye for yer hospitality. Do keep quiet about our alliance. I'm sure yer borders have ears, and we wouldn't want this information to get into the wrong hands."

I bowed my head and left the room. Corvis was waiting for me at the top of the stairs. "Your room is by ours. Unless, of course, you'd feel more comfortable elsewhere."

I snorted and shoved him away. "We are all adults here, no? Though I do sleep-murder, so be sure to have Sorlin in a rather exposed position tonight."

I could have sworn I saw a smile breech his lips as his shadows seemed to relax and flow steadily and away from his body. He noticed me staring, and they quickly retracted as we walked down the hall. "Goodnight, Eadha," he said before disappearing into his room. I lingered before entering my luxurious bedroom and retreating to bed.

⸶

I did not get more than two hours of sleep before I was in the bathroom, vomiting from a flashback my nightmare triggered. I was getting better; I was getting so much better until this mess. I tried to think of Lana, the twins, and Séamus, to keep me grounded, but their faces brought me back to that day. Images of Addax crept into my head, and how scared he looked when we told him how close he could have come to death had we not told him of the dangers ahead. If we had not informed him, Fossera could have tried to swindle him into joining their ranks, but as young as he might have been, he does not seem like the type to join such horrid creatures.

I started to grow angry at myself for thinking so low of the Fae and labeling them all as monsters. The few I have met were nothing like their ancestors and have seen their share of hardships as well. Most of their families' and friends' lives were cut short by family feuds, fights for power, or the occasional civil war. The fact that Addax could remain hopeful and keep a smile on his face after what we told him made my heart warm. I wanted to hate all the Sidhe, the Elites, but to me, Addax was just a bairn like Áine. These people have never personally wronged me; it would be immoral to detest them all for their forefathers' actions. Still, I would not let my guard down, I may not *hate* all of them, but I certainly do not trust them.

Since I would not get any sleep tonight, I rinsed out my mouth, glamoured myself, and left my room. The clock read three in the morning exactly, only three and half more hours to sunrise. The quietness of the land was starting to unsettle me. It felt as though the trees were watching every step I took as I walked into the forest and silently spoke to each other through the ground. I dared any Sluagh or Faery to attack me on my stroll. After my nightmare, the rush I was feeling in my body needed to be unleashed. On the map I had back home, the capital Elowen sat next to the sea only a few miles inland. A quick swim could do me some good.

My gift of sight began tracking a movement through the ground, something moving towards me. I quickly drew my swords and whipped around. Whatever was coming towards me seemed to run a few feet, disappear, then emerge a few feet ahead. "What the blazes?" I whispered to myself. It came closer and closer until Addax came stalking out of the tree that stood in front of me. I sighed with relief and sheathed my swords.

"Ye scared me," I said with a chuckle.

He raised an eyebrow and cocked his head. "How did you know I was coming?"

"How did ye know where to find me?"

Addax motioned around to all of the trees. "They are alive, you know. Trees, flowers, plants. They are my eyes to my entire court. I can hear them, make them grow, and they give me and my people a strength unmatched amongst my kind."

I tried to ignore how he did not say *our* kind as I am glamoured to appear Fae. I knew trees were alive, but if what he said was true, they could have seen me without my glamour and told him I was a fraud. I didn't want to press it. "Why are ye here?"

He looked around behind us and motioned for me to walk with him. "My territory is... wilder than the others. We have nasty Fae living here that aren't as civilized as myself and your companions. Faery is a broad term that encompasses all creatures on this side of the Circle. We have Shellycoats, Redcaps, Spriggans, you name it. The other courts drove them out, so we have always kept them safe here."

I looked at him with shock and a shiver went down my spine. I learned of those kinds of Fae in my lessons as a child, and they always chilled me to the bone. "Why? Why keep all of those things here?" I could not hide the subtle disgust in my voice.

Addax stiffened. "You know, I hate the terms

"lesser" and "Elite." We are all cut from the same cloth. Those creatures are my kind. They are all Fae, just like me, just like the High Lord you answer to. Just because they look different than us, does not mean they deserve to be treated like uncivilized monsters. They simply have their own ideas of right and wrong act accordingly...my forefathers never wanted our lands to become like the others. They wanted it to stay somewhat feral, and as nature intended it to be. So, I didn't want you out here alone, getting killed or killing the citizens of my land."

My face heated, and I looked ahead down the path we followed. The trees must have seen the blades I carried with me and alerted him. After taking in his words, I made my decision right then and there that I would not steal his stone. He had to have been the noblest Ruling Fae I have met and did not deserve that kind of deceit or trickery.

"It's quiet because you're blocking out their sounds, you know, the silence you hear. Most people do it automatically without realizing it."

How did he know I was questioning that? "I don't think I have the talent for hearing them." I was getting tired of walking, but I could not bring myself to turn back to the house and sleep. I did not want to have another nightmare.

Addax stopped and placed his hands on my shoulder. The slightest alarm rose in the back of my mind. "I think you are extremely connected to them. They can hear your thoughts loud and clear, just as they can hear mine. I'm not listening to all of them, but do consider minding what you think around here. I do not want to invade your privacy, I just can't block out their voices all the time."

I tried to keep my heartbeat steady as he picked up a flower and handed it to me. "Foxglove is toxic to humans, but since I can gather you are indeed glamouring yourself, I think you will be fine to eat it. The flower is known to help you not fall ill from being around Fae too long. Our energies can be quite taxing to those that are not of our kind. I suggest you keep some handy if you are going to be around us for a while. It should help with nightmares as well."

His voice was incredibly compassionate, and my anxiety eased. Addax knew this whole time that I was pretending to be something I was not, yet did not question me of it. Instead, he was genuinely concerned about my health. I blocked out my thoughts after giving a silent curse to the trees around me. "Thank ye. I appreciate it, I truly do."

He nodded and gave me a radiant smile. "I never have been able to hear anyone's thoughts before until you and Corv showed up today, so, forgive me. I am learning how to block it out."

I stopped and turned to him. "Ye hear Corvis's thoughts?"

"Not until today. The trees said you were connected to them in a way like myself but gave no answer as to why I could hear Corvis's. His thoughts are not as loud as yours and sound almost muffled. I would rather not leave you here alone, so I think we should turn back. I bet you are more than capable of handling yourself in these woods but some Fae only know to kill, and I don't want you killing any of them," Addax said kindly.

I nodded, looking ahead down the path, and saw a strange figure standing at the end of it. I could feel it through the ground, like a large man on a large horse, a sentry on rounds, no doubt, but my spine still went stiff. It did not feel right, and was walking in a sort of shamble.

"Ye have men patrolling around these parts, Addax?"

I looked to Addax, his skin paled, and he began to shake. His mouth fell open and he froze in place with eyes as wide as a full moon.

"That's impossible," he whispered.

"Addax, yer scaring me," I said, gripping my dagger so hard my knuckles turned white. The figure ahead stumbled and let out a disturbing, gurgling wheeze.

"Eadha, I need you to run."

CHAPTER TWELVE

Corvis

I woke up with a gasp, falling out of bed, and rushed to turn the overhead light on. Sorlin cursed and threw a pillow at me. "You're a terrible roommate, you know that? Turn that off," he groaned.

My hands went to my chest as my heart started racing and a wave of panic rushed my breathing. "Woah, hey, are you alright?" Sorlin asked with concern, leaping out of bed to my side.

I shook my head wildly. "No, I just-I'm panicking right now, and I don't know why," I panted out. I never had panic attacks. This was not normal.

Sorlin looked around the room and cocked an eyebrow. "Do you need water? Space? What happened?"

"I don't know, I just-" before I could finish my sentence, my vision blurred and went dark. Then, I was standing in the forest beside Addax, clutching his hands.

"Eadha, when I count to three, you need to run. Don't run for the estate. I cannot afford to lose any men. There is a freshwater river to the east. It withers in freshwater. Cross that river, then get help," he muttered in a low, hushed voice. *Eadha? Was I having a nightmare?*

"I'm not leaving ye, laddie," I said. *What? That's not my voice. Why can't I move?* My eyes slowly looked ahead and what stood in front of me was the foulest and most grotesque creature I thought I would go my whole life without seeing.

If one spoke its name, it would hunt them down for the rest of their lives until it killed them. It cannot be destroyed, only slowed down: the Nuckelavee. It had the body of a horse, with webbed front feet, long claws, and razor-sharp teeth in a jaw that unhinged at the corners of its skull. The torso of a bone-thin, human-esque figure was joined to its back at the waist. Its arms dragged on the ground and had just as formidable of a jaw as the horse it rode. I wanted to gag as the sound of blood trickled to the ground from its skinless body, but I held firm. Black blood pulsed through its yellow veins and poured over the exposed sinew and muscles.

A hand ripped me from my trance, and Sorlin appeared in front of me, yelling. I couldn't quite hear him until he lightly tapped my cheek. The ringing in my ear stopped, and his dark skin filled my still blurry vision. "Hey! Cor-vis! Can you hear me? Are you dead? Do you wish you *were* dead?"

"The Nucke-!" My hands clapped over my lips, and my eyes went wide as I stopped myself from uttering its name.

Sorlin jumped back and pinched his eyebrows together. "Uh, excuse me?"

"Eadha, she-shes is about to be killed by a...a Fae whose name we cannot speak. She's with Addax. We have to help them."

He tapped his chin as he mentally ran through what I could be talking about. "A Nuckelav-"

"Ahh! Ah no! Why would you say it? I just told you not to say it!" I cut him off and jumped to my sword.

"Well, well, hold on now, what if this is a...a sign, of sorts? That we should just let nature take its course with Eadha, you know? Let her spirit roam free amongst the earth as the gods intended? Whisk her out of our lives, perhaps?"

I stared at Sorlin with my mouth agape before beating him with a pillow and shoving him towards the windows. "Get out."

In the distance, I could hear a blood-curdling screech from the Nuckelavee, and we sprung out the window and into the air. "Corv, how did you know they were in trouble?"

I looked at him and shrugged. "I just knew." I couldn't tell him what really happened as I didn't know how to explain that somehow, I saw the event through Eadha's eyes. I didn't even know if that was a dream or not, but my racing heart would not relent. Sweat began to bead on my forehead as we called out their names.

"There! Eadha is crossing that river. Go get her, and I'll find Addax," Sorlin said as he raced away.

I plummeted down and met Eadha on the other side of the river. The anxiety I felt seemed to melt away within me, but it was still plastered onto Eadha's face. "There-there's a...it..." She waved an arm before putting her hands on her knees and vomiting.

"Did you say its name?" I asked frantically, patting her back.

She shook her head as she heaved again. "No. Why is that scum on these lands? The Mither o' the Sea is to confine it to the depths of the ocean during the summer months."

She was right. The Mither was in charge of keeping creatures that belonged to the watery depths off of dry land. The Nuckelavee were rare to see at all, but it was completely unheard of to see one roaming the lands in the summertime when the Sea Mither controlled the waters; unless she no longer did.

Eadha looked at me with wild eyes. "Ye think Sabriel has gained control of the seas?"

I shrugged. "It's possible if he- wait, how did you know what I was thinking?" Was that an ability she had yet to disclose to me? How many of my thoughts has she heard? Curse these wild lands and their magic that made no sense.

She looked around at the trees. "I just...listened. We have to go help Addax and Sorlin."

I nodded and extended a hand to her, but she pushed it away. "I can go on foot. Take to the skies," she ordered.

"Yes, ma'am." With a nod, I shot up into the sky.

I wasn't going to argue with her. She was probably the most capable warrior of ours, plus, Rigel agreed the Eadha was in charge. He wasn't there, so I had to listen to her. Since the Nuckelavee couldn't be killed, the only thing we could do was get Sorlin and Addax on the other side of the river. As I scanned the forest, I caught a glimpse of Addax sitting by a tree, clutching his side. Upon closer inspection, he had been slashed right through the muscle, exposing a few organs. Our immortal blood could partly heal us, but this would need the help of a real healer.

"Addax, I need to get you to the river." I began to pick him up but he grabbed my arm.

"Sorlin led the creature away when it struck me. Help him; the trees will take care of me," he grunted with a struggle, hoisting himself up.

I nodded to him and took off looking for Sorlin. "Please gods, let them be okay," I muttered to myself.

Sorlin deserved to be struck down by the hands of those he annoyed the most, not by the hands of some lesser Faery. My wings beat the air harder and harder until I crashed into the ground, finding Sorlin pinned against a tree by the beast, bleeding from his face and chest.

"Hey!" I screamed at the Nuckelavee. The torso screeched and hissed, arching back to me, but held Sorlin firm in its grasp. Using my ring, I summoned a bow and arrow and shot the human half of its body between the eyes. It let out the most haunting sound I had ever heard and pulled out the arrow, completely unphased.

Damn. Damn, damn, damn. *What the gods do I do?* I drew another arrow and fired, hitting the heart that was visible under its exposed muscle, but again it didn't die.

"You can't kill it, Corv! Ah!" The creature tightened its grip around Sorlin's neck, and blood began to pour from the wounds. If it held him any tighter, the talons were sure to puncture an artery.

All of a sudden, an urge to call out its name brewed somewhere within me. I had no intention of saying it, I knew the consequences of doing so, but I could not control the impulse. It was as if I were a puppet being controlled by an unseen master. My mouth twitched as I drew another arrow as I fought the urge and-

"Hey, Nuckelavee!" A female voice screamed.

I whipped my head around to find Eadha standing tall on a rock. *No...* The creature dropped Sorlin and howled at Eadha as she drew her dual swords. Sorlin looked at her with wide eyes and pressed a strip of fabric to his bleeding neck.

"Eadha! What are you doing?!" I called to her. She didn't look at me. She only turned her back and ran as the beast trampled the trees in its path to her. "Eadha!" I went running after her, but Sorlin grunted and fell.

"We need Áine...we need Áine right now. Addax got cut worse than me, and I already feel weak."

"Call us, ask us. She can hear us, so can you," a mass of small whispers assaulted my ears all at once, and I whipped my head around.

"Hello? Who's there?" I called out, drawing my sword.

"Corv?" Sorlin asked.

"We work only when called. We can fetch the Lady of Light from the Land of the Mist," the voices whispered to me again.

"Sorlin, are you hearing this?" I asked breathlessly, tightening my grip on the hilt of my sword. I whirled in a circle, trying to find the voice's origin, but I could have sworn it was all in my head.

"No. I do not hear anything. Are *you* listening to *me*?! We need to fetch Áine and Rigel!"

The whispers grew louder, quickening their speech. They came from all directions rushing at me in an eerie pulse. My fingers tangled and pulled at my hair as I clenched my jaw in a pathetic attempt to make the voices subside. I couldn't take it anymore.

"Get Áine!" I yelled

"As you wish, Anam Cara."

The forest became deathly silent as it once was.

"What? What does that mean?" I panicked and swore under my breath. I had to get Sorlin out of here, find Eadha, and make sure Addax was alright. I'll kill Sabriel with my bare hands; this was personal now. He had to have unleashed this creature onto us, but how did he know where we were? Was he watching us? Nevermind, it didn't matter right now.

Sorlin was my brother, and Eadha, well, we needed her. If Sabriel truly controlled the waters, none of the coastal courts were safe, including Tenebris. There were more than just one of these creatures, and they were the most deadly Fae. Sabriel could have released it in hopes of pressuring Addax to join him, or he was trying to thin as many courts' armies as he possibly could before invading.

I willed my shadows to encase me, but before I could succumb to their darkness, Áine and Rigel jumped out of the veil and ran to Sorlin.

"What in the living gods is going on? Why are you here? We waited hours for you in Cascata, and you have been in Arbres this whole time? What happened to Sorlin?" Rigel asked.

I shook my head. "No time to explain. Áine, heal Sorlin, and find Addax. He got slashed pretty bad as well. Rigel, come with me. Eadha is fighting a...well, you'll see."

He looked between us and nodded with a look of confusion across his face. "The next time you say I leave you two out of all the fun stuff, I don't want to hear anything about it. I'm wet and smell like fish while you're out here prancing through the woods. Akamu sends his regards, by the way."

I rolled my eyes and grabbed his arm, pulling him in a sprint alongside me. "Rigel, I respect you as my High Lord, but as my friend, I am telling you to shut up and run this way."

I ran as fast as I could. I had to find Eadha and

whispered a silent prayer to get to her alive. Not only was she the key to stopping Sabriel, but I harbored more selfish reasons as to why I couldn't bear to see her dead. The courts of Verbania no longer knew me by my name but as the Raven who lost his wings. My companions looked at me differently, always trying to help me when all I wanted was to go back to how things were. Even for how little she knew me, she could see that I was different yet treated me no differently than Sorlin, and I savored the feeling of normalcy it brought to me. I could even see us being friends until she left Verbenia.

By the time Rigel and I caught up to Eadha, she was crawling out of the river with blood flowing from her shoulder. Rigel hauled her up and inspected her once over. "Are you alright? What happened?"

She nodded. "A Nuckelavee was-,"

Rigel let out a high pitch squeal and cupped his hand over her mouth, "Why on the gods' earth would you just say that out loud? Did you say its name? Oh, gods, you just said its name. Well, my friend, it was nice knowing you. I wish you all the luck with-...wait, it's summer, it's impossible for them to be on land. Can someone please tell me what is going on and why I was left out?"

She shoved him away and scoffed. "Thank ye, genius, for yer insight, now shut yer gob. We think Sabriel has control of the seas, but I bet yer lad in Cascata would know more about that. His people have a thing for water, yeah?"

"Well, we will have to go back eventually. We didn't get the stone. Áine just started warming him up to us being allies. We didn't even get to speak of war," Rigel said defeatedly. "Did you get Addax's?"

I shook my head. "We were almost shot out of the sky on our way north. Addax was just attacked and didn't even know there was talk of war. I think we may be here a while."

"I need to check on Sorlin and Addax," Rigel opened the veil and waved us off.

I looked over to the bite mark on Eadha's shoulder and winced. "How did you manage to chase it away?"

She huffed. "I got on its back and plunged my swords into its neck to direct it to the river. Once it fell in, it just squealed and drifted away with the rapids. The head on that manky torso bit into my back. Go on without me. I'll manage to get back on my own."

"Well, at least let me take a look-" I asked, reaching out for her shoulder.

She quickly pulled away and shot me a deathly glare. "No. Just go."

I didn't need to know what she was hiding or why she did not wish for me to help her. I just didn't want her to walk around feeling even more exposed than she probably already did without her tattoos. I unclipped my sheath and pulled the tunic from my body, offering it to her.

Eadha apprehensively took the tunic and slopped it over her head. "Uh, thanks. I'll see ye back at the manor."

I turned to leave, but she called back to me, "Yer right by the way," she gave me a half-smile and picked at her nails nervously. "Ye don't look like a Raven who lost his wings to me. More like an oversized bat," she winked. "Now, I'm not listening to one more word these trees have to say." And with that, she disappeared into the veil.

So she was reading my thoughts. What other undisclosed magical abilities was she hiding from us? Then again, it did not seem like a reoccurring power. What did she say again? She just listened? I would have to circle back and make sure she knew I did not give her any permission to invade my mind. No matter, I needed to check on Sorlin. That was all that mattered to me at the moment. I let out an audible chuckle as her words rang through my thoughts.

"A bat?" I murmured to myself. I stretched out my wings and curled them in front to inspect them. "A bat indeed." I needed that humor, and I wondered what she was hiding under her shirt, envying that she had the ability to do so.

Looking back, the few times I have seen her since the first meeting, she had always worn high neck collars and a sleeveless coat over a cropped shirt. What could be so bad to go that far to hide? It was a sad thought; she knew what it felt like to be so ashamed by a part of her body that she felt the need to hide. I wanted her to know I'd be the last person to judge whatever it was. I tried not to dwell on the subject of Eadha, but as the days have passed since meeting her it was becoming harder to get her out of my mind. That was a dangerous thing, she was our ally and our support in this war and nothing more. It was unwise to bring feelings into war.

By the time I walked back to the estate, the sun had fully risen and Áine was sitting in the parlor holding her head in her hands. "Is everything alright?" I asked. That was a moronic question, considering the state she was in. She looked exhausted. Healing took an immense amount of energy, and Addax was hurt badly.

She sighed. "Oh, you know. You boys never let me

catch a break." I chuckled and sat beside her. "Oh my, was that a laugh I just heard? And not sarcasm? Who are you, and what have you done to Corvis?"

My eyes rolled. "You know, I do laugh sometimes."

"I wish you laughed more. You always look so...blank, and stern all the time." She rested her head on my shoulder, and I fought the urge to recoil.

"What can I say? I'm a man of few words and even fewer emotions."

I knew how badly Áine wanted to be friends with me. Rigel ran a rather casual court with his closest companions, and I knew she wanted to banter with me the same as Sorlin. Part of me worried that she thought I didn't like her, but it was just hard to tell her that was not the case. I would give my life for Áine. She had done so much for me through the years. It was difficult to form relationships when you grew up as rejected as I did.

"I just wish you would let someone in every now and again," she said with a yawn and stretched as she stood. "Well, Rige and I haven't slept yet. There was a party, Rigel was drinking, then we thought we were hallucinating when plants said you were in danger. Good thing Rigel knew of Addax's powers or I would have screamed and locked myself in a room. Goodnight-morning."

"Goodnight-morning to you as well," I said in return.

Addax must have willed the trees to speak to me in order to retrieve Rigel and Áine...but that didn't explain how Eadha heard them and heard what I was thinking through them. I would have to trust her word that she would no longer listen to my thoughts, I was far too exhausted to keep them at bay.

I wanted to crawl into my bed and sleep for the rest of the day like Rigel and Áine, but my blubbering roommate wouldn't let that happen. "So, you think the ladies will like this new scar?" Sorlin asked, pointing to the now healed gash on his neck.

I snorted. "What ladies? And no, that one just kind of looks like a love bite."

He threw a pillow at me. "Yeah, yeah. Hey, uh, so you were talking to yourself in the woods today. Kind of creepy. Wanna talk about that?"

He couldn't hear the trees earlier...I hoped he did; what was that word they called me? "I wasn't. The trees were, uh, talking to *me*."

The corners of his mouth pulled down as he nodded. "I see. Don't worry, I'll hold your hand when we drop you off at a home for the deranged." Maybe I was deranged. It could have all been an illusion, but Rigel and Áine came to my call.

"She yelled its name for me. She saved me. Oh gods, do I have to thank her?" Sorlin groaned and rubbed his hands over his face. "Will a nod of acknowledgment suffice?"

The door opened behind us, and Eadha gave a sarcastic grin. "No laddie, I want ye on yer knees giving me praise. That thing is going to be hunting me till I die now."

Sorlin rolled his eyes and scoffed. "In your dreams...why would you do it?"

Eadha's eyes met mine for a long moment before sighing. "I couldn't just let ye die. If it comes after me, I'll figure it out. At least I have my island as protection.

If it came after ye. Yer whole court would be in danger. Now, we have a long day with Addax if we want to get his stone. We are behind schedule, and I want my home back by autumn."

Her eyes were angry and almost lifeless as she walked out of the room, but I was sure that was due to the glamour wiping away the painting within them. I didn't like this place. The magic within this court didn't make sense. Rigel would sit up at night with me on the bad days and teach me some of the things he learned in his studies as a child. I remembered him telling me how the trees were sacred and they connect everything. Addax was one of, if not the most powerful High Lords because he wielded them. They could speak to him and give him news from all regions of the lands. No one could lie to the High Lord of Arbres.

But how could he have not heard of the war or threats going across Verbenia? I had to get answers. I had to talk to the trees again.

⸭

It was probably just shy of eight in the morning based on how the sun was positioned in the sky. Addax was still recovering, which allotted me enough time to take a walk before regrouping with Eadha to come up with a plan for the stone. I walked out of the manor just past the tree line and listened, but heard nothing.

I looked around and cleared my throat. "Um, hello?" No one answered me. The forest was calm yet unsettling, as if every noise that existed was absorbed by the trees to create an ominous silence.

"*Hello, Corvis,*" a sweet whisper clouded my mind, and the sounds of the forest unfurled in my ears.

I stiffened. "Why can I hear you? Why have you

not told Addax of the war?" I didn't have time to feel uneased by the powers at work here. I had a feeling something deeper was happening. If Sabriel now controlled the sea, what else could he control?

"Addax holds a great and coveted power. We have chosen to remain silent, for there are ears across dangerous waters."

I nodded. All Sabriel had to do was capture Addax and crack his head open like an egg to gain the knowledge of Verbenia. All of our plans, all of the battle tragedies of the other courts, was information at the fingertips of those willing to play dirty. Addax wasn't ignorant. Arbres remained neutral since the beginning of the continent so their knowledge wouldn't fall into the wrong hands. If that was the case, why did he agree to work with us, putting his life and all of Verbenia in danger?

"This land has been attacked. Our High Lord cares for the life of all living things. It pained him to see his people, his guards perish. He knows where the Sluagh dwell. He knows who controls them. However, if he knew of the war, he would have sought arms from his neighboring courts and been taken to the Dark Fae. You know where the light-wielders' allegiance lies."

Fossera, I knew it. We all knew. Did we just curse Addax by gaining his allegiance? I clenched my jaw and let out a long exhale. "How...how can I hear you? Why can Eadha hear my thoughts?"

"That is an answer we have provided for you. We cannot speak to you anymore. She will be listening."

"Who will be listening? Eadha?"

The sounds of the forest turned silent. Not even the sound of a chirping bird could be heard. What did they already tell me? They called me a word I already didn't remember, that was not an answer. I recalled our meeting just yesterday with Cazara and wondered if I did, in fact, hear into Eadha's thoughts for a split second and that we were somehow connected. I distinctly remembered her whispering not to leave her in Aerras alone, but did not see her lips move. And her eyes, I will never be able to forget her eyes and the utter fear they held. I've dreamed about her eyes before meeting her, but what did that mean?

I shook my head and tangled my fingers through my hair, letting out a groan of frustration. Enough. What I needed to do now was focus on my part in this mess. Eadha was a dangerous distraction, and I needed to block her out of my head. I gained some valuable information: the trees were protecting Addax. They didn't tell him about the danger to protect him from being slaughtered like a pig by Sabriel.

I wouldn't let that happen.

CHAPTER THIRTEEN

Eadha

"What took you so long? And where are the rest of them?" Vela asked as I broke through the veil to the palace.

"The flyboys and I were on our way back from Aerras till we got shot down over Arbres, we got attacked by a Nuckelavee, and now I'm grabbing some clothes because it looks like we're going to be in treeland for a while. Any other questions?" I rattled off to her.

She reeled back and opened her mouth to speak but shut it and raised her eyebrows. "What? How? The Mither- did you just say-... I guess judging by that look in your eyes, I know the answer. Well, don't mind me. Tell Rigel our borders are secure, but the Ravens are chomping at the bit for some answers. They are itching to attack something."

I scoffed, and my lips twitched. "Have them wait another fifty thousand years and then ask me if I give a shite about their waiting."

Vela brushed her short blonde hair behind her ears and put her hands up as she walked away. I did not want to lie to Addax today. The way he cared about the creatures that lived within his borders, the way he gave them refuge was enough for me to know he was a good man. I sighed with a heavy heart. He seemed genuine and maybe even caring, but who's to say if we called on him, or any other Fae, for help as we did all those years ago, they would even answer.

I browsed my closet of dresses and smiled. Thank the goddess for my mother forcing dresses on me and for my High Druid blood. Rigel said in order to keep most of the suspicions of me at bay I would have to dress like I fit in. Unfortunately, I did not do that in Aerras, but not much went according to plan there, and Addax already had some suspicions of me. The two servants, Thela and Cari, laid out a few options for me before I went to my room, but I was not the bumbling backward savage they thought I was, well, not entirely. Plus, all the backs on the dresses they chose were low, and I was not about to flaunt the damage that sat on top of my skin. I had been to war meetings. I have spoken on the council. A Laoch at heart but a High Druid by blood; I had just the dress to make them swoon.

The dress was long, sleeveless, and its silk hugged every curve; its neckline hugged the back of my neck but plunged down to my sternum. It was a deep emerald color, adorned with gold crystals scattered all around it. My Druid Stone, held safely in the bag tied around my waist. Last but not least, the glamour...seeing my tattoos disappear once again made me feel more naked than the thin fabric hugging my body. With a deep breath, I entered the veil back to my room in Arbres.

I looked like everything my parents probably wished for in a daughter. I looked elegant, soft, and feminine outside of my muscular frame. I took back anything I ever said about wanting to look like this. I wanted armor, leather, swords, something I could run in. I looked at my eyes and winced, as the part of me that reflected the gifts I was given from my masters were gone. I looked utterly normal, which was exactly what Rigel wanted. I brushed my hair out of its various braids to fall around my face and down my back. I did not realize how long it had grown.

When I left my room, it was one in the afternoon, and the downstairs was lively with chatter. I did not give myself a chance to turn back and change. The second I stepped into the room, everyone went silent.

Sorlin let out a whistle. "That dress looks kind of tight. How about you slip into something a bit more comfortable. The Otherworld, perhaps? I hear it's lovely this time of year."

Áine snapped her fingers and pointed to him. "Sorlin. You look stunning, Eadha."

That was quite a compliment coming from the woman who looked as if she were wearing the sun itself. Her dress was incredibly golden and glittery.

Addax's eyes were wide, and his lips slightly parted as he stood and bowed at the waist. "Thank you for saving me, my lady. I am in your debt."

My lips twitched as I forced a smile on my face. "No need. I'm no 'lady', Addax, but yer welcome."

"Got that right," Sorlin said through a fake cough. It took all of my strength not to yank his blood clean out of his body with the gift from Uisce, the Water Dragon, but I made a mental note to punch him in the jaw later.

I tried to keep my eyes from roaming to the leathery-winged man standing in the corner, but they had a mind of their own. He quickly averted his own when I met his gaze, but his shadows were twitching in a way I have never seen, and his cheeks flushed ever so slightly. I preferred the company of my Laoch brothers. They did not see you as anything other than the next chew toy to tear apart in the ring, no matter how beautiful they thought you to be.

Rigel cleared his throat and smiled. "Eadha, you'll be sad to know that your friend Sorlin will be leaving. Now, give him a hug and a kiss goodbye."

I could have retched right then and there. "Good riddance. And ye?" I nodded to Corvis, and his ever neutral expression was unchanged.

"Going with." I was taken back by the flatness of his voice. He always had a bit of staleness to him, but that was almost outright cold. He looked me over and walked out of the mansion. Sorlin followed behind him, making a kissy face and holding up his middle finger. I honestly hated that creature.

"Although the goings-on of early morning were not the most pleasant, that will not stop our celebrations today and tomorrow," Addax said proudly with beaming eyes.

Celebrations? Áine must have seen my face dropped her jaw in what could have only been shock. "Do you not celebrate Litha?" Rigel tapped her on the back, and she immediately regretted her outburst. I was supposed to be a Fae, of course I celebrated the holidays.

But my gods, was it already the twentieth of June? I only had two stones and two more months until September. How was I going to secure my homelands by fall? I nodded and smiled. "Aye, I do. Time must have slipped away from me. Ye must be excited," I said to Áine.

Litha was the summer solstice and the brightest day of the year. It was the climax of all fertility and abundance on earth. Addax and Áine were glowing. The

Lady of Light and the King of Trees in one court together, this was going to be some party.

Addax was wearing a tunic that closely resembled my dress in color and gold embellishments, with his crown of antlers standing proud on top of his golden hair. He extended a hand to me and smiled. "I would be honored for you to be my personal party guest today."

I looked around nervously at Rigel and Áine, who were both mouthing: "Do it. Do it. Get. The. Stone." I took his hand and nodded. He let out a triumphant yet bashful laugh.

"Well, this is my beautiful wife's favorite day of the year, and we have never spent it in such luscious lands before. You two go on without us. We will catch up." Before I could protest, Áine gave me a sympathetic smile and Rigel pulled them through the veil.

I did not care how nice Addax presented himself to me. My fight or flight was beginning to kick in as they left me alone in a crowd of Fae. I forced a smile and steadied my racing heart. If he tried anything, I could kill him instantly. I just needed to keep reminding myself to stay focused.

We took a stroll through the forest, and it was teeming with life. Fae of all kinds were running and jumping barefoot through the trees and gardens. I heard children's laughter and felt the presence of the trees and plants beneath my feet. Addax introduced me to many people, and we even ran over burning coals together. It was overwhelming, but I could not believe how much fun I was having. We Druids celebrated the eight holidays of the year, but doing so off of our homelands was not the same. We hardly put on parties such as this one and only spent them giving offerings and spending time with each other. I have not been able to cherish creation and bloom like this since the invasion fully. It was beautiful. A tear stung my eye and fell down my cheek; I felt so close yet so far away from home.

Addax appeared in front of me, and a thumb brushed my cheek. "Are you alright?" Concern glinted across his green eyes.

I simply nodded and quickly wiped my cheeks. "It's-it's so beautiful. It reminds me of home."

His white teeth shimmered in the golden waning sun as he smiled and grabbed my hands. "I'm glad you are enjoying it. It's normal for someone to be emotional on this day. You are standing on the most fertile lands of Verbenia on the day summer was born. I sometimes get overwhelmed too."

I looked up at him and pulled my hands away slowly. "Why aren't ye now?"

He bit his lip and placed his hand on the sturdy trunk of a nearby elder tree. "They are so quiet. They have been for a while. They didn't even tell me that *Fae* was on my land. Not all Fae have offensive magic, such as the fire-wielders of Eotia. I rely on my defense, and even that is slipping. It almost makes me feel powerless. Now that I know war could breach the continent, I am worried. I am truly worried, Eadha."

My heart broke for him as pain struck his face, but I was honored to hear such intimate thoughts from the High Lord. I knew that feeling all too well. He brushed out some wrinkles in his velvet tunic. The sun was setting, and I had not even begun looking for the stone, and I almost did not want to. "I want to show you something. Come with me."

I grabbed his outstretched hand, and he whisked

me away. The next thing I knew, I was on top of a hill looking over Elowen. My head spun, and I stumbled, but Addax quickly caught me. "Sorry, I should have warned you. Treewalking is a lot more abrasive than veilwalking."

"Treewalking, aye. Alright then. Where are we?" I asked, taking in the marvelous view. I could see the sun setting in the west and the house right in the middle of a sea of trees.

"I know you are glamoured to look Fae. I'm not going to ask, but I sense discomfort in you. I just want you to enjoy the rest of this evening without having to look over your shoulder all night."

My face heated, and I turned away. If Addax were a Druid, I could see my parents pushing me to marry him. I think I could love a man like Addax, but he was too gentle, like the first flower to bloom after a forest fire, and I was that flame, ready to scorch its petals once again. I could burn away any ounce of happiness he had ever felt without even trying. I was envious of how much life he had in his eyes, how much love he had in his heart. I did a double-take when a flicker of light caught my eye, and the trees slowly slumped into the ground, pulling me from my thoughts.

My mouth fell open as the whole region lit with bonfires and fireflies twinkled in the darkness of night. My mouth fell open, and a gasp escaped my lungs. It was just like how Covalla looked during this time of year. My friends and I would dress in such loose and flowing clothes as we lept over fires and danced under the stars for hours. On every holiday, my brother would team up with the twins and find ways to wreak havoc all over the island and get into all kinds of mischief.

"Let's go down, shall we?" Addax asked. I nodded, and he grabbed my hand as he sent us to the biggest bonfire right outside his manor. The music roared and creatures everywhere danced and dashed through the flame.

"Eadha!" Áine called to me, grabbing my arms. She was utterly glowing a rich golden hue against the dark of night, illuminating her golden bronze skin. Her powers must be at an all-time high as the brightest day of the year came to an end. "Dance with me," she pulled me into the dance ring and twirled around in my arms.

I groaned and jumped with her looking for Addax, but she grabbed my face and turned it to hers. "We found the stone. It's deep in the forest to the east in an old ruined temple. Well, it's not ruined, there is a whole chamber underground but it is heavily warded. I'm talking alarms, talking trees, sentries, everything."

"What? Really? That's what the two of ye were doing?" I asked as she pulled me into a dip.

"Yes. Talk to Rigel for the plan," she said, dropping me out of her arms.

I let out a yelp, but cool arms grabbed me and spun me upright. "Hello there." Rigel's silver eyes held the reflection of the fire and the sparkles in his silver hair twinkled against the flames. I tried to break away from him, but he held his grip firm.

"Not so fast. Here is the plan, meet us in the eastern forest after the court goes to sleep. We were able to see some guard shifts and mapped out a few ways around alarms. That's where your super-Druid-sensy powers come in. I'll be controlling the deerman, keeping him asleep, and making him think the stone has been lost for gods know how long."

"Wait, what? No, absolutely not-" Rigel spun me out of his arms, and I was scooped into a jumping dance with Áine once again. "Gah! Stop tossin' me about, ya bampot!"

She did not listen to me. "While Rigel is doing his thing, I think I can tap into Addax's likeness for a few minutes to get us in. We are both beings of fertility and abundance. Hopefully, that will be enough to-"

I covered her mouth with my hand. "No, I'm not stealing or lying to Addax. I can't do it. I'm just going to ask him for it."

She looked at me with wide eyes scoffed. "What? Oh no, we can't do that, not after what Corvis told us. Trust me, this is the best way for all involved and for Addax's safety. Hold on, hey!" Áine called to Rigel. "She wants to ask him for it!" She pushed me into the strong arms of Rigel once again.

I grew so angry the sweat on my forehead began to steam, and the fire began to pulse with my breathing. "You want to, what? You can't ask him for it. It's too dangerous."

I growled and tried to break free of the jumping dance, but he held my hands in place with his magic. "Addax knows everything the earth knows. If we tell him our plan and Sabriel captures him, Sabriel will know our plan. It's not the ideal situation, but it's what we have to work with. You said I get to direct my own people, well, this is an order. I'm sorry."

I pushed him away with all my might and let out a yell. The fire blasted up into the sky and the Fae clapped and cheered at the blaze. Sabriel would have to go through me to hurt Arbres. No more pain, no more suffering, no more lies to those who do not deserve it.

We cursed Addax by telling him information, but we curse ourselves if we lost him as an ally.

Áine and Rigel locked eyes with me. "Please. Just meet us just after dusk tomorrow, the party will die down by then, and we can talk about this. Please," Áine pleaded. A hot tear streaked down my cheek before I tore through the veil back to my room. The rest of my night was a waiting game for Addax to retreat to his bedroom.

I did not hold back my tears. I knew what I had to do. I just did not have the heart to do it.

⁑

The fires all extinguished as the sun rose and fell once again. Doors across the house opened and closed and the laughter began to cease until I was engulfed in the familiar silence of Arbres. I looked at the clock and read nine-thirty, time to go find Addax. I changed into my usual cropped tank and pants, strapped my weapons, and slipped just past the veil for stealth. Tears threatened my eyes as my glamour fell. For the first time in my life, an outsider was about to witness what I was truly capable of. I hoped I was not about to betray my people in the worst way possible.

I wandered down the halls until I felt the formidable force of Addax behind a gilded door at the end of a long hallway. He was sound asleep in his bed, sleeping away all of the drinks he consumed in the past days of celebration. I needed to make him listen, and to do that, he needed to be afraid of me. Addax needed to know everything.

I straddled his hips, put my hand over his mouth, and drew my sword to his neck. "I lied, yes. But now yer going to listen to me. I'll remove my hand if ye promise ye won't scream, but don't speak till I tell ye to." His eyes widened as he frantically gathered his bearings before nodding.

"Good. Ye ever heard of Druids, laddie?" He shook his head and sat up. "Yer looking at one. Kamber Island wasn't always what it was. It was my home till he invaded almost fifty thousand years ago, killing off my kind. If Sabriel succeeds in his plans to invade, we will be outnumbered and slaughtered like pigs. Ye know this. I came here for the stone given to yer forefathers by the great god Arawn."

He stirred under me and grunted, but I tightened my grip on his shoulder and drove my knees into his hips. "Get off of me. I knew there was something off about you. I prayed it wasn't anything malicious, but it looks like I was wrong. You're a liar and a manipulator. You all are. Gather your entourage and leave my grounds at once."

I shook my head and fought the tears from falling. "No. I went through the unimaginable for my people to not come this far and turn back. I'll prove what I am. I'm going to get off and put my sword away, but just let me show ye. If ye still don't believe me, drive this sword through my heart."

Addax nodded apprehensively. I released my grip and stood. I offered him the hilt of my sword, but he pushed it away. As I stood and took a low stance, a familiar scent of rosemary and lilac filled my nose, and I could feel Corvis's presence on the other side of the door. *Stay focused, Eadha.* I took a deep breath and gazed into Addax's eyes. "Ye have the power of trees, I have the power of the earth itself, of all the elements."

I slowly moved my hand, and ivy vines burst

through the window and coiled around his arms, pinning him to the bed. He looked down to his arms then up at me in bewilderment. "I command the waters of the world," I closed my eyes and called upon Uisce, the Dragon of the Water. "Guardian of the weeping waters, grant me yer reliance and flow. Let me heal bleeding wounds and be as wild as a dancing stream. Help release all the holds me back, and unleash the roar of the falls." I opened my eyes, and my body went fluid. The push and pull of the tide flowed through my veins. I moved my hands, and in an instant, the water from the air pulled into a razor-sharp stream, carefully slicing the ivy binds.

"Yer trees, yer earth, it is strong, but never underestimate the power of the rapids." Water wrapped around my hands, froze into daggers, then went flying towards Addax. Wind circled around us, and sparks danced around my fingertips. "I *am* the elements. *I* am the power of all the Dragons. I could kill ye. I could kill all of ye..." Tears streamed down my cheek, and the ice melted, showering down around a horrified Addax. "Yet I failed. I let my people die. I failed. We are in this because of *me*. Because I couldn't kill him, I couldn't stop him...I'm telling ye this because I couldn't bear to steal that stone from ye. Yer trees were silent to protect Verbenia from yer knowledge, but again, I was too weak to do it." I inhaled sharply as a sob tore through my lungs.

After he took a moment to recuperate, he slowly sat on the edge of his bed and rubbed his eyes. "How will this stone help you? What will happen to Verbenia if you can't stop him?"

I clicked my tongue and brushed the tears from my cheeks. "The whole Fae lands will burn and fall. The humans will die. Sabriel will control every inch of the land on either side of the Circle. I didn't lie about wanting yer allegiance Addax, we need ye. I just didn't tell ye the whole truth." I could see the look in his eyes, he was still skeptical, he did not trust me. I lied to him about who I was and why we were in his house. I would not trust me either.

I turned around and lifted the back of my shirt, exposing my back's mangled skin and the remnants of my first Laoch tattoo I received just before the invasion. I heard the air escape his lungs in shock.

"After my twin died in my arms, the battle was lost. I was taken prisoner...one hundred lashings. Twice. I was eighteen years old and lost everything." I turned to face him. "He was half as powerful as he is now and took out a race that would laugh at what ye call power. The stone will help me destroy his plans. Addax, I just want to go home. I want my brother to rest in the lands of my ancestors. I'm not supposed to be alive, I should have died that day, but since I am here, I will do whatever it takes to make this right."

Addax rose from the bed and gripped my shoulders. "I'm-I'm sorry, Eadha. I will keep your secrets. Sabriel could skin me alive, and I wouldn't share your plans. There is no way he can penetrate my memories. Only Rigel has that ability. The stone is-"

"Aye, like I said, we were planning on stealing it. We know where it is and how to get it, but Rigel can't know about this. I am technically a part of his court and I broke an order, and frankly, I just want to see them struggle a wee bit, see if they can get it themselves. Play along. If we trip alarms, send guards, send an angry letter, whatever ye want. I'll never forget this kindness.

Ye gained an ally within the Druids today."

He chuckled and nodded. "Thank you for not robbing me."

Addax paused for a moment, looking me in the eyes before pulling me into an embrace. I held onto him tight, savoring the feeling of touch I have gone so many years without. I gave him one last thank you and goodbye before rushing to my room.

From the windows, I could see guards rushing to the east. The moon was high in the sky, and it was far past dusk. Rigel must have gone ahead with the plan. I did not want Corvis to know that I could sense him outside the door the whole time, so once I got close to my room, I ripped him from the shadows and shoved him through the doorway.

"Ah-" he grunted as he hit the floor.

"Ye really have the baws to spy on me?" I asked as I held my blade to his chest.

"Eadha-" I kicked him in the chest, and he coughed before he could finish his sentence. "Rigel called me for manpower. When you didn't show up, he ordered me to look for you. I felt-"

Rigel burst through the door in full Vespairan battle gear, holding a green stone. "What part of 'meet us at around dusk' or 'gods damn alarms going off and sentries coming from every damn angle' do you not understand?" His silver eyes were angry and glowed ferociously in the darkness. Before I could say anything, he grabbed my wrist and pulled me into the veil. He was a slower walker than I was, but rage fueled his steps. I did not care. I did the right thing. Addax deserved the truth and I will stand by that until my death.

I did not stop to listen to the scolding I was about

to receive from Áine. I went straight into my room and collapsed onto the ground as sobs raked through my body. I have been numb for centuries, but now I felt raw. My body felt like an open wound doused in alcohol and everything hurt. Emotions poured out of me, and images of my brother flashed in my head, then I was numb again.

"It should have been me," the words escaped my mouth before I had the chance to catch them and my voice was hoarse from sobs. I was not strong enough for this. I had been here for not even two weeks and was already ruined from this journey. My daemons have been at bay, but their grip tightened around my throat. "Please let me give up. Just let me give up."

A strong hand braced my shoulder, and I jumped away. Corvis stared down at me with hurt in his eyes. "Get out," I choked out, pushing him away.

He stumbled back and grabbed my hand. "I know what it's like to feel how much pain you are in right now. I'm not going to ask you about it, just let me take you to where I like to go when I feel this way. It helps. You can cry as loud as you want, you can get it all out, and no one will bother you." He extended a hand to me; the stone mask cracked and fell before my eyes.

I wiped my face and contemplated for a moment but quickly realized I was a kettle about to blow its top. I grabbed Corvis's hand and he guided me to the balcony. "We'd have to fly there. Can I hold you?" He asked in a voice soft enough to banish the ache in my heart.

As I nodded, an arm slid around my shoulders, the other under my knees, and Corvis held me close to his chest. I closed my eyes, finding a strange comfort in his scent of lilac and rosemary ashes, and felt safe for the first time in years. I was not going to burden him with my troubles. I could handle this alone. I just needed to let out centuries of bottled up shame and anger.

Corvis's usually indecipherable persona melted as he held me with caution, and his face softened as my arms found their way around his neck.

"Hold on," he instructed as he unfurled his wings and took off into the sky.

CHAPTER FOURTEEN

Corvis

I held Eadha close as we flew over Oneiros, with her face nestled in my neck. I could feel tears falling onto my skin, but she kept her breath steady to hide the evidence of crying. I was unsure how to handle this situation, but I just needed to get her to the cavern and let her cry this out so I could leave her be. In the meantime, I pointed at a few buildings under us, trying to distract her.

"So, that's Mac's. Right over there." She looked over to the tavern below us. "Too many nights have I been peeled off that floor. A good guy named Macaulay owns it. He lets us get away with more than he should."

Her face didn't change. "Uh, right on that bridge down there, do you see the small chunk missing from the rail?" Eadha nodded and looked up for an explanation with bleary eyes. "One night when Sor and I were pissed drunk, I threw him into it and he fell over. He forgot he could fly and went in the river screaming that he was gonna drown and die." Chuckles escaped my chest as I remembered that night. He swore off alcohol forever and lasted about a day before he was back at Mac's.

"Why are ye doing this? Ye don't know me," she asked with a harsh tone.

My throat bobbed. "Because your dam broke. When mine does, and I know I won't be able to keep quiet, I go somewhere. My 'happy place', I guess you could call it. Also, Rigel and Áine were ready to tear you apart. I would have had to defend them if you decided to unleash whatever you were feeling onto them. I don't think I would have wanted to hurt you."

She exhaled slightly, and a smile tugged at the corners of her lips. "Nor I."

"Oh? You seemed so willing tonight. What saves me from a fate like Sorlin's when you two first met?" I asked in jest.

She sniffled and wiped her cheeks. "Sorlin's a bawbag, but he has heart. I see my best friend Séamus in him, and he could use a good arse-kicking. Yer more like me."

I wouldn't wish for anyone to be like me or feel the way I did at times. I doubt I was like her. I was not that strong. I broke down all the time in silence, and that is why I came here as often as I did. A tremble ran through me as I realized Eadha would be the first person I ever showed my hideout, a stranger I just met yet felt I have known a lifetime.

My heart rate quickened as we reached the ridge on the far side of the city. "Just let me move this." I pushed my makeshift door to the side and extended my hand to her, guiding her through. "It is going to be almost pitch black. Just keep walking until you see light."

"Pitch black indeed," she said as I closed the door. It wasn't long before the familiar glow reached my vision.

"It's better at night." I held my breath as she dropped in through the hole in the tunnel and gasped as she hit the ground. My happy place, the place I went to when I couldn't hold anything in anymore. It was the most beautiful place in Oneiros, with glowing crystals lining the walls and the dome of a cavern deep within the mountain. A roaring waterfall flowed out of a gaping hole in the ceiling and flowed down into a shallow blue pool.

The crystals reflected on Eadha's skin like diamonds set in alabaster sand. When I ran away from the war camps as a child, I stumbled into Oneiros and found this cavern. I hid in here from the Vespairan guards looking to hunt me down and drag me back where I belonged. Not even Rigel knew of its existence.

It sounded as though Eadha had been punched in the gut when she exhaled. "I've been to this place...in a dream. I have sat right there staring at this waterfall." She walked over to my pile of blankets, pillows, and books surrounding the makeshift living space. "Ye got the same wee bed and everything. That's not possible," she whispered.

There have been too many things going on that were impossible for me to argue. "I spend a lot of time here," too much time. Too many nights have I woken up in an inconsolable panic where I felt I had no escape. When the burden of my childhood, my wings, or my life weighed too much on my shoulders, I would get lost in a book or just cry by the pool and listen to the falls.

I nodded and sighed. "I'll come get you in the morning, but since you now know where it is, I'm sure you can veilwalk back."

She looked away from me and pursed her lips, looking almost pained by the idea. "Can...can ye stay?"

I pondered for a moment. I was not the best company to keep in these situations. I spent the better part of my life stifling my emotions. I didn't know the first thing when it came to consolation. But many nights, I have come here wishing I had someone to talk to, so I nodded and helped her sit down on my pile of blankets.

"So, among my people, we get our raven tattoos when we are initiated as warriors. I asked you once before what yours meant. It looks like we have all the time in the world now."

She wiped her face and looked over, understanding that I was trying to distract her. The pain on her face subsided for a few moments, and the stormy oceans in her eyes calmed. "Laoch, unlike myself, are their own breed. They originate from Druid blood, hence their abilities, but you are born into it and rarely inducted as an outsider. Our tattoos are given to us after acts of valor once we earn our first."

She was covered in blue intricate line work. My mind raced, thinking of the possible madness she had seen to earn them all. "Well, which was your initiation mark?"

Her left hand brushed over her right forearm that bore five linear dots. "Well, it is gone now...but after the invasion, I was given these. This represents the last four people that were taken prisoner that I rescued. My friends...and one more on the top of my hand for my twin brother who didn't make it," she sniffled, and her voice wavered.

In the Fae lands, Elite Fae rarely had children and were considered gifts from the gods. Lesser Faeries breed easier, and my kind breed like rabbits. If the Druids were anything like the Elites, having a twin would be unheard of. Losing one would be like losing half of yourself.

"Eadha, how old were you when this happened?" I had to know. There was no written history of the invasion, and Eadha didn't look a day older than twenty. Most immortals stopped aging around then, but some could look as old as a human's fifty.

She wiped a tear from her eye, but it was quickly replaced. "It was on my eighteenth birthday. I'll be fifty thousand come Mabon. Don't ask me how I survived this long because even now I'm not so sure. I spent the better part of a few centuries training with the Dragons, after that, time flew by. When the humans were having their wars, I would take a few Laoch to fight alongside our allies, and sometimes, I would sneak into distant lands and fight for those in need."

My gods, fifty thousand years on this earth. I couldn't have done it. There were days when I have sat on this same makeshift bed begging for the god of death to send his hounds to drag me away from this misery. My five hundred and sixty years were unbearable enough. I wondered what her full magic potential looked like, what she was truly capable of. When I waited outside of Addax's door, I could feel the raw power pouring out from her, but above all else, I wondered what fifty thousand years of Laoch training would look like against Sorlin.

I gently turned over her palms. With how she felt, it would be best to change the subject. "What of these?"

"Uisce, the Water Dragon rescued me when I escaped, and I found him later and asked to work with him." On the center of her palms was one large droplet shape, and running up to her elbows were images of various swirled fish and different knotted artworks that resembled waves of the ocean.

She brought her knees up and pointed to the tops of her feet, exposed by her dainty fabric shoes.

Blue mountains sat on them, under the roots of the tree trunk design from below her knee. "Cré, the Earth Dragon gave me these and the one over my eye. His marks go up to the tops of my thighs. With each skill I learn, I have to perform a task for them, whether it be saving someone, fighting in a battle, or retrieving something, and I get a new mark. I received the power of his element alongside strength and the gift of seeing through the rock."

Her legs flattened and she pulled her waistband down ever so slightly to show her full muscular abdomen. "Tine, the Fire Dragon, blessed me with passion and ferocity. I don't have many gifts from him." A blue sketched flame with what looks like lines of lightning above it took up her torso.

"Finally, Aer." She pointed to her biceps, which were covered with various blue swirls that resembled the drawing of blowing wind. I blinked in amazement. I didn't ask what she did to earn them, I didn't need to know, but it was impressive. "You are incredibly resilient, Eadha."

She shot me a glare and snorted. "No, I'm not. If it were up to me, I would have said goodbye to this world as soon as my brother did. They'll never say it, but I disappointed them, my parents, I know I did."

It took all of my restraint not to reach for her. Everything she just said I have told to myself in the mirror on more than one occasion. How could I tell her she wasn't a disappointment when I knew if she told me the same, I would laugh in her face?

"Why do you feel that way?" I figured that would be a safe question.

She shrugged and gazed into the pool in front of

her. "I don't fit in. My parents are beautiful, for one, all of the High Druids are, but they are especially alluring. So beautiful…they're proper and powerful beings who were granted magic by the creators of all things magic. My brother was the spitting image of them. All I wanted to do was run through the mud on a rainy day, throw axes at dead trees, and be a warrior. They are stuck with me now, this savage, broken thing," her lip quivered, and she turned away from me.

I clenched my jaw and cleared my throat. "I am not someone who dwells on vanity, but Eadha, you-you're radiant,and you have many marks proving your strength. I just wish you wouldn't hold back what you are truly capable of. "

Her side profile cracked with anger and she huffed. "The moment I show ye what I am capable of is the moment ye learn how to kill me. At least from past experience that is. Do ye forget where I am? I'm in enemy lands. I need to be able to protect myself."

"Eadha, we aren't your enemies. *I* am not your enemy. Why do you hate the Fae? Why do you-"

"Because they left us to die! The High Lord of Tenebris at the time sold us out. He told Sabriel of our treasures and cut a deal. Once I escaped, I washed up on the shores of Oneiros and was held prisoner again. He told me everything and I slaughtered him where he stood. Best not tell yer laddie, Rigel, about that," her voice was hostile and the setting sun in her eyes burned violently.

An overwhelming sense of worthlessness and dread came over my body. I found tears falling from my own eyes as I felt unworthy of kindness and an intense hatred. Much like in Aerras, these thoughts feel as though they were placed in my head by someone else and were not my own, not now at least.

I couldn't take it anymore. Rigel kept nagging *me* to take a break, but I could sense that the weight on Eadha's shoulders was breaking her back. She needed a break more than any of us. If she was going to feel worthless tonight, she wasn't going to feel it alone.

"About twenty years ago, Áine was captured by her father and brother. Sorlin and I went in to break her out, we didn't have Vela on our team yet, so Rigel had to watch over his court. I was captured by Farhan, Áine's father. Sorlin got overrun by guards, and he got captured. Farhan gave me a choice: take Sorlin's place or walk free alone. He ripped my wings out from me and healed new, bare wings to my back. I was already seen as lesser by the Ravens due to my half blood, but now...now there are very few who don't wish to tear me in half for soiling their name."

She whipped her head to me and I held her gaze, still mesmerized by the landscape painted within the borders of her irises. Eadha reached up and brushed my left wing. I studied her face and each swirl of blue marked on her milky skin. In the back of my mind, something snapped; all that existed in that moment was me and her together, and I stood on that cliff buried in her eyes overlooking the sea. I felt like I had come home.

"I like yer wings. Sorlin looks like a right fanny with his chicken feathers. I think yers are quite lovely. Reminds me of the Dragons. Ye seem very capable, Corvis. Before I came here my troops told me ye commanded spies. They said they barely got past ye. Being half wraith would be a gift to my Laoch and me." Her tears subsided, and her hand retracted from my wings as my shadows grew violent with her words, and any ounce of comfort I had begun to feel, fled.

"This 'gift' caused me so much pain growing up in the camp. I was thrown scraps for food, my shelter was whatever Sorlin could spare. The other boys pinned me down, pressed silver to my skin. Since I'm only half wraith, it didn't melt through it entirely, thank the gods it didn't scar me, but it was awful...I can't complain too much anymore. I have a seat on the High Lord's council. He is one of my best friends, and yet, I still manage to feel like you do now, so I'm sorry I can't give you more than an open ear."

She nodded and let out a soft chuckle. "No wonder we get along so well. Thank ye for distracting me. Ye didn't have to."

"No, but I wish I had a better distraction than books and a waterfall. We have our work cut out for us these coming months, so at least you have this place now. Feel free to use it when you need to."

Eadha tapped a few books and bit her lip. "So what are all these anyway?"

"When I was younger, I didn't have a mother to read me bedtime stories and make me feel safe and warm. So, on the days when I feel like I can't take it anymore, I read them out loud to myself. It brings me a sort of comfort. When that doesn't work, I lay out flat in a rainstorm and just let the water fall over me." I reached over and pulled out a few books.

She turned towards me and gave a small smile. "I do the same thing. My brother and I would read to each other. I read out his favorite books to him, and he would do the same for me. And I've laid out in every rainstorm

I have come by in my life." She put her hand on my arm. It wasn't like me to give in to the nonessential pleasure of company, but it was only for one night.

After this, Eadha could come here when she pleased, and I could start to distance myself from her. It wasn't healthy for me to get caught up in my emotions. Rigel needed me, and he needed me to be ruthless. We could feel sorry for ourselves on our own time after this mess.

Eadha rifled through my stack of books, a wide grin brimmed her face, and she let out a long whistle. "Hah, 'The Faery Dance'? Ye got a book on yer own kind?"

"Ravens aren't Fae."

"I'm sorry. Ye never really know what to call yerself, huh?" She asked in a low voice.

I shook my head. She couldn't have been more right. "Well, what about you? You call yourself a Laoch. You keep saying you turned savage, but I saw you in Arbres. You knew exactly how to play the part of a princess. And you fight with the Laoch, yet you work with Dragons much like a Druid." I regretted the statement as soon as it left my mouth.

"Much like yerself, I don't know what I am. I don't belong to either of them. I guess I am just a hybrid of my own."

There have been enough questions answered tonight. I picked up my book and spared us from re-living any other old tortures. "One evening in late November-"

Eadha gave me a light shove. "No, no, read it like ye mean it."

I smiled a real, full smile and began reading. Eadha's head made its way to my shoulder and her breathing slowed until she plunged into slumber. I didn't stop reading until the book was finished, then slowly laid her down and covered her with a blanket. Eadha should be my sentry, not my confidant. It was wrong to keep her this close and letting her in, I knew that. My eyes grew heavy, and the sounds of the waterfall cradled me to sleep.

I felt a weight move off of my chest and heard the splashing of water. For a moment, I forgot where I was until the foggy glimpses of the cavern entered my vision. The light illuminated Eadha's silhouette behind the waterfall. As I breached the falls, ice shards came flying towards my face, and I managed to summon a shield from my ring before they pierced my skull.

"Holy mother-goddess!" I exclaimed.

Eadha's eyes widened, then rolled once she realized it was me. "Ye best not be sharing that with the others."

"So you *do* have real elemental magic. Why did you tell Rigel otherwise?"

She shrugged and pulled at the high collar of her shirt. "Not magic, but I can't explain what it is though. Each Dragon gave me a piece of themselves to share their power. Ye can see it in my eyes," she tapped the corner of her eye softly. "I've seen you staring at them. They changed each time we agreed to work together, each piece of the landscape reflecting a new piece of the Dragons now living within me."

"Well, you know my secret," I said, waving an arm to the cavern around us. "I don't think Rigel needs to know the extent of your abilities outside of what you choose to share. Your secrets are safe. You can trust me."

She looked me up and down and sighed with a grimace on her face. "Corvis I think it's best if we keep our distance from each other. Ye did me a great service last night, and I thank ye for that, but as soon as this is over I'm gone. And if anyone stops me from doing whatever it takes for me to save my people, I'll kill them. Even *you*."

I took in her words and nodded as relief washed over me. I was glad I was not the one giving her this speech and that we were on the same page. Friendship was a dangerous game here, and at times I have even regretted getting close to Sorlin. If I ever lost him, I would not be able to recover from that. I never let myself get close enough to Rigel or Áine for that same reason. Everyone in my life, besides Sorlin, has been slaughtered. I've mourned too many people. I grew too tired. I made a silent vow to myself years ago that I would never find love, I would never make friendships, and I would do my work till I was put in my grave.

"Agreed. Sorlin has a gift for you, by the way. Another reason I took you out of the house. He would have made you beg for it last night," I said as I walked out of the cone of cascading water.

"A gift? What gift?" She called from behind me.

I motioned towards the tunnel that led out to the city and helped her up. "Cascata's stone. We managed to take it. That's why we left Arbres. Just act surprised."

I pushed the rock door open and took in the view of the city. I loved it here, I truly did. I will fight to the death to protect it.

"How about a race, laddie?" Eadha asked with an evil smile on her face, dangerously close to the edge of the cliff.

I dared to take another step, but she shimmied back more, ready to fall. "Eadha, if you fall, I will catch you, but I would rather not play these games," alarms went off in my head as I calculated how quickly I could get to her if she decided to jump off this mountain for whatever strange game she was playing.

"No need to catch me." She closed her eyes and took a deep breath. A sort of nimble glider made out of white, iridescent scaled wings and metal rods appeared in her hand.

My eyes widened slightly and a smile parted my lips. "What is-"

"A gift from Aer. Made it himself from his scales. I learned how to pick myself up with air, break my falls, jump farther and higher, and all the like. Once I carried myself over a great distance, I proved I deserved this. Less energy and the fastest flying ye'll see."

I didn't have to carry her last night, but she let me. I was sure it was only to avoid me knowing the extent of her abilities, but it is a moment of trust I will never forget. "Well, I am scared to ask what else you are hiding. So, are we racing or what?"

She smiled, ran off the cliff, and shot up into the sky.

⚜

Vela was on her feet and rushing to Eadha when we entered the house after a quite exhilarating fly. "I heard about the stunt you pulled. Would you like to explain yourself?" Her red eyes could have set ablaze in her skull with the fire in her voice.

Áine was not far behind her with a face pinched with anger. "I could have been killed. I risked everything to get this stone, and you just disappeared!"

Sorlin was the next to join in. "Guess all that time in the bedroom with Antlers didn't pay off, huh?" The lit candles around the room flicked and swelled with Eadha's ragged breathing.

"Sorlin, watch it," I said calmly.

Rigel appeared, holding a parchment in his hands and his jaw clenched. "An eternal feud. An eternal feud with Arbres, when we are about to enter an all-out war and need *every* court on our side. Well, that is just great. That sounds like a delicious recipe for success. Where have you two been?"

Eadha narrowed her gaze at Rigel and crossed her arms. "Listen here, ya knob. Ye pissed me right off at the fire. Addax saw and stopped me in the hall on my way to ye. He had questions. Corvis and I were out at the camps last night surveying the spies," she said violently. It was a lie, all of it. Unfortunatly, I knew what happened at the manor and knew what Rigel was about to do.

He looked at me, and a slight headache slid through my skull; my memories flashed before my eyes. I blocked out my memory of last night, but surrendered everything else. I had nothing to hide. I wisely wasn't listening to Eadha's conversation with Addax last night. Rigel has been crossed many times, I didn't blame him for going through my mind, but I learned how to block out memories from him. He trusted us with his life, so he never pushed past the barriers we built.

"Can you all give Corv and me a minute? Eadha, I'm sorry I doubted you, truly. Please don't take it personally. These are my people and my lands. I will protect them at all costs. I apologize," Rigel kept everything rather casual, but this was the most proper I had seen him in a long time.

Eadha lingered for a moment but nodded and left with the others. Rigel motioned for me to sit, and a lump rose in my throat. Whatever he saw, whatever I didn't block out, it wasn't good. "I saw a memory of yours I've never seen. I don't pry in your mind, you know that. I always ask permission, but this just came out of nowhere. I need to make sure you are okay."

"What did you see?" I asked breathlessly. I knew I never did anything to wrong him or the court and I couldn't think of anything else that would bring him this much concern.

"I saw you chained up, in blinding, unimaginable pain. People were screaming for you to be let go. You were sitting in a pool of blood and-"

"Rige, that was just a nightmare I've had," I cut him off. One of the newer, more terrifying nightmares.

He shook his head. "I wasn't looking for dreams, Corv, I was looking for memories with you and her, to see if she was telling the truth, and then that pops up? I am not just some novice at this. I kind of know what I am doing."

I leaned closer to him, utter confusion scouring through me. "Rige, it was a dream. I started having it a few years back, maybe once every few months. I will admit they have gotten more frequent within the past week." I blocked out the images before my brain recalled them.

"What other dreams have you had that seemed out of the ordinary?"

"I don't really want to talk about-"

"Corv, please. I wouldn't make you speak of this if it wasn't important." His face and tone softened.

I cleared my throat and looked out the door to the balcony. "I've been having dreams that feel like distant memories. I've been having...thoughts and feelings that are strange, like a random drive to do something or feelings that just aren't normal for me to have, as if someone with your abilities has been playing in my head." It sounded absurd to say these things out loud. This was happening because of Eadha. I had to separate us entirely. I needed to focus. I couldn't deal with more than my own struggles.

Rigel stared down at his hands, mouth slightly open, and nodded. "Well, Whatever is happening, we will figure it out. I am just glad nothing like that happened to you and that it was...just a dream. Well, go get Sorlin and let's plan our next move."

I nodded with relief that this conversation was over and left to find my brother.

CHAPTER FIFTEEN
Eadha

In the weeks following that night, my days were filled with training and planning with Áine and Rigel on how we were to infiltrate Eotia. When Corvis and Sorlin left Arbres in June, they went to Cascata and retrieved the High Lord's stone. Cazara helped twist the High Lord's hand, but he refused to lend us his arms. At some point in time, Rigel was going to venture into the Land of the Mist and convince him otherwise. Now that it was mid-August, we had only a few weeks until Mabon, and I promised our home back come fall, but it did not seem I had those cards in my hand.

I never went back to the cavern. I was too afraid of seeing Corvis there. I was rather cold to him ever since Arbres and felt a bit of guilt for it. I hated to admit I almost missed talking to him, and not just because his absence forced me to tame my boredom by speaking to Sorlin, who I still very much despised. But, sitting in the shadows and watching the group helped me work out a bit of the group dynamic. Vela was bound to Rigel when he called on her for a small battle between Fossera and Tenebris but has since stayed on her own accord. She was reserved but took up quite an interest in me.

I found myself sticking to her the most over these past weeks. I told her everything about the invasion, our struggles, what we have done to survive, and how we rebuilt our lands. I kept my magic a secret from her. I did not need her running to Rigel with the knowledge of my powers. Vela promised me that the history I gave her would not be seen by other eyes until I told her it was okay. I was grateful for that and found it easy to talk to her. She did not do anything other than listen; no advice, no emotions, just listened. I tried poking around her floor of the castle, but she was incredibly private and would not let me in her living quarters. It did not matter. I found other ways to keep busy.

I sat up in bed and stared out the window. It was warm and sunny outside, and the mysterious moon was in its rightful place as always. The ethereal strip of colorful light still danced in the skies. A knock sounded at my door, and Áine appeared. Her nose was bleeding, and her clothes were tattered.

"What happened?" I jumped up and ran to her side.

She waved me off and smiled as the blood disappeared. "We missed you in training today. And the day before that and the day before that as well. You know, you have been really stand-offish. Well, more than usual."

My heart rate slowed and I shoved her. The summer months have turned her skin a deeper shade of bronze and the gold hues shined more than ever. "I'm focusing. I don't have time to roll around in the dirt with ye."

She crossed her arms and brushed a loose honey lock away from her face. "Well, good thing for you, we have a lead. Meet me at Mac's in town. Your favorite winged buddies and our ruby eyed gem will be there. Play nice."

I raised an eyebrow. "And the doting husband?

Where has he been hiding?"

"He has been going back and forth between Cascata and Aerras. Corvis needs to meet with you today as well, actually, see him first. There have been more low profile attacks all across Verbenia. You two might need to do your sneaky business."

I shook my head. I could do it myself and did not need Corvis, but I respected Áine enough to do as she pleased. "If I must."

She snapped her fingers, and a flowing deep blue, beaded gown replaced her sparring outfit and clung to her body and pinned a matching veil in place. "Cheer up and live a little. I see the way he looks at you," I was about to speak, but she cut me off. "*And,* you to him."

"I suggest ye don't meddle in things ye know nothing about lass," I poorly hid the irritation in my voice.

She put her hands up and waltzed out my door. I did not have time for these childish endeavors. There were no looks or glances outside of curiosity. I gave a silent curse when I saw Corvis was waiting for me at the bottom of the stairs. I nodded to him, and he awkwardly waved to me. He was wearing a flowing midnight blue shirt with a plunging neckline, exposing part of his solid chest and striking red raven tattoo. His hair was just as tousled and shaggy as usual, his wings tucked in, and shadows drifted around him like feathers in the wind as he walked towards me. I noticed his typical shave shadow had grown out just a tad and was neatly trimmed.

I finally cracked the code to Corvis's shadows while keeping my distance from everyone. When he was relaxed, they floated gracefully with a mind of their own sweeping gently around him. When he was around the others or angered, they were held tight and stiff around him. Sorlin, on the other hand, was an entirely different story. He always wore his heart on his sleeve, but as I roamed the palace, I could see him writing in some sort of journal. I got the feeling that he was using his large personality to overcompensate for something; what exactly that was, I had not figured out yet.

"Well, shall we?" Corvis asked with an extended hand.

I batted it away and walked past him. "What mission are we going on exactly?" I asked.

"Well, we are going to meet up with Áine and Vela first. Then after that, you're coming with Sorlin and me to our camps outside the city. We have gotten reports of Fosseran sightings. If we catch one, we could have leverage for a stone. You call the shots, but we can discuss at brunch."

Corvis would occasionally point out a few shops or pubs that I should visit as we walked, but I had too much on my mind to pay attention. More Nuckelavee have been spotted around Verbenia, and just like we feared, many courts have seen a devastating amount of loss. I have been in close contact with Addax, and the lesser Faeries of other courts have all taken refuge within his borders. I worried about him. Last week, he wrote to me fearing that Fossera had seen this traffic and have started to gain interest in the knowledge he held. Farhan called on him for a meeting but I begged him not to go, and I have not heard from him since. My masters, the Dragons, have been silent as well.

I called to them many times in prayer and in ritual, but they have not answered. My magic was beginning to weaken because of it. The images in my eyes grew stale and lifeless. Without maintaining the working relationship, I could become as weak as the rest of my people who lost their divine connections. Something was happening, something big, and I could not do anything about it without the stones.

As we walked up to Mac's, a woman who was quite short and thin with skin that matched Rigel's silvery locks directed us to a patio that overlooked the city.

Sorlin groaned and rubbed his eyes. "Seriously, Corv? You brought *that* with you?"

"Shove it, bird boy," I said as I plopped down across from Vela.

Vela's red eyes met mine, and her face remained stern. "I'm glad you could make it. I can only stand to be around them alone for a few minutes."

"Oh Vela, you've managed just fine these past few decades. Let's all be adults and make this as quick and painless as possible," Áine smiled, but her voice was anything but friendly.

"Alright, Corv, take it away," Sorlin muttered as he looked over the menu. It was all so casual and reminded me of the times my circle, and I went to the tavern to conduct our meetings. I could not remember a time we actually met like the council did. I missed them, but I was glad to have a break from them. My tolerance for those twins only went so far. It was almost as if my thoughts were being heard across the ocean as my Stone gleamed at my side and a paper and pen appeared in front of me.

"Are ye alive?" I recognized the messy penmanship as Séamus's. I haven't heard from any of my friends since I left them in June, and my heart could have leaped

out of my chest with excitement. The others took a break from speaking and looked over at me for a moment.

"*Yes, piss off,*" was all I sent back.

The paper appeared with multiple different penmanships, scribbles, tears, and wrinkles from what looked like my friends fighting over the paper.

"*Pull yer socks up and get home for the island attack. We haven't all the time-*"

"*Eadha! Please! Lana tied me up to a tree for five days and-*"

"*I was only havin' him on, don't listen to Donnan. He was the one who was-*"

"*Have ye any Fae foods ye can send to us? Maybe a pint or two of their wine? OH! Maybe-*"

"*As I was saying, hurry up. Ye've been out faffin' about over there, and our armies grow restless.*"

I rolled my eyes and replied. "*Séamus, I'm working on it. Lana, if yer gonna tie up Donnan, don't let him live to tell me. Means ye didn't do the job right. Donnan, stop being a dunderheed. Dolan, I have no care for yer gluttonous ways.*"

The pen and paper did not reappear after I sent it, but I could not stifle the smile parting my lips. I missed my friends so much it pained me. I wondered if my parents cared that I was even gone as they have not sent any letters or spoken to me through the veil. For all I knew, they were already planning an attack against my better judgment and commanding the Laoch when they have no right to do so. A steaming plate of breakfast disrupted my thoughts as it appeared down in front of me.

"So," Corvis said with a mouth full of food, "Fosserans have been spotted near the northern borders of our lands. We need their stone, and Eotia's. We can see if they come sniffing around again, capture them, and get their stone. Or we can try and level with Eotia first."

Sorlin chewed his food and snorted. "If we go to Eotia first and manage to get their stone, there is a high possibility they will go to Fossera after. They have a blood bond."

"Well, what if we break their blood bond?" I mumbled with a mouth full of eggs.

Vela slammed her hands on the table and growled. "Can you all be civilized for once and chew your blasted food? It's not that hard to swallow before you talk!"

"Sorry, I don't have much practice swallowing," I snickered.

Corvis spat out his water, and Sorlin erupted into laughter before choking on his food.

"Great. I'm surrounded by children. Eadha, what did you say? Break their bond? I am a curse breaker and can't even break a bond like that," Áine asked me.

"Well, you know, Eadha, instead of sparing in the morning, you could practice sw-"

"Gods above Sorlin, not at the table! You, Eadha, talk, now!" Áine snapped.

After I wiped some tears from my eyes from laughing so hard, I cleared my throat. "Break their bond. Ye all go, convince them to help us, they say yes, I help ye break their bond." It would be difficult. I would have to manipulate their blood and use Áine's curse breaking ability to cut the Eotian's ties to Fossera.

Vela laughed and brushed her short blond hair behind her ear. Her fair face pinched with irritation. "That bond can't be broken. Unless you work with-"

"Blood. Aye. Ye let me handle that. But we cannot go anywhere with the Fosserans sniffing around the borders. And we cannot go to Eotia without Rigel. He will have to do the talking with you Áine." The barmaid took away my plate, and we all silently waited for her to clear the table.

Corvis looked at me, and his shadows twitched. "Eotia only works with Fossera because they are the smallest court, and they want ties with the most powerful one. In theory, that would be Tenebris, however, Rigel is the most docile. He would never slaughter his own people or partner with Sabriel for personal gain, therefore is seen as weak."

"Well if you wanna get technical, there was that one time he cried at the Yule gathering in Cascata and that just didn't sit right with the other Ruling Fae," Sorlin looked at me and put a hand up in mock secrecy. "He's a weepy drunk."

"Then we prove to them we are the most powerful," I said plainly.

Áine shook her head. "And be no better than Fossera? I won't do anything that will turn me into my father or jeopardize my people within *either* border. And I'm telling him you said that Sor."

Corvis looked at me as if he knew what I was

thinking. He knew I was more powerful than any of these Elites. "Ye have me. Let me handle it. All Ye have to do is get us the meeting. We may have to show up unannounced. The Fosserans cannot find out about this. We go to the northern border, sniff about, then head to Eotia. Rigel will have the final say on how to go about it, but I propose we do so in secrecy."

Áine nodded and stood, dragging Vela with her. "Alright, well. We are going to plot our plan then. Sor, meet Rigel in Cascata, you two plan to leave for the camps in a week. We should all meet up tonight here when Rigel returns and go over the big plans. It's happening. We are going to win this. I'm proud to work next to all of you. Stay safe."

I went stiff as Sorlin gave his smart mouth goodbyes and left me with Corvis. We exchanged a few glances before standing to leave. "As Áine said, plan to leave by the end of the week. I would rather not wait around the camp for a sighting. Have you-have you seen the city?" His face of stone started to crack as his mouth twitched, and his shadows whirled. I have spent enough time in solitary, it would not hurt to have some company.

"Not all of it. Lay it on me," I said with a smile. His face softened, even smiled as he liked arms with me.

We walked around the city in silence for the most part. He showed me his favorite spots and absolutely lit up as he spoke of all the reasons he loved them. I just watched him all day. I watched every smile, every frown. Everything felt normal, and I avoided him all these weeks for that reason. I did not come here for friends, but when I was with him, I had a chance to forget about the war and my past. It was refreshing.

For the past few blocks of walking, Corvis put his hands over my eyes and walked me through the veil. "I promise you'll want this to be a big reveal."

I waved my hands and stumbled forward. "Yeah, yeah. Get on with it."

"Alright. Look." He moved his hands away from my face, and I was standing in the middle of a field with white glowing orbs coming out from the ground.

"What-what is this place?" The orbs looked like a sea of white glowing roses.

"The moonflower fields. People call this court the Land of Darkness, but you're in the Court of the Moon. Some incredible celestial phenomena go on around here. This one just happens to be my favorite." He was right. The whole sky was illuminated and you could still see the stars. It was miraculous.

Corvis sat down in the field, looking utterly boyish with a coy smile on his face, and put a pointed hand in the air. "Rigel was named after that star riiight there. Brightest one in that constellation, but if you ask me, sometimes he doesn't live up to his name. I asked him to make me half a sandwich once, and he looked me dead in the eye and asked: 'but what would I do with the other half?' We got in a full-on fistfight over the fact that all he had to do was fold over one piece of bread and didn't speak for days," I burst out laughing with him as I played the scene in my head.

I have never seen him look so free, not even in flight. He stretched out his wings and looked up at gray clouds as they began to inch in front of the sun. It was at that moment I knew why I tried so relentlessly to keep my distance from him since the cavern. It had nothing to do with attachment; I was intimidated by him. I saw his dream, I felt the pain he went through, and yet he hated nothing. He could walk down the street and point to signs of beauty when all I saw was gray rock. When he would ask me if I had any favorite places on my island, I nearly gagged. I found no beauty in the world anymore. When he spoke of the Fosserans, he never daemonized them for who they were or what they did to him. He had his troubles, he may have even disliked the person he was, but he could still see the world around him in color.

"I'm sorry I have been cold to ye these past few weeks. I said we should keep our distance, but I was an arse." I said honestly.

Corvis chuckled. "No need to apologize. How have you been holding up? I saw the black eye you gave Sorlin last week. Of all the reasons to punch him in the face, 'breathing too loudly' is definitely a new one."

"He had it coming. But I could be better. I feel like we have just been sitting around when we could be out there, taking the stones and stopping Sabriel. I just have this...feeling. An uneasy feeling." I bit the inside of my cheek as the hairs on the back of my neck stood. I felt as if a sharp nail lightly trailed down my spine, sending my nerves into a fit of unease.

He turned on his side and propped his head on his elbow. "I have as well. It feels like the air right before a storm hits. Like you can just sense the electricity and that something is about to happen. I don't like it either, but you know what Rigel said, armies are being attacked in Arbres, Aerras and Cascata. It's almost as if Sabriel is planning something big for us, to catch us off guard. But I understand your concern."

No, he did not. I could not tell him I was worried about Addax, then he would know I went against Rigel's orders. Corvis may have waited for me that night, but I knew he did not hear what all was discussed between the two of us. I could not tell him my powers were suffering from not having been in contact with the Dragons. I was only here because they thought I could help them. If it turned out I could not be that person anymore, they would cast me out, and I would lose the manpower going into the island.

"I need a drink," I muttered as I rubbed my eyes. This was all too political for me. I understood the need to lay low, I knew the risks of storming the continent searching for the stones, but all this waiting made me nervous.

"That could be arranged," Corvis said plainly.

He looked as defeated as I felt. Over the past few weeks, I noticed his hair had been more unkempt than usual, and I could hear him walking around the palace at night when he should be sleeping. Whatever spy outings he has been on, I was not included, and that needed to change. Corvis probably knew more than me of what has been happening across the land, and that was information I needed. I broke my silent vow and decided that if I were to get anything done, I would have to spend time with the shadow of Verbenia. If he got close to me, despite the subtle warnings I have given him, it would be his fault.

I shrugged my shoulders. "Eh, I've kept worse company."

He nodded with a slight smile and rose to his knees with a loud groan, and I followed suit, heading in the direction of Mac's.

We sat in a booth by the river and ordered our liquors. "Should we toast?" Corvis asked.

I shrugged and held my cup to his. "To the years we've lost, and the future we'll conquer."

Corvis gazed intently into my eyes and gave me a warm, half-smile before pushing his glass to mine. I couldn't help but smile in return. Even if there was no hope in our futures, we needed to believe in something if we were to get through this war.

"You know, Fae spirits are not meant for outsiders. I'd hate to have to carry you home," he said with a playful look.

My eyebrow rose, and I picked up a second glass. "Is that a challenge? And I thought you 'weren't a Fae'?"

Corvis smiled and shrugged. "Close enough."

Clearly it was a challenge. Every drink I ordered Corvis matched until we were too drunk to know our names. We danced, we laughed, and we made utter fools of ourselves. I knew I was too intoxicated for the evening when Sorlin joined us and we did not fight once. The three of us staggered home, yelling and singing across the bridge. Sorlin crawled up the stairs, and the three of us could not figure out how to open his door, so he slept in the hallway. Thankfully, Corvis's door was already opened.

"Eadha, Eadha, this was the best night I had in a long time, all thanks to you," he said with a shaky voice and heavy slur.

I laughed horribly too loud. "Yer blootered, my friend."

He crashed down on his bed and pulled me with him in a fit of laughter. The room was spinning too violently for me to protest. "We are friends?" he asked in a tired voice with closed eyes.

I had a moment of clarity through my drunkenness and looked at his face. I kissed that face on the cheek while swinging in his arms tonight. I laughed with him when Sorlin fell off the bar, I cried with him when we shared our feeling of self-doubt as the barmaid chased us out. The room spun again, and I giggled. "Well, yes. We are friends, I guess."

He pulled his arm from under me and rubbed his face while shaking his head. "No, no, no, that's not good."

"What? Why?"

His head started to bob and his mouth went slack as sleep began to pull him away from me. "Because I don't want you to leave."

The shock from his words sobered me up enough to jolt and stare at him with disbelief. But my intoxication made my cheeks heat up and my mouth smile widely like an idiot as I laid my head on his chest and savored the sound of his heartbeat rumbling in my ears.

CHAPTER SIXTEEN

Eadha

We did not even make it three days before there was a Fosseran sighting up near the war camp. When we got the letter, I watched Sorlin go from the irksome dobber I knew to a cold-blooded army general in the blink of an eye. He ordered the Ravens not to engage and leave the rogues for Corvis to capture, but the letter they sent was alarming. The soldiers were looking for Áine and scoping out weak points throughout Tenebris to set up a stronghold to wait. When Rigel read the letter, the look of unadulterated rage on his face could have struck me dead alone. We did not know whether to keep Áine in the capital for her own protection or keep her in the war camps surrounded by Ravens. The sighting was of Fosserans alone with no Eotian warriors, so if she stayed in the camps during an attack, the Ravens would have no problem taking out the light-wielders.

The five of them were all arguing on what to do, even Vela, all shouting and debating on the best plan to keep their High Lady safe. As fond of Áine as I was, this was not a time for hiding.

"If ye want-" I started to speak, but their shouting drowned me out, "I said if ye want-" again, no one quit. "If yer quite done!" I shouted, and they all turned to me, "ah, there we go. We need to capture a Fosseran, and the Fosserans want Áine. Am I the only one who sees an opportunity here?"

Rigel was the first to give an aggressive step forward and a glare. "If you are suggesting what I think you are, go ahead and pack your bags and get out of my court."

I crossed my arms and let out a sarcastic chuckle. "Then yer just as shite of a ruler as I thought you to be."

His silver eyes glowed, and I knew if he could get into my mind, my brain would be melting out of my ear. "You want to use my wife as bait, and you are going to call me an inadequate ruler?"

Sorlin and Corvis exchanged a glance as if they were willing to hear this one out. Warriors knew how to make tough calls like this, to take emotions out of war. They knew what would be at stake if we did not know what the Fosserans were planning.

"No," I said and took a step closer, "I am telling a fully grown woman a plan and letting her decide."

Áine's throat bobbed and her honey eyes were wild. I knew she must have some challenging feelings harbored within her about her people, but I knew this was what needed to be done. After a few moments, she nodded, and Rigel gave her a bewildered look. "What, are you serious? You are going to risk this? After everything they have done to you, after everything they have done to Corv?"

"Don't you dare speak as if what happened to me had anything to do with Áine," Corvis said bitterly. The room went silent, and even the apathetic Vela held her mouth open with surprise. "Frankly, I find it insulting that I have more than proved I would give *anything* to protect the people of this court, and yet you think Áine would not be safe the entire time. For gods' sakes Rigel, we would have a Laoch and a camp full of Ravens!" His voice grew in volume, and his shadows jerked violently; he was furious.

Rigel made a move to speak but Corvis cut him off. "I don't know about any of you, but I not only agree with Eadha on this, but I am also done waiting around. People are dying, Rigel."

We were all stunned. The corners of my mouth twitched as I fought a smile forming on my lips. I never saw so much emotion in him before, so much passion. It was nice to finally have someone listening to me. I would have thought myself going mad from how these people ignored my input.

The two stared at each other, Rigel's eyes glowing. Sorlin patted Corvis on the shoulder and pulled him out of the room. Áine sighed and tenderly cupped Rigel's face. "Corvis is right. We need this. I'll be okay, my father will not lock me away again. Come with us if you have to,
Vela can stay here as always, and if anything happens, she can send for us."

The anger within him subsided, and he nodded, disappearing through the veil with Áine.

The camp was muddy, dreary, hostile, and stepping foot inside it was the happiest I had been since I came to Tenebris. It was just like the Laoch camp, only riddled with men and women who bore Sorlin's black feathered wings. It was easy to spot my two brutes, already punching a bag in the corner of the camp. As eyes began to settle on me, I became aware that I did not glamour myself and how ridiculous I must have looked to them. These people were dark in complexion with black armor and black wings, and I was a picture of white with bright blue tattoos—a perfect target.

"Ye alright lad?" I asked Corvis, interrupting his punching. Sorlin's mouth turned down tightly and he shook his head while making a cutting motion to his neck with his hand.

"Fine," he said curtly, but his shadows proved otherwise. I looked at Sorlin, and he motioned for me to follow him.

"I would just let it be. I have known Corvis his whole life, and worked for Rigel by his side for five centuries. Corvis has never spoken like that to Rigel. Even before his wings, which I'm sure you have heard about, he was still pretty reserved. When we argued, it was always civil on his end, and he would go stew over it later." Sorlin and I have gotten as close as we could for how little we cared for each other, but this was the most cordial he had ever been. He must care deeply for Corvis to be confiding in me so casually.

I leaned against a tree and looked over to Corvis. "I see. Why do ye think he got so angry?"

Sorlin shrugged. "I would be too if everyone always brought up my biggest failure after being a shame to my own race for my whole life."

My brows pinched together as I looked at him in disbelief. "Oh, don't look at me like that, this is how he feels. Our people abused the absolute piss out of him growing up. I was surprised he lived long enough to join the army with the crap they put him through. Now imagine going through all of that, being a half-breed that everyone looks to with contempt, then losing the one thing that made you a Raven to save someone from your court. I'd be pretty livid too if Rigel treated me like a victim. He didn't fail that day. Farhan gave him a choice. We were both captured. It could have been me, but he didn't let it happen."

I turned to Corvis and my heart sank. We had so much more in common than I thought. I gave myself up so my friends could escape during the invasion. As much as I did not want myself to get close to these people, I knew now that would be impossible. Corvis could not only relate to me, he knew exactly how it felt. He chose Sorlin over his wings.

I watched him punch the bag with fury until it was nothing more than dust, and his shadows spread far away from his body. We locked eyes, and he stormed off.

"You know, I'm-" he heaved and puffed his cheeks out, "I'm actually glad you're here," he gagged and dramatically lurched forward. "Oh, gods...that really came out of my mouth."

I kicked the dirt and scoffed. "That makes one of us."

"Seriously though. I don't hate you, I only dislike you. I mean, Corvis may be losing his mind, but I have never seen him so...open? Willing to talk to me? I don't know, emotional, I guess."

I raised an eyebrow and crossed my arms. "So, yer lover boy is talking to ye now, that means he's losing his head?"

He chuckled. "No, I'm grateful for that. In Arbres, he really freaked me out in the woods when I was injured. I thought I was delirious from blood loss, but I followed him later that night and found him talking to a tree. I guess he also told Rigel he was having thoughts that 'didn't feel like his own.'"

Trees? I hoped he did not hear my thoughts like I heard his. Addax told me I was connected to the trees, much like himself, and that was why I could hear them. How could Corvis? "Well, aren't ye a gossipy bunch. I'm just gonna go check on the lad. He looked upset. Why don't ye go make yerself useful and go scout out the woods."

The Ravens monitored my every move as I made my way to Corvis. I was not frightened, but it was apparent that no one was told I would be making an appearance in this camp. Corvis was speaking to another winged man who looked much older than him, and I cleared my throat.

"Wanna take a walk real quick?"

The man looked down at me and wrinkled his nose. "And who, or what, might you be and who gave you permission to enter my camp?"

I looked over my shoulder to be sure he was, in fact, speaking to *me* in such a way. Corvis raised his eyebrows slightly as if he could not wait to hear my response. "The cause of your impending dismemberment, at yer service. Corvis? Shall we?"

I turned to walk away but the stinging sound of a metal clash had me whirling around and raising my dagger. Corvis stared the man down with his orange eyes ablaze, his shadows twitching with what could only be rage, as his sword blocked the man's axe from crashing down into my head. Much like what would happen in the Laoch camp by such a sudden act of violence, the winged men and women gathered with their drawn swords.

"Cheap move, but I agree, the only way you could have killed her was with her back turned." Corvis lowered his sword and placed a strong arm around my shoulders as we walked through the camp, keeping an eye on the brawl hungry Ravens as we passed to an unoccupied area. "As a Laoch, you should have known that if you are going to tell people to shove off in the camp, you shouldn't turn your back."

"Aye, but why do I need to worry when I have ye by my side, eh bodyguard?" His face of stone did not crack, and his ember eyes scorched through my skull. "Look, I just wanted to be sure yer alright. Ye can say yer fine, but that pile of dust that used to be a punching bag says otherwise."

He looked away for a moment then back to me, but I knew he did not want to talk about it. Much like my friends at home, it pained me to see him so angry and hurt. When he woke up the morning after our drinking, he berated me wildly with questions on why I was in his bed, making sure nothing happened between us. I doubt he remembered me saying I thought of him as a friend and not just an ally, but I meant what I said. I gave him a hard, lingering squeeze to his arm and a smile.

His wall came crashing down as he visibly relaxed and unexpectedly grabbed my hand. "I have a very vague, very blurry image from a few nights ago of you telling me we're friends," he looked down at my hand and gave me a sad smile. "I don't lie to my friends. I'm fine."

I nodded and patted his shoulder, "Well, I'm going to wander about the forest and see if I can find any evidence of Fosserans." I did not wait for his reply before tearing through the veil just outside of the camp and tried to fight the blush forming under my cheeks.

Why did his words have this effect on me? My

mind traveled to past memories I have had with Corvis during these past two months. I recalled the small v-shaped wrinkles that form by his eyes the rare times he smiled, how he pursed his lips and widened his eyes whenever I offered him something sweet I was eating, and how whenever I walked into the room, his shadows would marvelously sprawl out and sway in the breeze.

I almost let my mind dwell on how it felt to fall asleep in his arms in the cavern, how safe I felt, and how I smiled every time he mumbled in his drunken sleep the night after Mac's. We were indeed friends, incredibly great friends. I shook my head and began to focus on the task at hand. This was no time for such intrusive thoughts.

The camp was on a peninsula of Tenebris that was relatively mountainous and considered its own territory entirely, much like the Laoch camps. Once I traveled to the outskirts, I was surrounded by a dense and rather gray forest, nothing like the woods of Arbres. There was no sign of life, no footprints in the mud, and no sign of any Fosserans, but I had a creeping feeling I was being watched. I planted my hand in the soil and waited, but I saw no bodies moving through the earth.

My magic was growing weaker, and has been since my masters fell silent. I needed to find a way to connect to them. If prayer was not working, I knew the only thing that would. I had all of the elements around me, thanks to the trickling stream just ahead and the small fire I lit with my hand. I sat down with one hand on the ground and the other in a blaze up to the sky as the sun's rays peaked through the treetops to kiss my cheeks, and I drifted into a deep dream-like state.

"Cré, Uisce, Aer, Tine. Where are ye? We need to

speak at once. Our connection is slipping, and I don't know what to do." I sat and waited. The closest Dragon to me right now was Uisce, living in the depths of the ocean to the west, but I could communicate with all of them spiritually. I was pleasantly surprised to feel the warmth of the fire brush my skin as the flame grew intensely, and the ferocity of its burn coursed through my body.

Tine's voice, like soft crackling embers, entered my mind. *"The Savage Child."* That is what they called me. Tine was the most elusive of the Dragons. He dwelled in an ancient volcano on a faraway island and rarely spoke to me.

"Great tender of the ever-burning flame, what is happening? I no longer feel yer presence, and my powers are slipping. I fear I will not be strong enough without them to take on Sabriel," I called out.

"We have been called away by our master. By this year's end, we will be leaving this world to dwell with the creators before us."

The rush of blood to my brain from my racing heart almost broke me out of my trace, but I fought to keep going. "The Otherworld? But why? We need ye, *I*, need ye. Who is yer master?"

"So many questions and so little patience. Our master sees all. She has seen death, ruin, and the downfall of all creatures. You will be wise to call the Tiarna and beg them to take you and your people to the Otherworld."

What master could the beings of the four elements possess? They never spoke of this "master" to me, nor were there any written texts of a fifth Dragon or a god of the Dragons. They were older than creation itself.

"Tine, I beg you. Give me more time. I will have

the rest of the stones by fall. There are only three left. We made an agreement, ye would fight with me."

"*The age of a great darkness is upon you, Savage Child. The only hope you have is to leave with us. We have been absent in making our preparations, but we are here. If you wish to stay this course, if you wish to burn, travel to the deepest chasm between this world and the next. You will find help.*"

"Why are ye so sure we will die? Tine, what is Sabriel releasing from the Well?" My voice cracked as I called out to him. I have never felt so much fear before in my life. Tine's rage coiled through the vessels in my body, and I felt as though I was being engulfed in flames. I did not dare scream or even take a breath as the pain ripped through me.

"*Balor.*"

The electricity from Tine's words did not have its chance to shoot through my nerves as a hand clasped around my lips, and two others bound my hands as I yelped. A rag was stuffed into my mouth as I was being dragged away and a leg kicked me onto my knees.

I was brought before a tall, sunkissed man with familiar honey pooled eyes and gold plated armor with images of the sun carved into the breastplate. "Where is she?" His dark voice commanded.

The rag was pulled from my mouth and I spat at his feet. This was Áine's brother; it had to have been.

"Where's who, ya bawbag? I've laid with a few women in my time, so ye'll need to be more specific."

He struck me across the face with the force of a brick wall, and his sentries pulled me back onto my knees. "You reek of my sister's scent," he drew a knife and held it to my neck. "I am not interested in these games. You will tell me where Lady Áine is, or I will cut your throat and let her find you here."

Curse these rope bindings. If they were metal chains, I could have destroyed them by now. The order from my father that I was not to use my magic on anyone that could sell us to Sabriel rang through my mind, but this man already had my likeness in his head. Being a Fosseran, he had the closest ties to Sabriel; the only option I had was to kill him.

"Áine? Hmm, Áine, Áine, nope. Can't say I know that name."

He curled his lip as he took in my scent. "Quiet," he struck me again. "What are you? I have never seen your kind before."

The sentry holding my arm scoffed. "Probably lesser scum from Arbres, no doubt."

Áine's brother narrowed his gaze. "No, she's not. My father would be quite pleased to know what other new beings Rigel has up his sleeve."

I jerked my arms but the guards held me tight. As I fought, I felt a spark ignite within, and the surge of my abilities came crashing down upon me again. The Dragons were back. Two men trotted to the man's side. "Norr, we picked up a trail leading south. Áine is being harbored in the barbarians' camp."

Norr waved a hand and opened up the veil. "Dispose of her, but keep the body," was all he commanded before he and all but four guards disappeared.

As soon as he left, I quickly flipped on my back, kicking the two sentries behind me down. I went to run, but a sword impaled my left side, puncturing a few vital organs and ripping my sleeveless jacket off with its exit. I only made it a few feet before they surrounded me. A woman lunged, and I lit my hands ablaze, burning my rope bindings, twirled my swords, and impaled the Fae in her stomach. His skin sizzled and hissed as I dragged the blade across, white-hot from the power of fire.

"Eotian magic!" The woman screamed as she fell to her knees. Curse my father, curse the rules, and curse Sabriel. None of these people were going to live long enough to speak of what I was about to do.

"Druid magic," I scissored off her head and sent a fury of flames around me.

I could heal my side, but I needed water. I needed to finish off these guards and get to the stream quickly. I took out one of the men in a blaze, but before my swords crashed down onto the other, I was blinded by a bright light, and instantly the air escaped my lungs as a slender blade retracted from my chest. I instinctively chucked a throwing axe to his head before cutting down the last man standing.

I fell to the ground gasping for air and coughing up the blood that was filling my lungs as a distant ghostly howl sounded in the distance. I was dying, and the hounds of the Otherworld were ready to snatch me away.

Not like this, I thought to myself. I tried to pull the water from the stream over to me, but I was too weak.

I ripped pieces of cloth from my shirt and shoved them into the wounds, flipped myself over onto my bleeding stomach, and began to crawl.

CHAPTER SEVENTEEN
Corvis

I waved down Rigel and Áine as they entered the camp. "See anything while you were out?" Áine had the brilliant idea of going out in the woods and leaving a trail for the Fosserans to follow, but Sorlin and Rigel agreed that they would not be stupid enough to enter a camp full of Ravens if they wished to leave breathing.

Rigel shook his head. "Went rather smoothly. No sightings, no rotten scents, are you sure your spies saw them?" Before I had the chance to respond, the camp's alarm sounded, and Vespairans all around took flight to the southern wall. I grabbed Áine, and Sorlin grabbed Rigel as we flew to the wall.

"I guess that answers your question," I called out to Rigel. We took our stance and my blood ran cold as Norr and his guards stood before our wall. I held onto Áine tightly, and Sorlin readied his blade.

"This will go one of two ways, dear friends. You give me my sister, and we leave peacefully, or my men and I set this whole camp on fire in the blink of an eye with everyone in it." Norr called out.

"He's bluffing. There are no Eotians in the shadows," I whispered to Rigel. He motioned with his head for us to fly down.

"Ah, Corvis, wings healed nicely, I see? They suit you, they really do," Norr sneered. My mouth twitched, and I clutched my blade.

"You know better than to cross our borders, Norr. Harming any of my men is an act of war." Rigel said calmly. I highly doubted that after these past two decades, Norr suddenly cared that Áine was married to Rigel and wished to bring her back. He was hiding something.

"I will not be fought over like some prize," Áine broke free of my grasp and drew her sword. "I left Norr. You stole me back and allowed our father to lock me in a cage and mutilate my friend. I will go with you when my heart stops beating in my chest. These are *my* lands to command now, and I am ordering you to leave."

Her brother laughed and inched closer to us. "As amusing as that was, dear sister, our father has instructed you to come home. It is not safe to be this close to the coast, and as your brother, I would hate to see you hurt."

My heart raced, and I shot a look at Sorlin. What was Sabriel planning? Have we run out of time? Áine took a step closer, and I looked to the shadows around me, ready to pull her in at any second.

"You think we are stupid? You think *I* am stupid? Your little bed warmer, Sabriel, is far mistaken if he thinks he has any chance setting foot on this continent. Do not think for one moment I won't cut you down brother, the Fosserans are not my people any longer."

"You think you know anything about what is happening, sister? You have a chance to leave, to live amongst the new race. You think you and your pathetic chickens have any chance of stopping what Sabriel is conjuring? The world will burn. If you wish to live, you will come with me. Since you are my sister, I will even make you a deal. By the fist of next month, you will make your decision, or I will make it for you."

As Áine shook with rage as the black swirl of Rigel's magic began to spread from her fingertips. I had only seen her do it once before when I was tortured. It was rare to find a connection such as Rigel and Áine's, but it made them connected in every way, including the ability to wield each other's powers.

"The people of Fossera and Tenebris are both my people, Norr. They are a part of me, and it would pain me to see harm come to either of them. Do not make me choose."

Her brother took a step back and opened the veil, and we all gasped. Never has a Fosseran been able to do such a thing. It was a dark magic that not many possessed. Rigel was the king of the night, and I was a half-wraith. It made sense for us to wield such a gift. How did Norr, a lightwielder, acquire such magic?

"First of the month, sister, I pray you make the right choice." He said before disappearing.

"Well, that went rather well if you ask me. Alright, I need those that dwell in the northern barracks to scour the land. If you find any of them, kill them." Sorlin instructed the Ravens.

"Rigel, we need those stones and we need them now. We knew he was planning something, but did you hear him? He wants Áine home because our lands are going to be the first to go. We need to-" a pain tore through my chest, and the wind released from my lungs as I fell to the ground. I gasped for breath and frantically pressed my body, assessing it for any blood.

"Corvis!" My three friends exclaimed in unison and rushed to my side. I clutched my heart, but no blood appeared on my hand. A strange feeling pulsed within me as if a piece of myself was teetering in and out of existence. *What in the gods' names just happened?*

I grunted and tried to catch my breath but suddenly became incredibly aware that Eadha never returned from the woods.

"Eadha," I whispered frantically, "Where is Eadha?" I looked up at Sorlin, and his eyes were wide as he shot into the air and flew above the forest to the south. I'd kill Norr myself if he was responsible for this. The pain lingered, but subsided enough for me to stand and pull Rigel to me. "Track her, I'll find you and meet you there," he slightly squinted his eyes and opened his mouth to speak but merely nodded and pulled Áine through the veil with him.

The Vespairans scattered back behind the wall, and I stumbled into the forest and clutched a tree. I was not sure if they would speak to me outside of Arbres, but I needed to try, I had to find her. "Where is Eadha?" I waited and waited but heard nothing. I stomped the ground and gripped the tree harder. "Gods above, tell me! Where is Eadha?!" I yelled. I was panicking, truly panicking.

"*By the stream, near the border of the camps and Tenebris,*" the eerie whispers of the trees crawled into my mind. They were incredibly weak and muffled as if our connection was fading.

"Thank you." I knew exactly where that was. I opened the veil and raced through while sending Rigel the coordinates to his mind.

When I emerged, Sorlin's face was twisted with rage and disgust as he leaned his head against a tree. I looked over to see a trail of blood leading the stream and Rigel standing a few feet away, face paled, and hand cupping his mouth. I sprinted over to find Eadha on her stomach and Áine working to heal the stab wound going through her chest. I felt the color drain from my face once my mind realized what I was looking at.

I knew whipping scars when I saw them, but this...her back was covered from neck to base in pink linear craters and bubbled up white scars all crisscrossing on top of each other. There were some areas where I could see she was hit too many times and lost patches of flesh. I felt nauseated as I recalled our time in Arbres and how she was vehemently against me assessing her wounds on her shoulder from the Nuckelavee.

Though there was a small strip of her bloodied shirt still intact, I knew there was not a single spot on her skin that was untouched. My stomach dropped when I saw that going down her back, was tattered, distressed remnants of blue tattooed wings.

Something clicked within me, I took a step closer, but Rigel grabbed my elbow and shook his head. Eadha groaned and turned over as Áine finished healing. Her eyes were red and clouded from being exposed to the Fosserans light magic. "Eadha, you need to take it easy. You were hurt and-"

"Get off of me," Eadha spat out and pushed Áine away.

I leaned over to Rigel. "You guys go. I'll get her back to the camp." He nodded to me and took Áine with him through the veil. Sorlin got the message and leaped into the air.

I did not know where to start and found it difficult to speak as I honestly did not have any words. "I-I felt the sword impale you. We came as quickly as we could."

She looked up at me and gave me a defeated laugh as she rubbed her dripping eyes. "They caught me while I was communicating with the Tine. Corvis, if we don't get these stones, the world will cease to exist. There is no hope. We will not be able to fight what Sabriel plans on letting out."

My jaw clenched, and I crouched down to her. After what Norr said, I gathered that what Sabriel was planning would be devastating but seeing Eadha look so shaken and afraid sent a cold chill through my body.

"What is it, Eadha?" I dared to ask.

A tear streamed down her cheek, and her mosaic eyes found mine. "Balor. Balor of the Baleful Eye."

I bit my lip and searched her eyes for an answer as to who that was. She sighed and rubbed her eyes, which were slowly regaining their clarity. "Balor was the king of an ancient and daemonic race that tormented the gods. He had a third eye in the middle of his forehead that caused destruction whenever it opened. He was killed by his grandson but could not be killed by any of the gods' weapons or magic. It's unknown how his grandson managed. The battle was before the time of the Druids."

Through their studies of history, I was sure Rigel and Áine would know who this being was, but if what Eadha spoke of was true and this Balor could not be killed when he roamed the earth before, I was sure his resurrection would only make him more powerful. I placed a hand on Eadha's shoulder and felt the rough textured skin under my fingertips and a hushed breath passed through my lips.

"Eadha-"

"Don't. Please don't," her voice cracked, and she

shook her head. I closed my eyes and rubbed them hard as a feeling of nausea and dizziness took over me, and plopped down onto the ground. *If anything happened to her...* I would normally curse myself for caring so much, but Eahda was more than just my ally. I could deny it all I wanted, but she was my friend, someone I could trust. I would protect my friends with my life and she was no exception. I didn't understand how much she could relate to me and my pain until now, and I resented every cold action I ever gave to her.

"Eadha?" I heard a young male voice call in the distance. I peeked over my hands to find Eadha in the same spot, unphased by the voice.

"Hey, did you hear that?" I asked, but she didn't turn to me. I glanced behind a tree but saw nothing. "Eadha did you-" when I turned back, Eadha was gone, and the forest suddenly went dark. I pulled out my sword and scanned my surroundings, walking slowly as I tried to stabilize my breathing. "What in the goddesses above..." I whispered.

"Eadha? Eadha?" The young male called out again, only it was closer and more frantic. I turned in a small circle feeling eerily exposed. It could have been her companions from her island, maybe they saw her get injured, but where did she go? She was right there in front of me, and I didn't hear her get up. If these cursed trees played more mind games on me, I would tear them up by the root with my bare hands. We did not have time for this.

I saw something rush between the foliage out of the corner of my eye, and I jumped around. "Hello? Show yourself!" I commanded. I heard phantom footsteps sprinting and circling around me but could not locate the source of the sound. I stepped further and further back until I collided with a tree, and the forest went black.

CHAPTER EIGHTEEN

Corvis

Hands braced my shoulders and shook me violently, waking me from my sleep. "Eadha? Eadha, wake up," Tadhg whispered with an alarmed voice.

I pushed him away and groaned. "Happy birthday to ye too, brother. Shove off. My back is aching from my tattoo, that is still fresh, I'll have ye know, and ye ruffled it up."

His hands pulled me up by my arms and turned me to face him. "It's pronounced you, and stop rolling your r's. But forget that. We have to go."

"Where are we going?" I rubbed my eyes and swung my legs out of bed. "Ceremonies starting already?"

By the grave look in my twin brother's eye, I knew something was wrong. "We have to meet mother and father. Quickly."

Tadhg waved his hand, and instantly, we were dressed in Laoch battle leathers and decorated with various weapons. My heart began to race as he dragged me along in a sprint. "Tadhg? What is happening? What is going on?"

"We are being attacked, now move." Attacked? He must have been joking. Who would be stupid enough to attack us? Whoever they were, they would not get far. My mother and father turned and embraced us as we burst through the doors of the war room.

My father brushed the hair from my face and willed it into a braid, holding my cheeks firmly. "Do you have your Stone?"

I nodded and furrowed my brows. "Aye, but father, what is-"

"There is no time, child. Forces are moving in as we speak, and I did not see them coming. They must have conjured some kind of spell to hide their movements and plannings. Eadha, go to the easternmost point of the city, Tadhg, the west. We are going to move the capital out of here. We have instructed as many people to flee here as possible, but the Laoch insisted on staying. There is a large island far to the northeast. Follow us through the veil and keep up." He released me and pushed me to move, but my head spun as I tried to wrap my head around all that was said.

"What? No, we should fight, not run. How many are there?" I asked flatly. I would not be running away like some feral rabbit with its tail between its legs. What was he thinking?

He shook his head, and anger stuck his face. "Their forces are greater than anything we have ever seen and have reached the northern beaches. Now go, I will not ask you again."

My body began to shake with a combination of fear and adrenaline as I grasped my Stone and headed east. The Fae should be here at any moment. We should not be flee-ing. Our armies were vast and with the help of Tenebris, we would be unstoppable. Once I was in place at the eastern tower, my hand connected with the stone and I screamed in pain as my family's magic ripped through my body. I was not as strong as they were. I struggled; the weight of the capital was crushing me as we moved through the veil.

I was too weak to stand up straight when I found my parents. "Are you children alright?" My mother asked as she inspected our weary bodies. We nodded and stood tall as we gathered our bearings.

"Good, we need to work on warding this whole island. Wards so strong that no man can see or stand on this soil unless they are brought by way of Druid Stone and magic. Come." My father reached for us, but I pulled away.

"No, our people are about to be slaughtered like pigs. I am going back." I pulled out my Stone, but his hand clasped around my wrist.

"You will do no such thing. We saved who we could, and now we will protect them. You will learn one day-"

"No, I won't 'learn one day.' I am a Laoch. It is my duty to protect my people. I am going to go walk as many people as I can out of there, and ye cannot stop me." I broke free of his grasp, and a deep breath filled my lungs. Before he could protest, I tore through the veil back to Covalla. As soon as I landed, it looked like a warzone and smelled of blood and death. Soldiers of ghastly looking creatures I guessed were Sluagh, were fighting the Laoch, Druids, and even plainsfolk, but I quickly spotted my friends.

"Oi, Eadha! Catch!" Donnan chucked dual swords he pulled out of a dead body in my direction and went back to fighting with his twin. Séamus and Lana were not too far from them.

"Séamus, Lana, we have to walk as many people as we can to an island far northeast of here. Yer Stones will pull ye to it. Fight, but get our people and our Laoch out of here." Their eyes held such panic and fear, but they nodded and began slicing through the crowds and veilwalking our people away.

"Eadha!" My brother's voice filled ears, and my heart sank.

"Get out of here!" I yelled to him as my swords connected to an enemy's chest.

"I'm with you. Tell me what I need to do." Tadhg began to fight the horde alongside me. He should not be here. He was not fit for battle. If we lost him, we would not only lose the heir, but I would not be able to live with myself if I brought him to his ruin.

"Yer the heir, ye can't be here, Tadhg."I quickly walked two Laoch through the veil, despite their protesting, and went back for my brother.

"I'm with you sister, tell me my duties," he grunted out in between impaling enemies.

I knew I would not win this argument; he was just as stubborn as me. "Don't die, and get as many people as ye can out. When ye feel too tired, ye leave."

I told every warlord I saw what we were doing and ordered their men to fall back. I then instructed every Druid I could find to grab a Laoch and a plainsfolk and walk them away. Soon there were so few of us standing on our home-land, and the fighting became harder. Getting swarmed was imminent. I could see my friends struggling to stay alive. They were battered, bloody, and dangerously outnumbered, while my brother was nowhere to be found. I could not keep going much longer and made peace with my ancestors as I accepted the fact that I was about to die.

"Time for ye to go!" I yelled at my friends, fighting off the surrounding crowd. They nodded but could not get away for long enough to open the veil without taking any enemies with them. "I'll fight them off! Ye go!" They all refused. I knew they would. We were going to fight and die together on this battlefield, and there was nothing I could do to stop it.

I killed off as many as I could before my legs and arms began to shake. "Too weak, too weak," I whispered in between fighting. I was about to fall over from exhaustion *and accept my fate when Tadhg appeared by my side.*

"We have to leave!" He grabbed my hand, and we ran through the crowd to my friends. We fought off the horde long enough to grasp hands and let Tadhg take us away. The darkness began to creep into my vision, and winds roared past my ears, but it all faded as Tadhg cried out and fell to the ground.

"Tadhg!" Donnan and Dolan yelled in unison as they attacked the archer that fired the arrow through my brother's heart. Séamus and Lana screamed as they circled us, fighting off the swarm. I held my brother in my arms, numb from shock.

"Tadhg, Tadhg, shh, breathe, yer-yer going to be okay," tears fell from my eyes as my hand covered his heart.

Blood escaped his lips as he coughed. "I can't say I-I never hoped I would go first. I knew I would never be able to lose you." He reached for my face with a smile, wiping away my tears. "B-but you are s-so much stronger than-than I am."

"Stop. Yer going to live. We are going to get ye out of here." I tried to keep my voice calm but failed. I prayed to whatever god would listen to me to not let this happen, to not take my brother away from me.

"Eadha! Get him out of here, ye two leave! It was a pleasure being yer friend and ally," Séamus yelled at me with tears in his eyes. My friends stood around us, fighting off the Sluagh.

The bond between my brother and I was fleeting, growing weaker and weaker as he took his last breaths. "Eadha, s-sing me to sleep one last time. P-p-please."

I shakily hummed to my brother, clutching my Stone. I was not going to let him die here. I used the last of my magic and sent him away through the veil before darkness took over my vision as my friends screamed my name.

The light faded in and out. My legs were dragging on the ground as two men held my arms. I groaned and tried to lift my head. I was being taken to the prison just outside of the now empty lands where the capital stood. Séamus, Lana, Donnan, and Dolan all shambled in chains alongside me. We were placed on the old wooden platform that was once used for public execution, and before me stood an Elite Fae male.

"All that is left from this invasion is a group of children? I should be ashamed of myself," his words chilled me to my bones. "Of course, as we examined the bodies...we found High Druids, yes, but not the Tiarna. Many savages and lessers but not the rulers I need. So, tell me, where did they flee?"

Donnan spat at the man and he laughed. "How such a refined people allowed you savages to breed, I will not understand. The capital is missing, and I assume a great deal of the population is as well. So, I will ask you one more time, where are the rulers of your kind?"

We agreed to die here together through unspoken words. We would go with pride and protect our people till the end. "Very well then. Ten lashings each and throw them in a cell. They will talk. I will enjoy breaking them." The massive crowd of Sluagh roared as two guards grabbed Séamus, taking him to the pole.

"No!" I screamed and thrashed against the guards. I refused to see another person I loved suffer. "Don't hurt him, don't ye dare hurt him!" I grunted, but the Elite Fae only laughed.

"Hush, you swine!" A guard struck my face.

Séamus thrashed and fought, but they chained him up and ripped the shirt from his back. "It's only ten, I can take it," he called out to me.

I did not care if it were only one. I would not stand for it. We lost too much today; my brother was dead. I did not care if I were about to be as well. "No! I'll take them! I'll take their lashings!"

The Fae froze and turned to me. "One hundred lashings?"

I nodded, my face fixed to stone. He roared with laughter and clapped his hands. "Why should I waste all the fun on you, girl?"

I broke free of the guard and looked him in the eye with disgust. "I am Eadha, daughter of Faolan and Aerona. Heir to the Tiarna throne. Ye want me, yes?"

Séamus screamed protests, but the guard beat him in the head with the hilt of his dagger and threw him with my other friends. I walked up to the block of wood, not breaking eye contact with Elite. "Where are your parents, love?" He asked. As I turned my back and knelt, the guards placed the shackles on me as I clenched every muscle I had.

I heard my friends begging, but my brain could not focus on their words. A hot breath traced my ear as the man leaned in close, tearing my shirt open and tracing a finger along my fresh tattoo. "Ah, raven's wings. The mark of a legendary warrior and an omen of death," he laughed. "Yet here you are, my prisoner. Don't worry, this mess will come right off. You can act brave and stay silent for your friends, but I will break you. I will find where your parents are, and you will not leave this island alive."

The whip kissed my back and sent a trickle of warmth cascading down my spine. I bit my lip and huffed out my nose, but I did not cry out, I would not give him that satisfaction. He grunted with each lash, putting all of his weight into it, and blood started to trickle down my legs by fifteen. "Where are they?" Whip. "Tell me!" Whip. "I will break you." Whip, whip, whip.

I coughed, and blood spattered from my throat. I lost count of how many lashes he had given me as my back started to go numb and my vision blurred. Fingers entwined with my hair and pulled my head up.

"Tell me where they are, and I will stop. You can't do much more of this," a dark voice filled my ears. Where was I? Another lash snapped me out of my shock momentarily. "Tell me!" Whip, whip, whip. Fifty, halfway there.

My friends. I looked over to see them screaming, sobbing, and begging the Fae to stop. My knees slipped on the wet floor, and I hung by my wrists. I had to get them out of here. My Stone...something came over me, within me, as if a spirit that was not mine made its way into my body. Stay awake, stay awake. Tadhg? Was that you? With every lash, my vision grew dimmer and dimmer. As I pulled against the shackles, I could have sworn the chain opened slightly.

"Tell me," whip, whip, whip. "Tell me!" Whip, whip, whip. "TELL ME! Ah-!" I heard the Fae slip and fall over, probably from the blood soaking the wood, and somehow I *pulled my shackles apart and collided with the ground.*

I did not have the strength to do more than pull out my Stone. I knew what I had to do. "Eadha, Eadha no...no!" Séamus yelled. I charged it to open the veil and threw it to Lana. Guards moved to grab them, but she cried and nodded, pulling my three companions to her, and disappeared. The whip connected to my back more times than I could count, and the world went black.

CHAPTER NINETEEN

Corvis

I jolted as a force collided with my cheek, and Eadha's seething face came into view. I had no sense of time, and I did not know where I was or what had just happened, but my stomach churned, and I retched.

"Serves ye right for rifling through my thoughts," Eadha's words were as sharp as a blade.

She turned to leave, but I grabbed her arm and yanked her a tad too hard, pulling her right into me. "No, I-I didn't. I was just sitting here, you were gone, I heard a voice, then everything went black and..." I was frantic and could not even believe my own words...the pain. The pain still lingered. The pain that Sabriel inflicted.

Eadha looked me up and down, and her face softened. "I was just thinking about...Sorlin was right, then? The trees, yer connected to them as well? I was thinking of my brother, and I heard ye in my head, then saw you slumped over by the tree."

I shook my head with wide eyes. "I'm not. I have been to Arbres before Addax even took power. This didn't start happening until-" I stopped and paused once I was stable enough to fully comprehend what just happened. Those were Eadha's memories. That dream I had months before I even knew who she was, that Rigel saw, it was her. It was what happened to her the day Sabriel invaded. How was that possible? I didn't care, not in the slightest.

I looked into her eyes and made a silent promise that no matter what happened after all of this mess, I would be sure she got the revenge she deserved. As long as she was with me, living in our court, she would never experience such pain ever again, but I couldn't do this. Whatever was happening between us, whatever was going on, it would only end in us failing this mission. I felt every slice from that whip, I felt her blood run down my back.

Eadha extended a hand and grunted as she pulled me to my feet. "I had a dream a few days after arriving that I had wings yanked from my back," I froze and stared at her. "I thought it was a weird, sadistic trick of yer High Lord's magic, that somehow he knew what happened to me...that in a way, *I* lost my wings. I only guessed it could have been yer dream, but I could not think of how it was possible."

I nodded and opened the veil. I did not know how to respond to her, so I chose to stay silent. I was feeling too many emotions all at once to process how to move forward. I was angry, confused, scared, and full of sorrow, with no way to determine which feelings were mine and which were Eadha's. Was she doing this on purpose? Could she actually be some kind of spy playing a sort of psychological warfare? She tried to speak to me, but I could only remain silent. If I spoke to her before Rigel, I would say something I would regret.

Eadha got the message and stormed off after giving me a various platter of insults. I grabbed Rigel by the elbow and shoved him into an empty tent. "Woah, Corv, a little 'hi Rigel, I would like to explain how I knew Eadha got skewered in the woods' would really be appreciated before you do your big-scary-emotionless-Corv-thing."

"You have to send Eadha away. Send her to Cazara, keep her here in the camp, I don't care. She can't stay with us."

Rigel's mouth fell open and shut as he staggered back. "If that is what you want, fine. We can make that work. What happened?'

I ran my fingers through my hair and kicked over a chair. "She is doing something to me, Rige. She is playing with my head, and I can't take it anymore. I distanced myself from her, we both distanced ourselves, and that only made it worse."

He looked at me as if I were a bumbling troll and sat down slowly. "Corv, Sorlin told me you were talking to trees. When did that start?"

I looked at him for a moment and furrowed my brow. Did he not just hear me? "Rigel, I'm not crazy, I-"

"I didn't say you were. I just want to know when it started."

"In Arbres. They said I could ask them to get you from Cascata. Why is that relevant? You aren't listening to me, Rigel, I am not okay with her being here anymore. It's dangerous." The volume of my voice increased as I grew irritated. Why would Sorlin tell that to Rigel? Did he think I was just going mad?

He bit his lip and propped his head up with his hand. "How did they speak to you?"

"I don't know they-they said...they called me a name in some foreign tongue, and that was that."

Rigel pressed his lips together and let out a small, half-hearted laugh.

"What-what is so funny?" I asked.

"About forty years ago, I had awful nightmares where I was trapped in a burning cage. Sometimes I would feel panicky all of a sudden, and no matter how far I walked, I felt like I was in a small space. When you got severely injured in training that one day, we didn't have enough time to get you to a healer, so I healed you. I never had that ability, but it came over me in the moment, and I healed you. Twenty years after that, I met Áine...the nightmares got worse, I felt trapped no matter where I went, I would collapse as if someone struck me right in the lungs."

I groaned and pulled at my hair. "Rigel, what is the point of your story?"

He held up a hand and pulled a chair in front of him, motioning me to sit. "When Áine was in trouble, I woke up in the middle of the night and just knew something was wrong. I felt her vocal cords ache from screaming, I felt her fingernails peeling off from clawing at her cage, and I felt her panic."

I resented Rigel for this conversation. I knew exactly where he was going with this and did not wish to pursue it any further. He would probably give me some long-winded speech about how I secretly loved Eadha and felt the need to send her away. He couldn't have been more wrong. We now had a clock ticking down to Sabriel's invasion with only three stones. We had no time for these childish stories.

"Rigel-"

"Corvis, you will listen to me-"

I stood up and batted the chair away. "No! You listen to me. Eadha knows what is coming out of that Well, some old daemonic being named Balor. He has the power to obliterate armies with a, rather literal, blink of an eye. Now we need to go to Eotia, break their bond with Fossera, and get the last stone from Eadha, all in three weeks. I gave my blood, sweat, tears, and *wings* to live the life that I have, and if you think I am going to let some," I felt a heat go through my body as anger overtook my sense. "Some wretched, ungodsly...child torturing, piece of scum take this away from me, you are mistaken!"

Rigel flinched at my aggression. Even I was surprised by my words. His silver eyes looked me up and down, but his face remained calm. "I understand your frustration Corv, this is my home too. We will continue as planned to make sure this 'Balor' stays in his hole. However, I just want you to know I do not think you are losing your mind, and I don't think Eadha is playing with it either. I am realizing now that this is not a conversation I should be having with you and you, unfortunately, need to work this out with Eadha on your own. I can't lose her Corvis. We still need her to fetch the stone her parents hold."

He was right. I was not thinking rationally and just needed a few rounds in the ring with Sorlin to straighten my head. Today, that image of Eadha, it messed with my mind in a way I could not explain. I felt too many emotions at once and lashed out at her for it. I was just so angry, and not with her, but Sabriel. I was disgusted that someone could do such atrocities to a child and enjoy it. I needed to apologize, but I also knew I needed to figure out how to control what was happening. One wrong move from either of us in this group could result in the deaths of many.

I walked up behind Áine and Eadha, and my eyes lingered on the tattered blue markings of wings on her back. "Don't worry, this mess will come right off," was what Sabriel said to Eadha, and those words were exactly what Farhan whispered into my ear when he broke off one of my wings. It was obvious that Eadha and I were connected, either by the veil or some other magic, but good thing Tenebris held one of the most powerful curse breakers I knew that surely could take care of this.

Before I reached the pair, a cluster of trees caught my eye. Aspens, my favorites. I gave an empty smile in their direction as I acknowledged their beautiful white bark and delicate leaves. I would read under those trees in this camp after I joined the army. I walked over and placed a hand on its sturdy trunk, and closed my eyes. I didn't think. I just needed some kind of answer to come to me. I replayed interactions between my friends, looking for something that would give me some answers on what was happening to me. A word stuck out to me, the title the trees called me in Arbres. I had indeed heard it before; I was only too plagued with fear from the Nuckelavee to realize it.

When Áine finally told us about Eadha, the night we returned from delivering the letter, she told us all about the time in the cave with her. I was not listening too intently as I was pouring over notes my spies sent me, but Áine turned to Rigel and said: "Well, at least I have a name for you now...Anam Cara." I felt time slow to a stop and everything seemed to click into place.

A gentle hand touched my shoulder and the scent of clove and honeysuckle filled my nose. "Ah, the aspen. Want to know something interesting?" Áine asked as she leaned against the tree, adjusting the navy blue veil over her head.

I smiled and sighed. "Of course, my Lady."

"Well, I listened in on Eadha's lessons to Vela. The Druids have an alphabet for their language called 'Ogham,' and each letter is represented by a tree. They would cut a twig from each tree, carve the letter on it and draw them as a way to predict the future."

I nodded and looked at the tree. "I see. Is this where you tell me my future then, oh wise one?"

She laughed and gave me a push. "Oh gods no, I don't remember what all the trees mean. I know this one, though," she pointed to the tree. "Aspen, it represents perseverance through fear, courage, and finding yourself, but is also an omen of imminent fear. It is the tree of Mabon, and in the old tongue, it's called," she took a pause and touched the white bark, "Eadha. Charming, isn't it? She was the firstborn, and her mother didn't know she was having twins, so she found it fitting to name her after the tree of Mabon *on* Mabon. I wish I knew the other trees though..."

My stomach sank, and electricity stung my cheeks. Áine carried on her ramble of trees, but I was not listening. I reflected further on what Áine told us that night about the "new word" she gave Rigel: "It's sweet really, she said you have your other half predetermined, and just have to find them. How precious?" Rigel felt Áine's pain, emotions and even had strange dreams just as I was.

I felt the sword go through Eadha's chest, I saw her dreams, I entered her mind. As far as I was aware, she has done the same. I had loved the aspen trees the second I saw them in this camp. I looked behind me and watched her fighting Sorlin and remembered the first time I saw my most pleasant dream in her mosaic eyes, how at the cavern I gazed into those same eyes and felt true peace in the midst of the chaos we saw the previous night. I remembered how easy it was to be vulnerable because I knew I did not have to be strong for her.

The trees did answer me that day. They told me how we were connected. Rigel knew. He knew the second I hit the ground today. I watched Eadha and the world seemed to slow. As she turned, I saw her tattered wing markings, and my own shivered in the summer breeze.

I felt unsteady as the blood drained from my face. I had no other half. This did not change a thing. In fact, it was a mistake. We still had a mission, and when this was all over, Eadha would still return home, and I would stay with my court, that is, if we even made it out of this alive. We had so much to do and so much to plan within these next coming weeks, and we all needed to be focused and be prepared to lose some lives. I knew one thing, I owed her an apology for earlier today.

I waited for Eadha and Sorlin to finish and cleared my throat. Eadha gave me a venomous look and crossed her arms. I would not tell her about my new revelation, nor would I pursue it any further. It was what was best for both of us.

"I just wanted to apologize for brushing you off earlier. I was shaken up from what had happened, but that is no excuse. You were hurting, and I left you alone, so for that, I am sorry." I kept my voice as even and flat as possible.

She looked me up and down and shrugged. "I've been on my own far longer than ye could imagine, and I don't expect that to change. Ye don't owe me anything. We have a job to do, so if ye wouldn't mind getting to it, that'd be great."

I did not need Rigel's dream-threading abilities to read her mind. She was livid with me, but it was for the best. As she said, we had a job to do. "I assume Áine told you about our encounter with her brother?"

She crossed her arms. "Aye. He saw me, Corvis, not glamoured and all. Are we certain Fossera has ties to Kamber Island?"

A shudder went through me. "I don't know, but if he saw you, then we need to proceed with caution."

She shook her head. "Let the bastard know I'm coming for him. He can't find our island without Druid magic, so if he knows of my existence, at least my people will be safe. I have to go take care of a few things, but I'll be back in time for Eotia."

She went to turn away, but my hand instinctively grabbed her arm. "There could be a price on your head. You can't just go traveling by yourself."

Eadha looked around and pulled me in close. "I'm worried about Addax. We have been in contact, and suddenly he stopped replying to my letters after sending something rather alarming."

I looked at her, and my eyebrow rose. When I went to Arbres from Cascata, I felt her in distress and waited for her to leave Addax's room. I thought she was distracting him or that he had figured out the true nature of her being there, but I was not going to eavesdrop on her conversation. Since Addax sent us a letter signaling the start of an eternal feud, I thought for sure my suspicions were correct.

"What do you mean you have been communicating? Have you been discussing the feud?"

She pulled me with her away from Sorlin, who

was walking nearby. "There is no feud. In the last letter he sent to me, Farhan called on him for a meeting. I told Addax not to go, but I did not get a reply."

I looked around and leaned in closer, our voices now nothing larger than a whisper. "What do you mean there is no feud? What did you do?"

"I went against Rigel's orders and asked him for the stone. I told him about our plan, and if Rigel found out about that, I'm sure it wouldn't end well. I asked him to play along, and now here we are. I'm worried he went to Fossera."

If Addax went to Fossera and got sold off to Sabriel, there was no point in acquiring the last stones. If Sabriel cracked his mind, then he would know we were coming. I pinched the bridge of my nose and sighed. "Okay, we go there, we look for him, and we come back. If he isn't there, we assume the worst and move on, understood?"

She scoffed. "*We* aren't doing anything."

"Eadha, I will not let you go by yourself. If you want to do this, it's with me or not at all." I didn't want to go. I didn't want to spend time alone with her and see whatever connection this was, grow, but I couldn't let her travel by herself and get captured by Fosserans. I would hate myself for it.

She begrudgingly nodded in Rigel's direction in a silent order to make up some excuse for our leaving. He was pacing back and forth, listening to Sorlin go over plans for Eotia. I cleared my throat. "Sorry to interrupt. Eadha and I will be meeting with a few spies that have valuable information on Fossera and Eotia. We should not be gone longer than a day. What do you have planned so far, Sor?"

He looked up from his map and sighed. "Sneaking in and grabbing the bloody rock is hardly an option. Eotia has few entry points, and all are heavily guarded. What information do your spies have? Did they say anything specific?"

I knew that look he was giving me. He did not believe a word I just said, but I was not about to tell him of Addax. Eadha telling Addax our plans not only put *him* in jeopardy, but the whole continent. I was sure he would have less than kind words to say. I shook my head to Sorlin and gave him a look to drop it, and Rigel was too anxious to notice my words. Sorlin nodded and waved me away, though I expected to hear much more from him when I got back.

If Addax was truly in danger, I was not sure what all we would be able to do to save him. If he was captured by Fossera, there would be no way Eadha and I could infiltrate their court on our own. We would be caught, and frankly, I had no desire to go near those lands ever again. I was not close with Addax though I knew him to be fairly kind. It would be a terrible loss for his court if anything were to happen to him. He had no next of kin to take his place, and Arbres's future would be unknown.

I knew two things though, I was going to have to save Addax with Eadha if possible, or find some way to keep Eadha from walking us to our graves.

CHAPTER TWENTY

Eadha

My stomach twisted as we tore through the veil. I did not think Addax would have been foolish enough to entertain a meeting with Fossera after all I told him. He would not have gone there willingly to sell information either. Not only did he have nothing to gain from an alliance with Fossera, but he cared for his lands so deeply it just would not make sense. I twisted on the fur of my sleeveless jacket as my newfound resentment for Corvis replaced my concern for Addax.

There was something off about him, and I did not know why. After all, he was the one who infiltrated *my* mind today and then stormed off as if *I* tormented him with the burden of my past. When the trees spoke to me in Arbres, they said nothing about Corvis. They only told me to "listen to what I needed to hear," but I had no time for such cryptic nonsense. I assumed hearing his thoughts was their doing, but I saw into his nightmares way before stepping foot into Arbres. I did not care, not anymore, I just wanted to find Addax and kiss these lands goodbye as soon as I possibly could.

When we left, the sun was starting to dim, but in the dense forests of Arbres, it was nearly pitch black. The path I remembered walking was gone, and the trees were so close to each other they nearly touched. It was dead silent, even more than ever before. I could not hear a single sign of life. This was Addax's doing; I knew it.

Corvis already had his sword drawn, and his shadows were pulled tight to his body, twitching and ready to grab whatever enemy dared to venture too close. I ignited a flame in the middle of my palm to light our way through the forest. Corvis looked at me briefly with wide eyes and continued to slowly move forward.

The trees in the distance seem to be shifting and moving, creating an ever-changing maze. "I don't like this," Corvis whispered.

"Aye," I agreed. It was unsettling. Something was clearly wrong. I knelt down and touched the ground, using Cré's gift of sight to find his estate. "Straight through this way. The trees are moving. Follow me."

We walked slowly, almost back to back, as we navigated the forest but were met by no guards or lesser Faeries. When the estate was in full view, there were no lights and the hair on the back of my neck stood. *Not good.*

"Eadha, I think we have gathered all we need. Addax isn't here," Corvis said in a stern voice.

I shook my head. "No, he had to have left something. He had to have hoped I would come for him."

Corvis took a deep breath in and followed me through the doors. It was empty as I suspected, but it put neither of us at ease. "Where are the guards? The servants?" I whispered. We walked up the stairs to his bedroom, but there was no note and no sign of a struggle.

"Eadha?" Corvis called and handed me a playing card with the image of a toad on the back. I raised an eyebrow and shrugged, not having the slightest clue why it was important. "There is a town in the west that has an inn with that symbol on it. Maybe he is there?"

I studied the six of hearts card. Addax has not replied to me in a week and a half. Whatever clue could be there may be gone. "Worth a shot, ye know how to get there?"

He shrugged. "We will probably have to fly. I won't be able to navigate that mess out there. I do not wish to be in the veil if any rats from Kamber are here." His tone was unsympathetic and stale as if he would rather be anywhere but here, and it irritated me down to my core. I had a good feeling that if the roles were reversed, Addax would help Corvis in a heartbeat.

He walked to the balcony and shot into the air, and I followed with my glider. Even this high in the air, I could only see an ocean of trees with few lights down below me. There were few villages that, by the looks of the clusters of lights below, were rather quaint and far from each other. The town we were flying to was the closest to the estate and still took some time to travel to. Although it was small, it was by no means a poor town. The buildings were all carved from stone and the people wore elaborate clothing; children were running and playing in the street. I noticed that the people of Arbres had no distinct features and all looked vastly different from each other. It truly was the land for the lost souls of Verbenia. I wish I stumbled upon Addax five years ago in the woods. Oneiros was beautiful, but this simple lifestyle was one that I missed.

"This is it. Eadha, do you know what day it is today?" Corvis asked as we approached the lively inn.

I gave him a dumbfounded look. "I have been a bit too preoccupied to worry about the calendar, my friend."

He paused for a moment. "Good to know we are

still friends."

"For now. Was there a point to yer question?" I rolled my eyes. I was still angry at Corvis, but it would pass. If it was indeed an accident that he entered my mind, I had no reason to be upset with him. There was a childish part of me that wanted to be comforted after what had happened today, but that was a fault of my own. Corvis owed me nothing, and I was just as shocked when I entered his nightmare and felt his wings crack off of his back. I let out a silent breath as a shiver ran across my shoulders.

"Well, it's Saturday, and better yet, the twentieth. Before Sorlin was banned, Addax would invite us to a small gathering on the twentieth of each month and give his personal sentries the night off. This is the closest inn. We found the card. Addax could very well be here."

I wanted to believe that, but there was a feeling of dread in the pit of my stomach that made me think otherwise. I opened the door, and it was filled with tree warriors who were all laughing and shouting while drinking their fill. I pushed my way through the crowd to an older man tending the desk. "I'm looking for Addax. Is he here?"

The man looked up at me apathetically. "No, ma'am. If you are looking for a room, we are at capacity,"

I muttered a few curse words under my breath and made my way to the bar. "Well, what now?" I asked.

Corvis ordered us drinks and shrugged. "Addax clearly gave them the night off as always. I don't think there is any foul play here."

Something just was not sitting right with me. I pulled out the six of hearts and looked it over, and on the back, there was a word written over the toad's face in the very fine print. "What does 'Asrai' mean?" I asked.

He took a long gulp of ale. "It's a small lesser Fae that lives in water. They melt away when exposed to light. Why?"

"Why would that be written on the only playing card in his room?"

Corvis took the card from me and examined it, dropped a few coins on the bartop, and went back to the man at the desk. "Is room six available, sir?" he asked.

The man went a tad still and looked between the two of us. "No. No rooms available tonight, as I said. We fill up on the nights the guard is released."

I pushed in front of Corvis and slammed my fist on the wood. "We would like to go to room six, please, although I think the magic word ye are looking for is 'Asrai.'"

The man's throat bobbed up and down as he handed us a key. "The room is only for the High Lord's private affairs...I am not supposed to-"

I took it and smiled. "Good thing the High Lord sent us." The man blubbered out a few nonsensical protests, but I grabbed Corvis's hand and pulled him up the stairs.

"Ten coins says he is in there drinking the night away with women of the night," he muttered.

I unlocked the heavy wooden door, and my heart sank. The room was torn to pieces as if a wild animal was set loose. My hand extended to Covis, and coins jangled into my palm. I gave him a glare, and the overhead light twinkled on as the door shut. "It looks like someone came in through the window and grabbed him in his sleep," I muttered.

A tug pulled in my chest, and guilt dredged my body. I should have come as soon as Addax sent that letter saying Fossera wanted to meet with him. The room was stale and rather chilly, thanks to the dying summer. The fireplace on the far edge has not been lit at all today. On his desk was a note. As I read, anger raged through my blood.

"Listen to this: 'Eadha, if yer reading this, then my suspicions were correct that I was being stalked. I dropped the card, hoping ye would come after my silence. I do not know who it is or what they want, but if I am captured, do not come looking for me. I delegate the rule of my court to Rigel until a successor is chosen by the trees. They will know when and if I should perish, Addax.' We have to go. We are going to Fossera right now and-"

"Eadha, It's the middle of the night. We both had exhausting days, clearly Addax has been missing for some time now, and we don't even know who took him. There are two courts south of here that work for each other and will kill us in a heartbeat. I want to find him too, but we need to start looking in the morning."

He was right. I knew he was. My muscles were screaming at me to rest, and my mind was barely functioning. "Alright, well, hand me a blanket and a pillow. I'll curl up on the rug."

Corvis gave me a small laugh and shook his head as high orange eyes flashed in the moonlight. "I'll take the floor, Eadha." He began to take a disheveled sheet off the bed but stopped with a grave look creeping onto his face.

"What is it?" I pulled the sheet and gasped as I saw the bed had various burns spread throughout. "Eotians...should that makes us feel better or worse?"

He took a deep breath, and his shadows pulled in tight to his body. "That's a great question," he ripped off the sheets from the bed and laid down onto the floor.

"He probably charmed the trees to make it harder to be followed. Guess that didn't help." I muttered as I jumped onto the foot of the bed, staring down at Corvis. "How can ye hear the trees, Corvis?"

He chuckled and flared his magnificent wings out to the side so he could flip onto his back. "A question I have been asking myself since the first time we came here. How come you can?"

"I have the power of the earth. It only makes sense I guess. Addax guided me a bit to listen to them."

"Do you fancy him? Addax?" Corvis asked me.

"Wouldn't ye like to know?" I chuckled and threw a pillow at him.

I thought about it. Maybe I did fancy him. He was a beautiful man with a beautiful spirit, kind and gentle, a complete opposite of myself. There were very few men I found myself having an attraction to. I have gotten involved with a few Druids and Laoch throughout the years, but none ever stuck. I recalled the recurring dream I have some nights, although it was rare, of a wedding day with a faceless man, the man lost in the shadows. Perhaps the face will be revealed when the time was right, or maybe not at all. I was happy in the time I spent with Addax, but he did not make me feel alive.

"What about ye? Have any women lined up, or are ye too busy with Sorlin to look?"

He shot me an annoyed look and rubbed his eyes. "Nothing permanent or recurring if that is what you are asking. It's...it's not in the cards for me. Go to sleep. You'll need every ounce of rest for what we have to do tomorrow."

My interest was far too peaked to turn over and rest my eyes. "Why do ye say that?"

He sighed and turned towards me. "Fae tend to stick to their own kind, and Vespairans value pure blood. For one or two nights, I get by just fine, anything longer?" He shook his head. "I don't mind. I never want anything permanent."

"Why not?"

"Eadha, go to bed."

I chuckled, swung my legs over the edge of the bed, and crashed into his shoulder. "We're all maybe gonna die by the hands of an ancient daemon, might as well start getting soft on me."

He bit his lip and turned toward the ceiling. "Well, I am glad our critical search for a High Lord taken hostage has turned into a gossipy sleepover."

I nudged him and let out a laugh. "Out with it."

Corvis looked at me intently, and his ember eyes seemed to glow in the moonlight. "I lie to myself and say it's because I wouldn't be able to handle losing a love, but I have become numb to loss over the years. It's really because I don't know if I could love anyone when I don't particularly love or even like myself. I have such negative thoughts, scary even. I'm an epidemic of darkness, consuming all light in sight. I will not burden anyone with that."

I blinked and froze for a moment. I was not expecting such honesty from him. It seemed every time he opened his mouth, I saw more and more of myself in him. Corvis had a long life ahead of him. He deserved to be happy. He was a half-wraith with blood that would be sought after by my kind, and his wings meant nothing. He could still fly. That should have been all that mattered to his people. My hand moved to my shoulder, pressing into the lines of scars across my back where the tattoo of my wings once sat. It was given to me as a symbol that I would be the most fierce warrior the Lacoh have seen, and it was taken away from me. I understood his pain so deeply, but still could not imagine the burden he must have carried.

I breathlessly found myself placing a hand on his knee and returning his burning gaze. "Ye'll find someone who isn't afraid of the dark, Corvis."

"I guess we shall see," he lifted his chin in the direction of the bed, "Get some sleep. Who knows what we will be up against tomorrow."

I nodded and flopped down onto my back, but my racing mind wouldn't let me fall asleep. I thought of Corvis often, more than I would ever admit to anyone. I sat up a moment and gazed at his face, fallen with slumber. Sometimes no matter how angry I acted, seeing him from across the room still managed to tug the corners of my lips upwards. Over the course of these few months, we have had our ups and downs, but I still considered him a friend, and I would fight for his happiness much like I would for my friends back at home.

After Eotia, we would have to face Fossera. I could not let Corvis or Áine step foot onto those lands. I would have to go there by myself and find a way to sneak away from the group and infiltrate the court. I already planned on doing this on my own. I promised no harm would come to my friends. These people, this man that slept on the floor beside me, were my friends. I would be keeping that promise.

Tomorrow, I will show the High Lord and Lady of Eotia that Fossera's magic is mere child's play to what I was capable of. After today I was done hiding. I wanted the earth to throb with the force of the Druids, I wanted the winds to carry the scream of the Laoch, and I wanted Sabriel to know I was coming for him. He could prepare all he wanted or try to ward against me.

I would break down every wall. I would tear through every inch of magic to get to him. I was the daughter of the Tiarna, I was the general of the Laoch army, and now I carried the allegiance of half the Fae lands. Nothing could stop me.

I woke with a start, momentarily forgetting where I was, and peered over the bed to find Corvis sitting up and lacing up his shoes. He was no longer wearing his loosely fitted long-sleeved shirt. He wore his tight battle gear, and his black ring was glowing with power. He looked up to me and nodded. "Good morning. If I could make one suggestion, Eotia is completely underground and riddled with molten rock and flames. Fur is a tad bit flammable."

I looked down at the sleeveless jacket I wore and sighed. I shrugged it off and was left with my blue sleeveless shirt and tight gray pants, perfect for a fight. Corvis gave me a slight smile, extending a hand, and helped me out of bed. "Eadha, if we can't find Addax, we leave. Today is not the day we look for the stone."

I nodded as a silent lie, and he gave a look as if he understood. There was too much at risk to keep making these trips. "We will have to veilwalk. The lands on top of Eotia are flat and barren. We would be seen from a mile away in the skies." As he opened the veil, I noticed his shadows were extremely tight and twitched violently; he was nervous.

We were traveling dangerously close both to the coast, and to Fossera, and would need to move quickly. *Ye won't be captured, Corvis, I promise*, I thought to myself. Corvis stiffened and clenched his jaw as if he heard every word.

"There is one area topside with minimal guard posts. Their people work in the shadows, so they don't come up during the day too often, but it will be extremely dangerous underground. Eotia is the home of wraiths. They will be able to see you regardless of stealth if you are not careful."

Anxiety tightened around my stomach, but I stifled it away. I took his hand, and Corvis led me through the veil until we landed onto a flat gray rock that extended for miles. He started speaking of finding an entrance, but below my feet, I saw the entire court of Eotia. I saw sentries doing laps, children running, and a peculiarly familiar figure standing many feet right below us. I bent down and placed my hand on the ground. Every so often, the figure would move slightly, and the image of wings appeared in my head.

"We have a problem."

Corvis raised an eyebrow and tilted his head. "I see a winged figure down there. I can only see shapes with this gift, so either there is a Sluagh down there, or it is our feathered friend. Did Rigel tell you he was coming here today?"

He scrunched his face as if it helped him remember. "When I told Rigel we were leaving, Sorlin was going over some plans for Eotia, but I don't think they would leave without us. Either way, we both have stealth. Let's find a way in and-"

I already saw a route in. I grabbed Corvis and walked through the veil just east of where we stood. Once my feet touched the ground, I took a deep breath and plunged my fist into the rock, creating a tunnel all the way down.

I looked up to Corvis, who pursed his lips, and nodded. "Well, there we go. I am going to take my shadow form down there, but you will be able to see me if you slip behind the veil."

His shadows expanded from his body, swirling delicately and encasing him into a mass of black smoke until he was nothing more than a vague figure of a man. He extended a hand, and for a moment, I froze and whipped my eyes back and forth from his hand to his head. My heart skipped a beat, and I felt my lips part as my mind wandered to a distant memory. I have seen this hand in a dream, a hand made of soft blooming shadows. I shook my head and cleared my throat as I pulled out my Druid Stone. I slipped behind the veil as the shadows around Corvis slowly dissipated, and his familiar ember eyes met mine.

"Are you ready?" He asked in a dark voice. I could not manage to find my words, but I nodded and grabbed his hand as we marched down the tunnel.

Heat caressed my cheeks, and orange lights stung my eyes as the ghostly city entered my vision. I fought hard for my knees to keep the weight of my body supported as I struggled to take in the images in front of me.

CHAPTER TWENTY-ONE

Corvis

Eadha looked as though she could faint at any moment as we came closer and closer to the end of the tunnel. Molten rivers and falls roared, and the smell of sulfur stung my nose. I never have been inside of Eotia, only have ever walked over it topside. I always had a fear that because of my wraith blood, I could walk in here and never walk out. Eadha managed to tunnel us right into the palace in the capital city Dife and straight into the belly of the beast.

"Stay close to me. If we come by any wraiths, you won't be able to fight them," I said as I pulled Eadha by the waist closer to me. I held onto her as if my life depended on it just so I could feel she was there. Wraiths existed between this side of the veil and behind it, so in my shadow form, even though Eadha could see me, I was not fully there with her and would be slow to defend her if she were attacked. She was going to stay connected to my hip during the duration of this sneaking and I would protect her with my sword or even my own body if it came to it.

I felt as though lightning was setting my nerves ablaze walking through the palace corridors. Almost every corner we turned, a guard was walking with a wraith as if they were expecting us, as if they were expecting me. Something didn't feel right.

I felt a tug on my shirt, and Eadha pulled me into

a tight crack in the wall, and my body tensed. "It's Sor-lin. Sorlin, Rigel, and Áine. Just up ahead in the throne room, past those doors."

I let out an exasperated gasp as her chest pressed up against mine in this bloody crevasse. "How do you know?"

Eadha lifted her arm and touched the palm of her hand to the rock behind her. "The image is clearer down here. I can see the bastard clear as day. I also see some sort of jail deeper below. If you go to Rigel, I could get to the jail and-"

"No. Absolutely not. We are not separating. You can't fight wraiths. They are only shadows."

She peered out of the crack and shrugged. "I see them clear as day behind the veil just as I can see ye."

"That's impossible. Only wraiths can see other-" I paused and glanced down at the scar I could see on the back of her shoulder. The connection...we shared more than pain and emotion, just like we shared magical abil-ities. "Nevermind. I don't care if you can see them or not. It is too dangerous. You cannot go down there by yourself."

The look in her mosaic eyes told me all I needed to know; she would go with or without me, and there was no stopping her. A pain started deep within my chest as she gave me a squeeze on my shoulder and knocked an opening in the wall behind her. "I'll be able to see if anything happens to ye. I'll grab Addax if he is there and come straight back."

I clenched my jaw and nodded. Eadha slipped into the opening, and it shut before I could beg her to stay. The pain in my chest persisted, and concern dripped through my body like a vicious poison, but I needed to focus. I made a mental note to speak with Áine on how to break this bond so my life could return to normal.

I shimmied out of the hole and plunged myself fully into the veil and right to Rigel's side. Sorlin and Rigel jumped, reaching for their weapons before realizing it was me standing in front of them.

"*Where in gods' names were you, and where did you come from?*" Rigel spoke into my mind.

I opened my mouth to speak but the High Lord, Nago, and his Lady Jada appeared on their thrones. We all jumped and bowed our heads to them. Eotians were the most captivating Fae I had seen, and their presence never ceased to leave me stunned. They smiled at us, their white teeth glistening against their midnight skin. Nago's crown flared red with the fire behind him as it stood proudly on top of his short twisted hair and wore an elegant black suit. Jada's hair was long and coiled back like a fierce storm over a stilled mind, and her golden crown adorned with thorns seemed to smile with her. The red dress she wore dripped over her like the blood she was sure to spill from our veins. Both wore various necklaces and bracelets made from what I could only imagine was bone. They were stunning yet caused my blood to turn cold despite being surrounded by flames.

"Ah, so the Court of Darkness *did* receive my letter last night. So pale and delicate for the 'Master of the Night.' Perhaps we could hold onto the title, keep it nice and warm," Jada lit a flame in the center of her palm. "In case anything should happen to you."

"What can I say, darling? I'm a star. My title will not be going anywhere unless you know something I do not," Rigel said playfully, but the tension through his body was anything but.

Out of the corner of my eye, I saw a few guards enter the throne chambers and a few wraiths as well. I looked to Sorlin, who gave me a side-eye, acknowledging he saw it too. Jada chuckled. "You know what they say about stars. They tend to fall."

I slowly crossed my arms so my hand was closer to my sword. Rigel's face fell, but he still kept a calm composure. "Why did you call me here?"

Nago placed his chin on his hand and smiled, twiddling with a few shells in his hand. "We know you have been traveling to the courts throughout Verbenia, for what, we do not know. There is no point in lying to you about what is happening in our lands. We are going to be attacked, and you can either escape death and join us, or move out of our way."

Sorlin laughed. "Ah, so you are warming Sabriel's bed as well? Sounds about right. I hear he adores under-performance. And with the smallest court in Verbenia having the smallest-"

"Sorlin!" Rigel snapped.

Jada looked at her husband and smiled. "No, actually, just doing what we need to protect our court. Now!"

A shadowy rope tied around my arms and violently yanked me to the wraith now standing beside the throne next to Nago. "What the- release me!" I demanded as I strained against the shadows that pinned my arms and legs together.

Sorlin's eyes widened and a mixture of fear and panic struck his face as he pulled his sword from its sheath. Rigel and Áine moved to pounce, but guards crowded around them with blades to their necks.

"I will present you with two options, Rigel: you

can leave here unharmed without your half-breed, or you can die. It's rather simple, and the choice is yours."

No matter how hard I struggled, I couldn't break free. I moved in and out of my shadow form, but the bindings held their place. What did they want from me? Where was Eadha? Rigel was seething with anger, his silver eyes flashed, and the guards around him knelt to their knees, quivering with whatever horrors he placed into their minds. Nago drew a blade and shot a stream of flames to his feet.

"You can shift my reality Rigel, but flames have no master once they leave my hands. You could hurt one of your loved ones terribly," Nago explained.

"Is this why you called me here? Just to steal my spy?"

Jada chuckled and admired her long, black-painted nails. "You may see us as evil, and that is fine. However, we will do *whatever* we have to, cut down *whoever* we have to, to keep our lands safe. Your spy is a rare half-wraith with a peculiar aura around him...or so says our dearest companion, Norr."

"You have hybrids. I know you do. You don't need me," I grunted.

"Have you seen any hybrids, dear Corvis?" Nago asked. "You have not, because they do not live past their teenage years. They get sick and pass away once the wraith blood sets in. You, however, are not only alive but harboring a peculiar magic. A magic we need to guard our city," Nago turned to Rigel. "You have no idea what will be happening within the next year, and you cannot stop it. If Farhan wants to dabble in the dark arts, let him, we will join him. But we will not do it without a sort of...insurance, for our kind."

Áine looked at me with sad eyes. "My people are liars. There is nothing more than the aura of a Raven and the shadows he possesses."

Rigel knew when we were lying, and he gave her a look I have seen one too many times. My heart sank and I met Áine's gaze of honey, wondering what she could see in me that she hasn't told me about.

"As you said, Lady of Light, your people are liars. You can try and hide from your lineage, but you are a Fosseran and, in turn, bound to me. You cannot lie to a blood-bound soul. I can see it. You still have your chance to leave. I do not wish to kill all of you," Nago said with a smile.

"We aren't going anywhere without my brother," Sorlin growled.

"Just go. I'll be out of here in no time." I would escape. I always did.

Nago laughed and sighed deeply. "I am the king of the wraiths and shadows. Do you think we haven't learned how to keep them at bay?"

My wrists burned as something clamped onto them. "Agh!"

"Of course, since you are a half-breed, the silver won't kill you, but it will hurt quite a bit. Your exit slips have now expired, my dears," Nago sent a flame to my group of companions, and a ring of fire corralled them. "Now, we can find out together what sort of mysteries lie beneath this dapper young man's skin."

"No, no, you let them leave, you let them leave right now!" I demanded.

"Nago, you don't want this. You want your people, your lands, to be safe. I can promise that no harm will come to them. Farhan and Sabriel will destroy you, and you know it!" Áine cried out.

Jada clicked her tongue. "We joined Farhan for safety and safety he will give us."

"Then why do this? Why do this unless you had a once of doubt that you were in danger? Do you even know what Sabriel is planning?" Áine asked.

"Sabriel wants to unify the world under one rule. One rule, one law, no chaos. He wants to expand the lands of the Fae, break us out of our realm, and destroy the Faery Circles binding us here to create the supreme race of Faery. No lessers, no mixed breeds, and no humans to get in his way."

Sorlin chuckled. "Oh, okay, phew, and here I thought you were just a bunch of idiots playing Lord of the Lands."

A crack sounded in my ears, and the pain of a broken bone seared my hand as I wailed. "Norr told us pain would be the easiest way to unearth whatever is living within you," said Nago.

My friends' looks of horror changed to anger as the wraith broke another bone in my hand. I panted slowly to keep calm. "There- there's nothing within me. I am just a hybrid. My father was just a guard in the Vespairan camps, and my mother was a wraith. They met here during the few wars Tenebris waged with Eotia, that's it!"

Nago chuckled. "We know about your incredibly unremarkable parents, dear half-breed. Your mother is a whore, and your father is dead, but that doesn't explain what you have lingering under your skin."

My mother is alive? Nago knows my mother? I pulled on my restraints and turned to Rigel, who looked as though he could burst into flames at any moment.

His eyes flashed, Nago and Jada grimaced. They shielded their eyes and spewed flames everywhere, burning Rigel.

"Enough! Rigel, just leave!" Sweat dripped into my eyes, and Jada growled. The wraith broke more bones in my arm, and I bit my lip so hard I tasted blood.

"Nago, maybe the Raven within is holding him back. Perhaps we should learn a lesson from our beloved blood brother." Jada rose from her seat and stalked over to me. "Pain is one thing, but we are trying to unleash whatever primal power he has deep within his bones. The power clearly isn't that of a Raven, so let's take the Raven, out of our half-breed."

A finger traced my wings, and my eyes widened. I thrashed against my restrained and grunted. "No, stay away from me! There is no power!"

Rigel, Áine, and Sorlin were yelling over each other, and Nago sent another blast of fire their way. "You can trick my mind all you want Rigel, it will only hurt you."

Not again, no gods, not again. Jada gripped my wing, and her warm breath played against my ear. "This time, there won't be anyone to heal you."

A large quake in the ground distracted Jada momentarily and threw us off balance. *Eadha, I hope that was you.*

CHAPTER TWENTY-TWO

Eadha

I shook my head to get rid of the image of Corvis's hand. It had to have been a coincidence, but there have been too many strange goings-on for me to believe otherwise. Either way, now was not the time to think of such things. Addax needed me. I worried about Corvis briefly, but at least he was meeting the others. He would be protected. I was not as worried about the wraiths as he was. My dagger was made of silver, exactly what I needed to give them a final blow. I blessed my abilities to tunnel my way through the rock, but as I got closer and closer to the jail, I would need to be out looking for Addax.

I made a small hole just past the entrance of the jail and saw a lone Elite female guard making rounds. I waited for her to come within my reach and burst from the rock, snatching her back in with me.

"Shh, shh, no sense making a fuss," I whispered. I placed my arm across her neck and held her until her thrashing and muffled yells slowed and subsided. I waited to see if there were any other guards crossing this path, but thankfully, the hallway was empty.

I slowly left the safety of the rocky walls and slid against them in the shadows. Every corner I turned had a guard or a wraith making rounds and had to be taken out with stealth, but that was not the problem. I could feel how deep and how many cells were in this jail. They were filled with all kinds of Fae, and many of them were Elites. I could not see where exactly Addax was being held or if he was even here. I turned a corner, and three wraiths were standing at the entrance of a door with several locks, and behind it were fewer cells spread further apart from each other. Surely Addax could be back there. I slipped just behind the veil and saw their true forms. They were a group of large, ghastly-looking men that walked in intricate rounds so every inch of the hallway was guarded. There would be no sneaking past them.

I felt the ground, and the floor underneath me was just as guarded. My hand touched the rough skin on my upper back, and I sighed. I hoped and prayed to my Dragons that Corvis was safe. I should have told him to leave without me if the events turned unfavorable. I left the veil, drew my dagger, and picked up a rock, flinging it in the direction of the guards.

They let out a collective howl and I slipped back into the veil so I could see their true forms. As I peered around the corner, one of the wraiths was heading towards me, and two others came to the sound of their call. I clutched my dagger, regulated my breath, and when the wraith turned the corner, I plunged it into his heart.

There was no way to do this with stealth. Wraiths screamed their souls out when stabbed with silver. The whole floor would be alerted to my presence either way. I kicked him away and jumped around the corner, stabbing another wraith, then I was surrounded. The screams bewildered my mind. It was hard to keep focused. I was dancing with the shadows as I struggled to take them out. More and more flooded into the hallway and quickly surrounded me, but I was relentless.

One must have gotten too close to me because suddenly, a rope of shadow clutched my wrist and pulled me towards a female wraith. I dug my heels into the ground as I resited her force, but soon more tethers held me in place.

"Foolish lesser Faery, you think you can kill all of us?" The female's orange eyes flared with ferocity as her ghostly voice echoed the hall. My elemental magic would be useless on them, but I had to think of something fast. I rattled my brain, and for some reason, the only image I could find was Corvis. I felt something slither through my veins, and before I could realize what was happening, the tether around me broke, and I sprang for the door. I used the winds to propel me forward and peeled the metal away, slipping through the hole before twisting it shut. It had to have been forged from silver because the wraiths were not able to slip past it.

I looked at my shaking hands and panted. I thought my eyes were playing tricks on me, but as I blinked, I saw a tendril of black shadow recede into the palms of my hands. I froze, but the clicking of boots echoing through the hall in which I stood jolted me back into reality. I pressed my palm to the floor and found a lone Fae in the far back of this room. I hid from the guards rushing to the wraiths outside the door and knew I did not have much time. I looked through all of the cells I passed, but no sign of Addax. At the end of the hall, I spotted a small unguarded door. *That has to be him back there,* I thought. There was nowhere else to go.

There seemed to be no wraiths in this lot, so I slipped behind the veil and made a break for the door I believed Addax to be behind. As I opened the door, I saw a body curled up against the wall, not moving.

"Addax?" I whispered. I clutched my dagger and approached the figure slowly. "It's me, Eadha."

I knelt down and turned the body over, and a gasp of relief escaped my lungs as Addax groaned. He looked awful, like he had been to the Otherworld and back. His once exquisite face, now bloodied and bruised. He had various stabs and burns on his skin that looked recent. This just happened. His immortal blood was already working to heal him. I looked around and noticed a pot of water in the far corner of the room. I took a deep breath and summoned the stream to curl around my hand. I pressed the water against all of his wounds and slowly healed them.

"E-Eadha?" He croaked out.

I nodded and finished up healing his face. "Aye, what happened, Addax?"

He sat up and groaned. "I knew Farhan wanted a meeting, but I rejected it. I could feel a presence in my forest...I knew you would be able to find my note with the card I left."

I nodded and stared into the palms of my hand. "Addax, have the trees been speaking to ye?"

He nodded. "Now that I know everything, they have no reason to keep secrets from me. I did not say a word of you or your quest, Eadha. I swear on my life."

I snorted. "I did not think ye would. I have a question, though. Ye said ye could hear my thoughts because I was connected to the trees in the same way ye were, correct?"

"Yes. Why?"

"How come ye could hear Corvis's?"

"I-I don't know, actually. I was stunned when I heard yours, and even more shocked when I heard his. Why?"

I shook my head. This was not the time to speak about this. "No reason. Addax, we need to get you out of here."

I went to grab his arm, but he pulled away and looked at me with horrified eyes. "Eadha, wait. I told you not to come looking for me. Did you come here alone?"

The injuries to his head must have healed, seeing as though he just realized I was standing next to him. "Addax, I wasn't going to let ye die here. I brought Corvis with me and-"

"Eadha," he grabbed my shoulders. "I thought this would have been a trap, but my suspicions were confirmed when I heard guards talking outside my cell."

Anxiety pooled in my stomach and I locked eyes with Addax. "Explain."

"Nago captured me, but Farhan did not order him to. There were wraiths in my court hiding in the shadows at Litha. They not only saw you and me together, but you and Corvis. They captured me to get to him. If I spoke of the plan you were hatching, that would only have been a plus for Nago."

I stammered and dug my nails into the palms of my hands. "Why would he want Corvis?"

"Nago isn't like Farhan. He wants power, but he is not willing to sacrifice his court for it. I didn't hear much, just that they were expecting Corvis to come for me."

I nodded and pulled out my Stone. "Alright, well, let's get ye out of here so I can find him."

"No, I'll fight with you. I promised you my allegiance." The fog was just starting to settle in Addax's mind. There was no way I could let him help me.

"Addax, ye got yer skull knocked in. Yer court needs ye back, and Rigel still doesn't know of our agreement," I started to shift the veil but Addax grabbed the Stone from my hand.

"I am helping you, Eadha. That's final. Do you have any silver?"

"Only my dagger. There has to be at least a dozen wraiths out there. Ye won't be able to help me much without a weapon."

"Give me the dagger, I'll fight the wraiths, and you fight the Elites." As I handed my dagger to Addax, a horde of footsteps clattered down the hall to the door.

Before they could turn the key, I grabbed Addax and kicked a hole in the rock under our feet, dropping us onto the floor below. We were surrounded by a flowing river of molten rock with a small sliver of land keeping us from an unpleasant death. "Get moving. Quickly. Get to the other side." I shoved Addax, and he made a break for it.

Sentries started filing in from the hole I created and shuffled their way toward me. "Eadha! I found a door, hurry!" Addax yelled.

I took a deep breath, formed a firm stance, and closed my eyes, waiting for the right moment to strike. Once no more soldiers dropped in, I felt the strength of the mountain build in my arms. With a flick of my wrists, I used my gift from Cré to release the energy and broke off the rock on which they ran before they could reach me. The rock cracked ferociously and crumbled beneath their feet, sending them into the flowing river of flames. Their screams echoed in the distance, but as the ground under me began to shake, I whipped my head forward. I took out the whole wall from which they emerged. A chunk of the mountain was missing.

I did not have time to celebrate our small victory as fissures had begun to form in the walls around us. "Eadha! We have to go! Now!" Addax called.

"Oh, shite..." I muttered. A rock fell and splashed the lava. I yelped and quickly pulled a wall of liquid rock to shield me. I looked at the river carefully, and a thought popped into my head. I shifted my weight and willed the scalding liquid to harden until it was solid. "That's it...I can do this," I whispered.

The floor rumbled violently, and the ceiling cracked. "Eadha!"

"Go!" I yelled at Addax. I threw my hands up and caught the rock before it came crashing down. I screamed as pain tore through my body, and I held the blasted city up with my powers of the earth. My mind threatened to send me back to the day of the invasion when I veilwalked the capital off of the island but fought hard to stand firm. I had to do this. I had to save Corvis.

Addax rushed over to me. "What can I do? Is there anything I can do?"

My arms trembled, sweat dampened my hair, and ran down my face. "Go, so ye don't get crushed. I'll be fine. I can tunnel further down-"

"Eadha, there are innocent lives up there. If this collapses-"

"I know!" I snapped. I looked to the wall I formed with the lava. If I could hold up the floor above me with one arm, I could manipulate the molten rock to create columns and reinforcements on the walls.

I released one of my arms and the rock aggressively shook. "Ah!" I yelped as I quickly caught the slipping ceiling. "I can do this. I can do this," I whispered. I gathered all my strength and focused it on my dominant arm, and with a deep breath, I released the other.

There were few times I have experienced this amount of pain. It felt like my body was being ripped apart by hungry wolves. I was grunting and convulsing, but I was able to catch a current of the liquid as the magic of the Dragons flowed through me. I managed to make four columns before I felt a warmth drip from my nose and a metallic taste stained my tongue. I released the city I was holding together above me and quickly hardened more molten rock to the walls for support. My knees shook, and as I felt the rock stabilize I dropped to the ground.

The screech of wraiths filled my ears and Addax pulled me up, bracing my arm around his neck to get us through the door that I then barricaded shut. He set me down against the wall and took a cloth to my nose, wiping away the blood. "Eadha, that was...miraculous. All of Dife could have come crashing down."

"I think I'm gonna be sick," I mumbled. I closed my eyes, but the darkness behind my lids snapped away the clouds forming in my mind. "Corvis," I whispered. "We have to get to Corvis. I left him in the palace. We have to go."

"Do you need a minute?"

I ignored Addax and placed my hand on the rock behind me. The images were faint as my body was incredibly weak. Corvis and I had been unconsciously hearing each other's thoughts and witnessing memories...even though I did not want to believe it, I had broken free from the wraiths by using shadow magic. I had dreams of him before I knew he walked this earth. I wondered if there was a way I could intentionally connect to him.

I closed my eyes and touched the rock once again, letting images of our time together flow into my head, all of the laughs, the tears, and even aggression. Slowly through the rock, a picture appeared. It was Corvis, bound and kneeling before a woman with her hands on his wings. The sweat on my body began to sizzle and steam as the heat of my rage cascaded over me.

I ignored all of the pain, stood tall, gathered all of the strength I had, and extended my hand to Addax. "Give me yer hand," I ordered. He obliged with a nod. I turned over his palm and swirled my finger above it. "Áine is more powerful than her brother. I could feel it. If we want to break the blood bond between Farhan and this High Lord, we will need her curse-breaking abilities-" I looked at the droplets I had tattooed on my palms and remembered my training with Uisce.

Once I felt Addax's blood responding to my command, a smile brimmed my face as a single drop pooled in his hand. "And my blood magic."

CHAPTER TWENTY-THREE

Corvis

The rumbling stopped almost as soon as it had begun. Nago nodded for sentries to investigate and Rigel took advantage of the break in the tension. "Jada, Nago, Farhan cannot give you the power you seek. Sabriel is going to destroy everything. He is looking to destroy and enslave anyone he can."

No matter how hard I thrashed, my own shadows couldn't free me from the binds. Jada growled, "Seeing how you all are not leaving here alive," she snapped her fingers and the sentries formed a line in front of my companions with their palms ablaze, "surely you can understand the need to protect your people. We were promised power, and we will take the necessary precautions to get it. Besides, the wraiths belong to *our* court."

"And the Ravens belong to *mine*," Rigel snapped.

Jada clicked her tongue. "Good thing he won't be one much longer, although these ghastly things are anything but Raven," she said while stroking my wings.

I tensed every muscle in my body and braced for Jada to break them, but an unsettling feeling stirred in my stomach; we were not alone. Sorlin glanced around the room, slowly reaching for his sword as a strange force brewed in the air. Nago slowly rose from his throne, and Jada moved to his side.

The wraith who held me in place quivered and

retreated back. Its shadows that held me vanished. I went to run away, but I couldn't move. I looked around the room and noticed everyone was struggling to move their legs.

"What is the meaning of this?" Jada asked coldly.

A disturbing feeling spread deep through my bones. It felt as if ropes were slithering under my skin and taking control of me like some sort of puppet. "Rigel?" My voice broke as I saw the same look of horror on his face. Our knees buckled, and our hands slapped the ground, but the Eotians remained standing.

"Sabriel?" Nago asked in a voice just above a whisper as he and Jada struggled to move. My body went stiff, but the comforting scent of a rainy cedar forest filled my nose. Addax and Eadha appeared at the foot of the thrones. Her frosty braids were crazy on top of her head like a furious snowstorm and drenched in sweat.

"Oh, much worse, laddie." As she moved her right hand and flicked her palm open, Jada and Nago were forced into their seats. Her left hand was in a tense claw to her side. I wanted to be relieved to see her but the wrathful look on her face incited a deep fear within me. It was the look of a true savage warrior, the face of a Laoch.

"You insolent, sniveling-"

Eadha cut Nago off with a vicious smile. "Shut yer gob and give me the stone of Arawn before I snap yer neck." Her voice was hoarse and vengeful.

Nago struggled to move his arms as his hands began to glow with heat. Eadha rolled her eyes and slowly moved her fingers into a fist. Nago began to sputter and his eyes grew large.

"Guards! How dare you just stand there, kill her!"

Jada cried.

One guard awkwardly hobbled up, yelping and questioning how his feet were moving. "Here ye go, lassie, here is yer guard," Eadha moved her hand in a swift motion, and blood flew from his body through his skin, dropping him to the ground white as death itself, gurgling. Jada screamed as Eadha sprayed the room with blood. I looked away and gagged. I have seen horrors, I have inflicted devastating mutilations through interrogation, but this was a sight I would not be able to unsee.

"That is how easy it is for me to kill ye if you don't do as I say. I don't even need to look at ye."

When I first sparred with Eadha, I knew she was holding back. I could feel the force she truly was, but I never expected this. The ferocity of a Laoch combined with the magic of a High Druid bred the most terrifying thing I have ever laid my eyes on. Sorlin and Rigel were not holding up well to the gruesome scene before them. Neither was Áine. Addax pulled out Eadha's silver dagger as wraiths appeared.

"Call them off," Eadha commanded.

"L-leave us," Nago choked out. Eadha released her hold on his neck and he coughed, gasping for air. "W-what do you want?"

"Many, many things. Ye want power? I got power. I have the power to send yer whole city the pits of the Otherworld. Ye are going to give me the stone of Arawn, and pledge yerselves to me, and the Court of the Moon."

"We are bound to Fossera and therefore bound to Sabriel. We never agreed to aid him. Farhan tricked us. He said Sabriel merely wanted a meeting to speak about breaking the Circle, but when we went to his island, he told us his plans. We are scared. We don't want our people to die!" Jada pleaded.

"I don't really care. Ye'll give me the stone, then Áine and I will break yer bond and bind ye to us. Or, ye can die."

Jada nodded. "It's in our treasure hold."

Eadha released a guard, and Addax held the knife to his throat. "Take me to it. Try anything funny and, well, I think you can guess where that will leave you," he said as he motioned to the blood-spattered walls and marched the guard out.

Sorlin looked as if he could pass out at any moment and all I could do was stare at Eadha. "Áine, come here," Áine was released and walked apprehensively to Eadha's side. "Get ready to break the bond," Eadha said to her, and Áine nodded.

Eadha moved both of her hands to the front of her, Nago and Jada matched her movements, and blood seeped from their palms. Áine shuddered and slowly began chipping away at the bond.

Eadha's nose began to bleed, and her knees shook. She looked completely drained. She took out two vials from her pocket and collected a few drops from the Ruling Fae. "Charm it. If they break the bond, they die."

The vials turned to gold in Áine's hands, and Nago and Jada presented two relatively small yarn dolls that resembled them and handed them to Eadha. "Farhan will see these disappear from his keep since the bond broke. He will come for us," Nago explained.

As Eadha took the dolls, the pressure released from my body and I fell forward. "We will deal with Farhan next. He won't hurt ye."

"Who *are* you?"

"The keeper of yer souls. This will be released

once we no longer see ye as a threat. I suggest ye do yer due diligence and prove that to us sooner rather than later."

Addax came jogging into the room, holding a black and gold stone. "I got it," he said as he tossed it to Eadha.

"Right then, we'll be off. I'll see Addax home. Any lesser Fae that ye have locked in those prisons will be released on his word. I hope that is clear."

Jada and Nago exchanged a glance and nodded. Eadha struggled to open the veil and her knees buckled. I went to her, but Addax caught her in his arms and helped her through the veil. I watched him like a hawk until it closed.

Rigel brushed a hand through his hair and rushed to me. Now that whatever hold Eadha had me under was gone, the pain of my broken bones was blinding. "Are you alright Corvis?"

"Yes, you?"

"I will be," he turned and punched Nago in the jaw, sending him back into the throne. "Better now."

His silver eyes glowed, and a purple mist sprang from his hands, circling Jada and Nago. They shuddered as they surrendered to whatever nightmare Rigel was inflicting. "You will pay for what you did. Eadha might see this as finished, but not me. I extended you an olive branch. We could have helped you without any of this happening. You could have told us Farhan tricked you, and we would have listened. Now, your life is in the hands of that manic psychopath. Congratulations. Let's get out of here, everyone."

He released the Ruling Fae and opened the veil, grabbing Áine. I went over to Sorlin. "Are you okay?" He asked me.

I grabbed his arm. "As Rigel said: I will be."

As we entered the war camp, my friends surrounded me, asking me about my well-being, but the weight of the day collapsed onto my shoulders, and I stared at Áine as she healed my bones. "How long did you know?" I asked her.

Sorlin furrowed his brows and looked around at us. Áine's throat bobbed and she sighed. "I-I knew once I saw you two in the same room together, you share an energy between you. I told Rigel-"

"But not me."

"Corvis-" she started.

"Do you have any idea what I have been going through because of this? I have my own battles to conquer, Áine. Did you really think throwing someone else's into the mix was good for me?" My voice rose slightly, and Rigel clenched his jaw.

"Áine didn't tell me until we found Eadha in the woods, Corv. We didn't 'throw' anything onto you. Eadha came to help us, we all wanted it, and she has done a lot. Áine only had suspicions until she was sure of it."

Sorlin cleared his throat. "What are we talking about here? Can I have a turn? We are all being incredibly calm for having the entirety of a man's blood all over us, that was pulled right out from his skin, I'll have you know. And why was Antlers there?"

I gave Sorlin a grave look, and he threw his arms in the air and shut up. "So that's it then. She is my Anam Cara?"

Áine shrugged. "It's not what you think. It just means you two are eternally connected. You two can hate each other or be great friends, but in the end, the connection is there for a reason. It helps you in ways you can't even imagine. It is such a rare, beautiful thing."

"Break it," I said sternly. Rigel pulled Sorlin away to give us privacy.

"I can't. It is an ancient bond. Druid legend says the gods picked it for a reason, and I think-" Áine said with sad eyes.

"Áine, having this almost got me *killed* today," I slowed my breathing. "If you can't break it, how do I stop it?"

She sighed and put a hand on my shoulder. "Corvis, you heard Nago and Jada, half-wraiths die by the time they are teenagers. I think...I think you are alive because you share a part of Eadha."

I froze and stared intently into Áine's honey eyes. I pondered for a moment before realizing I have never seen any half-wraiths before. If Áine somehow managed to break the bond, would I cease to exist? If Eadha dies, would I die as well?

"I see that look in your eye Corvis. No, I don't think if Eadha dies, you would too. However, if I broke the bond, if I somehow found a way to, yes, I think you would. You see, Eadha said that even if your other half perishes, their soul still lives on within you. It's why the pain can be unbearable when you lose them. I can see why you wouldn't want this, you have been through so much, but just try to see the positives."

I could name so many reasons why I didn't

want this cursed bond, but the biggest reason wasn't even about me. I couldn't put Eadha through any more pain than she has already experienced in her life. I would hate myself for it until the day I died if I hurt her or burdened her with my troubles.

Every day I feel our energies growing closer and closer, so I needed to learn more about this, but the only way to do that was to speak with Eadha, and that was out of the question. Áine said I could hate her, and the connection would still be there, and as the days carried on, I realized that I hate is the farthest thing I could feel for her, no matter how hard I tried.

The veil shifted, and as I turned around, Eadha fell into me and wrapped her arms around my neck. The destructive woman, as forceful as the moon itself, now could barely lift her head up to meet my gaze. "Are, are ye alright?"

Relief washed over me and I nodded, placing a hand on the back of her head and holding her tighter than I intended to. "Because of you, yes. What about you?" She went limp as her legs gave out, and I caught her, scooping her up into my arms. "Eadha?"

Áine placed a warm, glowing hand on her back. "Gods, it feels like she got ripped apart on the inside. She'll be fine, just needs a lot of rest and a healing session or two. Take her to the palace, we are finishing up here anyways. I'll meet you there."

I tore open the veil and Vela was waiting in the parlor. "Goddess above, what happened to her?" She asked as she jumped out of her chair.

"Long story, we are all fine. Eotia was a trap.

They took Addax, but we got him back."

"Addax? What did they want with Addax? Is our feud over now?" She asked as she crossed her arms.

"Eadha can explain everything once she is well. The others should be back shortly." I dismissed her and started up the stairs, and she relented her questioning once Áine, Rigel, and Sorlin took her attention away from me.

I laid Eadha onto her bed and pulled a chair next to her. She groaned and opened her eyes, meeting my gaze. She didn't speak, only looked at me in a way she never has before. The waves painted into the portrait of her eyes softly brushed against the rock, and clouds steadily drifted past the burning sun. She looked at me as if she saw me for the first time.

"Well, that'll show them, won't it?" She asked with a laugh.

I let out a weak huff of air. "A little overkill, don't you think?"

She shook her head and narrowed her gaze. "No. Not for what they were going to do to ye,"

"I am in your debt, Eadha."

She smiled and shut her eyes. "As I have said, ye owe me nothing, Corvis."

I clenched my jaw and just stared as her chest rose and fell with heavy, sleep-filled breaths. Whatever the gods had planned with this connection, it was rather cruel. For the first time in my life, I was able to be myself around something more than the walls of my room, and it was incredibly liberating. Eadha made me feel a warmth I never thought I would feel. She protected me viciously today and endangered herself and her people doing so. No matter how many times she says I owe her nothing, it was a lie. I, quite literally, owed her my life. My eyes met her face, and I studied every swirl of blue marked on it.

When I looked at Eadha, I saw unbridled courage. I saw a sincerity as pure as the water from a fresh spring and a passion that burned hotter than the sun. I looked at her and saw the thorn of a rose, protecting the dainty petals from those that sought to pluck it from the ground. She was the lightning that blazed the sky in a storm, the unrestrained gale that pushed the waves of the oceans higher than mountains, her own force of gravity...yet I looked at her, and saw the drop of first morning dew that crested a blade of grass, and the soft leaves of a tree gently dancing in the breeze. I looked at her, and saw the unmatched beauty of the stars painting a night sky.

I did not want to love Eadha but I was pulled in like the tide from the moment I saw her. I could not give her something I knew nothing of, something I didn't even have for myself. She deserved the world, and I could only give her a pebble.

CHAPTER TWENTY-FOUR

Eadha

I kept my eyes closed long after slumber fled my body. It was the first moment of peace I had in a while to mull over all that has happened in the time I have spent away from home, but most importantly, what was happening between Corvis and me. My eyes opened, and I stared at the palm of my hand, trying to will the shadows I used in Eotia to appear, but nothing happened.

I pinched my eyes shut and rubbed them harder than I intended while swearing under my breath. There were a few explanations as to what was happening. The veil had a strange way of connecting those that were able to walk past it, or the magic of these lands could be pulling us together to save it, but our connection was deeper than that. I could ignore it all I wanted, but he lit up for me like a beacon in the darkness when my powers were too weak to see through the rock. I used his magic; I shared his dreams.

We had two weeks before we faced Farhan in Fossera, and stealing a stone from my parents now seemed to be the lesser of the two trials. I needed to go home for many reasons: I needed the stone, I needed to see my friends, but most importantly, I needed to speak to my mother about what was happening to me. I felt like I knew the reason for these strange occurrences, but I did not want to believe it or accept it. Also, as much as

I hated it, I needed to collect Séamus to help me steal the stone from Farhan and infiltrate Kamber Island. The thought of Séamus coming with sent a nauseated feeling through my stomach, but with him back on the land of the gods, his connection to his goddess would be reformed and we would be unstoppable.

That's what I needed to focus on, my original mission, the reason why I was here. Connection or no connection, I did not come here for Corvis. I needed to bring my people home and stop Sabriel. I turned in bed and nearly jumped out of my skin when I saw Corvis sleeping like the dead in a chair beside my bed.

I picked up a pillow and chucked it at his head. "Get up, ya lug."

He jumped and looked wildly around the room. "Eadha. How are you feeling?"

I shrugged. "Fine. I'm leaving, I need to go back to my island. I need my parents' stone, and I need to get someone to help take the island."

I swung out of bed and started packing, but Corvis was quickly on my heels. "I thought we were going to take care of Verbenia before getting your parents' trove?"

I chuckled sarcastically. "*We* weren't to be doing anything. This is *my* mission. Yer simply helping me."

The look in his burning eyes showed that comment hurt him, and I regretted saying it the second it left my mouth. He clenched his jaw and nodded. "Well, don't let me stop you."

My hand reached out and grabbed his arm on its own accord as a thought entered my head. He stiffened but did not look back at me. If I were to ask my mother what was happening to me, to us, she would have to read him too. He would have to come with me. "I'm sorry. I didn't mean it like that."

He pulled his hand away. "No, you did. And that is okay. I know you don't want to be here, Eadha, you don't need to apologize for your feelings."

The truth was I did enjoy being there. I have made friends, but I was beginning to get distracted by them. As soon as this was done, I would only see them at festivals and communicate through letters. "I didn't at first, yes, but that is not why I am leaving. I need to go get my friend Séamus. He can help us in Fossera."

Corvis nodded, and his wings flexed as he relaxed. "I wish you luck. How long will you be away?"

"Come with me," I blurted out faster than I wanted to. I could not think of a more convincing way to ask him other than coming right out with it.

He turned to me and pinched his eyebrows together. "I have a job here. I can't just travel to distant places as I please. My lands have already been threatened."

"It will only be a day or two, I promise. My parents do not know I am doing this. I will have to steal their stone, and I will need help." It was not a complete lie, though it was far from the truth.

He took a few moments to think about it and let out a long sigh as he motioned for me to lead the way. I pulled out my Druid Stone and tried to find my home, but I was still weak from the amount of magic I used yesterday. It was not as simple to just veilwalk there. I had to feel the connection and be pulled by it. I focused and began to feel the magic of my parents wrapping around me like a warm blanket. Because I was so weak, concentration was key; I could not take my eyes off the

Stone.

I grabbed Corvis's hand and smiled. Never in my life did I think I would be happy to go to that island. "Yer about to be the first outside in fifty thousand years."

He looked nervous. His shadows were stationary and held close to his body. The veil had opened, but I was so focused I did not know someone entered my room until I saw Sorlin clamp his hand down on Corvis's shoulder.

"Not so fast you two. Listen, I'm not going to be angry, but my blade sharpener is missing, and the last time any of you two were in my room-"

"Sorlin, let go!" I yelled at him, but it was too late. If I broke away, there was a good chance I would not be able to open the path back home. The magic encased us, and we plunged through the veil. Sorlin was hollering. His long black locks were whipping his face as he held on to Corvis for dear life. I was going to kill him, I have threatened him with it before, but I was serious this time. I navigated my way, feeling the pull of my people, and felt my feet touch down onto cobblestone.

Corvis merely looked windblown, but Sorlin was a bit green as he held onto his brother's shoulders. His amber yellow eyes were wide as he looked around, and his coily hair stood up around his head. My lip curled, and I suppressed my burning rage as I pulled him by the collar of his shirt to meet my face.

"Ya raging eejit! Are ye mental?"

"Where the-what in the goddess above happened?" He stammered as he looked around and tamed his hair. I groaned and pushed him away, taking in where exactly we were. I looked around and saw the old weathered sign of the tavern my friends and I spent most of our free time in. Druids and plainsfolk all stopped and gawked at the two winged men, and a few Laoch started reaching for their weapons until they saw me.

"Mother, what is that?" A small child stopped and pointed. I waved to her mother and smiled as my cheeks heated red. Surely someone was already off to tell the Tiarna their daughter came strolling back in with two brutish strangers.

I pulled the two men and pushed them through the doors. "Get yer hides inside, now," I seethed. Glasses were flying and fights were going on in every corner, but the yelling, screaming and singing all stopped as we walked through the doors.

"Well, where are they then?" I called out. Everyone stared at me and looked at the two men I was with. Corvis was tense, his shadows jerking, Sorlin's fingers twitched over his sword.

"Eadha!" A familiar voice yelled out. Donnan came running and nearly knocked me over as he embraced me in a tight hug, pressing my face into his chest. I wanted to push him off, but I did not see him before I left in June as he was recovering from injuries. I hugged him back and clutched his dark shaggy locks.

"I am so glad yer back, Lana's tried to kill me. She's tied me up and thrown me in a river, dragged me from her horse down a stone road and- what the gods are ye lookin' at, eh Birdman?" He sized up Sorlin and spun a knife into his hand.

I pushed him off and smacked him. "Donnan, don't be a pox. Where are the rest of them? Curse ye Donnan, stop staring at them!" I pulled his face to meet mine, but his eyes did not leave the men for a second.

"I don't like the Birdman, Eadha. Or the other one with the...black things around him."

I groaned and pinched my nose as the familiar 'twin headache' had begun to spread across my head. "Donnan!" I snapped.

"Oh, they're at the northern barracks. Will ye at least tell me why we have Birdmen here?" He asked. Sorlin was about to make a remark, but with a room full of Laoch and Druids, it was in his best interest to stay quiet. Sorlin was big, but Donnan was thin and the fastest thing I had ever seen. It was a fight I would pay to see, but not here.

"Tell them to meet me at the palace in my room," I pulled Corvis and Sorlin to me and soared through the veil.

"Who was the pipsqueak, and when do I get to kill him?" Sorlin grumbled.

I laughed. "Oh, by all means, go right ahead. The twins don't die. Trust me, we have been trying for years. *You*," I pushed his chest, "Get no say and are not allowed to touch anything. Ye shouldn't even be here."

"Well, stop stealing my things, and maybe I *wouldn't* have to be here."

I looked to Corvis, who quickly stifled his small chuckle and avoided eye contact with me as he blushed. I think it was the first time I have ever seen him do such a thing.

"Who're the birds?" Dolan announced as Lana pushed him out of the veil.

Donnan put his arm around his twin's shoulders as he pointed to them. "That, Dolan, is Birdman and his brother Scary-Shadowman."

Sorlin curled his lip and lunged, but I stuck my

arm out in front of him. "*They* are Sorlin and Corvis. They have full permission to beat ye to dirt if ye piss them off."

"I like yer wings," Lana said as she circled Corvis. He clenched his jaw and nodded.

Séamus stepped out from the veil and before his feet hit the ground, I leaped into his arms and wrapped my legs around his waist, burying my face into his fiery curled locks. I could not contain how happy I was to see my best friend.

I fought the tears pooling in my eyes as he stroked my back and whispered, "Ye made it back."

I nodded and slid back down to the floor. "Aye, for now. I came to steal ye back with me. We only need two more stones, the Tiarna's and the stone from Fossera." I turned to my friends. "I'm here now, and if things do not go right when I speak to my parents, then option two is to send in the twins for a distraction. Will ye come back with me, Séamus?"

He lingered for a moment before giving me a soft smile and a nod. I patted him on the arm. "Séamus, Lana, take them to the Druid spies. Donnan, Dolan, piss off." I shut the door behind me as I made my way to my parents.

I did not know how I was going to speak with them about this. I did not want to lie or steal from them, but I was going against all plans they had set in place for the invasion. My stomach knotted up and I bit my fingers as I entered the throne room.

I sighed with a bit of relief. They were not there. I took in the room for a moment and smiled as my eyes fell on the enchanted mural behind the thrones. It grew and changed as we did and was as alive as the world around it. The image of my brother never changed though, never aged, and stayed as still as death. I placed my hand on his chest, and a tear dropped down my cheek. We were so close to going home. He would finally be at peace in the tomb of my family and have a proper burial. My people's pain would end, and we would be powerful once again. I looked at the painting of myself; the image stopped smiling many years ago. I made a silent promise to the girl staring back at me that I would make her smile again. I would find the inner child that has long been lost and bring her home.

I furrowed my brow and noticed that behind the thrones, there was one too many candles lit. There were only supposed be eternal flames lit for each member of my family and our forefathers. I tried to use my fire magic to extinguish the new flame, but it stood tall. I pinched it between my fingers, and it persisted in burning. "Hm," I snorted.

"You're back, and you brought outsiders," my father's cold voice made me jump as I turned to face him. My parents were as radiant as ever in their deep green and gold robes. My stomach flipped as my mother smiled and held her arms out to me. I missed her.

I gave her a quick embrace and faced my father. I had not seen him since our fight before I left, but I wasn't mad at him. I actually missed his scoldings. "Aye. I could sit here and lie to ye about why I came back but-"

"You have been collecting the stones of Arawn's cauldron and have come for this?" He held out a gleaming gold stone and smirked at me. "I may not have as much magic as I used to, dear daughter, but I speak to my patron every day. He is not happy." I caught the stone as he chucked it at me and could not find any words to speak.

"I am sorry to inform you that you will not be able to handle the power of the cauldron without being burned alive by its raw power," he continued.

"This is no time for me to be punished by a petty god, father. Tell him I am doing what needs to be done to stop Sabriel," I said flatly. If I died destroying the Well, I would see that as a win for me. It did not matter so long as Sabriel was stopped.

My mother placed a hand on my shoulder and looked at me with sad eyes. "Eadha, the cauldron will kill you before you even conjured enough magic to destroy the Well. It's not that Arawn is punishing you. He is angry because he does not want to see you dead. It is not your time yet."

I laughed. "Mother, I am long past my 'time'. What do I need to do to accomplish this?"

My parents exchanged a look and motioned for me to sit. "The only people strong enough to wield the full magic of the gods, are the Tiarna. Druids go into working relationships with the gods, yes, and get a mere fraction of the power from it. We are not powerful enough to use that cauldron because of how much magic we use to keep our lands hidden." My mother said gravely.

I shook my head. "Well, I have those I work with already. I cannot be Tiarna. The god and goddess never wanted me to be, they wanted Tadhg."

"They wanted Tadhg because they needed a powerful Druid to work with them when it was our time to cross over," my father stated. "They never wanted him to be Tiarna. They are the most powerful of the gods, yes, but there are older and more formidable beings that walked this earth even before them."

My heart began to race, and I bit my lip. "What are ye saying, the Dragons? I have worked with them for centuries and never once heard the word 'Tiarna' leave their mouths."

"Because you do not work with all of them. The Tiarna is simply the most powerful Druid entrusted to protect their people. With the power of the Dragons, that will be you. The journey of the Tiarna is one they must take alone. We could not help you find your way," my mother explained, "But one of you masters has already given you enough information that you need."

"Yer saying there *is* a fifth Dragon? I thought Arawn and Macha selected the Tiarna themselves..." I raked my mind and replayed every conversation I have had with the Dragons in the last decade and found nothing. The only time they spoke to me recently was when Tine told me they were leaving me before the war. He told me...*his* master was calling them away.

"Tine told me, if I chose to stay on this course, I would find help in the deepest chasm between our world and the next. Is that where this fifth Dragon dwells? Where is that?" There was no way I would be able to find this Dragon and retrieve the last stone before Mabon. Even if I did find the beast, I would not take the title Tiarna.

"Eadha, please do not stay this course. I have had visions after every stone you stole, and all I saw was death, ruin, and war. There is no stopping Sabriel from opening the Well. I see no path in which it is avoided. Find this Dragon, take the throne, and then lead our people in battle like you are meant to. *That* is your destiny." My father looked at me intensely but I detected fear in his voice. Fear from the thought of losing his last child.

"Then why give me this?" I held up the stone. "If yer telling me, I can't use the cauldron, why give this to me?"

He clenched his jaw. "In case you need it. You are an adult and the soon to be leader of your people. You are free to make your own decisions," he grabbed my arm and raised his hand over the torc I wore on my left wrist. It moved and shifted, bending into a new shape, the shape of a coiled dragon. On its back were six stones: one that represented each Dragon and my father's Druid Stone now embedded into the white gold, the middle bed was empty as it would soon hold the stone of the Tiarna that I only could assume would be given to me by the fifth Dragon.

"No, I don't want this. This isn't mine," I stammered.

My mother crouched down and put her hands on my knees. "You need to do what is best for your people. We knew the second you were born, you would be our heir. We needed you to find your own path to it." She took off her necklace that was secured tightly around her neck that signified her status and tied it around mine: a simple blue sash with the talisman of the Tiarna. "Please, do not cut your path short trying to destroy that Well before you have everything you need."

I stood and turned to the painting, now with my head bearing the family crown. I tried to stifle my panic and the fear in my eyes as I faced my parents, who were beaming. This was not supposed to happen. I did not come here for this. The room started spinning as fear raced through my heart. Everything was happening so fast I had no time to breathe or process what was happening. I could not do this. My brother was to be standing here and accepting this title.

My father smiled and bowed his head. "Once you find your fifth master, and perhaps once this war is over, there will be a more formal celebration. Tiarna, Eadha, The Savage Queen. Become the leader of our people, and bring us to victory."

CHAPTER TWENTY-FIVE
Eadha

I did not know whether to cry, scream, or run as my parents stared at me. I knew what needed to be done. I knew one day there would be a new Tiarna, and it would either be me or someone from the council. I said I would do anything to bring my people home and if this is what it took to accomplish that, then fine. What was most important right now was taking the island and finding a way to do it. I did not have time to go searching the depths of the earth for a Dragon. I had the power of Séamus and my new Fae allies. There would be enough power on that island to run the world, and I just knew we could manage it.

My mother placed a hand on my shoulder and crouched beside me as my father left us. "I am sorry we never told you, Eadha. Your father was the successor of his mother and had two brothers. He was the youngest and discovered right away he would be the Tiarna. When we married, I found my path to the title on my own, much as you have. I did not have any living family, and the goddess did not call on me at first."

I shook my head. "I do not wish to speak on this anymore."

"What else troubles your mind, child?" She asked.

"Is father yer Anam Cara?" The words came out of me quicker than the water from a broken dam. I had my speculations of the connection I had to Corvis, but once I saw that shadowy hand reaching for me, my heart had dropped, and it was almost as if I knew but did not want to admit it to myself. I prayed to the goddesses above to spare me of it and let this connection simply be a tie in the veil, but I was not naive.

"No, he is not. I simply just love him. We have a bond, but nothing more magical than ordinary love," she paused and looked at the painting behind me. "Do you have suspicions that you have found yours?"

My head shot up, and I glared at her. "What do ye mean 'found' mine?"

"If you are asking me if I have one, should I not assume you do as well? You never speak of such things. Is it Séamus?"

I burst out in a bit of a laughing fit as I took in her question. "Mother, I don't even know if Séamus has ever taken a lover in his lifetime. He is my closest companion, not someone who shares my soul...I love Séamus, I am not *in* love with him."

"You do not need to love your Anam Cara. They could be anyone from a family member to a stranger. You exist to help each other in times of great need. In fact, you could even hate them. Lana's mother has this bond with a Laoch, and they truly detested each other. But, in times of great battle, she was there to heal him, and he was there to protect her. I do not remember his name, but he fell during the invasion, and it pained her deeply. It is a bond that exists in every race and every realm."

Her words brought me no comfort. I needed to leave. I needed to run away and never look back. My worst nightmare was coming true. The title I loathed was slowly becoming mine, and now I have yet another person in my life that could burn when my flames ran too hot, or weep when they extinguished.

I could ignore this bond, I have done it in the past, but it never relented. Maybe I was in denial, maybe I thought I did not deserve such a thing in my life, but either way, this was too trivial to think about in times of possible war. Once Sabriel was taken care of, I would be leaving the Fae lands for good. The nature of the connection I had to Corvis would not matter once this was done.

"I need to be off. I have outsiders waiting for me."

When I stood, my mother grabbed my arm and pulled me into a tight embrace. "Your father will never say it, but he is so terrified to lose you. It comes off as anger and apathy, but it is only anger for having to worry so much for his last living child. Eadha, no matter what path you chose to take with this invasion, I need you to promise me you will do whatever it takes to stop Sabriel. Your father saw who he intends to release. If he wins, the world will burn, and no amount of our magic can hide us from Balor of the Baleful eye."

I stiffened and pulled away from her. Her piercing blue eyes held a melancholic passion that pierced my heart. "I give ye my word, Tiarna, that I will stop him. Balor will not see the light of day."

She touched her now bare neck. "That is a title I no longer answer to."

I was walking rather leisurely to my room until the sound of shouting and broken glass resonated in the halls. "Shite," I groaned as I quickened my pace with an eye roll.

I opened my door to find Donnan in a headlock given by Corvis, and Sorlin had his hands around Dolan's throat as Séamus attempted to restrain him with a rather amused smile on his face. Lana was lazily flipping the pages of a book, unbothered by the commotion in the room. I slammed the door shut, and the men halted their beatings to look up at me. Corvis and Sorlin dropped the twins and readjusted their raven black locks.

Séamus pushed past Sorlin with wide eyes, and his mouth dropped. "Y-ye've been crowned?"

The twins froze, and Lana shut her book abruptly before the three scrambled to Séamus's side. "No, I am not, nor will I ever be. I am refusing the title as planned."

"Yer wearing yer mother's necklace and have a different torc. What do ye mean ye aren't the Tiarna?" Dolan asked.

I held up my wrist. "Missing a stone. I have to find it before being crowned, which I will *not* be doing. This is not a title I was meant to bear. Go do whatever ye like. I got the stone of Arawn from my parents, but I need to spend a few moments to myself. Do not leave the palace grounds, and if I hear *any* fighting, I'll kill ye all myself."

My friends exchanged glances and bowed their heads in respect to me for the first time. My stomach churned, and I clenched my jaw. There was no need for it, I was not the Tiarna, not officially. Although, wearing these new pieces said otherwise.

As they shuffled out the room, Sorlin muttered, "Ruler or not, I want my blade sharpener back."

Corvis paused and bowed his head, his ember eyes never leaving mine before exiting the room. My cheeks stung, and I shut my door behind him. The air was thick with an imminent storm. I clutched my torc and stared at my father's Druid Stone, now shrunken and placed on the back of the white gold Dragon. It felt alive as it gazed up at me with contempt as if it knew it did not belong on my wrist. I concentrated, and it produced its radiant glow, promptly opening the veil, sending me right to the courtyard and onto my back as I waited for the rain.

I broke. My chest heaved as my breathing quickened. I needed a plan, and for the first time in many years, I had no idea how to move forward. If I spent time looking for this Dragon as my father wished, Sabriel could unleash Balor, and we would not be prepared for the ruin to come. If I went to the island before acquiring the magic of the Tiarna, I could perish and take my friends down with me. I was lied to my whole life. My parents knew I was stronger than Tadhg, yet let me believe it was him to be crowned. Did my twin know about this?

I recalled my lessons as a child and remembered learning the history of the Tiarna. My father's blood and his ancestors held the title simply because they were strong magical conduits. It was never the gods that chose the Tiarna. They were just the only beings the High Druids worked with. The Dragons helped create this world, birthed from starlight itself, and still walked the earth. Who could the fifth Dragon be? Tine said she was their master, but there were only four elements.

Rain softly pelted my body as the clouds rolled in high in the sky. I closed my eyes and let something, any image, come to my mind. I waited and waited, then the intrusive image of Corvis graced my thoughts, reminding me of yet another problem I had. I still did not know if my suspicions were correct, but if they were, it was a problem. This battle very well could be my last, and he did not deserve to live with that burden. Corvis still smiled and was still grateful he drew breath in the morning. He lost his wings yet still flew. I was imprisoned to the ground for most of my life until he taught me to trust the winds again. I wanted Corvis to be happy. I wanted him to see how he was everything he said he was not.

The sound of leather sliding against concrete made me aware that I was not alone. I did not have to look up to know it was Séamus. He laid down beside me and raised an eyebrow. "Those men ye brought have quite a spirit in them."

I chuckled. "Ye have no idea."

"Eadha, I know what must be going through yer mind right now, but I need ye to know that ye deserve this. Ye unified our people for the first time in history, and ye would give yer last dying breath for them."

I nodded. He was not wrong, and I knew that. I would not trust anyone other than my family to guard and protect our people. I turned on my side and placed an arm around Séamus's chest. "I don't know what to do, Séamus."

He sighed. "Start by letting yerself be loved by everyone around ye and go from there. We all need to learn how to do that."

A sadness fell over me. It was so easy for me to get caught up in my emotions, not realizing my closest friends lost their home as well and even lost a great deal of magic. "I'm sorry, Séamus. I'm sorry for thinking I had to go through this myself all of these years. If I had opened up more and not pushed ye away-"

"We are fine, Eadha. Everyone heals at their own pace and there is no shame in it. Yer a great leader, and we happily follow ye. Now, what else is troubling ye? I know it can't only be the title."

"Something I need to figure out on my own. Where are Sorlin and Corvis?"

"Lana took the lot of them to the northern barracks. The big one wanted to spar before heading back," he turned to the sky and smiled. "A wild one he is. The other reminds me of ye. Yer both so reserved but will jump into a fight like a feral animal at a moment's notice. Is there a reason he looks different than, what was his name, Sorlin? They mentioned they were brothers."

I stood with a grunt and helped Séamus to his feet. "Corvis is half wraith, and he lost his wings a decade or so back."

Séamus chuckled. "Maybe ye have more in common than I thought. Shall we?" I grabbed his outstretched hand and walked us leisurely through the veil. I told him all of the gear he would have to pack and told him all about Tenebris and the new friends I found there. He was apprehensive in joining, as he should have been considering the history we had with the court, but ultimately accepted the position to accompany us to Kamber Island.

"I will say one thing," he said as we entered the ring to join the others. "I will not be leaving ye on that island ever again. If we fail, we fail together." I nodded and yet again lied to my friend. He deserved the best life he could live, all of my companions did, even if that meant without me. We will not be failing this time. We were ready, or at least I was.

Corvis and Sorlin were watching a three-way fight between Lana, Donnan, and Dolan. "Alright, yer with me," Séamus pointed to Sorlin. He nodded with a smile and drew his sword. If Sorlin had a hard time beating me, I could not wait to see him face Séamus. It was quite amusing to see the two next to each other. Sorlin's golden dark skin made Séamus look as pale as a ghost. I was right when I thought Séamus was taller than Sorlin, but not by much.

"What about ye?" I asked Corvis.

He shook his head. "I don't think I want to fight right now."

"Me neither." I stood next to him and silence and watched my friends were all laughing and beating each other raw. Séamus was gleaming as he fell into a waltz of fury and blades with Sorlin. His damp hair turned to a tarnished orange mop of soft curls like waves of autumn wheat blowing in the wind. He looked so healthy and almost happy that it made my heart smile. I looked over all of his markings as I reflected on how far he had come. Séamus had few blue tattoos, but they were large, much like him. The bear on his torso flexed, and his muscles glistened in the rain as he beat Sorlin.

In the time that I was gone, he had become so much more elegant in his fighting and quicker on his feet. He must have assumed I would not be coming back and trained twice as hard in case he became the general. Either way, I was proud.

Lana looked more fierce than ever and has gained more muscle than I had ever seen her with. She turned her fragile body that she let wither away during the autumn months, into a solid force not to be trifled with. The twins, as carefree as ever, had trouble keeping up with her. My friends were out for blood, and they could take on any force with ease and grace.

The rain was still beating down and I looked to Corvis. I was always amazed at how perfectly content he looked at all times. I have seen his dreams and heard his insecurities, but through all of that, he could still stand to show me all of the places within his lands that brought a smile to his face of stone. He remained loyal to Áine after what the Fosserans did to him, and that was a loyalty I did not think I could ever give to the Fae, even when they have shown me nothing but kindness.

But above all else, I found solace in the very darkness I had been running from. His shadows have haunted my dreams for centuries. He looked down at me with his eyes the color of hot coals and cleared his throat. "After we stop Sabriel, are you planning an attack on the island?"

I nodded. "I will have the twins and Lana at the ready once we destroy the Well. Séamus works with Badbh. When he steps foot on those lands, he will be unstoppable."

Corvis looked at me for a moment and chuckled. "*Badbh Catha*," he said proudly.

I was taken back. My eyebrows rose high enough to touch my hairline. "What do ye know of the Battle Crow?"

He took off an old pendant he wore around his neck with the image of a woman and raven carved into it. I bit my lip and looked up at him. He pulled his loosely fitted shirt down to expose the red raven tattooed on his muscular chest. "The Vespairans believe we are descendant from her. We pray to her and honor her in battle. I told you we weren't Fae," he smiled and gave me a small wink.

I clenched my jaw and worried what other things he knew about Druid culture. If he already knew about the bond, I would want to know, but I did not want to risk asking him about it if he did not.

I let out a piercing whistle, and everyone paused. "Say yer goodbyes to Séamus. Lana, be ready to walk through the veil at a moment's notice when we call on ye three to join us at the island. Bring as many Laoch as ye can muster. Since Séamus and I will be gone, yer the acting general." Lana tensed her body but slowly nodded. It was a weight I knew she could handle.

Séamus made his teary goodbyes and held onto Sorlin as I opened the veil for the four of us. I looked back to Lana and the twins and gave them a pained smile as we made our way back to Tenebris.

"Just know that whatever Eadha said about us is a lie. Stick with me, and you'll be fine," Sorlin said as he pushed the door to the palace open.

Corvis and I burst out laughing. "Stick with him if you want to end up with a bloody nose from Eadha is what he means to say," Corvis exclaimed.

I quickly untied my necklace and hid my torc in my pocket. I did not need Vela to see that I carried the necklace of the Tiarna, I did not need her questions. It was hard to miss. It was a magnificent gold talisman bearing the sigil of my people. The only thing I was missing was my father's crown putting a highlighted target onto my back, but his Stone alone was enough to manage that.

Séamus was as stiff as a board and surveyed every one of my winged companions' movements as they walked through the house. I clutched his hand tightly as I knew exactly how he felt. Rigel and Áine were going over plans for Fossera with Vela when they looked up at us in utter shock.

"Well, look at this. Another one just for me?" Vela asked with a sultry smile as she tousled her blonde hair. Séamus knew right away what she was and curled his lip, ignoring that she even spoke to him.

"What the overbearing spawn of the Otherworld means to say, is welcome. I am Rigel, this is my wife, Áine, and that is Vela. Yes, she does bite." Rigel's silver eyes glinted as he rose to shake Séamus's hand.

"Séamus. Second in command of the Laoch army and born of High Druid blood," His voice was much lower than usual, and his muscles tensed.

"Who do you work with?" Vela asked.

"Badbh," he replied flatly. Sorlin raised an eyebrow in shock, and his face held an expression I could not read.

Rigel nodded. "Impressive. The house is all yours. All I ask is that if someone gets killed, please do not make my servants clean up the mess. I apologize there is no room made up at this moment, but it is in the works as we speak."

The tension in the room was as crisp as a ripe apple. I patted Séamus on the shoulder. "Alright, I have a plan for Fossera. We go there on the first of September and use Áine, Rigel, and myself as a distraction while Séamus, Sorlin, and Corvis look for the last stone. Séamus knows what to look for, and I will protect Áine with my life. Any questions?"

I looked around the room, but everyone seemed to nod in agreement. "When I see my father, I want to be the one to speak. I have a lot to say," Áine said forcefully. Rigel wrapped an arm around her waist and gave her a sympathetic smile.

"I'm going to go let my friend settle in. It has been a long day for all of us." I turned with Séamus and paused. "Oh wait, I almost forgot," I slammed my fist into Sorlin's face with a forceful grunt. He staggered back and clutched his nose with utter shock. "Don't ever come in my room without knocking again, understand? And yes, I stole yer blade sharpener."

"I am going to-" Corvis grabbed him before he could lunge at me, and I gave him the radiant image of my middle finger before running up the stairs with Séamus.

We laughed, and I led him down my wing with joy overflowing my heart. I loved that he was here, that I had a piece of my home to keep me sane, but the circumstances surrounding his presence could have made me sick on the floor. I was to bring him back to that island and face Sabriel. It was a fate that had always been written in the stars, but no amount of time could have prepared us for it. I made sure he was comfortable and reassured him that he could trust Rigel. He was still quite tense, but I left him be and retreated to my room only to find Corvis sitting on my bed.

"I am not giving it back to him," I said as I leaned against my door.

He chuckled and motioned for me to sit next to him. "I never got to thank you for saving my life in Eotia."

I rolled my eyes and plopped down beside him. "Corvis, we have been over this."

He gazed at me intensely, his face of stone unchanging. "Thank you, Eadha."

There was no need to thank me. I was a member of his court, even if only temporarily. It was my duty to protect and help them. Corvis was not going to drop this conversation, and I knew that, so I nodded as an acknowledgment. As I studied his face, I wondered if it would be a truly awful thing to have him as my Anam Cara. He was a beautiful man with a heart almost as big as Séamus's. We fit together like two pieces of the same strange, broken puzzle, and I tolerated him more than any of the others. I think we could potentially be an incredibly unstoppable force. If I did give into this connection, that is all he would be to me. I could not help but laugh at myself as I wondered if that were true.

I recalled all of the times my gaze has shifted from his eye to lips while he was speaking or the times I caught myself staring at him from across the room. I was beginning to question how I did feel about Corvis because I genuinely did not know. There were times I hated him, but times when I was glad we were the only two people in a room together.

"What was the purpose of me coming with today?" He asked in a low voice.

I did not know how to answer that question. I brought him there for my mother to confirm the nature of the connection, but I could not bring myself to allow the answer to be said. I wanted to live in the blissful ignorance of never knowing. I would rather just wait this out for as long as possible so I could just go home and live in peace. All I wanted, all I craved, was the sweet comfort of peace. I could not possibly gain that from retaining any connection to the Fae lands.

"I..." I could not think of any words as I lost myself in his burning stare.

His face softened, and he gave my shoulder a friendly squeeze. "Well, no matter. Thank you for bringing me, as strange as it was."

He rose to leave and paused before walking out the door. "I think...I-your brother was right, Eadha. I think you are going to be the greatest ruler your people have seen."

Air escaped my lungs as the tightness I felt released. My eyes welded and I panted, trying to wrap my head around the words Corvis just spoke to me. I clutched my mother's necklace and remembered holding my twin in my arms as he died. My soul ached as I realized that no matter how far I ran, the title was mine now, and there was no going back. I buried my face into a pillow and screamed as loud as I could, punching my bed. If I had to lead my people, I would do it with pride.

I just hoped Séamus was as prepared to take the title when I destroy the Well, and myself in the process.

CHAPTER TWENTY-SIX

Corvis

We had five days until the first of September, and in the week that had passed, we all spent every ounce of free time training and going over the plans. Having two Laoch under one roof with Sorlin was a recipe for disaster. He had been excessively insufferable. I could count the number of times I had to peel Eadha off of him on both of my hands. She explained that her soon to be crown needed to remain between us until she completed her journey to become Tiarna, and Sorlin was having a blast holding it over her head. Séamus had kept his distance from all of us for the most part but had taken quite nicely to Sorlin, who was uncharacteristically cold to him. Maybe it was due to Sorlin being the polar opposite of him, but ever since Séamus joined us, he has been quite distant. Though it was nice to have him out of my hair long enough for me to think.

I had spent a lot of time alone trying to ease my nerves about going back to Fossera and seeing Farhan again. I knew I would be safe with my allies, but a shiver of pain still traced the base of my wings. I could give all the advice in the world to Eadha, but following it was a different story.

I was in the library study pouring over the map of the palace of the capital city Cyra when Séamus appeared in front of me. I was startled for a moment, but once my mind caught up to my eyes, I gave him a forced smile. He was larger than Sorlin, which I did not think was possible, and his blue tattoos were different that Eadha's. He had few blue-knotted animals and shapes taking up large portions of his skin, but his face was bare.

"Hello, Séamus, are you looking for Eadha?"

He shook his head. "No. Sorlin and I both agree we should not wait till the first to infiltrate Fossera. They will be ready and waiting for us."

I thought about that possibility. Farhan was cunning, but I bet no matter when we came, he would be expecting us. "I have yet to find a possible treasure hold on these maps. If we leave before I do, we run the risk of getting caught as we spend more time searching for the stone. Have you spoken to Eadha to get her thoughts on this?"

He pulled a chair up and sat across from me. "No. Eadha has been a little too...intense, as of the last few days."

I have done my best to distance myself from her since we came back from her island, but I did notice her temper had been rather short. "I see, well, I agree with you, but you do not know Farhan like I do. He has been trying to get Áine home for decades and will stop at nothing to do so. Any time we travel there, he will be expecting us. I am not worried about this meeting. We have two Laoch and two Ruling Fae."

Séamus nodded and sighed. "Aye. I still think that we would fare better going sooner. What if he has Sabriel there waiting for us?"

"There was something about Norr when he came to give us the ultimatum. He seemed like his regular scheming self, but he also seemed different, almost afraid. I think the Fosserans bit off a little more than they could chew with Sabriel and want Áine there to protect her." It was an assumption I told Áine in the days following the altercation, and she agreed she saw it too. Whatever we were walking into in Fossera, there was a good chance it could end in our favor.

"Let's talk to Áine and Eadha and see what they think about your plan. You have a little more leverage with your friend to sway her stance on this."

"Ye'd be surprised. Eadha can be incredibly immovable." Séamus tensed for a moment as the door to the study swung opened but relaxed once he saw Sorlin.

"I talked to Rigel and he said that we move on my word. I think it would be best if we leave tomorrow and show up unannounced." Sorlin pulled the map over to him. I looked at Séamus, who was studying Sorlin intently but casually averted his eyes when they met mine. "Here, here, and here are the three places it could be according to Áine but that is as close as we have to a lead. In the meantime, I have another plan."

I raised an eyebrow and slapped his hand away from my map to inspect his markings. "And what would that be?"

"Alcohol," he said as he dropped a fist onto the table.

"No," I said flatly. None of us needed to take on Farhan tomorrow inebriated.

"We could all die in about a week and you don't want to have one last trip to Mac's? You can bring your new-found eternal love, and we can all-"

"Sorlin," I snapped at him.

He realized as soon as he said those words that we were not in familiar company and cleared his throat as he looked to Séamus, whose interest was thoroughly peaked. "I think we could all just use a drink or two. All of us, even the madame of darkness herself, Vela."

"If it will get you to shut your mouth, fine. I'll meet you there tonight. Get out." Sorlin threw his arms up and mouthed an apology, and I thought of how I could inflict a scar to match the other he had over his mouth.

"Ye have a woman then, Corvis?" Séamus asked. I didn't know if it was a Druid's personality trait to be so forward, but the few I have met all seemed to share it.

I shook my head. "If you are going drinking with Sorlin, you should prepare now. Eat food, drink water, and say a silent prayer for your organs in the morning."

"That answered my question then. Why don't ye bring her out? Sorlin said it best, it could be our last few days standing."

"Well, as Eadha not so politely says: Sorlin is a 'bawbag' so, there's that," I mumbled as I collected my documents.

"She's a lovely woman, that one," I sensed where this conversation was going, but before I could speak, Séamus continued, "Sorlin said, 'eternal love.' Big words for someone who doesn't have a love."

"Again, Sorlin is not the brightest star in the sky; he doesn't know what he's talking about." I walked past him but heard his footsteps behind me. I told Sorlin about mine and Eadha's bond and now thoroughly regretted it, but I needed advice. I had finally come to terms that I would ask Eadha about it when the time was right after this was over. She didn't deserve something like this hidden from her.

"Love can mean many things. I love Lana, but I am

not in love with her, same as Eadha. Maybe ye do, in fact, have a love then."

I groaned and turned to face him. "What do you want me to say, Séamus?"

He raised his eyebrows and clicked his tongue. "How are ye Eadha?"

I jumped and turned around and to see Eadha with a furrowed brow marching down the hallway. "Sorlin says we are moving tomorrow?" She asked us.

"Aye, did he tell ye we are going to a tavern tonight?"

She nodded. "I'll see ye there." I watched as she turned and walked away. When I turned to face Séamus, he had already closed the veil behind him. "Druids," I muttered.

They had a trend of being so cryptic, but I could only assume when you have lived a life as long as they have, you would develop that over time. Séamus was right though, I would do anything to ensure the rest of Eadha's days were at least tolerable and hopefully pleasant. I would fight with every bone in my body to ensure she reclaims her home.

As I walked into my room, I headed over to my covered mirror and touched the soft cloth hanging over it. I gave it a tug and looked at the man staring back at me. I examined my billowing shadows and thought back to Eotia when Nago insinuated my mother was alive and somewhere in Dife. Perhaps when this was all over, I would seek her out. That break Rigel has always pushed me to take may be up for consideration. I looked at my wings and recalled all that I told Eadha last week and tried to see them for what they were. I have these wings because I took my brother's place, and I would do it all over again. I flexed and stretched them out to fully inspect.

I had taken Tenebris and my life for granted. Within these borders, I found a family that I had pushed away but still loved me as their own. I never allowed myself to get close to anyone because I was sure at the first chance I had, I would give my life to the battlefield and honor the goddess in which my people worshiped. But since meeting Eadha, I realized I did not want to end my life, I just wished a part of me dead. The part that never hugged Áine when she stretched out her arms to me, the part that never told Rigel just how bad I was suffering, and the part that felt unworthy of the bond between Eadha and myself. I was not ready to take on this change, but I knew where I could start.

I took a bath to calm my nerves as the sun set. This was possibly the last night of normalcy we were going to have for a long time, and I was going to enjoy it. I combed my hair for the first time in a long while and put on a loose-fitting shirt with a deep neckline that exposed my tattoo, and drank whatever liquor I had in my room. Everyone had already left, and I debated whether I should even go, but I had to.

I walked along the bridge at a leisurely pace and took in the breathtaking full moon. The purple and green lights danced across the sky as people ran past me, laughing and oblivious to the horrors that could come should we fail. Rigel was not cruel enough to keep his people in the dark, he informed them of the threat, but they trusted he would do everything he could to stop it.

When I opened the doors to Mac's, Rigel and Sorlin were already in a drunken embrace, dancing in the middle of the tavern. Séamus was not far behind, laughing and enjoying his time with Eadha while Vela sipped on some wine with Áine keeping her company and looked utterly embarrassed by their companions. It was against Áine's morals to drink, but boy, she looked like she needed one.

"Corvis! You came!" Áine beamed. I smiled and found myself an ale before joining the ladies in their booth. "Just in time too, my husband is making an absolute fool of himself out there."

I raised my glass. "As we all should. How are you feeling about tomorrow?"

She laughed. "Ask me tomorrow, and then we'll talk."

Sorlin stumbled over and pulled Séamus away from Eadha as the song concluded and a new one began. The ladies went on about birthdays, holidays, and other celebrations they would celebrate once the threat of war passed while I drank as much as I could to gain the courage to walk over to Eadha. I was as ready as I could be.

"I am late by an hour, and those three are already drunk," I said as I clanked my glass against hers.

Eadha laughed. "What do ye expect? Ye look good and warm yerself." She furrowed her brows before reaching up and running her fingers through my hair, tousling it out of place. "That's better." The music slowed into an intimate swing.

I drank the rest of my courage inspiring liquid and reached my hand out to her. "Dance with me," I asked. She hesitated for a moment but took my hand. I slowly spun her around before placing her arms around my neck.

"Well, look at that," Eadha tilted her head to the side, and I chuckled as I watched Rigel pull Séamus and Sorlin to him in a teary drunken embrace. "True love unfurling right before our eyes...are ye going to be okay tomorrow?"

I nodded. "I have to be. We need that stone, and I think it's time Áine knocked her father down a peg or two."

"Ye don't have to be alright, Corvis. Ye of all people should know that."

"Okay, truth is I am terrified. I know that if anything goes wrong tomorrow, the path to a future without war will not be so straight and narrow. But I know I will do everything in my power to find that stone and get Séamus and Sorlin out alive." I looked into her mosaic eyes and sent myself back to that grassy cliff in my dreams, the only moments of true bliss I have known. If I did not do this now, I knew I never would. I pulled Eadha close to me and opened the veil, sending us to the glowing cavern.

She gasped as her inebriated mind caught up with the abrupt change in scenery. "Alright, I'll bite. What's going on?" She backed away nervously and hovered a hand close to the dagger on her hip.

As I looked into her eyes, I was sent back to that moment of her holding her twin in her arms as he died. I felt the fear, the anger, the anguish as she sent his body away through the veil. The pain was a deep, primal ache of pure heartbreak that still lingered in my chest since that day in the woods. I felt her entire body tremble as the Sluagh chained her to the post and the heat of the blood running down her back when all she could think about was her friends and family. Eadha did not need this right now. She did not need a man to tell her of some connection that at the end of the day meant nothing. I loved Eadha much like I loved any of my other companions. What she needed was to go home, and I needed to use this connection to bring her closer to that.

I studied her pale face, every line on the tattoo covering her mosaic eye, and decided this would be the last time I would allow us to be this close to each other, but I brought her here for a reason, so at least I could say my peace.

"May I speak freely for a moment?"

She shot me a look that could have sent me to an early grave. "Corvis, if ye ever ask me for permission to speak again, I'll put a rock through yer front teeth...I'm not crowned yet, and I never will be."

I bit the inside of my cheek and mulled over my words carefully as I sat down. "When we spoke last, you looked upset that I told you I thought you would make a great leader, almost like you didn't believe me."

Eadha inched away from me and scowled. "Because it's not yer place to say such things. I never said I didn't-"

"But you do feel that way. I see it in your face, I saw it when you came back from speaking with your parents, and I see it now. You feel unworthy of the crown because you feel responsible for what happened to your people," the alcohol I consumed made me bolder than ever as I was fully aware that what I was about to say could lead to a bloody fight.

"Corvis-" I grabbed her hands and held them tight. She needed to listen to what I had to say. I was not going to allow her to think so low of herself anymore.

"Let me speak, please. You only believe this because life has done terrible things to you, Eadha. You turned cold to defend yourself from the pain it has brought on you. Trust me, I know. It is easy to feel guilty, I know it took me a long time to not feel that same way. I may not like who I am, but I know I did not cause myself to end up the way I did," I looked into the landscape within her eyes and paused for a moment, "I just want you to know, you are so deeply an amazing leader, and that guilt you feel proves it. It shows how passionately you care for your people. I pray to the Battle Crow herself that goodness enters your life when this is over, to wash away that which has devastated you."

Her eyes widened, and she pulled her hands away from mine, stammering and stumbling over her words. I didn't care if she hated me after this moment. I just needed her to know that once we parted ways, I knew she was going to do great things. I could see her eyes begin to glass over, and her frosty cheeks turned into the most alluring rose color.

After what felt like an eternity, she chuckled softly and placed her hand on my thigh. I drew a sharp breath and held it as my muscles tensed. Eadha looked up at me and bit her lip.

"Corvis...ye see life in ways I wish I could. I hope ye know that."

"I hope one day you see it through my eyes then, *my Lady*."

Eadha reached her hand up to caress my face, and I froze, pulling away ever so slightly. It felt like lightning was going through my veins, and alarms were silently ringing in my head as the intoxicating scent of cedar and fresh rain filled my nose. I would be lying if I said there were times I did not yearn for moments like this. Many times have I caught myself gazing at her and wondered what her lips felt like against mine, but this was not right. Eadha would be leaving, and I refused to make her life harder than it had to be. But not only that, she was officially a ruler, a queen of her nation, and I was the exact opposite.

She leaned in so close that I could taste her liquor-filled breath on my tongue. I clutched her hand and cleared my throat. "Eadha, with all due respect, you are drunk. I don't think we are in the right headspace to..."

She lingered for a moment but nodded and pulled away, and I could have sworn I saw a bit of an ache as she did so. "Aye, well...let's be off then."

I helped her up from the makeshift chair and was about to open the veil when Eadha's hand braced my neck and pulled my mouth to hers. My entire body went stiff, but I found myself savoring her taste. I felt a warmth spread through my body and felt utterly electric as my cheeks heated. It was wrong, this should not have been happening, but I could not find it in me to pull away from her embrace. My hands made their way to her waist, and I didn't realize how small she was until bending down to her level. I always pictured her so much larger in my eyes because of the forbidding magic pouring off of her body on any given day.

I pulled Eadha closer to me, but the lack of space between us did not satisfy my craving for her touch. My hand traveled up her strong back to grip the nape of her neck, pushing her against the nearest rock wall. I felt a rumble escape her chest that was tightly pressed to mine. A hand gripped my hair and pulled, and our kiss quickened ferociously as Eadha's tongue graced my lips. It was my turn to release a low moan into her mouth. I swiftly pulled her up by the knees and wrapped her legs around my waist. I've never felt a kiss so exhilarating, so passionate. I was absolutely enthralled and at her mercy. Her teeth pinched my bottom lip and sent me spiraling as she gently clawed the back of my neck.

Eadha broke our embrace as quickly as she started it, and I pressed the palm of my hand into the rock wall to keep me steady as I gripped under her thighs. My cheeks heated, and my breath was ragged as she stared at me while sliding down the wall.

"I'm sorry, I-I just had to know," she gasped.

I didn't want to know whatever revelation she was looking for or if she found it. It was not my place. I, however, learned all I needed to. It was going to take a lot of strength to keep this from ever happening again.

I nodded and cleared my throat as I stepped away from her, awkwardly adjusting my pants. "Alright, well...shall we?"

I opened the veil and motioned to leave, and Eadha almost looked disappointed. I had a feeling this was the last moment of intimacy we would share, and I was not sure if I was grateful for it or not. Every part of her fit so perfectly into my hands like expertly molded clay and I didn't know if I could let that go, but I would for her.

As soon as we stepped into Mac's, Vela was sitting in her booth with a horrified look in her eye, and Áine was shaking her head, pulling a piece of her veil over her face with a look of embarrassment. Séamus and Sorlin were in a full-blown brawl on the bartop, and Rigel was in a one-man line dance with tears in his eyes. A regular night out at Mac's, I would say. I turned to make a joke to Eadha, but she was already on top of Sorlin and peeling him off her friend.

"C-Corvish, get in here!" Rigel slurred as he pulled me into a tight embrace. I picked up an ale from the passing barmaid and downed it in one gulp.

"You see, this-" I motioned up and down his face, "is why I said we shouldn't go out tonight. The world is on the line."

He stuck his finger in my face and shushed me. "Look at them over there," he pointed to our group of three, pummeling each other behind the bar. "They are having fun. I-I want to have fun. We never have fun." I rolled my eyes and shrugged, letting the Rigel hand me drink after drink as the night carried on. The tavern slowly emptied, and all that was left was the four of us in a pile on the floor.

"Alright, g-give me your best, best way to die. Go," Sorlin slurred out. I did not hear the words he was saying as I laid on my back, watching the ceiling spin. I lazily held Eadha's hair as she heaved to the side of me.

"I've always wanted to sled down the eastern mountain range. If I go, I'm going out with a thrrrill," Rigel said with a chuckle. Eadha mumbled something incomprehensible, and my drunken mouth stung as her kiss lingered on my lips.

"If I could give my life to save any of those that I loved, th-then I would consider my life fulfilled." Who was that speaking? Oh yeah, Séamus.

"A-are we going to die at the island?" I heard a

thump and then Sorlin grunting in pain. Rigel must have hit him to get him to shut his mouth.

"We are going to Fossera, we are going to the island and then we are coming home. Now shut up and let me sleep." I mumbled.

CHAPTER TWENTY-SEVEN

Eadha

The images of last night were blurry. We all woke up on the floor of the pub and shamefully walked home to receive a harsh scolding from Áine and Vela. It was worth it to have one night before our lives possibly changed forever. What happened in the following days would not only determine our future, but also the world. The gravity of the situation hit me as Séamus and I were dressing into our battle leathers and strapping our weapons. If we failed in retrieving this stone, there would be no way we could destroy the Well, and the only option would be to take Sabriel and his fleets on right then and there.

"Do ye remember what ye did last night, old friend?" I asked as he tied my leathers up my back.

"I do not even remember going to a pub last night. Why?"

"I came in and saw Sorlin and ye going at it," when I turned to look at him, his face had fallen for a moment before giving me a short snort and the shaking of his head.

"Ye were right about that one. He's a right fanny." Séamus was not easily bothered. In fact, he was the most level-headed person I knew. Whatever Sorlin had said must have gotten under his skin. The day after I had brought Séamus to Tenebris, Sorlin had been a tad rude to him. They were mirror opposites in every way, but somehow, Séamus had still tolerated him more than I ever could have.

"Well...ye can tell me about it," I said in a low voice.

Séamus froze and stiffened as he looked absently at his hands. "I-"
he cleared his throat, "it was nothing. The music picked up and...well I asked him for a dance. I don't remember what was said, but somewhere between dancing and drinking, we ended up brawling."

I gave him an inquisitive look before the corners of my mouth turned up, and he shoved me. I let the conversation die. He would talk to me about it when he wanted to. "Well, good luck down there today. Ye listen to me: ye protect Corvis with yer life. Farhan was the one who ripped his wings from his back. Do not get caught," I did not intend my voice to be so harsh to my dear friend, but I would rather be cursed than see Corvis suffer by the hands of that man as he once did.

Séamus nodded. "Do ye love him?"

"I-... I kissed him last night. I...no, I don't. We are connected in a way I cannot explain, but..." I did not know if that was a lie or not. My mind told me my words were true, but my heart said otherwise. That kiss last night, I needed it to be sure I knew I did not love him, and I was almost positive that was true, but the memory of his taste was burned into my tongue like a brand I never wanted to fade. If I saw those lips on anyone else, I would not react so nicely.

My friend's green eyes grew wide before a smile brimmed his face. "Listen, if I can't look at ye, then ye can't look at me like that, Séamus," I said as I fought a smile.

"What happens when this is over? Between the two of ye's?"

"Nothing. I rebuild our home and govern our people. I'm not coming back to these lands for anything other than business." The truth tasted like vinegar as it fled my mouth. I considered these people my friends, but at the end of the day, they were my allies. We owed each other nothing after this mess was resolved. Of course, if Corvis ever needed me for an emergency, I would come if he called.

Áine was waiting for us at the bottom of the stairs in the most glorious outfit I had ever seen. It was a golden robe speckled with glittery suns and adorned with rubies. She pinned a brooch of a blazing ruby sun onto the wrap she had just finished fastening to her head. She was showing her father that she was no child he could command. She was a woman who could end his life in seconds if she so chose. Rigel was in his regular simple black tunic, which was striking against his silvery hair, and his Ravens were dressed to kill.

"Alright, my father has no idea we are coming. The only thing we are doing is distracting him and his guards so the three of you can get the stone. We need to do this as quickly as possible."

We all nodded, and Áine continued, "The three of us will go in first. You three give us about fifteen minutes before following. Rigel, Eadha, let's go," I swallowed hard and gave Séamus a hopeful smile before walking through the veil with Rigel and Áine.

The city of Cyra was immaculate. The landscape was filled with golden glittery sand, and all the buildings were stark white with beautiful golden orbs decorating them. Although the summer sun was fading in

Oneiros, it was sweltering here. I was amazed by how the Ruling Fae of each court used their magic to keep their lands so vastly different on this large continent. Guards were lined up at the palace entrance with weapons drawn as they commanded us to halt.

"You will let me through to speak to my father immediately, or you will not have the breath to halt me ever again," Áine's once candied voice was now menacing and dark. The guards lowered their weapons and opened the gate. I saw out of the corner of my eye one guard disappearing into the veil, likely to warn Farhan we have come.

Áine did not wait for anyone to lead her. She pushed us past the guards and threw open the doors to her father's chambers with the grace of a phoenix and stood before him. He was the spitting image of her and brother Norr, and the woman I assumed to be her mother raised her eyebrows in shock as we approached the thrones. I looked around and studied every guard, feeling my way through the ground to their bodies, marking weak points, and calculating the best plan of attack in my head.

"What do you think you are doing, father?" Áine demanded.

The man had darker hair than Áine and a thick beard to match, but shared her golden, glittery, bronze skin. He pushed his swirled locks back and smiled. He was charming, and if he was not one of my worst enemies at this moment, I would call him strikingly handsome. "Áine, my sunshine, I am so glad you have made the right choice."

"The only choice I made was to come here and demand to know what you *think* you are doing. I advise you to answer my questions as I ask them," the rage and hurt in her voice was unmeasurable. The last time she set foot in these halls was the same day she watched her father mutilate her close companion.

Áine's snake of a brother emerged from a room to the right and looked at me with a baffled yet calculated look in his eye. He must have known I was responsible for killing his men. I gave him a small wink before turning my attention to the High Lord.

"You will not speak to me in such a way," Farahn commanded.

"I am a Ruling Lady and will speak to my equals in any way I see fit. What are you doing with Sabriel, and why are you-"

"You will lower your voice at once," Farhan spit out.

"I am speaking, and you do not have permission to silence me. If you interrupt me again, the taste of blood will stain your tongue. What are you doing with Sabriel and why are you demanding I come home?"

I could have heard a pin drop in the silence that birthed in the room. Rigel tucked in the corner of his mouth, likely to stop him from smiling, but the look of pride for his wife was plastered onto his face.

"Sabriel offered us a deal, the nature in which is no concern of the wild beasts that trailed in behind you," the woman who spoke looked nothing like Áine. Her face was rather round and not as angular as hers.

Áine gave me a dismissing nod. I walked behind her, grabbed Rigel, and pulled him with me just behind the veil. "What are you doing?" He asked.

"Shh. Just listen." Guards walked all around us and confirmed we were in fact, "gone."

"I am happy you chose the right path, Áine. We wanted you here to keep you safe. The world will be shifting to a new age," Farhan said simply as if the imminent destruction of the world was a minor inconvenience to himself.

"An age of fear, destruction, and war. That is what you support?" Áine kept her face composed, but I could tell she was disgusted by his words.

"We are not destroying anything. You can sit in your Land of Darkness and play queen all you want, but you do not know how to govern a people. We know what Sabriel is planning. We are not aiding him, we are protecting our lands from his wrath."

Much like Nago and Jada were attempting to protect their people from Sabriel, it seemed as though Farahan was doing the same, but I did not believe it for a second. There was something else going on, and Áine needed to push to find out.

"You know he is planning on destroying the world, yet you sit here and do nothing?" Áine asked with a raised voice.

"No. We know Sabriel wants power, and he can have it. There is no army that can take down Sabriel, so why try? If I happened to get land or jewels for my compliance, so be it. In fact, I told him he could have whatever he wanted, and all I asked in return was to level that stain of land on which you dwell first and bestow no harm onto you."

A felt the veil shift as Rigel's fury bloomed. He clenched his fist and made a move to leave, but I grabbed his arm. This was Áine's fight, not ours.

"You-you told that creature to destroy my home and kill my people?"

"*This* is your home," the woman beside Farhan explained with a wave of her hand.

Áine turned to the woman slowly and narrowed her gaze. "Ima, you will never speak in my presence again, you good for nothing whore."

My mouth dropped, and eyes widened. Farhan stood and lit the room with a blinding light. "Enough! Guards, see Áine to her room at once."

Áine drew her sword and the dark magic of Rigel emaciated from her palms. "I do not want to hurt you, father, but no one is going to touch me. Sabriel is tricking you. Are you too ignorant to see that? You speak of me not knowing how to govern, but I am working tirelessly to prevent this war, so my people are safe. You are my father. I do not want to see you dead. I beg of you, please join me."

Farhan laughed and clapped his hands. "Always with the dramatics. You should be on your knees, begging Sabriel to take you in as he did myself and Nago, but of course, you cursed that poor man to death. I do not know how you did it, but I know you broke the blood bond between us. Did you give him the same pathetically hopeful speech of stopping the war and saving the day? Or is he just as naive as you are?"

Áine blasted him with the purple magic, and his eyes rolled to the back of his head. "I have been silent for too long," she turned to her brother, who was beginning to look utterly conflicted. "Norr, I pray that when this sniveling coward dies, I don't have to see you dead as well. Learn from his mistakes and make our nation respected again,"

Norr shook his head. "You know nothing, sister."

Guards had surrounded Áine, but she stood tall.

As the trance she had Farhan under faded, he shook with anger. "You dare bring that filthy magic into my lands?" He unsheathed his sword and stalked over to her.

"Maybe I should take a page out of your book, father, and heal your head onto the body of a swine. It would fit you quite nicely."

Farhan connected his blade with Áine's, and they were off. Norr looked sheepishly around the room and disappeared. "Rigel, go help her. I need to see what that one knows."

"Be careful," he muttered before leaving the veil.

"Aye."

⫴

Norr was pacing and sweating. As I emerged from the veil, he drew his sword, but I batted it out of his hand and shoved him to the wall by his neck. "Surprised to see me again, laddie?" The confident man that had me kneeling in the woods was gone.

"He's lying," he said in a panicked voice.

"About what? Quickly before I rip out yer throat."

"He-he sold his soul to Sabriel. He made him do it. My father is not a good man, but is not malevolent."

I felt my eyebrows pinch together as I pushed Norr into a chair and held a knife to his throat. "Tell me everything."

"Sabriel needs a vessel for something. Do you have all of the stones of Arawn? Are they with you?"

My heart sank, and my hand instinctively touched the bag I never took off of my hip. "I don't have yers. How did you-"

"Find it, and do not let any of them leave your sight. Let me see your bag."

I bellowed out a laugh. "Really? Ye think this 'I'm on yer side' thing is working on me? Do ye have any idea how old I am, laddie?"

"Sabriel does."

My face fell, and I jumped back. My heart started racing, and I felt as though I could fall over right then. "What?"

"He knows a Druid is attempting to find the stones. I don't know if he is aware it is you or not. Half of my father's soul is being held by Sabriel, and I have no idea what he is planning on shoving into his body. I hate Rigel for taking my sister away and soiling our blood-line, and I hate you for helping him. But I do not want to see my father dead or the world's end. Sabriel invited my father to a meeting and trapped him about the same time I saw you in the woods. I did not speak anything of you. I do not know how Sabirel knows a Druid is here in Verbenia."

I placed my hand on his chest and felt his heart. Cré taught me how to read if someone was lying or not. It did not race as he looked me in the eyes. I had to believe he was telling the truth. I said a silent prayer to my Dragons and any god willing to listen that I was not about to curse our mission by trusting him.

"If I save yer father, he leaves Áine alone. Goddess above she is happy and has a bond with that man ye will never be able to understand. He is one of the greatest leaders I have seen, and he is lucky to have Áine as a wife. Do ye understand?"

Norr nodded and held out his hand. "Give me your bag." I hesitated but surrendered it. "We are master curse breakers, but also master charmers. I need a drop of your blood." I pointed my finger and commanded a drop to emerge just above my skin and let it fall into the outstretched bag.

"There, only you are able to see and handle the contents of this bag should it ever get stolen." He turned it over, but nothing fell out, reached inside and pulled out the lining.

I took it from him and saw all six jewels were nestled into their places. I looked up at him and nodded. "Thank ye, Norr. I have men scouring the grounds as we speak for that jewel. Do ye know where it is?"

He shook his head. "I have never seen it. Leave here and keep this quiet. Do not tell anyone of this meeting. As of right now, you cannot trust anyone in Verbenia," he gave me a pat on the shoulder and left me alone.

Norr's words stung me down to my soul. Every ounce of comfort I have found in the people I have met has fled, and I felt as I did the day I stepped foot into Oneiros, alone in hostile territory. If someone in the city was contacting Sabriel, then that could mean Rigel's lands would be the first to fall. I did not want to believe someone from his court would do such a thing, but I had no choice but to treat everyone as a spy...*a spy...*

No, no, it was not Corvis. I refused to believe it was him. That servant Cari always looked at me funny, and never spoke to me. It could have been her, but that was too easy. I raked my mind of everyone that knew who and what I was. It had to have been someone who was either with me all the time or had eyes on me as I walked through the lands. My eyes shut hard, and my hands slammed into my head as my stomach turned sour. *No, no, no, no.*

It had to have been him. It had to be Addax.

CHAPTER TWENTY-EIGHT

Corvis

"Since we are all here, I just want to say I am sorry for whatever I said last night. It wasn't me, it was the alcohol," Sorlin whispered obscenely loud as we crawled through the tunnels of Cyra. Since neither Séamus nor Sorlin had stealth, we had no choice but to sneak in together.

"Sorlin, if you utter one more word in this gods-forsaken tunnel, I will kick your teeth right out from your gums," I was not afraid of tight spaces, but I was not particularly fond of them either. My wings had to wrap around my body in order to fit, and all I wanted was peace and quiet until we were at our destination.

"I forgive ye," Séamus whispered back.

I stopped in my tracks and looked behind me at both of them. Their eyes met mine, and Sorlin mouthed an apology of sorts. I memorized the map of the city, and if all went as planned, we would emerge into the first treasure hold soon. We paused and waited to hear any noise, but it sounded utterly empty. I shifted onto my back and kicked off the panel covering our exit. As I slowly rose, there was no guard in sight.

"Huh, well, so much for a welcome party," it was times like these that I forgot Sorlin was the menacing general of our aerial army. Sneaking was a word that didn't exist in his dictionary.

"Just stay against the wall and keep your eyes on

our flank. Séamus, get in the middle." Every corridor we walked down, there were no guards. The air in the room was surprisingly free of tension, and no guards were hiding in the shadows. Whatever was happening, it was not an ambush.

We turned the corner to a vault, and Sorlin looked around and shrugged. "Corvis, I'm not gonna lie, your job is pretty nice outside of crawling for a few miles. See as the *general* I have to-"

"Sorlin. Shut. Up. Now." I opened the door to the vault, and it held treasures and gems, but nothing that caught Séamus's eye. We checked every room leisurely, even tossed around a few gems before pocketing them, but there was no stone and no guards. Sorlin whistled and shouted in the echoing corridors, and Séamus slapped him on the back to hear his yelp reverberate down halls. We flipped coins and skipped them around, broke a few vases, and went through every room in no time at all.

"Should we check the other keep? In the eastern courtyard?" Séamus asked.

I shrugged. "Well, we have to find it. If it wasn't here, it has to be there."

"Should we get back in the hole, or...?"

"Let's um, let's walk carefully," I replied to Sorlin. This was strange. There were no alarms, no traps, no nothing. We walked across the courtyard as if we belonged there and did not run into anyone. Whatever distraction Áine was causing must have been a good one.

Sorlin plucked an apple from a tree and turned in a small circle before looking at me and shrugging. If he gave me any hassle about my job being easy after this, I would make sure he would go to bed and wake up under water the next day.

We walked into the temple, and Séamus froze. "That's it. That's a statue of Arawn. It'll be there."

We looked around and approached the statue. Séamus inspected the large statue and pressed down on some sort of lever. The structure creaked and shuddered as it opened and revealed a small glass case covering an empty pedestal. I clutched my sword and spun around, "This has to be a trap. The stone is missing, and there are no guards."

"There was one more treasure hold in the palace," Sorlin said.

I shook my head. "No, there are fresh fingerprints disturbing the dust on that case. Someone has already taken it." I kicked the statue door closed and muttered a few curses under my breath. Áine said under no circumstances should we come to her side in the palace. The only thing we could do was turn back to Tenebris.

"Let's go back. Whoever took that stone knew we were coming for it. We need to tell Eadha. It took us a long time to get through those tunnels. They may already be back," Séamus said.

"Well, hold on a second. I think we should check out the palace. It may not be there, but it could be."

"We have orders, Sorlin. We are only to look here and then leave," I explained.

"But Áine pointed to three locations. One of those was in the palace. Let's just go-"

I held my hand up to silence him as the faint sound of running footsteps reached my ears. I grabbed my two companions and pulled them behind the statue after shutting it. Norr was running to the statute and paused at its base. He pulled the lever and sighed a breath of relief.

"Thank the gods," he muttered as he closed it. I looked to the two men, and Sorlin furrowed his brow and motioned his head for us to investigate. Norr was alone. It would be easy to take him out if needed. As he walked away, I sent my shadows after him, wrapping around his ankle and pulling him down. He grunted and whipped around as we jumped from behind the statue.

"What are you still doing here? Why are you attacking me?" He asked with utter shock was plastered onto his face.

"Why are we attacking you? Is that a serious question?" Sorlin mocked.

"Where is the stone, Norr?" I asked as my shadows pulled him closer.

He looked at us with absolute confusion. "You have it, don't you?" My eyes widened, and I looked back at the statue then to him. I motioned for Sorlin and Séamus to keep watch over him as I inspected the statue. I held my finger against the imprint in the dust and spiraled into further confusion. I could lift the glass case with one hand but whoever took the stone needed two.

"We didn't take it, Norr," I called back.

He got up, and his eyes widened. "Then who did?"

When we exited the veil, Áine was being comforted by Rigel while Vela and Eadha were pacing the room. Eadha pounced on me, grabbing me by my high leather collar. "Give it to me. Give it to me now."

I stumbled back and grabbed her hands gently. "Eadha, the stone was missing."

Her eyes grew large, and she gasped. "What? What do ye mean it was missing? Go back and look again."

"It's true, it was not in its rightful place. We looked in every room, but no one stopped us. There were no guards or alarms," Séamus explained.

Eadha started to tremble, and she clutched her stomach. "No, no this-this can't be happening. This can't be happening,"

"Eadha, listen-"

A blade spun into her hand, and she held it to my chest. "Do not touch me. Do not take one step closer."

"Hey! Calm down. We fall to our back up, remember? Kill Sabriel first, deal with the Well later," Rigel called from the couch.

"Ye don't understand. I will not be able to kill Sabriel without that cauldron," the panic in her voice and her eyes was enough to make my heart race.

"Even with the crown?" Séamus asked.

The room went silent, and Áine perked her head up. "Crown? As in Tiarna?"

Eadha shook her head wildly, and the whole house shook. "Stop talking and let me think!" Rigel and Vela exchanged a look, and Eadha dug her fingers into her hair, mumbling and muttering. "We go tomorrow. We cannot risk sitting here any longer. We can't go back and look for that stone. We just have to go."

"What about my father?" Áine asked.

"He'll be fine. Just-"

"No, I know my father, and I know how to handle him. That man was not my father."

Sorlin was looking wildly around the room. What happened at that meeting? Eadha's breathing became erratic, and she clutched the table to support her body. I could feel my chest tightening as her panic crept into my body.

"Eadha, give us a plan, and we will follow you. We need to focus on Sabriel right now and how the last stone we need is now missing." Áine looked at me as if I betrayed her, but she had to have known what was now at stake.

"If we stay here and wait, something bad will happen. We will leave tomorrow before dawn."

"What do you mean? What did you do?" Vela questioned Eadha aggressively.

"I made a mistake. I went against yer command, Rigel, and told Addax everything. I told him who I was, what we were doing, and that we needed his stone. There was no feud. It was a facade, so ye wouldn't find out. Nago and Jada were so terrified of their people dying, and I believed they captured him, yes to get to Corvis, but also to make sure Addax couldn't speak to Sabriel again. I mean, how did that Nuckelavee know where to find us? It was him all along..."

Rigel looked terrifyingly calm. If something terrible was about to happen, I did not know which side to be on. Eadha betrayed my High Lord and possibly put my home and these lands in danger, but I could not imagine Addax doing such a thing. "Rigel, before you say anything, Addax is young, incredibly young. He protects his lands and harbors the unwanted of our kind. I doubt he would do this."

"No one is that nice just because. It was a front. It had to have been." Sorlin said in a low voice. I looked at him and gave him a gesture to stop talking, but he only stared me down.

"Well, you heard her. We go before dawn. You, Eadha, are to never enter these lands again. If I see your face, I will order my men to kill you on sight. I suggest we all rest for the journey we have ahead of us. Sorlin, sleep with Séamus tonight. Corvis with Eadha. Do not let them out of your sight. Everyone go to your rooms and stay there until we leave."

I felt a pressure in my head, but Rigel did not ask for permission to enter. My reality had begun to shift, and the room spun until just him, and I stood in the dark. "I am not going to ask you where your allegiance lies, because I know I would follow Áine to the ends of the world no matter what. I am, however, ordering you not to do anything stupid. I do not want to lose you, Corvis, but Eadha put my lands in danger."

"It just, it doesn't make sense. Addax has no personal gain from this. In fact, I saw the way he looked at Eadha. He considers her a friend. I don't think he would betray her like this. I am your head spy. I interrogate every person you have me capture. I have learned a thing or two about personalities."

"If it wasn't Addax, then we can talk about that one some other day *if we live*. We are marching onto that island with our whole plan out the door. I am sending my *wife* and my closest friends to possibly march to their deaths because of something she did. Watch her, and do not let her out of your sight." His silver eyes flashed, and I was standing back in the room, leading Eadha up the flight of stairs.

Norr was shocked that the stone was missing, and when he found out we did not take it, he became hysterical. Addax is smaller in stature than Rigel, the prints could have been his, but they still seemed too small.

I could feel Eadha shaking as I held her arm and closed the door to her room behind us. "I-I failed us. I failed my people I-... I trusted him and now-"

"Eadha, I am telling you I do not for one moment believe Addax would do this. He is a kind man, a gentle ruler, and exceptionally caring of all life. I would not feel good about stealing from him either. It could be anyone. I don't think Norr is in the right state of mind, I ran into him, and he was as shocked the stone was missing as I was, but could be lying."

She violently wiped her tears and pushed me away as I approached her. "No, that man was *afraid*. Did ye hear Áine? She said that wasn't her father, and she was right. Norr is afraid for him and for his people and I felt it in his heart that he was not lying."

"What do we do then?"

"Nothing. If what ye say is true and ye think Addax innocent, then the spy is one of *you*."

I snorted. "What, you think it's me?" I took a step closer and she grasped her dagger.

"I'm not interested in speaking anymore. I guess we will see tomorrow."

"Eadha, this is absurd. It could have been anyone who has seen you. It could have been Nago, but it was not one of us. These people are my family. I know them."

"Well, they aren't mine," she pushed me away again, sending me into the bed. "Get back!" She yelled.

"Eadha, you did not fail, and we did not fail you."

She went to push me again, but I grasped her hand and pulled her into me. I was not going to let her succumb to the darkness growing in her heart. She wedged her leg between us and kicked me in the stomach to get away. I fell to the ground with a grunt but grabbed her leg, pulling her down with me. Eadha tried to kick my hand away, but I pulled her to me, wrestling to get my arms and legs around her until all she could do was struggle to free herself.

"You didn't fail Eadha, you did what you thought was right, and I believe you made the right choice. We are going to be fine tomorrow, with or without the stone. We are going to kill Sabriel," I panted out.

I could feel her hot tears on my arm as she cried. "I can't do it. I can't kill him. I can't...I can't."

A pain stung my chest as it tightened. Her sorrow began to crawl into me, and it was unfathomable. She had come so far; we all had. We were not going to fail tomorrow. "We are going to go to the island, look for Sabriel, and take him out. We have the power of Badbh and a Tiarna."

She shook her head quickly. "I am *not* the Tiarna. I do not have the power of all the Dragons. They are leaving this world, and when they do, I will be powerless. I had to stop Sabriel and stop this war to keep them here, but it looks like that future isn't written in the Staves for me."

"Everything is written in the Staves for you. Are you forgetting your name? Your mother named you after the aspen tree for a reason. Your destiny is anything but fulfilled."

She chuckled sarcastically. "Every Ogham Stave can be reversed." I lessened my hold on her, but she didn't move. "I'm glad I met ye Corvis. I truly am."

I looked down at the top of her snow-white hair. "Me too, Eadha, me too." In that moment of holding her to me, I knew I did not want her to leave once this was over.

CHAPTER TWENTY-NINE

Eadha

I was awoken by Corvis, and my stomach flipped. It was time. I did not know if I was ready or not, but I had to be. I was about to face the man who took everything from me and kill him with pleasure. When I joined the others downstairs, they could hardly look at me, but Corvis kept his hand on the small of my back, and Sorlin cleared his throat. "We do not know what is going on, and all we have is each other. We will fight to keep everyone safe and deal with the drama of court politics after."

Corvis looked him in the eye and gave him a nod of thanks. He did not have to answer for me to understand that he believed me to be innocent. Vela grabbed my hand and squeezed it hard. "If you cursed my people, Laoch, I will be the first to gut you."

"Look at you, going soft on us," Corvis joked coldly.

She gave him a look with her red eyes filled with murder and silently advised him to keep his mouth shut. Vela technically worked for Rigel more or less against her will, but it was obvious she cared for him and his court.

I touched the charmed bag on my hip and nodded to our group. "I will make sure ye all walk out of there alive. I say we walk through the veil to the northern shore, closest to his palace. We will not split up; we will not play the hero. We are going to do our job and get out. If we hunt him in a pack and use my gift of sight, we should manage to corner him."

I needed to plan as if I was not coming back from this alive, and in my heart, I knew I would not. I clutched my mother's necklace in my fist and stealthily hid it in Séamus's pocket as I hugged him. "Fight hard and die a quick death, my friend," I tousled his autumn red curls for what could be the last time.

Áine gave me a grave look and nodded. We were as ready as we were ever going to be, I looked at Corvis and my heart dropped. I pray this would not be the last time I looked upon his face. Sorlin clutched Séamus and Áine to Rigel before slipping into the veil.

"Corvis, Uisce lives in the waters surrounding the island. If anything should happen to me, call on him."

He nodded, but I knew he did not understand our connection enough to know that my magic lived within him somewhere. His throat bobbed, and when he clutched my hand, he turned into the stone-cold warrior I met when I first came to Tenebris and vanished through the veil.

The second my feet reached the sandy shores of the island, I felt alive. Séamus stood tall and stretched out his arms. The power of the gods and goddesses our people worked with came rushing to be claimed by the Druids who once stood on these lands. A black smoke seeped out of Séamus's hands, and a sword and shield took its place as a crow sounded from afar. Badbh was here. Her magic flooded Séamus, and he looked ready for blood. The island became alive and aware its owners had come home. I drew my bow and arrow and took out the few marching Sluagh that were patrolling the beaches, then shifted the sands to engulf their bodies.

Sorlin watched in amazement as Séamus took out the next wave of patrols in mere seconds. I plunged my hands into the sands, the image was foggy, but I could see no more winged beasts in the area. "Move forward. Stay low. There are scouts in the towers."

I took the lead with Sorlin as the commanding generals we were, leading our people to the base of the castle. I placed my hands on the stone, and the images swarmed my head. I saw him. I saw Sabriel. I expected to shake and turn sour in my stomach by my hands heated as rage tore through my body. I was not afraid, and I would not be leaving this island until life fled his body.

A squeal from behind made me jump, but Áine swiftly beheaded the two Sluagh who caught us lurking. I nodded to her and willed the wall to drop so we could file into the castle. "That was too easy," Sorlin muttered.

I agreed. Something did not seem right. The air was thick and tense, yet Sabriel was sipping wine in the comforts of this castle, unbothered by our presence. The island's energy was shifting and pulling Séamus and me as if it were begging us to stay and save it. I knew Sabriel felt it; it was impossible not to.

A cool black shadow graced my arm for a moment, and I smiled. I did not need Corvis's help to stay calm, I was prepared, but I appreciated him more than he could know. "I see him. He is in a grand hall eating with his beasts. There are so many Sluagh, hundreds, all milling about in there. I don't think we can take them all. I say we go to the Well."

"Are ye mad, Eadha? Ye said yerself ye can't destroy the Well without the cauldron's magic," Séamus whispered.

"I have six of seven stones. The cauldron could still work, just not at full power. If I combine my magic with it, maybe we could have a chance. But, I do know we are not taking on those creatures alone." It was a risk we needed to take if we had any kind of chance to destroy this Well, we needed to do it before heading to Sabriel.

"Where is the Well?" Rigel asked. *Good, he did not oppose the plan.*

"This castle was built around the courtyard that held it." I placed my hand on the rock and felt the power of the Well pulsing through the stone. "It's in the middle of the castle, in the throne chambers. I-I don't see the cauldron."

Rigel gripped my shoulders and spun me to him. "Can you destroy the Well without it?"

I rattled my brain, but I did not have an answer. "I can try."

He nodded. "Then let's try. I am not interested in fighting off a horde of bleached bats today, so let's do this quickly and quietly."

I led the way as we ran through the halls. I had thought of all the ways I would enjoy killing Sabriel, but that would have to wait. The lives of Verbenia and the human realms were more precious than my revenge. The Well was protected by the goddess Bríg, and I knew no one who shared her magic. I knew little of the goddess through studies as a child and did not know a way to break through the wards around it, but I needed to try.

The throne room entrance was guarded by many Sluagh. I crouched down and lined my bow with three arrows, aiming them across my body. "On my mark, ye run and take them out with little noise. Get closer," I commanded the group. They moved forward as close as they could and crouched down low.

I took a deep breath and released my arrows, impaling three Slaugh right between the eyes. We ran out as fast as lightning, there were minimal shrieks from the beasts, and before we knew it, we opened the throne room doors. A frenzy of violence unfolded as the guards yelled and swung their swords. We needed to work faster, we would have been heard by now, and it was only a matter of time before Sabriel came waltzing in here. I ran in first with my dual swords and took out the leaders of the guard while my friends finished the rest. The whole place smelled of death and rot, and the Well stood ominously in the middle of the room. I rested my hand on its stone and shuddered. Not even the might of Cré himself would be able to break it.

"It's made of stone, but nothing from this world. I can't break it with my magic alone." I tried to use my own Druid abilities, but it would not budge. Through the floor, I felt Sabriel still sitting a few levels down. "Alright, I say we find the cauldron. I could still make it work if we just-"

I needed to think. The cauldron could not have been far. It was the most powerful piece of magic on this island. Sabriel surely had to have tried to use it to open the Well without the magic of the Tiarna. He had been stewing here for centuries, so I guessed a slew of magical troves were somewhere close that could be used. The cauldron had to have been close by or even in this room. I could not see it as it probably hid itself from my gift of sight, but I just had a feeling it was here. I looked around the room and saw a torch that seemed deceptively ordinary.

"Hold on," I drew my sword and slowly made my way to it, and pulled down the makeshift lever and a door opened. Through the pitch black corridor, I could hear the ominous sound of a rolling boil. "It's here! The cauldron is down here. Stay there, and let me take a look."

"I'm coming with you," Corvis exclaimed as he turned towards our group, "Séamus watch the door, Sorlin, watch Áine and Rigel."

There was going to be no arguing with Corvis as he jogged over to me. I nodded and lit a fire in the palm of my hand, and led him down the hall. I looked up as he clutched his sword and wondered what he thought of all this.

"Corvis, something just doesn't feel right to me."

"What do you mean?" He asked. The sounds of the cauldron grew louder, and a distant glow grew in my vision.

"Ye can feel the shift on this island by the second, yet Sabriel is drinking with his filth. Of course, he could think himself to be so untouchable he truly has no idea we are here."

He snorted and looked at me with a smile. "Let's hope it's the latter."

When we entered the room with the cauldron, I felt a presence in there with me as if Arawn himself were staring me down to my soul. It was enormous and bubbled violently. I reached for my bag and caught Corvis peering inside of it.

"Norr charmed it. Only I can see and touch what is inside."

He nodded and smirked as he lifted me to the

cauldron's brim to the seven empty slots. I fumbled in my bag and carefully placed each one. As I clicked them into place, the cauldron bubbled ferociously, and I could feel the hair on the back of my neck stand as a dark magic filled the air. As I placed the sixth stone, there was no explosion of power, the god himself did not come crawling from the liquid inside, and I had no idea how to harness whatever magic the cauldron held.

I hoisted myself up to stair down into the mysterious green liquid and felt some sort of pull, calling me to go in. I placed my hand into the liquid and felt Corvis pull me back.

"Are you insane?"

I pushed him away and shushed him. "I just-I don't know, there is something in here." It took more willpower than I was willing to admit not to dive head-first into the ethereal pool. As welcoming as the waters were, there was also a nasty feeling in the back of my mind that I did not belong there, as if I were soiling the pure magic of the cauldron. When I pulled my hand out, it was not wet. I tried cupping the liquid in my hand, but none left the cast iron pot. I put my arm further in, and not even my sleeve dampened. I felt no change, no magic, nothing leave the confines of the cauldron.

"What is happening?" Corvis asked.

I sighed. "Nothing. Absolutely nothing. There is something here, I can feel it. I just don't know how to get it."

Corvis gently pulled me down after gathering up the last of the stones and placing them into my bag. A finger made its way to my chin and pulled my eyes to meet his. "This isn't over. The Well was a no-go, fine. The cauldron didn't work, okay. We are going to take him down today."

Those were the words that kept me from diving away into dark thoughts. I nodded and gave his arm a tight squeeze. When this was all over, it was going to be hard to say goodbye. I fought hard for my mind not to drift back to the night at the cavern, but it was the only memory keeping me grounded. Corvis pulled one of my swords from its sheath on my back and held it to me in a symbol of solidarity. I grasped it, holding his burning gaze for a moment and jogged back to the others.

I saw a few new bodies on the floor, and Rigel finished off a guard before we emerged from the secret room and closed the door. "Tell me you have something, please," The look in Rigel's eyes made my soul ache.

He was a skilled fighter, but not a warrior. He lived in a small cottage in the outskirts of his city and wore simple clothes. All he wanted to do in his life was watch over his people and love his wife. All of this death and blood was getting to him, and the future ruin of Verbenia would tear him apart should we fail.

I shook my head and crouched to the stone. "No, I'm sorry. The cauldron will not work without the last stone. Sabriel hasn't moved at all. It's...strange."

"I say we go there. We can take him and his beasts," Áine said exasperatedly.

"Sluagh are strong and do not go down so easily. Plus, Sabriel has a magic we do not know the nature of. It would be suicide," Séamus explained.

I thought carefully about our next move but came up short. I thought back to what Norr said to me, that his father sold his soul to Sabriel for something. To do such a thing, one would need a soul charm of sorts. I wondered if Sabriel sold his soul to Balor in exchange for magic, then maybe, just maybe, that charm could be somewhere here. If we found it and destroyed it, it could be a way to stop him. "Alright, I think we just-"

"Eadha, Rigel, psst!" We jumped and turned with our weapons raised to find Vela scurrying across the room frantically with a black eye and a bloody nose. "Tenebris, it's under attack. They came as soon as you left. I couldn't fight them all off. I have a protective shield over Oneiros that will last long enough for the Vespairan armies to fly in. We need to leave now before it is too late!"

Rigel looked at me as if I was the one who had ordered the attack and a shiver ran down my spine...this was my fault, I did this. Corvis and Sorlin looked horrified and stiffened as they clutched their blades. "We are leaving. Now. My people are sitting there like a deer in the crosshairs," Rigel seethed.

"How did he know we were leaving?" I asked. It made no sense. Addax needed trees to hear and see the goings-on of Verbenia, and there were none near the palace. Corvis wanted to believe him to be innocent, and maybe I was starting to as well, but it did not make sense. The night I first met him when the Nuckelavee attack, it came as if it knew where I was. Addax would have had to know of our motives that night to want me dead. And if he was behind this betrayal, why would he have given me his tone?

"I guess there is more to your *friend* than meets the eye," Vela spat out at me.

If we left now, there would be no chance of getting to Sabriel. He knew we were here; he probably would put up enough wards to keep us from even crossing the ocean. *Wait, wards?* Where were the wards when we first came?

"Áine, did ye break any wards to allow us onto the island?" I asked.

She shook her head. How could there have been no wards if he knew we were coming this whole time? Unless Sabriel *let* us in. This was a trap. We were trapped here like animals in a cage. My brain raced as I tried to think of a plan and something crossed my mind.

"Eadha, look at this," Corvis said. I walked over and looked at a small black brick of wax embedded into the stone.

"It's, uh," I turned it and brushed off some debris to see a familiar symbol of a sun that sent a chill through my spine. "Shite-" I went to chuck it, but it did not matter. It was too late. The spell jar exploded in my hand, and a fiery cloud of magic surrounded me.

"Eadha?!" Séamus yelled. I coughed and waved a hand around, wondering what spell was just cast onto me.

"I'm fine, I'm fine." Corvis was right by my side, looking me over and making sure I was okay. I heard the snap of a bow and pulled him down in the blink of an eye. "Archers!"

We scrambled behind the Well as a volley of arrows rained down on us. We all took out our bows and picked off the guards one by one, but more came charging in. Sorlin jumped in front and used the magic from his ring to forge a shield as we weaved in and out to kill the pack of Sluagh.

I fell to the ground, but no images came to my mind. "What?" I whispered. I jumped to Sorlin's side and the Sluagh stopped firing. I brought my arms up in a strong motion but the earth beneath me did not bend to my will. I stared at my palms with disbelief and tried to ignite them, but not even a spark graced my fingers. The Sluagh laughed, and panic rushed through me.

Suddenly, the face that has haunted every nightmare since I was eighteen broke from the shadows smiling and clapping. Sabriel looked me up and down, his malevolent eyes filled with astonishment. I fought my thoughts from going to the dark places of mind. He was just as I remembered: long brown hair, plain brown eyes, and an angular face. He aged more than any Elite Fae I have ever seen. He had lines by his eyes as he smiled and slight traces of gray in his hair.

"Get behind me," Séamus pulled me to his side but I refused to hide. He took away my magic with a charm forged by a Fosseran.

"The savage child of the Druid Tiarna. My, you haven't aged a day. I didn't believe it when I first heard of your return. I thought you were dead."

We all stopped and stared. I looked to Rigel, and he clutched Áine with fear in his silver eyes. The necklace Sabriel wore around his neck was glowing a radiant gold and orange. It had to have been Farhan's soul. "Ye know nothing of Druid magic. How did you take away my powers?" I demanded. I kept my voice direct and even, but the fury coursing through me shook my breathing.

"Ha, I found someone who knew everything, of course. I know everything about you, Eadha. I hope we can put what happened between us all those years ago aside and end this civilly," his voice was like a needle against my eardrum, "Grab her."

We all took a defensive stance and raised our weapons as the Sluagh came flowing in. Séamus recited an incantation and exploded into a mass of battle power. He was astonishingly fast and plowed through the group of serpents with the grace of a humming-bird's wings. Sorlin ran to his side, forging his own shield and weapons. Rigel radiated a blinding white light and began to bend the minds of every beast in the room. I whipped my swords out and began tearing through the crowd. I did not need my magic to beat them, but there were so many.

When I caught a glance at Sabriel, he was having two guards haul in somebody with a bag over their head. "Stop!" I yelled, but no one heard me. "Stop!" I screamed. We all paused and looked to Sabriel, who looked disgustingly amused.

"I thought that might have gotten your attention. I am prepared to offer you a trade. You, for him." He shucked off the bag to reveal Farhan, beaten, and bloody. His dark brown locks were stained red, and the face that once looked so similar to Áine was swollen and almost unrecognizable.

Áine gasped and released a sob. "Father," she whispered.

"I'll give you five seconds to decide, then I fire at one of your companions."

"Deal," I said without hesitation. I had a hunch that if I played my cards just right, we could all get out of here okay. I remembered the words Norr spoke to me carefully and knew I was making the right choice. Everything clicked and I knew what to do. "Release him to Rigel." If Rigel kept his hands on Farhan, he may still have a chance to live.

Sabriel threw his body down to us and he landed with a grunt of pain. Rigel rushed over and took him into his arms. "Eadha, stop. What are you doing?" Corvis held onto my arm, but I gave him the weapons in my hands.

"Remember what I told ye before leaving," I said quickly before a strong clawed hand clamped down around my arm and pulled me away.

Séamus grabbed my arm and tugged. "No! We are not giving ye to him!" I pulled my hand away and a tear fell from his eye. I hated to see it, I hated to worry him, but I knew what I was doing. I was going to get everyone out of here alive, even if that meant without me.

"I have to say I am incredibly disappointed in you Eadha, I was expecting a fight." Sabriel crooned.

"I have no reason to fight. Yer not going to kill my friends." My heart started beating faster than my brain could handle, and my hands trembled.

Sabriel must have sensed my anxiety. He placed his flat palm on my chest and smiled. "Ah, the pleasant tremble of fear. It is a beautiful thing."

"Don't you touch her," Corvis growled. A guard aimed his bow up to his face and hissed.

"Let the ritual begin!" Sabriel boomed. Sluagh began painting sigils onto the floor and lit a ceremonial fire in front of the Well. They were going to try to open it, and a smile played at my cheeks. Sabriel grabbed my hand and sliced my palm with an athame as he walked me over to the fire. My friends were horrified, Séamus looked like he was going to collapse.

Sabriel spoke the ancient tongue of my people and praised Bríg. "With my power, and the power of the Tiarna..."

I did not care to hear what else he had to say. Sabriel might have taken away *my* magic, but I had the powers of someone else burned into my soul. *"Corvis, can ye hear me?"* I forced the words into his mind. I looked at him, and he nodded slowly. I felt him trying to make his way into my mind, but he could not concentrate enough to speak back. *"Ye made me a promise that ye would protect Séamus. Ye better keep that promise and get him out of here alive."* His eyes widened, and I could see his chest rise and fall at an alarming rate.

"May the great Balor walk out of his immortal prison, let him walk free, I command it to be!" Sabriel grabbed the back of my neck and forced a few drops of my blood onto the top of the Well.

"Sorry to interrupt, but I hear this spell only works with the blood of the Tiarna. Ye should probably go get some," I said sarcastically.

He pulled my hair and held a knife to my throat. "Eadha!" Corvis went running for me and was caught by two Sluagh. I thrashed against Sabriel, but the might of earth was gone from my body. I was not a natural-born Laoch. I did not have their otherwordly strength to break free.

"Do not hurt him. If you hurt him, I will-"

"You'll what, kill me? Darling, I would love to watch you try. Open the Well before he loses his wings permanently." There it was, the confirmation I needed to know exactly what was going on around here. There was only one way Sabriel could have known about Corvis.

"I can't open the Well. I am *not* the Tiarna. Ye saw it yerself, my blood did nothing." He snarled and leaned my head over the Well with the knife to my throat.

"Then I will get more blood."

"She's telling the truth! Look at her bracelet.

There is a stone missing. She doesn't have all of the magic to become Tiarna. Let her go!" Corvis pleaded.

Sabriel grabbed my arm to inspect, and his eyes shot to my group of companions. "Why you lying-" I kicked his knees forward, grabbed his knife, and threw it with all my might to the heart of the wolf hiding amongst the sheep.

Vela's ruby eyes flashed open wide before catching the knife before it could pierce her chest. My blood ran cold. She smiled as she twirled the knife and drove deep into Rigel's chest.

CHAPTER THIRTY

Eadha

"No!" Áine shrieked as her husband collapsed into her arms, sputtering and breathing raggedly. Sorlin stood shocked before lunging at Vela, but she waved her hand and drove him into the wall with a force stronger than a windstorm. I became nauseated when I heard the sound of crunching bone, and his black feathered wings bent in ways they were not meant to.

Séamus rushed to his side, and Corvis hollered as his brother became surrounded by Sluagh. A force collided with my face, and I was knocked to the ground with Sabriel above me.

"Enough!" The walls shook as his voice filled the room. "You told me she became Tiarna."

All this time, every piece of history I told her and every in and out of my magic that she wrote down, Vela sold to Sabriel. I was stupid. How could I not see this? Norr said Sabriel needed a vessel, and all this time it was for Vela. He left a piece of Farhan's soul so she could retain his magic as she took over his body. I had three options: kill Sabriel and risk my friends dying in a horde of Sluagh, kill Vela and be trapped here by Sabriel, or kill Farhan so Vela was stuck in her Fae body and could be dealt with by Áine.

Vela dragged Farhan by his hair with her as she sized up Sabriel. "I heard from the lumberjack over there that she *was*, and then princess confirmed it yesterday.

You wanted me to relay information, I did."

"Ye worked for my family! Ye knew us, and ye still worked with him, ya treacherous swine!" My voice was raw and burning as I screamed at her. Red clouded my vision as I looked behind her and saw Áine ripped from Rigel as she attempted to heal him. I locked eyes with Corvis and gave him a nod. I needed him to know what he had to do.

"I did, but I work for power. The Druids were gone, and Sabriel took their place. It was meant to be."

Vela reached for the necklace around Sabriels neck, but I used the hidden blade attached to my shoe to puncture her thigh. She scoffed and recoiled as she clutched the blood coming from her leg. I knew if I stabbed her, it would only hurt the woman she was possessing. I knew how to kill a daemon but did not have the tools to do it.

She laughed, "Go ahead, stab me through the heart. I'll find a new body before you can take a breath."

"Yer not touching that soul. Why do ye want Farhan's magic?"

Vela looked at me smugly and shrugged. "I guess I don't."

She clutched Farhan's head and twisted it, and a lethal snap filled my ears. The golden light around Sabriels neck flickered and disappeared. Áine screamed and sobbed as she thrashed against the Sluagh that held her in place.

"I just need someone else's magic so I can amplify it. In fact, Sabriel my dear," she brought her lips to his and kissed him lightly. I could have retched right then and there. "Since this creature is not the Tiarna, I could enter her. A daemon wielding the power of the Dragons, we will be unstoppable."

Corvis was struggling to get to Áine, and Rigel was barely moving. Sabriel picked me up by my hair. "I need the blood of the Tiarna."

"Leaving a part of her soul will give me her memories. I would be able to locate the Tiarna and bring them to you."

Sabriel held out the jewel on his necklace, and I thrashed to get away but Vela held me in place. "No! No!" I fought.

I tried to conjure the earth, but it was no use. I was cursed, and my magic was gone for however long Vela deemed fit. Since the spell was crafted with the seal of Fossera, the only person who could reverse it was Áine, and she was too far away. I stabilized my breathing and thought long and hard about what I could do. I did not need magic or weapons. I was the general of the Laoch army.

I used all of my force to kick my legs up to Sabriel's neck and flung him away before tackling Vela. The Sluagh pounced, but I fought them off. The goal now, was to get everyone out of here alive. I could deal with Sabriel later. Sharp nails grasped my shoulders, and Vela pinned me to the ground. I looked at Corvis, who managed to break away from his captors for long enough to get to Rigel and protect his High Lord.

I kicked Vela off with the blade on my shoe but it only made her laugh. If I killed this body she was in, it could buy me enough time to think. She grabbed my ankle and straddled on top of me, holding the soul catcher. As she whispered an incantation, I began to feel sick. I saw my life leave my body through my chest and both my best and darkest memories flashed in my eyes.

I saw Tadhg laughing and swinging from a tree, I saw my mother holding me while I was sick, and my father teaching me how to use my Druid Stone. I saw Tadhg die and every other small battle I fought with my four friends from Covalla.

Then I saw Corvis. I saw him emerge from the shadow of my dreams. I saw every small smile he has ever given me and the small lines that form by his mouth when he laughs. I saw the times when we fought and apologized, and every moment he made me feel like I was the only person in the room with his intense eyes of burning embers. I felt his lips against mine and his taste on my tongue.

I could hear Séamus screaming my name like he did on this same island many years ago, and my eyes shot open. I bucked Vela off of me and grabbed her throat. "Where-where is the rest of your soul?" She choked out.

My soul. She did not have enough to take before it would kill me, and I had too much of it left for her to possess me and take my magic. I looked over to Corvis, who shared a piece of me, and Vela followed my gaze, pulling out a dagger. She went to jump, but I grabbed her and pushed her to the ground. The hounds of Arawn would have to drag me to the Otherworld right then and there before I would let any harm come to him. Sabriel called in more Sluagh, and my allies were fighting for their lives.

Corvis ran to put Rigel next to Sorlin and shielded them as Séamus fought to get Áine. There was no way out of this. I fought Vela hard, but my muscles were screaming as I attempted to keep up with her. I was incredibly weak. As her small hands circled around my neck, I stood on one foot and detached the blade from my shoe before plunging it into hers.

She fell to the ground clutching her throat before choking to death. The daemon exited the body, but I grabbed the necklace before she could take refuge. Sabriel screamed as he charged me, punching me with an ungodly force, and levitating my body with his magic. "What's the matter, afraid yer plaything will have to find an ugly replacement?" I mocked.

He laughed. "Surrender yourself to me, and I will let them live. They will have their chance to die when their lands burn, but I want you. Now." I looked around the room and my friends were on their last legs. If Rigel did not make it out of here, soon he would die. Corvis and Séamus were surrounded, and Áine was too hysterical to fight anymore. My heart ached, and a tear stung my eyes.

Magic circled my throat, and I clawed at my neck. I locked eyes with Sabriel and croaked, "Go ahead and kill me. I would rather lose my life by your hands than beg for it at your feet."

The ground began to rumble in violent bursts. The Sluagh hushed and their eyes widened, and Corvis looked at me with a smile of relief. As Sabriel was preoccupied, I slithered my legs to him and tackled him down, shaking and pushing my last knife closer to his heart. A loud crash shook the room, and the dawning sun burned my eyes, but I kept pushing. This was going to end here.

A roar as forceful as a waterfall sounded in the distance, and rock came crashing down around us. Sabriel did not yield. I managed one last push of strength and stabbed the knife into his shoulder. He yelped and threw my body into the floor. The ground rumbled again, shaking as if an earthquake was rolling through. *Cré.*

The stone beneath me split and cracked. "Fight back, you fools! Kill them!" Sabriel yelled before lunging and punching me. As I fell, I heard the clanking of glass skidding onto the floor and the soul catcher was rolling away. Sabriel and I scrambled for it. I would get closer and he would pull me away. If I had the piece of my soul back, I would be able to kill him.

"Corvis!" Áine shrieked. I looked over and saw a blade protruding from his stomach.

I looked between him and the necklace. If I was quick enough, I could race to the necklace then over to him, but I knew I would not be able to manage it. My heart ached as I turned away from Corvis, and tears stung my eyes. I could not let Sabriel have my soul. "I'm so sorry," I whispered and powered my way to it.

Just as I reached my hand out, a knife plunged through it, and a force sat on my back. I yelled out in pain, and Sabriel picked up the necklace. The ground shook violently, the crack in the earth began to widen.

"Corvis, tell him to stop!" I yelled with a hoarse voice.

He could not hear me. Sabriel must have seen what was happening. He picked me up by my neck to toss me into the pit, but threw me across the room with a force so strong I managed to grab the other side of the trench. I clawed at the ground, but half of my body had slipped into the crack.

I looked back to Sabriel who's plane of earth was receding back and down quickly; Sluagh all ran to his side. Below me was a violent rumble of molten rock from the volcano that created this island. A Sluagh inched further and further to the edge, waiting to catch me if I fell. My hand was in too much pain. I could not hold onto the ledge anymore. I shut my eyes and let go.

"No!" I heard Corvis scream, and he caught my hand. He was weak. I could see it in his eyes and feel it as I held his shaking hand. He could not hold me for long.

"Corvis? Where is Séamus?" I asked between pants.

"He-he walked everyone out through the veil when they rock split. It's just me left and I am not leaving you." My hand was aching and the blood was slipping my grip as the plates of earth moved further and further apart.

"They have my soul Corvis. Vela is still alive. If she gets it, my people will die. She knows everything about Tenebris too. I can't leave."

He shook his head and attempted to pull me up but cried out in pain as he clutched his bleeding stomach. I looked down to see the plate that Sabriel was standing on was moving closer and closer to the lava below. "When I let go, tell Cré to stop. I can't talk to them anymore. I- I don't know if you know what ye are to me, but ye have to do it."

"You are *not* letting go!" He yelled, "Eadha, don't do this! I can't-I don't want to-"

"Shh." My magic was gone, but I could feel another deep within me, swirling under my skin. If I could connect my shadows to his, I could send him through the veil.

"Corvis, when I saw Jada about to rip off yer wings, I knew right then and there that ye meant something more to me than an ally."

"Stop it," he warned.

My hand was slipping, and I could not hold on much longer. Sluagh with wings came rushing into Sabriel's side, ready to fly up to grab me and kill Corvis.

As I looked into Corvis's eyes and saw his shadows, the piece of his soul within me ignited. I reached up with my left palm and grabbed his arm.

"Ye have to go now, Corvis. Please don't succumb to the darkness of yer shadows again. Do it for me." I concentrated all of my power and felt the cool brush of darkness tickle my palms.

Corvis tried so hard to pull me up, but he only lost more blood every time he tried. I knew this was the only way to get him out of here. "Eadha, I have waited a lifetime for you. If you let go of my hand, I will follow you into the next, I swear it. Don't you let go."

"I'm sorry," I cried before I released my grip. As I fell, I shot a stream of shadows up to Corvis, encasing him until they pulled him through the veil. I knew I was either going to plunge into the sea of molten rock below or be skewered by the outstretched claws of the Sluagh below.

Time seemed to slow as I fell, and the heat of the volcano graced my skin. I did not know which death I preferred, but either way, I was at peace. My friends were safe, and in my eyes, that means I won here. I knew they would fight with every breath and every drop of blood to protect this world. If I survived this, the worst adversary Sabriel ever could imagine would be living in his prison, waiting for the right moment to strike.

I closed my eyes and let density decide where I would go.

CHAPTER THIRTY-ONE

Corvis

I landed with a thud on a cold marble floor and heard Áine gasp. "Where in the god's names is the healer?! Séamus, go to him!"

"No... no, no, no," I patted the floor under me and with panicked and shaky hands. "No!" I yelled. She was right here. I held onto her, I was holding on, and she...she...

"Corvis?" Séamus spun me around and looked me in the eye. "Where is she? Where is Eadha?"

"Séamus!" A female voice called. That girl with the three blue slashed over her eyes was looking down at me with the two twins at her side.

"She let go...she let go...I had her, I was holding on, I just needed more time, I-" I looked down at my hands that were covered in Eadha's blood.

Séamus's eyes grew large, and his mouth trembled before crashing onto his knees and letting out a painful scream.

"Eadha is...is Eadha dead?" The girl asked as she looked between us.

I clutched my hand over my heart and tried to find something, anything from her, but I felt nothing. I did not know if she was alive or dead. The polarizing fragment of her soul that I once could feel was now gone. It was lifeless and stale. I touched my lips as I remembered that one night of intimacy I took for granted and hugged my body tightly. Eadha was gone. I was not strong enough to pull her up. My heart ached, and my breath caught in my chest as tears fell to the ground, and my stomach lurched.

"She let go," was all I could choke out in between heaves. I looked over to Rigel, who was as still as death. "No," I grunted and went to move, but pain spread through my body.

"Yer hurt," the woman said in a small voice. What was her name? She looked to Áine and crouched down to me. "With a Fosseran here, I think I can..." She placed her hands over my wound and healed it slowly. I couldn't feel the pain of my would slowly sealing.

I was cold and numb as I trembled violently. I felt like I was encased with ice then seared with white-hot iron. As soon as she was done, I crawled to Rigel and brushed his silver hair off his pale face. Rigel was more to me than my employer or my High Lord. He was my friend and my brother. I felt his neck, a weak pulse beat against my finger, and I cried with relief.

Sorlin was moaning and groaning in pain beside him, panting and crying. "I'm sorry, Sorlin. I'm coming, I'm coming, I swear-I just, I can't lose him," Áine said through her tears.

The woman and Séamus ran to Sorlin. "This is going to hurt. I'm sorry-" The woman grasped his wings, and Sorlin screamed out in pain.

Séamus clutched his hand and held it to his chest. "Deep breaths, breathe. Look at me, stay awake, friend."

I got up and marched to the window, but the twins stood in front of me. "Ye cannot leave Shadow-man," said the man with a blue knotted bird on his neck.

"She-she wouldn't want it." The other, with a blue

line down the center of his face, reached out for me, but I pulled away. If I went back there for Eadha, I would be killed before I even touched the sand on the shore.

Tears fell down from my face, and I wiped them away only for more to take their place. "I can't leave her there. What if she is alive?" Sorlin screamed behind me and sobbed as the woman broke his already healed bones and set them back. I flinched and let out a shuddered breath.

One of the twins gave me a small smile. "She's with her brother now. I think she is happier than she has ever been. If she isn't dead, then...then she will be soon, Shadowman. Look at yer brother, Birdman, and yer Lord. If ye go back, that is what will happen again," the man with the blue line started to cry, and his brother held him.

He was right, and I hated him for it. If we went back now, we would be killed. I closed my eyes and felt the pull of the Dragon that answered my plea. *Cré, stop your destruction*, I willed to him. If Eadha was alive, his carnage would kill her. I looked at my friends and new allies and was filled with a wrath I have never felt before. We were broken, destroyed, and dying because of that man. Áine would surely have to leave and inform her step-mother of Fahran's passing and decide what to do with the throne.

Rigel would recover, and when he did I prayed he doesn't turn into anything like the other High Lords. If Sabriel found the location of Eadha's home, the Tiarna, we would lose, and there would be no stopping him.

I couldn't stand it. The walls were closing in on me, and I felt disgusted by the thought of leaving her to rot. "We have to go back. We have to stop him!"

Áine looked to me and curled her lip with her hands covering Rigel's heart. "There is no stopping him! Vela knows everything about Tenebris. Every entrance, every stronghold, and every citizen. We need to just wait for whatever Sabriel is planning and stand our ground. *That* is what we are doing. I am your High Lady; *that* is an order Corvis. I'm sorry your Anam Cara is dead, but you have a duty to this court and to the people in it. We need to protect them."

Séamus's eyes widened as he heard the words come from Áine's mouth. Eadha did not tell him of our connection—*my Anam Cara.* The memory of an eighteen-year-old Eadha chained to a pole to be whipped to death played in my mind, and my stomach turned sour. If she lived, if we left her on that island, I was sure she would be subjected to more extreme horrors. I began to panic and shut my eyes, but all I could see was her face twisted in pain.

Séamus didn't nod or shake his head. He simply looked at me as if to say, "We will figure it out." I believed him. I knew we would figure it out even if I had to swim to the island myself to get her back.

Whether it be plotting our own graves on the battlefield or going back to face Sabriel once more, we would be ready. Sabriel was not going to step foot on these lands or anywhere in Verbenia as long as I drew breath. If he did, they would be the last steps he ever took. We needed to unify the courts and solidify an army. That was the first step we had to take to secure our homelands. Fossera would most likely be up in flames, and Norr would surely blame us for the demise of his father.

I walked out to the balcony and looked across

the ocean. "I'm coming for you, Eadha. No matter what world your soul now dwells, I am coming."

I was no longer the spy of this court. I was a man ready to bleed for his people.

PRONUNCIATION GUIDE

Áine: Awn-Ya
Eadha: Eh-A
Rigel: Ry-Jel
Faolan: Fay-Lin
Tadhg: T-Iyg
Badbh Catha: B-Ayev-Ca-Ha

- Creatures

Sluagh: Sloo-Uh
Sidhe: Sh-Ee
Nuckelavee: Did you not read the book?! don't say it out loud!
Cré: C-ray
Tine: Tin-a
Uisce: eeSh-Ca

ACKNOWLEDGEMENT

I just would like to say, that if you are reading this right now, you have made me the happiest person in the world and I am so grateful to have had you as a reader. You have made my dreams come true and have inspired me to keep going as an author. I genuinely hope you stay with me on my journey of writing for the many books to come.

I want to take this time to thank a few people. First, I want to thank my mom and dad for believing in me and believing that I could do this. I am not a writer, I did not go to school for this. I was just a depressed girl in the middle of quarantine that thought of a story and began to write. If my dad never told me to keep going, I don't think I would have made it this far. I love you both and I hope I made you proud with this.

I want to thank my amazing beta readers who gave me the confidence to publish this piece and my beautiful and amazing friend Allison. Allison, without you, I really do not think I would have made it through college. My favorite memory I have with you, besides Six Flags of course, is me sitting on the floor of a practice room sobbing hysterically and you staring at me and finally saying: "You know what? I think we should go to The Rain Forest Café. It would be a nice change in scenery." You were there for me through all of my ups and downs and I hope to have you in my life for many years to come.

Lastly, I want to thank a professor I had. I do not know if you will see this, but I just want to say that you were the only teacher who took the time to help me when I was struggling instead of telling me to quit. You never told me to think about changing schools, saying "it's never too late," and you never told me that I would never find a job in music. Even though I really didn't understand a single thing that ever came out of your mouth, you took the time to sit with me every week and break down all of the stupid questions I had. One of the reasons I knew I could do this was because of you. I will never forget your patience and kindness. -Don

ABOUT THE AUTHOR

As of 2021, Jordon Genetski is enrolled in the Chicago College of Performing Arts to pursue a degree in Classical Vocal Performance and Music Education. She pulled inspiration from J. R. R. Tolkien, Laura Thalassa, and research in Celtic mythology to write her novel "Elder". She currently lives in Chicago with her two sons, Fritz and Toby, that are in fact cats.

Get connected:

Her website: www.jordongenetski.com

Her Instagram: @jo_18g

Her TikTok: @jo_18g